T0146489

"Just let me go."

"No." Apparently finished with the conversation, he swung his torso and lifted, landing her squarely behind him.

Her ass hit the leather seat. Damn it. How in the world had she forgotten his strength? Even for a demon, his was unreal. He'd lifted her with one hand, and he wasn't even breathing hard. Before she could protest and burn his ears off, he ignited the engine and roared into the street.

She yelped and grabbed his dress shirt with both hands, leaning in for balance.

Nick Veis handled a Ducati like he did everything else in life . . . using control edged with a hint of violence. The contrast between the elegant demon official that he showed the world and the primal being lurking inside him showed just how far he'd come since this latest war had ended. But the elegance was merely a mask for the cold predator lurking beneath.

She wasn't the same wide-eyed girl he'd played with before. It had taken years, but she was as tough as they came, and she could handle him.

Wicked Burn

Realm Enforcers, Book 3

REBECCA ZANETTI

LYRICAL PRESS

Kensington Publishing Corp.

www.kensingtonbooks.com

LYRICAL PRESS BOOKS are published by

Kensington Publishing Corp.
119 West 40th Street
New York, NY 10018

All Kensington titles, imprints, and distributed lines are available at special quantity discounts for bulk purchases for sales promotions, premiums, fund-raising, educational, or institutional use.

Special book excerpts or customized printings can also be created to fit specific needs. For details, write or phone the office of the Kensington sales manager: Kensington Publishing Corp., 119 West 40th Street, New York, NY 10018, attn: Sales Department; phone 1-800-221-2647.

LYRIC PRESS and the Lyrical logo are Reg. U.S. Pat. & TM Off.

First electronic edition: June 2016

ISBN-13: 978-1-60183-515-4
ISBN-10: 1-60183-515-9

First print edition: June 2016

ISBN-13: 978-1-60183-516-1
ISBN-10: 1-60183-516-7

This one's for Jessica Namson,
a truly amazing friend.

ACKNOWLEDGMENTS

I have many people to thank for help in getting this third Realm Enforcer book to readers, and I sincerely apologize to anyone I've forgotten;

Thank you to Big Tone for giving me tons to write about and for being supportive from the very first time I sat down to write. Thanks also to Gabe and Karlina for being such awesome kids and for making life so much fun;

Thank you to my talented agents, Caitlin Blasdell and Liza Dawson, who have been with me from the first book and who have supported, guided, and protected me in this wild industry;

Thank you to my amazing editor, Alicia Condon, who is unflappable, willing to take a risk, and is always a wonderful sounding board;

Thank you to the Kensington gang: Steven Zacharius, Adam Zacharius, Alexandra Nicolajsen, Vida Engstrand, Michelle Forde, Jane Nutter, Justine Willis, Lauren Jernigan, Fiona Jayde, and Arthur Maisel;

Thank you to my fantastic street team, Rebecca's Rebels, and especially Elizabeth E. Neal and Minga Portillo. Thanks also to Jillian Stein for the amazing work;

And thanks also to my constant support system: Gail and Jim English, Debbie and Travis Smith, Stephanie and Don West, Brandie and Mike Chapman, Jessica and Jonah Namson, and Kathy and Herb Zanetti.

Prologue

A century ago

Nicholai Veis leaned against the interior wall of the rock and clay cottage, the ring nearly burning a hole in his pocket. Peace surrounded him in the silent dwelling, and even he, a former demon soldier, could feel the magic of Ireland outside the door.

He loved Ireland.

Or maybe it was the witch who'd captured his heart that made him embrace the magic of the place.

He reached for the ring to admire. Stunning. A three-carat Alexandrite gem surrounded by pure silver. It would look lovely on Simone's finger. His nerves increased. Would she like the cottage? It was small, but for now, small would work.

Energy shifted outside the door. He paused and then shoved the ring inside his pocket, reaching for a dagger in his boot.

The knock on the door surprised him. Frowning, he crossed the empty main room and pulled it open. "Prophet Lily," he murmured, looking immediately over her head to see Dage Kayrs, the King of the Realm. "And the king." He had met both of them during peace talks after the last war. Tension uncoiled in his gut.

Even worse, dreams had been plaguing him lately in which Lily showed up and changed his entire life from light to dark. The dreams could not be omens. He wouldn't let them be.

Lily smiled up at him, her stunning blue eyes lacking their usual sparkle. "I'm sorry to just appear, but the matter is urgent." The weak sun shone on her nearly white-blond hair, which the wind instantly lifted. She shivered.

He drew her inside immediately, recognizing her scent of wild strawberries. Even in the dreams she smelled like the sweet fruit. "I'll start a fire." A stone fireplace made up the entire northern wall.

She shook her head. "I won't be here long."

Nick lifted an eyebrow at the king, who hadn't moved. Dage Kayrs was six-and-a-half feet of hard soldier with dark silver eyes and jet-black hair. He'd had to step up as king after the war, or rather during it, and the toll showed in his world-weary gaze. "Are you coming in?" Nick asked.

Dage shook his head. "I'm just the transport. Lily said you needed to speak privately." Even the king obeyed the tiny prophet. Yet he cleared his throat. "The Realm and the demon nation are allies for now, so I ask you to guarantee her safety."

Nick's chest heated. "I wouldn't harm a prophet, king."

"Understood." Dage jumped up on a stone wall to sit.

Besides, Nick was leaving the demon nation. Well, perhaps not leaving, but he was finished working for them. It was time to mate Simone and start a new life in Ireland, where she could pursue her ambition of working for the Coven Nine, the ruling body of the witches. "Do you think it odd that you're the only vampire to be able to teleport across the world?" Nick asked.

Dage shrugged. "Nope. I've got a gift."

Nick barely kept from rolling his eyes. Someday the king would have to face the fact that there was a demon in his family tree—demons were known for being able to teleport by altering dimensions. Unfortunately, Nick wasn't one of the demons who had that ability. "All right." He shut the door and turned to face the tiny woman.

Lily fluttered her small hands together. The prophet marking wound up her neck in a graceful arc. She was one of three people chosen by fate to wear the mark and administer wisdom to all immortals. "I am so very sorry about this."

Nick drew in a deep breath and gestured toward the rock ledge fronting the fireplace. "I haven't had time to buy furniture, so that's the only seat."

She perched and spread her yellow skirts out. "I had a vision, Nicholai." Her gaze remained on her hands.

Chills, sharper than normal, clawed down his back. In every bad dream, she had said the same words. "Is something bad going to happen to Simone?"

"No." Lily took a deep breath. "Well, that depends on you."

Ah hell. His head dropped forward. "I'm out, Lily. My uncle is right-hand to Suri, who now leads the demon nation. They have a plan, and they're strong."

"Your uncle is a sadist, and even he pales in comparison to Suri," Lily whispered. "They can't be allowed to follow their plans."

Nick looked up, his muscles tightening through his abdomen. "Demons rule by lineage, and I don't have the right bloodline. Even if I wanted to challenge Suri, and even if I had a chance in hell of beating him in a death match, I'm not of his line. I can't rule."

"I know," she whispered. "But you, and only you, can make sure the right person does."

He frowned, imaginary weights beginning to shove his shoulders down. Suri had two sisters; one was crazy-evil and the other too gentle to lead. "Who is the right person?"

"He hasn't been born yet, and he won't be unless you are in the right place to maneuver fate." A tear slid down Lily's face. "Several key moments have to come together, and even if you commit yourself fully, I don't know that you'll succeed. But you're the only chance."

He coughed out heated air, his mind burning. "Lily, I'm not in a position to do anything."

"If your uncle died, you would be," she whispered, her voice breaking.

He jerked back. "My first act to fulfill some impossible destiny is to murder my only living relative in this world?"

"Yes." She met his gaze levelly, but her dismay was palpable in the small room. "You'd be next in line to advise Suri. Oh, Nick. I've seen some of the terrible things you'll have to do in order to keep that place."

"No." He wouldn't give up his soul. "The ends can't justify those means."

"They do." She shook her head. "A terrible plague is coming in the future, one that will decimate the immortal world, especially vampire mates and the witches. I've seen it in visions. Only one person can stop it, and if he isn't born, there is *no* stopping it."

"Witches?" Nick asked, weakness sweeping through his knees.

"Yes. Even Simone." More tears gathered in Lily's eyes. "I hate this. I hate everything about this, but I've seen it, Nicholai. How bad it could get."

He backed away from her until he reached the far wall. "Suri is evil, Lily," he croaked.

"I know." She shook her head, and a couple of tears fell. "You'll have to go against everything you are to work with him."

Nick breathed out. "Who has to be born? Who is this savior?"

Lily bit her lip. "I can't see all of it. All I know is that a group of vampires will attack demon headquarters, and you have to be in a position to allow them to take Felicity. She must go with them."

Nick narrowed his gaze. "You want me to allow Suri's youngest sister, the only one with an ounce of kindness, to be taken by rogue vampires?"

"Yes. Then when she comes back, her son, the oldest one, must be protected at all costs. He's the one."

Bollocks. "You're telling me that a demon-vampire half-breed is the one who will save the immortal world from a plague so horrendous that fate wants me to give up my life, most likely my soul, in order to protect him?"

"Yes."

"I can't put Simone in that kind of danger." Hell. He didn't want himself in it.

Lily swallowed. "There's more."

Of course there was. "Tell me." Nick was done playing nice.

"I can't see you after the boy takes power. That doesn't mean you're not still alive, but . . ."

Dread felt like needles as it pricked beneath Nick's skin. "So I'll be dead."

"I don't know."

If he mated Simone, she'd never be able to take another mate, even if he was dead. Plus, if he committed to such a deadly plan, anybody he cared about would be a weakness to use against him. Which was more than likely why fate thought him perfect. "If I leave her, I'll break her heart." His was already shattering.

"I know." Lily stood. "I've given you the facts, but only you can decide." She crossed the room and leaned up to press a kiss to his cheek.

"Does the king know?" Nick asked.

"No. He has his own part to play, and he can't know any of this." Lily turned for the door.

Nick closed his eyes and tried to keep from throwing up. "If I do this, I need to know Simone will be taken care of. The king is a strong leader." He hated to make the suggestion, but at least Nick wouldn't have to see Dage ever again, especially with Simone. He reopened his eyelids.

Lily nodded. "I'll try to secure her with Dage, but sometimes fate has other plans." She opened the door. "Dage will return tomorrow for your answer, and if you decide to follow fate's plan, he'll teleport you to demon headquarters. Again, I'm so very sorry." The door closed on a sob she couldn't quite mask.

Nick buried his face in his hands. Oh, he'd felt the change coming. Fate had visited him, as well, but he'd chosen to ignore the dreams.

There really wasn't a choice for him, not if the plague would also someday get Simone. He had to make sure the worst didn't happen—leaving her was the only option. Even if he survived, he wouldn't be the same person she loved now. He couldn't be and still stand beside Suri.

He took the ring out again to see it sparkle in the dim light. "Good-bye," he whispered to a future that could've been his.

Chapter 1

Modern Day

Fury wasn't a strong enough word to describe the heat coursing through Simone Brightston as she strode out the front door of her Seattle penthouse building, a too-calm demon on her heels. Even through her anger, instinct whispered that a calm demon was a hundred times more dangerous than any raging warrior—which only pissed her off more.

And this demon . . . she didn't know. The devoted suitor of a century ago had been replaced by the cold and deadly warrior behind her.

"This way." Without waiting for her to acquiesce, Nicholai Veis wrapped one warm hand around her arm and turned her toward a black Ducati, sleek and sparkling, waiting by the curb in the morning hour.

She jerked free and arched one perfectly manicured eyebrow. "You're riding bikes now?"

His lids lifted in a curiously deliberate way to reveal those black as midnight eyes. "When in Rome." Low and cultured, his voice gave no hint as to his baser nature.

But she knew. Oh, she knew him and the animal he barely kept in check. He'd broken her heart once without a hitch in his stride, but that was nothing compared to the horrendous things he'd done in the name of the demon nation since. "Seattle is hardly Rome, and this has gone on long enough." In the building, she'd left family who needed her help. Family who'd pretty much betrayed her by asking Nick to secure her somewhere safe.

"Get on the bike, Simone, or I'll put you on the bike." His tone didn't falter a bit, remaining rough and harsh.

She paused and turned to more fully face him, curiosity winding through her anger. Could she take him? As a witch, a powerful one, she could reshape matter by applying quantum physics, and she could burn his ass with plasma. For well over a century, she'd trained.

Yet so had he. Demons could attack minds, and this one could fight physically with the prowess of a shifter and the precision of a vampire.

He waited patiently, that gaze knowing. A killer more than comfortable in his own skin. "Is this really the place?"

"Excuse me?"

"The battle coming. Witch against demon, your powers against mine. You against . . . me." He leaned in, and the scent of an oncoming storm came with him. "Are you sure you're ready?"

"Oh, I'm ready." She let her voice go husky and threat fill her eyes.

He smiled then. A quick flash of teeth against his bronze face, turning harsh angles into masculine beauty. He had the blond hair, black eyes, and mangled vocal cords of a pure-bred demon, but even among his own people, Nick Veis was something . . . more. He'd done it all, he'd seen it all . . . hell, most folks thought he'd planned it all.

From the downfall of dictators to the protection of fate's chosen ones . . . Nicholai Veis was the male to call. He fought with no remorse and killed more easily than he breathed.

Even though she was a tall woman, he looked down several inches at her, somehow not towering. Nick had the rare ability to seem peaceful, when he was anything but. He ran his hand down her arm to her wrist. "If we fight here, your cousins will come running, and they have enough going on."

She drew in air, her mind spinning. "That is exactly my point. Demon Prince Logan Kyllwood has been kidnapped, and as advisor to the Kyllwoods, you should help save him and not worry about me."

There it was. A flicker of the boiling feelings that must be ripping Nick apart showed in his eyes before being quickly veiled. "Zane Kyllwood can get his brother back, especially with your cousins assisting in the rescue."

Aye. Witch Enforcers and demon soldiers working together? The kidnapper didn't stand a chance. Yet Simone lifted her chin anyway. "I do not require your assistance."

"That's unfortunate." Keeping his grip on her arm firm, he threw one leg over the bike. "Get on, Simone. We'll go to the mat later." His phone buzzed, and he used his free hand to retrieve it from his pocket to read the face. His eyebrows lifted. "The Guard will be here in two minutes."

"Good." She set her stance. The Guard, an elite Irish force tasked with policing the witch nation, was arriving to take her into custody, and as a member of the Coven Nine, she was prepared to state her case to the ruling body of witches; after all, she was one of them. Of course, she'd known at some time she'd have to face charges, just not the ones being issued at the moment. "I'm not running."

"I'll fight them, and I'll win." Arrogance, hard-won, stamped his face.

Aye, he probably would win, even though the Guard were some of the best Irish soldiers the Coven employed. "You'll start a war between our peoples."

"Yes." His hold tightened. "Not only that, but if the Guard catches you here, right outside of your building, where the witch Enforcers are currently preparing for battle to help demons, the Guard will know the Enforcers disobeyed orders to contain you. Your cousins will face treason charges."

Dread slammed into her abdomen. She swallowed. "I'm a self-centered bitch, and you know it. My cousins created their own demise."

He chuckled then, easily zeroing in on her weakness. "Oh, I agree you're a bitch, Simone, but you're so far from self-centered it isn't in the ballpark. You'd do anything for those cousins, and your façade doesn't fool me now any more than it did last time we met."

She tried to eye the area around them for some escape, but nothing was apparent. The male was right in that she'd give her own life for Kell, Daire, or Adam, who were her cousins and three of the Coven Enforcers. "Just let me go."

"No." Apparently finished with the conversation, he swung his torso and lifted her, landing her squarely behind him.

Her ass hit the leather seat. Damn it. How in the world had she forgotten his strength? Even for a demon, his was unreal. To lift her with one hand, and he wasn't even breathing hard. Before she could protest and burn his ears off, he ignited the engine and roared into the street.

She yelped and grabbed his dress shirt with both hands, leaning in for balance.

Nick Veis handled a Ducati like he did everything else in life . . . using control edged with a hint of violence. The contrast between the elegant demon official that he showed the world and the primal being lurking inside him showed just how far he'd come since this latest war had ended. The elegance was merely a mask for the cold predator lurking beneath.

She wasn't the same wide-eyed girl he'd played with before. It had taken years, but she was as tough as they came, and she could handle him. "Let me go." She leaned up to hiss in his ear while allowing plasma to course along her hands. Creating flames out of oxygen calmed her.

The fire bit into the back of his dark shirt, and smoke rose.

"Dammit, Simone," he bit back, swerving to avoid a school bus.

She allowed the fire to dissipate. Burning him held little appeal at the moment, with him driving and her life in his hands. But the sight of the perfect handprints burned into his shirt made her smile.

Leaning into him, she allowed herself just one moment to feel. The chill of a Seattle morning, still misty and damp, had no power over the warmth from the demon. Firm lines and smooth muscle filled her palms. It had been over a century since she'd touched him, and if anything, he felt harder than ever. Streamlined and tough.

As a soldier, he was unbeatable . . . but his true strength lay in strategy. Zane Kyllwood now ruled the demon nation because Nicholai Veis had protected, groomed, and then defended him until it was time to take over.

There was a moment, centuries ago, when she had believed that Nick would sacrifice his entire future for her. How wrong she'd been, and there was no going back. Even now, with peace ruling, Nick was one cold bastard.

"You're out of my life," Simone whispered, more to herself than to the warrior.

He stiffened and turned his head to the side, deftly driving around a series of potholes. "No, I'm not, and you'd better get used to that fact right now."

Why the hell was he doing this? She opened her mouth to say something, anything, when a flash of silver caught her eye, and a black SUV careened out of the nearest alley.

The Guard had found her.

Nick hit the brakes, dodged around a honking compact car, and gunned the engine. The bike leaped forward with a growl of power.

His nape tickled, and he focused on the moment.

The SUV veered left behind him, fully visible and making a move.

Not good. Totally not good in a fucked way. Witches were masterminds at dropping nets on prey, and if they were showing themselves, they'd already created a nice little trap in downtown Seattle.

He'd rushed right into it the second he'd gotten the call that Simone was in danger.

He increased his speed, and a woman with an armful of shopping bags screamed and jumped out of his way. The tension from the woman holding him so tightly ratcheted up his heart rate, so he took a deep breath and allowed his body to relax, banishing all emotion.

Another SUV tore away from the curb, nearly clipping his back tire.

He sped up, and towering buildings blurred together on both sides of the street. Not one of his sources had reported Guard members entering the country, so they'd flown in under the radar. The witch Enforcers were unaware of their presence, and there was no way to interpret that as a good thing, considering the Enforcers and Guard usually worked in tandem.

Nick allowed adrenaline to flood his system, effectively sharpening his reflexes and senses. A whir above him stiffened his shoulders. A Black Hawk? The Guard had gone all out.

The helicopter maneuvered gracefully through the buildings, keeping above him, tracking easily.

Honking cars and screeching brakes pierced the day behind him as the SUVs kept pace.

"Pull over," Simone hissed into his ear. "We can't outrun them."

No, but perhaps they could get to safety of a sort. Even the Guard wouldn't risk a full immortal fight with human witnesses. So he kept driving, avoiding a wreck, knowing full well the risk he took.

The skyscrapers turned to three-story buildings. Then homes. Finally, trees began lining both sides of the road and filling the air with the scent of pine.

"Where are you going?" Simone whispered against his ear, her breath hot.

A shiver wound through his body to his groin. Jesus. He was about to take on a cadre of witches, and his cock wanted to play? Simone Brightston had always destroyed his system.

It was a relief to know that she still could. In his darkest moments, he'd wondered whether he'd ever find his way back to warmth. "I have a cabin prepared for you." At least then, they'd have a chance.

The roar of pipes echoed through the trees, and within seconds, men on careening Harleys and dirt bikes surrounded them.

Nick hunched over the bike. "Hold on," he yelled.

Her thighs tightened on his, and she slipped both arms around his waist to hug tight.

Two men moved in on either side of them, and he smelled shifter. What the hell? Turning, he eyed the closest threat. Lucas Bryant? A grizzly bear lieutenant? What the fuck?

Lucas narrowed his dark eyes and jerked his head toward the rider on the other side.

Nick glanced the other way to see another man draw a gun from his jeans. The shifter smiled.

Nick shook his head.

The shifter lowered the gun toward Nick's front tire.

Damn it. Nick leaned to the left and kicked out with his right leg, hitting the guy in the ribs. The male's eyes widened, and he flew off his bike with an animalistic bellow, his bike dropping and spinning around in his wake.

Nick yanked to the side, swerved to avoid the shifter's head, and drove straight into the forest.

Simone screamed and tucked her face against his neck, her hold tightening until his ribs protested.

Branches whipped into them, and the bike skidded on wet pine needles. Instinct guided him as much as his enhanced senses, but he didn't know these woods. The bear shifters careening through the trees in his wake certainly did.

His only hope was to outrun them and find shelter. The Guard's helicopter was visible through the treetops, but at least he'd lost the SUVs.

The bike hit a patch of tree roots and shot up in the air. He held tight and corrected when they came down, jerking the handlebars before opening the throttle again. The trees thickened, providing cover but less visibility.

"Where are you going?" Simone yelled into his neck.

There were more weapons at his cabin, if he could just outrun the shifters. He turned right, barely missing a sapling, and then snapped around another tree. Branches scraped his cheek, and his left eye watered, so he used his right.

Lucas Bryant flew out of a bunch of cottonwoods, his bike in the air and his gun already firing.

Nick tried to jerk away, but a bullet sliced into his front tire. The explosion was deafening.

Panic swept him. They pitched into the air. He turned, enfolded Simone, and wrapped himself around her as much as possible, protecting her head with his arms. They flew through the forest, hitting trees and branches.

Pain exploded through his back.

His head impacted with a tree, and stars flashed behind his closed lids.

Something shattered in his shoulder a second before agony ripped through his neck. Simone's screams echoed in his head, gravity took over, and his skull cracked.

Unconsciousness took him before he felt the ground.

Chapter 2

Simone wiped blood off of Nick's forehead, wincing at the gash across his left temple. Her entire body ached as if put through a meat grinder, and she could only imagine the damage he'd sustained in shielding her.

His sprawled body overwhelmed the leather couch in the Grizzly Motorcycle Club's main recreation room. The tingle of healing tissue wafted up from his still-unconscious body as his skull no doubt repaired itself. Hopefully. His right femur protruded from a rip in his jeans, and his left shoulder appeared misshapen, as if the bones had shattered.

For now, his body seemed to be concentrating on healing his brain before he awoke. She'd caught a glimpse of his demolished Ducati before the Grizzlies had loaded them up on bikes in the forest.

Man, was he going to be furious.

She looked around, trying to find an escape route.

The biggest plasma television she'd ever seen stretched across one wall, while a pool table, dartboards, and video game consoles were strategically placed around a bar loaded with liquor. The place smelled like leather and wood polish.

Windows took up the north wall, allowing gray Seattle daylight inside. Guard members were stationed at each corner of the room, stances set, their concentration solely on her.

Outside, several more Guard members were strategically placed to contain her as they waited for transport back to Ireland.

She worked within their system, but she'd always done things her own way. When the Coven Nine hadn't wanted to move forward, she'd moved them, and when she couldn't, she'd broken more than one rule. Aye, she'd face up to that.

But not today.

She could sense bear shifters also patrolling the area outside. Where was their leader? He hadn't been among the shifters on bikes. She needed to find him.

Nick gasped and sat up. "What the fuck?"

Simone winced and planted a hand on his good thigh to keep him still. "Don't move until you fix your body."

He leaned over and exhaled. "Holy fuck." Pain cascaded off him. "Next time, we wear helmets," he groaned.

She nodded.

He leaned back and shut his eyes. "Is there anything immediate I need to do?" His voice emerged weak but determined.

"No. Heal your body, and then we'll figure everything out. We're at Grizzly headquarters."

"Is Bear around?"

"No," Simone whispered. "I haven't seen him, and when I asked for him when we first arrived, Lucas said he was out of town."

"Lucas is his second in command?" Nick gasped. His leg snapped back into place, and he grunted.

"Yes." Simone allowed plasma to heat down her arm to her hand, concentrating on keeping the level low before placing her palm on his newly healed leg.

He groaned in pleasure this time.

"Work on your shoulder, and I'll finish healing your thigh," she said, altering oxygen molecules into healing heat and weaving it through the muscle and ligaments. Right now, as much as she hated it, he was her only ally.

He breathed out. "This would go faster if you let me in your head."

Hell to the absolute no. Once a witch loosened those mental shields and let another immortal in, especially a mind attacking demon, she'd be vulnerable for life. Simone would never trust a man that much. Ever. "Not a chance." She heated his thigh.

"With you so close, I ache a little farther up. Heat there?" he mumbled, his lips nearly forming a grin.

She bit her lip. He did not get to flirt with her. Ever. "No."

"Jeez. I did save you." His shoulder changed shape and realigned itself.

She moved her hand over his cracked ribs. "You shouldn't have tried to protect me from the Guard in the first place." The Guard was well trained and powerful, and as tough as Nick was, he couldn't beat ten of them. Beneath her hand, his ribs healed.

She leaned back, her energy draining. "You okay?" Not that she cared about him, but he had to be able to fight if they got the chance.

"Yes." He extended his right hand, revealing three broken fingers. His chest moved as he inhaled and exhaled evenly, and one by one, the fingers snapped back into place. Pain blazed from him, but his expression didn't alter.

Man, he was tough.

A ruckus started up outside, and the door flew open to bang against the wall.

Nick leaped in front of Simone, covering her.

"What the holy fuck is the Irish Guard doing in my rec room?" Bear stepped into the room, irritation sizzling from his honey-brown eyes, and his square jaw set hard. His shaggy brown hair appeared as if he'd been pulling on it, and his clothes looked well worn to the point of being older than the shifter. He paused. "Simone?"

She stood and angled to Nick's side. "B-Bear. Hi." Shit. She'd almost used his real name.

Nick stiffened. "I take it you know each other."

"You could say that." Size-sixteen motorcycle boots clomped as the leader of the entire bear shifter nation entered the room. "Lucas?" he bellowed.

Nick glanced down at Simone, and she shrugged. "Long story." One she had no intention of sharing. Nobody knew about her connection to Bear. Sometimes the truth needed to remain buried.

A door off the bar opened, and Lucas stalked into the room. "You're back."

Bear growled and sounded like the grizzly he truly was. "All I wanted was a few days to catch fish and relax, and instead, I get a frantic call that I have an injured demon leader and a witch from the Council of the Coven Nine held captive in my headquarters."

"I'm not the demon leader," Nick said evenly. "Zane Kyllwood is."

"You're close enough, which makes this a fucking problem. What's going on?" Bear asked Lucas, his hands on his hips.

Lucas crossed around the bar. "The Coven Nine called and asked for assistance in detaining a rogue witch. We didn't know it was Simone until we, ah, captured her in the forest." He frowned, puzzlement stamping his rugged features. "We're allies with the Coven Nine, right?"

Bear slowly nodded. "I thought we were." He glanced at the Guard soldiers standing at obvious attention. "Simone? What's going on? You are still a member of the Nine, right?"

She nodded. "Aye, but somebody has manufactured a lot of evidence against me, trying to prove that I've committed treason in a few different ways."

Bear snorted.

"I know, but apparently the evidence is good enough that the Guard has been sent to fetch me for trial." Her mind spun, but the only way out of the current disaster was for her to go peacefully. "I'm ready and willing to face the charges, Bear." So long as she could finish up a couple of Coven Nine projects first. She kept her gaze direct and her voice level. If she asked him to intervene, he might, and she couldn't have that. Not right now. And if he said no, she'd understand, but it'd still hurt. So it was better not to ask.

"And the demon?" he asked softly.

"Misguided attempt to save her ass." Nick crossed broad arms. "I take it you two, ah . . ."

Simone nodded. Better for him to think that.

Bear's eyes widened. "Me and Simone? No. Ewwww."

Simone shook her head. God. He was such an ass sometimes. "Shut up, both of you."

Nick wiped more blood off his forehead. "I don't understand."

Bear looked at him, then at her, and then back at Nick. "We go way back, have worked together, and that's it. We're friends." He grimaced on the last word. "As much as I have friends. I mean, if I have to have them. It's not like—"

"Bear," Simone snapped. "Shut up." The Guard soldiers were watching him, curiosity and suspicion obvious in their expressions.

No mission on record had Simone working with a bear shifter. Or any shifter, for that matter.

"*Zaychik moy?*" Nick eyed the guards. "You have some explaining to do."

Bear barked out a laugh. "Little bunny?" His eyebrows arched. "Um, that's an interesting nickname. You're not exactly bunny-like, now, are you? What the heck?"

She rolled her eyes. Why did Bear give two craps about a silly nickname? "I like rabbits." There was a time, a century or so ago, when she'd raised them. They liked her, too. Although she definitely regretted sharing that information with Nick during a vulnerable, postcoital, forever-together moment. Those sure as hell didn't last.

"Bunny. You like rabbits." Bear rubbed his chin, his gaze inscrutable. "Did you tell him that during sex?"

Now wasn't the time. "Shut. Up. Bear." Simone allowed morphing blue plasma to dance down her arms.

The soldiers stiffened around them.

Bear held both hands up, not even remotely appearing harmless. Even wearing faded jeans so old they were more white than blue and a T-shirt with Harry Potter on the front, the animal in bear was more than evident. "Okay. Back to business. What does a trial entail?"

"Just a normal trial," she said, not liking the calculating gaze Nick was shooting her way. "The prosecution will present evidence, and I'll defend myself. It'll be fine."

Nick coughed. "Bullshit."

"Excuse me?" Simone snuffed out her plasma.

"A conviction for treason means your powers are blasted out of you, or it can mean death." Nick flashed his teeth. "Bear, if you want your *old friend* to survive, you'll help us out of here before her transport arrives."

The soldier guarding the door shook his head. "Any action to prevent our mission is tantamount to a declaration of war."

"Like I give a fuck." Bear kept his gaze on Simone.

Nick gave the equivalent of a demon growl. "I concur with Bear."

The soldier snarled. "Unless Zane Kyllwood condemns your

actions, demon, the Coven Nine will declare war on the entire demon nation. Again."

Unfortunately, the soldier had a good grasp on the political situation.

Nick set his stance. "Zane Kyllwood has no idea I'm with Simone, and he certainly did not approve my actions. This is all me and not the demon nation." He studied Bear. "You in or out?"

Bear lifted one dark eyebrow. "Simone?"

"I need to face these charges." She tried her damnedest to keep panic from her voice. "We just finished a war . . . Let's not start another one quite yet."

"True." Bear shrugged. "Yet, I'm in."

He'd barely gotten the words out before the lead guard hit him with a plasma ball in the center of the chest. Bear flew through the air and slammed into the bar. He rose, beginning to shift, and the other three guards pummeled him with plasma until he dropped unconscious.

Lucas ran forward and faced the same attack to save his boss. One of the guards drew a gun and shot him several times in the chest. He clutched his arm and fell, falling on his face, out cold.

Nick growled. Vibrations of air from him, dark and menacing, pierced the oxygen. The Guard soldiers cried out, two of them grabbing their temples. One fell to the ground, his body convulsing.

Simone panted, her eyes widening at the nightmarish scene. Turning, she watched Nick's eyelids droop as he managed the demon mind attack and ripped through their brains. "Stop it," she whispered.

"No."

She glanced over at Bear, who was out cold and bleeding freely. Thank goodness the wounds were in the chest. Shifters had a hard time recuperating from head shots. And politically, he was all right. No matter how the day ended, at least he'd be protected because he hadn't had a chance to do anything amounting to a declaration of war. But man, was he going to be pissed.

A second soldier dropped unconscious to the ground from Nick's attack.

The third tried to form plasma down his arms, but the flames sputtered.

God, Nick had gotten even more powerful through the years. Most demons could perpetrate mind attacks, but not to this degree. They shot both images and pain into their victims' brains, which could be destroyed forever. "Nick. Stop it." Even though the Guard was after her, these were her people, and they were just doing their jobs.

He ignored her, his chin lowering.

A helicopter set down outside the wide block of windows, and several Guard soldiers jumped out.

There was no escape, and they'd kill Nick.

Simone sucked in air and drew on all her power. Nick was concentrating hard on the soldiers and didn't turn her way. The bastard wasn't leaving her a choice. She concentrated, drawing on the power of the universe and the molecular compounds around her, creating plasma out of oxygen. Taking a breath, she threw a ball of plasma at his back.

The fire hit hard and knocked him into the sofa.

He jumped up and spun around, red spiraling into his face. "What the hell?"

Winding her arms, she propelled ball after ball at him, burning his clothes, but stopping short of a truly damaging shot, just in case she needed his help getting out of there. She hit his arms, his shoulders, his legs. He growled, twisting and turning from the blows, but not attacking her mind.

She'd counted on him not harming her. Physically, anyway.

Bootsteps pounded outside the building. Damn it. To keep him alive, she had to knock him out before they entered the room. Not for one second did she question her need to save his life.

So she twisted her aim for his face.

He ducked, and the fireball smashed into the door, throwing it off the hinges. Bellowing, he lunged for her, hitting her mid-center and taking her down with a tackle that stole her breath. He landed on top of her, his furious face an inch from hers. "Do not make me hurt you."

Hurt her? He'd just bruised her entire body. She sent flames down her arms.

"Damn it." He flipped her over, planted a knee in the small of her back, and clasped her wrists together, ignoring the fire. Seconds later, something strong wrapped around her wrists and up her forearms.

He stood and jerked her to her feet.

Her mouth gaped open. He'd tied her hands behind her back with his damn belt. Then she smiled. Idiot. She changed the oxygen and increased the heat of her flames, burning the leather completely away.

Her hands remained tied.

Her smile slid away.

He leaned in, rubbing the burn marks along his hand. His gaze was hotter than any flame she could create. "Do you really think I fetched you without some protection from your fire?"

She jerked against the restraints. "You dick." His belt had been leather over coiled steel.

He smiled, and so much threat lived in the expression that she stopped struggling.

The door burst open, and several soldiers ran inside. Guard soldiers.

Plasma flew from the first three, each shooting a different color of fire, all hitting Nick mid-chest. He dropped. The smell of burned fabric and flesh scorched the air.

Simone screamed. "Stop. By the power of the Coven Nine, stop the attack."

The solder in front shook his head. "You don't currently speak for the Nine."

Nick slowly stood, his face a frightening white, his body smoldering.

Simone stared. Nobody, and that meant *nobody*, should've been able to stand after that attack. Nick had a strength that was unreal. "Stop," she whispered.

He lowered his chin, no doubt starting a mind attack.

Five soldiers faced him, and fire flashed out, all different colors. Such fire would kill a non-witch. Simone reacted without thought, throwing herself in front of the injured demon. Fire and then pain detonated throughout her chest.

Nick caught her before she hit the floor, and the last thing she heard as the darkness claimed her was him bellowing her name.

Chapter 3

The blast he'd taken had short-circuited his nervous system, and he hadn't been at a hundred percent before the hit. Nick kept his face stoic as he lifted Simone while baring his fangs. Several of the Guard soldiers took a step back.

A demon rarely let the fangs show, and the sight was supposed to be chill-inducing. However, he wasn't strong enough to manage a mass mind attack, and they all probably knew it. "This is war," he said softly, not missing the roll of fear through the air.

"So be it." The lead soldier stepped to the side, tall and stoic. "Carry her to the transport, or I will."

A low growl rumbled up from Nick's chest. "You touch her, and your brain will never be the same." He hadn't cheated death for more than a century to lose her now. By her breathing, she was healing from the blasts, thank goodness.

The soldier didn't blink. "Just take her to transport and get in. You're under arrest for harboring a fugitive, or for fleeing with a fugitive, or for just pissing me off. I don't give a shit. Right now, you're coming with us whether you like it or not."

Either the guy wanted everything taken care of in Ireland, or he was smart enough to know that Nick wasn't letting Simone out of his sight. Good thing. Facing the Coven Nine held little appeal to Nick, especially since they'd most likely call for his death, but he couldn't let Simone go alone. Somebody had done an exceptional job of setting her up. Though he would sacrifice for her, he had to protect his people, as well. He had to distance himself from Zane and the demon nation. "I'm working alone and not under Kyllwood authority."

"I'm sure that's how it'll come down, whether or not it's true," the soldier sighed, gesturing again for the door. "Let's go."

Yeah, that's probably exactly how it'd come down. The witches could take care of him without eliciting war from the demons . . . if Zane acted like a politician instead of a soldier or a friend. Unfortunately, Zane sucked at being a politician and was an incredibly loyal friend. At the moment, he was on a mission to save his younger brother from a kidnapper, so at least he was otherwise occupied and couldn't be drawn into the disaster right away.

As if on cue, Nick's phone buzzed. He freed his hand, dug it out from his back pocket, and glanced at the face. "I have to take this if you want to avoid immediate war." God, he hoped Zane was all right.

The soldier huffed. "Make it fast."

"Plan to." Nick shifted most of Simone's weight to his other arm before sliding the phone against his ear. "Zane?"

"Yeah. We're good. Got my brother back, and he's fine."

Relief coursed through Nick, even though he was surrounded by armed soldiers. "Good to hear. Ah, I'm in a situation and am heading to Ireland for a bit."

Silence ticked for a second. "Define *situation*."

"Simone's in trouble, and I'm just helping out. You need to lead the nation and excommunicate me."

More silence . . . this one heavy. "The Guard must've found you, right? Where are you? I can be there in a second."

Oh, hell no. Zane, like many demons, had the ability to teleport from one place to another, and he'd just done that at least twice to save Logan. Another jump would be unhealthy, as would facing down the many guards around Nick. "It doesn't matter. Just trust me."

"I do trust you, but you taught me that backup is a good thing. Plus, the Enforcers are here, and their job is to protect Simone."

Nick closed his eyes and breathed before facing the guards again. Damn, he wished he had the ability to teleport, but not all demons could, and that was a sad fact of life. "That would tear the witch nation apart, and Simone would be furious. Stay there and do your job. I'll do mine."

"You sound funny. What's happened? Did somebody attack you?" Zane's voice rose, fury vibrating. "Have you been hit with plasma?"

"I'm fine, *Mom*." Nick's sarcastic tone failed since his voice cracked. Damn it. "Do your job, Kyllwood. You've worked too hard to get where you are and you need to let me handle this." They both had sacrificed way too much. Hell. Nick wasn't even sure he remembered how to be gentle, much less kind after the way he'd lived the last century. He clicked off just as Zane started in with an impressive tirade of threats. God, friends could be a pain in the ass sometimes.

The lead soldier nodded. "You did the right thing."

"No shit." Nick stepped over one of the still-unconscious men just as the lead soldier bent down and hauled Bear up and over his shoulder with a pained grunt. "What the hell are you doing?"

"He's coming, too."

Big mistake. "You can't kidnap the head of the Grizzly nation without starting a war with all the shifters." What the hell was wrong with this guy? Nick eyed Lucas, who was bleeding on the floor. He'd heal from the injuries but not soon enough to lend assistance to his leader. "Put Bear down."

"No. His people are scouting the outer territories, and mine the inner. I can have him in the helicopter before they even know he's gone."

"And? The war?" Nick asked.

The soldier turned, his knees bending under Bear's weight. "He was going to attack us, so he started the skirmish. His connection to Simone is unknown, and my instincts tell me it's important. So he comes to Ireland."

Nick pressed his lips shut. They'd have to take the helicopter to the airport, and by then, perhaps both Bear and Simone would be conscious. It might be easier to wage a battle away from headquarters and before embarking on a plane. "Your funeral, asshole." He moved past the soldier, keeping Simone tucked against his chest and hoping to hell he didn't pass out while holding her.

Even in his damaged state, the woman felt right in his arms. Her spicy scent of wild roses filtered up, and something deep inside him, in a place he usually ignored, settled. Yeah. Only Simone could do that. He had wondered whether he'd ever experience the feeling again, or whether he'd recognize it if he did.

One step in front of the other. One more. He kept his gait steady, even while blue dots jerked across his vision. Blue? Why would dots be blue?

Fire still burned in his chest, and his ears might as well be stuffed with cotton.

His boots must be touching the concrete, although he could barely feel his legs. The combined plasma hits had messed with his entire system, and he needed to rest and heal. So did Simone and Bear, for that matter. Gravel crunched, and the sun shone weakly down, shining off the black SUV.

A dented compact slid into view and quickly stopped. A woman with streaks of purple in her hair jumped out, her eyes a furious blue. "What's going on here?" she yelled, retrieving a knife from her back pocket.

"Private matter," a shorter soldier said, reaching her in seconds.

Nick opened his mouth, but his voice had disappeared. The human female was probably just a friend to the Grizzly Motorcycle Club, which explained how she'd gotten by the shifters guarding the perimeter. "Leave," he whispered.

She shoved the soldier away and ran over to Simone. "Simone? What's wrong with her?" The knife glinted in the sun as she lifted it, concern and fear wafting from her. "What did you do?"

Nick edged to the side to protect Simone from the knife, just in case. "Wasn't me. Who are you?"

The woman glanced at the men rapidly surrounding her, at Bear slung over the lead soldier's shoulder, and then up at Nick. "I don't know what's going on here, but you're not taking Simone." The woman reached for a phone from her pocket, keeping the knife level and ready to strike. "I'm Tori Monzelle. My sister is Lexi Monzelle with the Seattle Police Department, and I'm calling her."

Nick shouted a warning, but the shorter soldier had already grabbed the nerve point in the female's neck and pressed. She spun around with impressive speed, her knife flashing out and catching the witch across the arm.

He bellowed and jumped to the side, dodging in and grabbing her nerve cluster again, this time hard. Her eyelids fluttered shut, and she dropped. The soldier caught her easily, ignoring his bleeding arm. "Shall I leave her inside?"

The lead soldier grunted, trying to shove Bear up his shoulder. "Sister to Lexi Monzelle? Isn't that the Enforcer's mate? Kellach Dunne's mate?"

Damn it. So that's who the human female was. Nick had heard she was dating Lucas Bryant, which explained her presence at headquarters. His vision went black, so he held perfectly still. "Yes, and I doubt you also want to kidnap a human. Especially one with ties to not only the Seattle Police Department but to the Enforcers. She's dating Bryant, so leave her here with him. You know. The bear shifter you left bleeding out on the floor inside."

The soldier smiled, sweat dripping down his face. "She comes with us until we figure this all out."

Nick shook his head. "You're fucking crazy." Or arrogant. Witches rarely gave a shit about the laws of other species, and this guy certainly proved the rule. "Sometimes I forget how much I dislike you fuckin' witches," he muttered. A soldier opened a door to the SUV, and he hitched forward. He slid into the backseat, and Simone didn't even stir. He quickly removed her restraints and settled her safely against his chest.

She was one witch he didn't hate, although she'd pretty much wanted to rip his heart out and feed it to the hogs. Not that he could blame her. Not really.

The soldier chucked a still-bleeding Bear into the back of the SUV, and the entire vehicle shuddered in protest. The unconscious female was placed next to Nick, her head slumping against his shoulder.

He must have blacked out during the drive, because he suddenly realized they'd arrived at the private section of the airport. His growl when a soldier tried to take Simone from him had the guy backing away, hand inching toward a weapon. Grunting, Nick stretched from the vehicle and hefted the still-silent witch across the tarmac and up the steps of a private Jetstream, while a soldier carried Tori Monzelle.

"We're locking you in the back," the lead soldier said, his voice sounding tinny and far away.

Nick nodded, needing more than ever to sit down but unwilling to show any weakness.

Tori chose that moment to awaken, look around the plane, and start screaming.

"Shut up," the soldier carrying her said, grimacing.

She struggled furiously, her face filling with red, her legs kicking out. "You don't understand. God. Get me off this plane. Not near the cockpit. Oh God. Not near the cockpit. We won't make it."

The soldier pinched her neck again, and she went limp with a soft whimper.

"Tie her up and throw a blanket over her on the sofa," the lead soldier ordered. "Take everybody else to the back. We're behind schedule."

Nick eyed the soldier as he placed Tori on a sofa with a blanket. She'd be all right for the flight, and he needed to heal before trying to rescue anybody. With such an obvious phobia about flying, she'd be better off unconscious for the duration.

Pain sliced through his torso from his ignored injures. He turned and staggered behind the two guys carrying Bear to a rather spacious bedroom. They rolled the unconscious shifter onto the bed and backed away, locking the door securely from the other side. Bear started snoring.

Good sign.

Nick gently placed Simone on the bed, his strength rapidly dwindling. Then he glanced around the area for any weapon. Nothing. There also wasn't anything to block the door. While he'd be out-gunned by the soldiers, he still wanted warning if anybody tried to enter the room while he was healing. So he grabbed Bear's shoulders and yanked him from the bed. The bullet holes in his chest seemed to have finally closed, because the blood had stopped flowing.

The shifter hit the floor hard, and Nick winced. He coughed but continued to drag Bear in front of the door. "Sorry, Bear."

Bear fell sideways, his head *thunk*ing on the thick carpet, his body easily blocking the door. His eyes didn't open, and his snoring deepened.

That would work.

Nick stumbled back to the bed and fell facedown next to Simone. He just needed a couple hours of sleep to heal. At that point, he'd figure out what to do next.

Simone mumbled something and curled into him. The scent of wild roses surrounded him, and he fell asleep with a smile tickling his lips.

Chapter 4

Simone struggled in her sleep, trying desperately to avoid the dream from taking her under. But after her injuries, her subconscious wasn't strong enough. Once again, the dream won.

She was been climbing the stairs to her new apartment overlooking the Liffey, her limbs heavy and her heart aching. Nicholai had left her only a week before, his eyes a chilling arctic as he told her it was over. They were over.

She'd pleaded with him, offering to leave Ireland and live with his people. For him, she'd gladly give up her own destiny of ruling the Coven Nine.

He'd said she had been a nice fuck, but he needed to return to real women. Demons only.

She'd given him her virginity, and he'd given her pain. Thank God she hadn't allowed him into her mind, or she'd be vulnerable even to the present time.

Now, a week later, she'd been appointed for life to the Coven Nine. She'd rise to the top and become powerful, relying only on herself and not on any man. She'd learned that one the hard way.

Tonight she'd even celebrate by herself, although her damn cousins were making her attend a family dinner in her honor the next night.

Her hands were full of fresh bread and produce she'd purchased from street vendors. She was so caught up in her musings, she didn't notice the presence of others in her flat until she'd shut the door and walked halfway to the kitchen.

"Simone Brightston." The deep voice echoed around the room.

She'd dropped the groceries, pivoting to defend herself. Two males faced her, one adult and one a teenager. Brown shaggy hair, brown eyes, both fit. "Who the hell are you?"

The kid cleared his throat. *"I'm Beauregard."*

All right. The kid had bruises down the side of his face that seemed to continue into his oversized shirt. "What happened to your face?"

The kid flushed and looked away.

"You are Simone. I heard about your council appointment." The adult looked her over. His lip twisted.

Her appointment had made news all around the world. *"All right."*

He breathed out. *"Vivienne Northcutt is your mother."*

Awareness tingled through the air. Something familiar and yet not really. Simone slid one foot behind the other, in case she needed to kick. "Who are you?" she asked again, wondering whether she could get to the door before he attacked. She could scream, but the Enforcers weren't back home yet, so her breath would be wasted.

Something told her that wasting breath wouldn't be a good idea with the male facing her.

She concentrated, trying to feel beneath his skin. Not a witch or a demon. She knew those signatures. A vampire? Possibly, but it didn't feel quite right. "I'm not going to ask you again," she said grimly.

He smiled then, showing long canines. *"I like your grit."*

The kid seemed to relax. *"Just answer his question, would you?"*

Simone edged slightly toward the door. *"Vivienne is my mother."*

The adult lifted his chin and inhaled, his nostrils flaring. *"I can smell her on you. You are part witch."*

Simone had stilled. *Part witch? "I'm all witch."*

"Is that what she told you?" the adult asked. "Where did you get the last name of Brightston?"

Her mother had said that she was a bright light in Viv's life. It wasn't uncommon for witches to use new first and last names for their offspring. *"None of your business. Who are you?" Her knees began to tremble.*

"I'm Roman. Has your mother ever mentioned me?"

Simone tensed to go for the knife in her right boot. *"No. Sorry."*

He pulled out a green gun—one that shot lasers. *Immortal weapons had always been eons ahead of human ones. "That's all right. Though you'd think the fact that I impregnated her would've made her track me down."*

"What?" Simone asked, her gaze going to the barrel.

The kid's eyes widened. "You said you wouldn't hurt her."

"Shut up." Roman swung, much faster than Simone would've expected, and smashed the kid in the temple.

The teen dropped like a weight tossed into a river and kept going, crashing right out the window. The impact of his body hitting the ground below rolled in with the wind.

Simone gasped. "What have you done?"

"The stupid prick knows not to question me." Roman's broad shoulders hunched, and his eyes darkened to beyond black. "You need to come with me."

The words took a moment to penetrate her shocked mind. The lunatic wanted to kidnap her? "My family won't pay a ransom." There was no way this male was her father, was there? "So leave."

"I'm your family now." Roman's eyes narrowed. "Your mother obviously has done a horrendous job, considering you're about to be mated to a demon. I saw the land deeds for the cozy little cottage."

All right, the guy was crazy. "The demon is long gone. Get out, or I'm going to hurt you." Her voice quavered, and she infused strength into it.

He sighed. "I don't want to shoot you, but I will. Then you can heal at home. Your new home."

Fire lanced down her arms, but before she could throw plasma, he pulled the trigger.

A bullet struck Simone's chest, and pain exploded through her torso and down her shoulder. She cried out and fell to one knee, gasping for air. It wouldn't kill her, but recuperation would take a while.

Fire danced down her arms, and she started to throw, going into a survival mode she'd only heard about. Hissing and throwing fire, she yanked her knife free of her boot and lunged at her attacker.

Something smashed hard into her face, and darkness assailed her. Then nothing. No sights, no sounds, no feelings.

Sometime later, she came awake, her entire body hurting. Groaning, she sat up to see Roman's lifeless corpse sprawled across her floor. The blood around where his head should've been had already congealed.

Bile rose in her throat.

She sucked it down and then saw his head beneath her table.

Oh God. Somehow, she'd killed him. She tried to crawl forward and reached the window, grabbing the sill to look down at the cobblestones. Blood marred the area, but the kid had disappeared; he must still be alive.

"Um, lady? I was out cold for a while." The kid limped inside, and his eyes widened. "Oh my God. You killed him."

Had she? She must have. "I'm sorry," she whispered, trying to stand up.

He reached her and helped her, already strong at his young age. "As a father, he failed both of us. I'm sorry, too." Blood matted the kid's shaggy hair.

Dots covered her vision, and she tried to remain upright. "Was he really my father?"

"Aye. Sorry about that." The kid shook his head. "What now?"

Simone swallowed. "Now we get help from my mother. She has a lot of questions to answer for me."

Beauregard nodded. "I have family across the sea, and I don't want to stay here anymore."

"We'll get you there, sweetie. I promise."

Simone awoke from the dream with a heavy weight on her chest. Holding perfectly still, she opened her eyes, her senses going on full alert. She glanced down. A thickly muscled arm was thrown across the tops of her breasts.

The smell of a storm about to strike, pine-filled and wild, surrounded her.

Nicholai.

Sadness swamped her for the briefest of seconds. There was a time, not too long ago, when she'd belonged next to him. She looked toward her left. He lay on his stomach, sprawled carelessly across most of the bed, his arm over her. Broad muscles made up his back and tapered down to his trim waist. His head was turned away from her, and it took every ounce of her self-control to keep from running her fingers through his dark blond hair. He'd grown it almost to his shoulders, giving him a bit of a pirate look.

A rumbling broke through her musings, destroying the silence. "What the hell?" she whispered.

"Bear snores." Nick turned his head, his dark eyes sleepy, lines cut into the sides of his mouth. The air around them nearly sparkled from the healing waves cascading from both of them. "How are you?"

"Finding it difficult to breathe with you trapping me in the bed," she whispered, trying to clear her mind.

Nick lifted an eyebrow. "There was a time you liked me trapping you in bed."

Heat coursed through her, zinging around her abdomen and landing in a very private place. "That was then." She pushed his arm off and tried to sit up to get a better look at the shifter lying against the door with one boot kicked off. "What in the world is Bear doing on the floor?"

Nick rolled over and sat up, a dimple playing in his right cheek. "I needed a doorstop."

Humor bubbled through her, totally inappropriate for the moment. She cleared her throat. "The plane isn't moving."

"Landed about five minutes ago." Nick scrubbed both hands down his face, ending at the shadow lining his jaw. "I figure they're waiting for more soldiers before letting us out."

That quickly, all humor deserted her. "Listen, Nick——"

"No." He pushed from the bed and gently kicked Bear in the leg. "This is not a place to argue."

Oh, he didn't get to dictate anything. "I don't want or need your help. When we get out of here, you will leave me alone." She could atone for her own sins while fighting the trumped-up charges.

"Bullshit."

"Well." She got up, too, irritation pricking along her back to her neck. "Get the fuck out of my life, Veis."

He half-turned. "Baby, you want to lose the attitude right now." There was the stone-cold killer whispered about by frightened immortals.

Rolling her eyes would be undignified, so she tamped down her anger. "Don't call me baby."

"Then don't be stupid." He kicked Bear harder.

"Whatever we had was over a century ago, because of you, and you've given up any claim on me. Please go back to the demon nation and let me take care of myself." Her family had no right to ask for his help.

His chin lowered then, the movement deliberate and a little threatening. "Wrong."

Her foot itched with the ridiculous need to stomp. She plastered on a simpering smile. "Excuse me?"

He chuckled demon low. "Trying hard to rein in that temper, are you? How long do you think you'll last?"

Heat flowed through her veins along with anger, ready to be freed in the force of fire. She licked her lips. "My temper is well controlled these days, Nicholai."

"Now that's a pity . . . and probably untrue."

"What am I wrong about?"

"What we had is not over. I have not given up any claim on you." Every once in a while, his century-ago Russian accent returned, the sound deep and mysterious.

Her mouth opened and then snapped shut.

A muscle ticked in his neck. "I let you go because I had no choice and figured I wouldn't live to see peace. Yet I have, you're unattached for a reason, and now, your time of freedom is up."

She blinked. Time was up? Panic threatened to choke her, and she shook her head. "You're crazy."

"There is no doubt about that, and I also know I'm not as smooth as I used to be. It has been too long since I tried kindness." Even with the matter-of-fact tone, his voice roughened as he leaned down and pinched Bear's nose closed.

The shifter jumped up, swatting away Nick's hand. "What the fuck?" He leaped to his feet and stumbled back into the wall, hair raising on his arms. Dark hair.

"Don't shift," Simone hissed, backing away. The force of the change inside the small room would be painful.

His brown gaze focused on her, and he straightened his shoulders. The darker hair receded. "Where. Am. I?" he growled, the sound more animal than human.

"My guess?" Nick took a step back, obviously giving Bear some room to contain himself. "Ireland?"

Bear breathed out, his gaze remaining on Simone's. "I can't be in Ireland," he whispered. "You know that."

"I know." Simone held up both hands to placate him. Life had just gotten way out of control, and she couldn't see a way to fix everything. "It's okay, though. I promise. Nobody knows anything about you being here. You haven't broken the contract."

"I'm not worried about myself, and you know it." He shook his head, fury darkening his honeyed eyes to nearly black. "I knew I shouldn't let the Enforcers into Seattle. I just *knew* it."

She winced. "Aye." Were his eyes changing color? Bear's eyes never changed color. What in the world? Something was wrong with the lighting.

"Fuck it, Simone." Bear knocked his head back against the wall. "I signed a contract, and if your mother knows I breached it, no matter what the reason, I'll lose all of my holdings."

"She probably already knows, but we'll just get you out of here, and she'll ignore the situation." Fear settled in her stomach, and she tried to keep her voice soft.

Bear growled low. "I have other enemies in Ireland that you don't even know about. They'll try to take my fuckin' head."

Simone stepped back. "Who?"

He shook his head. "None of your business."

Ouch. That kind of hurt.

Nick's gaze hardened as he looked from Bear to Simone. "It's time to catch me up, little bunny."

Bear pushed off from the door. "Not your monkey, not your circus. Both of you stay out of my business." He turned and set his stance. "Get ready."

Simone moved forward. "Bear—"

He planted his boot in the center of the door, and it flew right off the hinges and through the plane. Guns cocked. Simone peered around him to see at least four soldiers with green guns pointed at Bear. The kind of guns that shot lasers that turned into metal upon hitting immortal flesh. Plasma was too unstable for a plane.

Bear looked down at his hole-riddled sock. "What happened to my other boot?"

Simone grabbed the boot and hit him in the hip with it.

Nick grasped her arm and pushed her none too gently behind him.

"This will be explained," he said softly enough that only she and Bear could hear it.

Bear turned full around, his back to the weapons. "Simone? Does he know anything?"

She tried not to grimace. "No. Of course not."

Nick inhaled sharply.

As she took in Nick's raised eyebrows, she knew without question he wouldn't let it go. No matter what happened next, Nicholai Veis would get his answers, and right now, protecting Bear was all that mattered. So she leaned up on her toes and set her mouth next to Nick's ear. "Bear's real name is Beauregard, and he's my brother," she whispered.

Chapter 5

Ireland smelled the same. Nicholai Veis sat in a waiting area far underground in the secret Coven Nine location after a shower and change of clothing. The witches did insist on their comforts, now, didn't they? At the moment, Simone was probably getting dressed somewhere else. The second she returned, she was explaining her statement about Bear to him. It didn't make a lick of sense.

But he liked her strong and pissed. For so long, he'd carried the image of her pale and sad in his mind. From the day he'd broken her heart. The worst day in his entire life, and that said something.

There was so much blood on his hands, they'd never be clean. He'd chosen his path, and even today, he wondered which moment had tipped his soul into darkness. Was it when he'd turned away from Simone? Or was it the next hour, right after the king had delivered him to demon headquarters?

Nick leaned his head back against the wall and closed his eyes, forcing himself to face that day. Only by facing the past did he have a chance of remembering to love again. God, he wanted Simone, but how the hell could he find his way back to her?

Dage had teleported him to demon headquarters, right outside Nick's rooms. "Jesus," Nick had muttered, stepping back from the king. "You can come right in past our defenses."

"You might want to remember that fact," Dage said, his silver eyes somber. "I don't know what Lily told you, but if you ever need my assistance, you know where to find me." He zipped out of sight.

Nick took a deep breath, went inside to arm himself, and then strode almost casually through the labyrinth of tunnels to reach his uncle's rooms. It wasn't too late to turn back. The image of Simone, tears in her eyes as he rejected her, wouldn't leave his mind.

He rapped quickly on the stone door and waited for his uncle to bellow permission to enter.

Turn back. Turn back. Turn back.

Nick ignored his inner whispers and walked inside his uncle's main office, instantly assailed by the smell of flowers on fire. Opium. His uncle had made smoking the sweet-smelling stuff a sport.

"Nicholai." Uncle Henry stood behind his desk, a map of the new world spread across the stone surface. "I thought you went to Ireland with your tail between your legs."

"I changed my mind." Nick shut the door and crossed the room, bypassing a series of chairs.

Henry's gaze narrowed, and shrewd black eyes took his measure. At about seven centuries old, Henry had honed his warrior's body to pure muscle. His blond hair reached his shoulders, and he'd tied it back with leather. "The witch rejected you, huh?" He threw back his head and laughed.

"No. I decided it couldn't work. The witch is too ambitious to be my mate." Nick reached the desk and surveyed the maps. "What's this?"

"New world with a new breed of human females." Henry smacked his too-red lips together. "Suri and I are thinking about going hunting."

They needed laws in place to protect females of all species from demons. "Doesn't sound like much sport," Nick murmured.

Henry shrugged. "'Tisn't. But the end result is always so much fun." He reached across the desk and smacked Nick in the arm. "Maybe I'll go hunt that witch first and show her what a real man can do."

Nick's stomach rolled. "I don't think so." He grabbed Henry's arm, yanked, and pulled his uncle right over the desk. The demon weighed a ton, but gravity helped.

Henry hit the floor, rolled, and came up swinging.

The first hit to the face nearly knocked Nick across the desk. Pain exploded as his cheekbone cracked. He countered with a punch to Henry's nose. Blood sprayed.

Henry roared and yanked a razor-sharp knife from his back, swinging for Nick's neck. "You bastard," Henry hissed.

"Not really. Mum and Pops were married," Nick countered, slashing across Henry's forearm. His parents had died during the last war, as had many demons. Heat filled him along with purpose. Now he was committed, like it or not.

Henry snarled and tackled Nick, taking him down. His head bounced against rock, and stars flashed behind his eyes. Twisting his body, Simone in his head, he slammed his knife up and into Henry's throat.

Henry's eyes widened, and blood gurgled from his mouth. Angling to the side, he shoved his knife between Nick's ribs.

Agony ripped through Nick's body. "Fuck." Drawing on a darkness he hadn't realized lived inside him, he shoved harder until the hilt of his knife rested against Henry's neck. Pushing up, Nick reversed their positions, twisting and slashing until Henry's head rolled away from his massive body.

Oh God. Nick turned and puked. Then, wearily, his soul actually slipping away, he stood and wiped the knife off on his pants. Coldness settled down his body.

He staggered toward Henry's head and grasped it by the hair. His stomach rolled. What had he done?

This would either work or get him killed, and right now, he wasn't sure of the better outcome. The walk through tunnels to Suri's office took an eternity, and he left droplets of blood the entire way. He shoved open the rock door without knocking.

Suri looked up from his desk. He was centuries old but appeared about twenty; the only sign of his true age was an ancient glint in his eyes. "What the hell?"

Nick strode inside and dropped Henry's head on the desk. The neck impacted first with an odd squishing sound. It would take time and terrible deeds to gain Suri's full trust, but now Nick was committed. God help him. "I think you have an opening in your organization."

Nick was yanked back to the present day as the door opened. He returned from the past to see Simone sauntering in to sit on a thousand-year-old sofa against the rock wall, her green velvet skirt topped by a classic bustier lined with diamonds. She'd pulled her hair up with a fine ribbon, revealing her smooth neck and pounding pulse. A ruby choker, one probably worth millions, glowed against her pale skin.

He cleared his throat, trying to banish the darkness from the past. "I figured you'd go for a modern pencil skirt and blouse to face the accusations."

Her gaze, dark and feminine, moved to his as she opened a ledger on her lap. "I have more power in this outfit."

Yes, yes, she did. The woman wore beauty as a shield and wielded it like a knife. He'd always respected her for the gift and for never trying to be anything but who she was . . . a stunning, brilliant, vain, independent, sarcastic, loyal witch. There weren't enough adjectives in the universe to truly describe her. "We haven't had a chance to discuss the bomb you dropped on me earlier."

"Now isn't the time, Nicholai," she murmured, her hands flattened on the ledger. She drew a pen from her pocket to make notations.

"What are you doing?"

She glanced up, her eyes refocusing. "We've been working on an economical package to assist younger witches wishing to attend human universities. The humans have discovered new advances in science that we can use." Her eyes gleamed. The woman loved strategy and, well, money. He'd always known that.

"You're working." The woman was about to face serious legal charges, and she was working?

"Of course." She frowned. "I have to get this finished."

Oh, first they were going to talk, damn it. How in the hell could she and Bear be siblings? The only way would be for them to share a father. Was Simone part bear shifter?

The door opened, and a guard shoved Bear inside.

"Where's Tori Monzelle?" Simone asked, half-rising and setting the ledger on the sofa.

Bear shrugged. "Dunno."

Simone sat back down and swallowed. "They won't hurt her." Doubt infused her tone.

Bear had changed into pressed black slacks with a bourbon-colored button-down shirt that matched his eyes. An aqua-colored tie hung from his right pocket. "I jumped into the shower, and they took my jeans." He sounded more bewildered than angry.

"One must dress to meet the fucking Coven Nine," Nick ground out, looking down at his pressed black pants and shirt with matching tie. "Whoever chose the clothes lacks imagination."

Bear lifted prominent eyebrows. "Huh. Well, I got blue and light brown. Maybe they went on personality. The all black?" He pointed to Nick's form. "Demon, I guess. Cranky demon."

The damn bear couldn't even speak in complete sentences. Rather, he chose not to. Nick set his hands in his pockets as casually as possible to prevent himself from going for the shifter's throat. "Want to tell me how this all came out?"

Bear crossed the room to drop into one of two chairs aligned at a ninety-degree angle from the sofa. A marble table was set before him. He looked around the otherwise bare room. "No weapons here."

Nick had already scoped out the room. "None."

Bear appeared to be bored beyond belief, but a tension emanated from him that nearly choked the entire room. "Why don't you sit down, demon?"

"Why don't you tell me what has you so upset, shifter?" Nick returned evenly.

Bear kicked back and slammed his boots on the table. "I don't like Ireland."

Nick barely kept from wincing as the priceless table cracked. "Everyone likes Ireland. It's green and cheerful." He tried to read the thoughts of the two immortals, but both could keep him out. "Somebody needs to explain the familial connection," he muttered.

Simone stiffened and swung her gaze to Nick. "The story isn't that long. My mother had a one-night stand with Bear's father, who seemed to have a gift of procreation without mating."

Nick blinked. "The bear shifter wasn't mated to either of your mothers?"

"Nope," Bear said. "Talented asshole, right?"

Incredibly rare, actually. Nick shook his head. "How long have you two known?"

"About a hundred years." Bear shook out his leg in the pressed pants.

Ouch. Simone hadn't even thought of confiding in him, but it wasn't like he could blame her. "Where's your father now?" Nick asked.

"Dead," Bear said simply.

Okay. So many questions. Nick frowned. "How did your father keep Simone's lineage a secret? It's nearly impossible these days."

"He was great with secrets." Bear plucked at a loose string on his pants.

Nick slipped his thumbs in his pockets. "What aren't you two telling me? How did your father die?" Something wasn't quite adding up.

Simone shook her head. "He died so far in the past, let's let him rest."

"I investigated for years, but never found the truth." Bear scratched his head, ruffling his thick hair. The scent of a lie filled the room.

Nick cut Simone a hard look, and she pressed her lips together. "*Zaychik moy?* Come on. Give me the truth."

Her eyes darkened. "He was a real dick who showed up and tried to kidnap me shortly after you deserted me. I ended up killing him." Her hands visibly shook on the ledger.

Instinct whipped through Nick like nails. "Wait a minute. When?"

"In my place about a century ago." She shrugged.

Oh God. "Broken window, blood on floor, huge guy with a green gun?" Nick's gaze narrowed as his mind clicked facts into place.

Bear jerked his head around. "How did you know that?"

"I was the one who killed him." Nick leaned back, awareness rushing into him. "I knew Simone was in danger, I showed up, and I saw him shoot you. I killed him, thinking he was an assassin targeting the Nine."

Simone blinked and shook her head. "What the hell are you pulling?"

"Nothing. The timing is right." Shit. He'd killed their father.

Bear shook his head. "You're a damn liar, demon."

Anger swelled in Nick. He was many things, tons of them bad, but not a liar. "Whether Simone likes it or not, she and I have a connection that was never quite severed. I felt her in danger and had a friend teleport me to Ireland." They'd only just broken up, and he'd still been able to sense her emotions. Or perhaps fate had been helping him out. Who knew?

"Bullshit," Bear said, while Simone looked on with widening eyes.

The damn shifter was about two seconds from getting his head torn off his body. "I heard a fight and rushed in just as Simone went down. So I killed the attacker."

Simone slowly shook her head. "I know I passed out, but I still thought——"

"No," Nick said gently.

Fire lashed through her eyes. "Why the hell didn't you tell me?"

"I had to get out of there before the Enforcers showed up." Nick winced. "I didn't think it mattered." Sometimes he forgot that not everyone lived with so much blood on their hands. He had just killed his uncle, along with several of his uncle's backers, and one more hadn't made an impression. Maybe he'd been doomed from that point, anyway. "I kept in touch with the Nine afterward, and no announcement was ever made, so I figured the Enforcers had taken care of the entire issue."

"Unbelievable," Bear muttered.

"Sorry, Bear. What did you do next?" Nick asked, his mind reeling.

"I got on with life with the bear shifters." Bear rolled his neck. "It wasn't like Roman and I were close."

Roman? Their father had been named Roman. "I'm sorry," Nick whispered.

Sympathy glimmered in Simone's eyes for the briefest of seconds before it was banished. Her gaze swung to Nick.

He gave a barely perceptible nod. Although he'd been there to defend Simone against her father's attempt to kidnap her, probably nobody had defended Bear in his childhood. "Your father, ah, raised you?"

"Yep." Bear stood and stuck his hands in his pockets. "I want my jeans back."

"I'll make sure they're returned to you," Simone said softly.

Nick eyed Bear. "Your mother?"

"Um, a bear shifter who didn't live through childbirth," Bear returned. "They weren't mated."

How very odd. Nick rocked back on his heels. While it wasn't unheard of for an immortal to impregnate someone without a mating bond, it was extremely rare. To be able to do so with two different females, of different species, was impossible. "That's amazing."

"The old man was one of a kind," Bear said, turning to study a Brenna Dunne oil painting on the far wall.

Land mine there. Something told Nick that Bear wasn't being completely forthcoming, but Nick couldn't exactly blame him. He cleared his throat, watching carefully for Bear to lose it. "You mentioned you have enemies other than the Nine in Ireland. Who?"

Bear shook his head, his gaze almost haunted. "Not talkin' about it."

Fine. "What contract with the Nine were you talking about when we were in the plane earlier?"

Bear slowly turned, his eyes seeming darker than usual. Much darker. "When the truth came out about Simone being part shifter, I signed a contract with the Coven Nine, or rather, her mama, that I would never reveal Simone's lineage, and that I'd get the hell out of Ireland."

Nick shook his head. The damn witches, their egos, and their dangerous ambitions. Maybe it had been a mistake to encourage Simone to follow hers. Look where it had gotten her. "Let me guess. If you reveal the truth, or if you set foot in Ireland, you forfeit everything you have?"

"Yep," Bear said.

"Figures." Nick glanced at Simone. "Vivienne wanted me to sign such a contract when Simone and I, ah, decided to break up. I said no." He couldn't help the sarcasm dripping from his words.

Simone rolled her eyes. "Yeah. *We* broke up. Asshole."

He deserved that, but now, something different glimmered in her eyes. Would the fact that he'd saved her life soften her toward him? God, he hoped so. "I guess Viv's plan for you to mate with a full-bred witch and not one of us mongrels hasn't come to fruition?" Nick kept his voice level, but bitterness still ate through him.

Bear snorted. "You ended it because of Viv?"

"No. I had a job to do that didn't allow any entanglements, and I truly thought it was for Simone's best," Nick said.

"You fucking prick," Simone spat. "Nobody protects me for my own good. We are so done."

Nick turned and met her gaze evenly, feeling hope for the first time in way too long. They'd both been through rough times, but maybe this was their reward. Perhaps, just perhaps, fate was rewarding him with a second chance. "We are by no means over," he murmured.

The clouds disappeared from Bear's eyes. "You're not over?" His entire body visibly relaxed. Then he threw back his head and laughed, long and loud.

Chapter 6

The door opened, and a soldier gestured toward Simone. "Ms. Brightston? It's time for you to face the Coven Nine."

"Councilwoman Brightston," Nick said evenly, stepping in front of her.

The soldier flushed. "My apologies, Councilwoman. It's time to meet the members."

"I *am* one of the members of the Coven Nine." She stood, her chin high.

"Yes, ma'am." The soldier stepped back.

Both Nick and Bear moved into motion, and the soldier shook his head. "Ms. Brightston alone."

"No." Nick stepped in front of her. "Pursuant to Coven Law, Title Eighteen, Section Four, Subsection D, Councilwoman Brightston is allowed a representative at the reading of any charges. I'm her representative."

Simone paused. "You've been studying Coven law?"

He looked over his shoulder. "I figured it would come in handy at some point. Look. It has." He turned back to face the guard.

The guard sputtered and then drew his shoulders up. "You're a demon."

"No shit." Nick planted both hands on his hips. "Nowhere in the Coven laws does it specify that only witches can serve as representatives. So get the hell out of my way before I melt your small brain out of your ears."

Simone cleared her throat. "Nick, I can handle this."

"You're not handling this on your own." He didn't bother to look over his shoulder this time.

"I agree," Bear said, moving to her side.

Okay, that wouldn't work. She patted his arm. "Both of you need to butt out."

Nick turned then, facing her fully and ignoring the guard. "We can do this the easy way or my way, woman."

Fire gathered inside her. Damn it. She had to stay calm, and right now, Nick was as solid as a brick wall. She couldn't go through him. "Excuse me?" Her voice dripped with sarcasm.

"We go nicely, or you enter the chambers over my shoulder. Either way, I'm going." His jaw hardened to what looked like sheer rock.

Bear leaned around her to get her attention. "I hate to agree with the demon, but you can't go by yourself. We should all go."

Simone nearly cracked a tooth by clenching her teeth. She had to protect Bear. "All right. Nick can come as my representative, but Bear, you need to stay here."

"Why?" Nick asked.

"Because my mother has a bounty on his head," Simone snapped. Damn men. She shoved a wayward tendril of hair out of her eyes. "Plus, apparently he has other enemies here that he hasn't shared with us."

"Everything is fine," Bear muttered.

"Sure it is." Simone shoved Nick in the back. "If we're going to go, let's do this." She forced a smile for her brother. They'd stayed in touch through the years, but she'd always wanted to be closer. "By the way, I've missed you."

His ears turned red. "Me too."

"Jesus." Nick reached back for her hand and started forward, all but dragging her along. She tried to tug free, and his grip tightened.

"Let go," she hissed, drawing up alongside him.

"No." His stride didn't shorten, and she had to quicken her pace to keep from tripping.

The familiar rock around her did little to soothe her nerves, yet she kept her face set in calm lines. They passed priceless oil paintings, sculptures, and prints set perfectly against the smooth rock walls, while immaculate maroon carpets cushioned their steps. The guard led them through the labyrinth of underground tunnels, obviously one of the few soldiers who knew the path.

"Tell me about entering the council rooms," Nick said, his gaze straying to a Vicente Voltolini landscape on the far wall.

"What do you mean?" Simone asked.

"The veil. Tell me about the veil and how to survive going through it." His hand tightened around hers.

She tripped as they reached the end of the tunnel, and the guard maneuvered a bunch of rocks against the stone into the correct formation.

The stone slowly slid open. "Wait in there for them to get you," the guard said. "Ma'am," he added quickly when Nick snarled.

Nick led the way inside a waiting room set with plush blue furniture, gold accents, and a Persian rug. "You witches sure like it fancy," he muttered, releasing her hand and crossing to the closed door on the other side. "Tell me about the veil." He turned to face her, arms crossed.

She slowly shook her head, awareness crashing through her. "You're expecting to go through the veil?"

His head tilted ever so slightly. "Well, yes. We're entering the chambers, right?"

"Yes." Heat filled her lungs. The veil was a protective shield of cosmic forces that protected the entrance to the chamber, and it could rip a person apart without leaving a trace. He'd thought to brave the veil just to be her representative? Why? Why would he take such a chance? "The only non-witch ever to survive the veil was Conn Kayrs, and he had been mated to witch Moira Dunne for a century. He barely survived."

"I know. Now tell me what I need to understand," Nick said, his eyes blazing.

"Nick." She shook her head. "You're not going through the veil." She held up a hand to stop him as he began to argue. "We put in a back door to the chamber after Moira insisted that Conn accompany her on missions." Moira, Simone's cousin, was an Enforcer, and her vampire mate just had to tag along. "This is the back entrance. No veils."

He blinked and uncrossed his arms. "That's a security risk."

"One we had to take." She lifted a shoulder. "There's plenty of security, in case you missed the crazy maze we had to go through to get here. Plus, there were several coded doors we went through before reaching the last room." The emotional armor shielding her started to crack, and she scrambled to hold herself together. "You really can't have meant to risk your life like that."

He moved then, coming at her. "You're not doing this alone."

She shook her head, wanting to back up, but her feet remained frozen in place. "Nick, no—"

"Yes." He paused in front of her, gently grasping her chin. "I'm familiar with your laws, all laws, actually. I will represent you, but you have to make me one promise."

Butterflies blasted through her abdomen. "What promise?"

"If it looks like things are going south, and I have a chance to get you out of Ireland, you let me."

What? She tried to shake her head, but he held her easily in place. "I'm not running. What are you planning?"

"Backup plan, *Zaychik moy*." His gaze dropped to her mouth. "I always have a backup plan. You know that."

She swallowed, suddenly feeling too warm. "I will not run."

"You'll do what I tell you to do, if it means surviving." No give showed on his face.

Temper, finally, took over her emotions. Flames shot down her arms. "You do not tell me what to do."

"There it is." He leaned down and brushed his lips over hers. "Keep that anger with you today. I have a feeling we'll both need it."

Her temper flew. Oh yeah? Man, she was tired of him messing with her equilibrium. She was Simone Brightston, for Christ's sake. Time to throw him off balance. She grabbed the back of his head and lifted up, angling her lips perfectly inside of his. Her eyelids fluttered shut, and she slid her tongue inside his mouth.

He stiffened, his lips nearly pressing into a line.

She smiled just enough to let him know he couldn't fool her. Nicholai Veis had forgotten whom he was dealing with. She wasn't some wilting human female who wouldn't bite back. She was Simone Brightston, member of the Coven Nine, and a badass, bitchy witch. Her tongue flicked along his bottom lip, then she slowly, so damn slowly, moved away.

She leaned back, satisfaction relaxing every muscle in her body. If the demon thought he could take the upper hand with her, he'd forgotten her power.

His lids were half-closed, and a fire burned in those dark eyes. Crimson darkened his high cheekbones, and his nostrils flared like a panther catching a scent. Tension emanated from him in waves.

Her mouth curved in a smile. Triumph felt good.

Then he moved.

Faster than any shifter, he clamped both hands on her arms and lifted, shoving her against the rock wall. She let out a startled *eek*, her hands fluttering in protest to his rigid biceps.

Held half a foot off the ground, she barely had time to register her position before his mouth crashed down on hers.

Fire exploded inside her, burning and spiraling out. He kissed her hard, going deep, banishing every thought she'd ever had. Sensations, dark and demanding, softened her muscles. She moaned, overtaken with impossible need.

Hunger, so strong it clawed, stole all rationality from her.

The pain of the instant craving fired through her, bringing a shot of true fear. Her body was taking over, and nothing else mattered.

As if he sensed her fear, he softened his assault, reducing the pressure and drawing her away from the edge. His mouth still worked hers, showing her the devastating pleasure to be found in his gentleness. The warmth spiraled around and spread through her chest.

He brushed his knuckles across the tops of her breasts.

They ached, heavy and full, her nipples hardening to sharp points.

He released her mouth, and she gasped in breath. Her lungs wouldn't fill with air. His thumb slid beneath her bustier and ran across a nipple.

She gasped, and her legs trembled.

He watched her, lust shining in those dark eyes. Several deep breaths moved his broad chest.

She swallowed. Instinct kept her still. One move, just one movement, and they wouldn't be able to stop. *She* wouldn't be able to stop.

Slowly, with perfect control, he lowered her to the ground.

The second her feet touched, reality slammed home. "We can't do this," she whispered, her voice hoarse.

He released her and stepped back. "Not here, anyway."

"Not anywhere."

"Why not?" He straightened his tie, his gaze unrelenting.

Was he kidding her? "You're a bastard."

"Not technically, but I sure as hell acted like one. I've explained that. Fate gave me no other choice. Plus, you've had a century to forgive me. Time's up."

Panic still threatened to swamp her. "I appreciate that you saved me with my nutjob father." Truth be told, she wasn't happy she hadn't taken him out herself. "But you and I were finished a long time ago."

He shook his head. "The war is over, we're allies, you've forgiven me, and now it's time to deal, little bunny."

That's exactly what scared her. She'd never been able to handle Nicholai Veis, and now, with the Guard after her, wasn't the time to try. "No."

He lifted an eyebrow. "You've never been a coward. Now's not the time to start."

What an ass. She parted her lips to say something, anything, but the outside door opened.

Nick fully understood Simone's reluctance to delve back into the quagmire of their wild relationship, but sometimes risks paid off. He'd seen it happen with Zane, and although Nick had maneuvered the chess pieces the best he knew how, he still never expected to succeed the way they had. Zane was now mated and even had a daughter.

Sometimes life worked out, even for the wounded and desperate.

He fought the urge to step in front of Simone just in case an attack waited on the other end of what turned out to be a long hallway. These were her people, and she had to face them without a shield.

For the moment, anyway.

If anybody threatened her, he'd become more than a mere shield.

Dim light filtered down and barely pierced the darkness on either side of the hall.

"Keep your steps on the carpet," Simone whispered back. "One inch off, and weapons discharge from the walls."

Fucking witches. "Great," Nick drawled, his shoulders tightening to stone. Magic, the ancient and rational kind, surrounded him with threat. While the veil might be somewhere else, power vibrated against his skin, raising goose bumps. There was no doubt his energy, that of a demon, did not belong in this place.

A door at the end slid open silently, and he followed Simone into the underground chamber very few non-witches had ever seen.

The headquarters of the Council of the Coven Nine.

Even with magic nipping at him, he was somewhat disappointed. In the center of the room was a raised rock dais complete with long counter and nine high-backed velvet chairs. Empty chairs. Twin tables, divided by a walkway, faced the dais. Just like a modern courtroom. "Shouldn't there be bats flying around and cats howling?" he whispered.

Simone's shoulders straightened, and she approached the nearest table, drawing out a seat. Nick naturally sought out the exits, but there weren't any. A quick glance behind him confirmed that the door he'd passed through no longer existed.

Wonderful.

He slid out the seat next to Simone and drummed his fingers on the stone. "Where is everybody?"

She stared straight ahead and clasped her hands together on the table. "We like to make an entrance."

Oh yeah. The smooth wall behind the chairs parted, and three people walked through to take seats facing them. Peter Gallagher, Nessa Lansa, and Sal Donny, all members of the Nine, calmly watched him. He'd read extensive dossiers on Peter and Sal, but he'd never met them in person. Nessa had just been appointed to fill a vacancy, and he didn't know anything about her. The door slid closed.

Simone drew in a sharp breath and stood.

"What?" Nick whispered, also standing.

She shook her head and visibly swallowed.

"Where are the other five members?" Nick asked, his back rigid. Even though Simone obviously couldn't sit on the council right now, there should still be eight people passing judgment.

Peter sat in the middle at the head council's position. "This is not common knowledge, but Council members Louise Fronts and Frances Murphy were attacked a fortnight ago with darts filled with planekite. Many darts, and they're both in comas." Anger lowered the witch's voice to a growl. "The outlook is not good."

Simone shook her head. "I'm so sorry, Peter. Did they catch the attackers?"

"Not yet," Nessa responded, shoving thick black hair from her face. Her deep blue eyes nearly glowed in the candlelight, and Nick made a mental note to have her investigated. "The Guard is hunting them, and we're thinking of recalling the Enforcers."

"After this matter is taken care of," Peter said, his dark eyes somber.

Simone nodded.

Nick needed to follow up on his people's search for the manufacturer of planekite, which was the only mineral in existence that could kill a witch. Somebody was after the witches, and he vowed he'd find out who, if the Enforcers didn't track the bastard down first.

Simone cleared her throat. "Please send my regards to Louise and Frances."

Nick didn't like the subtext he wasn't quite catching. "What about your mother, aunt, and cousin Brenna?" All three women served on the Council, and he'd counted on their votes to free Simone, considering they were her family.

Simone cleared her throat. "If they've been excused from this duty, there's only one reason."

Oh, he wasn't going to like this. "What's the reason?"

Simone's chin lifted, but she kept her focus on the Council. "The accusers are seeking the death penalty."

Chapter 7

Simone kept her posture straight and her gaze inscrutable. The underground candlelight danced around, no doubt enhancing her beauty. She had no illusions about her looks and had used them often to her advantage. There were two men sitting in judgment and one woman, and she hoped it would be hard for the men to kill beauty. Punish perhaps, but not end. As for Nessa, she was a complete mystery.

A side door opened from nowhere, and Colman Foley, dressed in a slate-gray suit with red power tie, walked in with stacks of files in his hands. At about five centuries old, Colman had been the Coven prosecutor for several centuries. His hair was black and curly, his eyes a dark brown, his skin a smooth mocha, and he was a genius at building up a case to prove guilt.

He nodded at Simone and set the files next to her. "Here's everything we were sent and the materials we've compiled. For your defense." Then he took his place behind his table.

Nick leaned down. "This is all so civilized."

She nodded. "Whoever is out to get me sent the materials to the Coven Nine, which had to investigate. Nobody here wishes me harm, but they'll all do their jobs. Colman has a duty to follow the evidence."

Nick drew out his phone and tapped the face. "I can't get service."

Simone gave him a look.

"Oh." He glanced around. His tech guys had created devices that could broadcast from this far underground, and he needed to be more prepared next time. "Okay. Once we're aboveground, I'll have dossiers put together on the council members as well as the prosecutor. By tomorrow I'll know every single weakness they have." His voice rumbled with anticipation.

"You love strategy, don't you?" she asked.

"Yes."

The side wall opened again, and a burst of energy in the form of Moira Dunne-Kayrs rushed inside, curly red hair flowing and wild. Her sister, Brenna Dunne-Kayrs, entered more sedately, her brown hair up in a fancy clip. The two, Simone's cousins, immediately flanked her, with Moira edging between Simone and Nick.

Simone glanced from one to the other. "What in the world?"

Peter Gallagher banged an ancient gavel on the stone. "Moira Dunne, you are an Enforcer and have not been called before the Council yet. Brenna Dunne, you have been excused from your Council duties for the duration of these proceedings. Neither one of you should be here right now."

To Simone's surprise, Brenna stepped forward first. "With all due respect, Peter, you forgot the *Kayrs* at the end of our names. We married brothers, you know." Her voice was polite but direct.

Simone bit back a smile.

"My apologies. Sometimes I forget the vampires exist." Peter was just as polite in his sarcasm.

"That's unwise." Brenna had dressed in a flowing gray dress the exact color of her eyes and appeared calm and serene. "I am here as the representative for Simone Brightston."

Simone touched her arm. "You can't do that, Bren." Her heart warmed, and she shoved emotion away. Brenna had to remain neutral.

"Sure I can." Brenna eyed Nick, who was watching the proceedings with a slightly bored expression. "Apparently there are two of us representing you."

Simone shook her head. "You can't take that risk. If things go bad, you'll lose credibility on the Council." Not to mention the emotional hit Brenna would take. "You're pregnant, three months if I remember, and you need to distance yourself from this stress and turmoil." Though Simone would always remember the sacrifice sweet Brenna was trying to make.

Brenna turned to face her fully, a gentle smile curving her lips. "Shut the fuck up, Simone. I have a job to do, and I'll knock you on your ass if you get in my way." She kept her voice low. "I love you, you're family, and I'm going to protect you whether you like it or not."

Simone blinked. Had Brenna just said "*fuck*"? "Geez. Being mated to a vampire has turned you raunchy, Bren."

"You have no idea." Brenna leaned in even more. "Are you going to allow me to help you? Or do I get nasty?" An odd purple flame danced down her arm to sputter out.

Simone frowned. "What in the world was that?" Bren's flames were usually green or blue.

"Pregnancy." Brenna rolled her eyes. "It has totally messed with everything. So stop ticking me off, or I'll accidentally start shooting plasma."

"Enough of this. I appreciate the offer, but I don't need help." Simone turned her voice curt and her gaze arrogant. "Now, toddle home to the vampires and prepare your nest for that baby. Or whatever occupies your time these days." She turned away to face the Council, her stomach roiling. While she hated to hurt Brenna's feelings, there was too much at stake to allow the pregnant witch to stay.

Heat and sudden pain flared along Simone's arm. She yelped and edged to the side, her gaze widening as she turned back to Brenna.

"Oops," Brenna said, no remorse on her face, reaching out to snuff out the fire she'd lobbed.

Simone rubbed a round burn on her forearm. "You're supposed to be the nice one," she hissed quietly.

Brenna lifted a graceful shoulder. "Eh. Nice is overrated. The bitchy act won't work with me, so knock it off." She turned to face the dais. "I love you and I'm here to help. Deal with it."

Simone's mouth opened and then shut with a sharp *snap*. Brenna had always seen through her outer shields, which was why they were close. Her insides tried to turn all mushy with love and gratitude, but she kept her face set. "Fine, but if it gets dangerous, you're leaving."

"Uh-huh." Brenna smiled for the three council members and raised her voice. "Simone has accepted my offer of representation."

Peter cleared his throat. "That's unwise for you personally, but not against the rules. The Enforcer hasn't been called, however."

Moira stepped forward, irritation all but buzzing from her. "The

Enforcer has a name, Pete. While the remaining Enforcers are in Seattle tracking down the main distributor of Apollo, I'm here in official capacity to protect Simone Brightston."

Peter blinked. "Excuse me?"

Simone moved to stop Moira from speaking, but the wild witch held up a hand to halt her. "Simone is a member of the Council Nine, and if she's innocent, which I believe she is, then somebody has gone to an enormous amount of trouble to set her up. She's in danger, and it's the Enforcers' job to protect Coven members in danger. Thus I am here."

Nick leaned in to Simone. "Isn't family a pain in the ass?" Somehow, although he probably tried to hide it, he sounded a bit melancholy. The poor guy had never had a family, having lost his parents centuries ago.

Simone nodded. "There's no way to get them to leave."

Peter studied Moira, who met his gaze levelly. Finally, he nodded. "Very well, but if the Coven Nine decides to send you on a mission elsewhere, do not forget your alliance." Peter banged the gavel down. "Let's get this started. Please read the charges."

The prosecutor nodded. "The charges are simple. Simone Brightston is guilty of committing treason, the first-degree murder of humans by using planekite darts, and the attempted murder of witches. The charges are made more serious by the fact that Coven Nine members have been attacked with planekite, thus requiring imposition of death on the guilty party."

Simone's head buzzed. At least all the charges were trumped up and not based on the actual laws she'd broken. Yet. It all seemed so casual and normal, yet the prosecutor, in following the law, was asking for her head to be removed from her body. She should be terrified or even angry. But shock drew her away from the proceedings in a way that felt impersonal.

"This is bullshit," Moira muttered beneath her breath.

Brenna smiled. "We demand a proffer of proof."

The prosecutor clasped his hands at his back. "I've compiled all proof and handed the papers over in manila files, but I'm willing to give a brief recap. For more than a century, Simone has transferred money through different accounts and funded various endeavors, the latest being the mining of planekite, which, as you know, is the mineral that kills witches."

"You've traced Simone's money to the planekite mining and distribution?" Brenna challenged.

"Yes. The mineral has been used to create Apollo, the drug killing humans in Seattle, as well as inserted into darts and shot at our Coven Nine members." The prosecutor rocked back on his designer loafers. "We have signatures, e-mails, texts, and other records that show Ms. Brightston was not only aware of the mines but actively set this plan in motion."

"Why?" Moira demanded. "Why in the world would Simone do such a thing?"

The prosecutor shook his head. "Our theory as to motive will be revealed at trial. For now, every bit of evidence we've collected has been turned over to the defense. We request a trial date."

Peter leaned forward. "Pursuant to Coven law, a trial date is set for Monday."

"Five days from now?" Nick shook his head. "That's ridiculous. Five days isn't enough time to go through and counter this stack of nonsense." He pointed to the files. "This is a death penalty case."

Simone jabbed him in the ribs and winced as her elbow ached. "It's our way." She cleared her throat. "I accept the trial date and enter a plea of not guilty for the record."

"Plea so entered," Peter said.

The prosecutor stood straighter. "Through Councilwoman Brightston's tenure on the Coven Nine, she has pursued progress and her own personal vision in a way that has undermined other council members and the organization as a whole. We don't have evidence yet, but we are investigating her in this area, as well."

Ballocks. Simone remained stoic. Sure, she'd gone for right over tradition more than once. Had she broken a law or two? Maybe. Okay. Definitely.

"Very well," Peter said with a short nod.

Yeah, they'd butted heads more than once. Simone lifted her chin. "I look forward to answering those charges. In the meantime, members of the Guard kidnapped a human female and a bear shifter when they took me in. The shifter, Bear, and the human, Tori Monzelle, need to be released and returned to Seattle," she said.

The prosecutor placed both hands on his table and leaned forward. "Both the bear shifter and the human female attacked our soldiers. They must stand in judgment."

Simone fought to keep her fire at bay. "The bear shifter was protecting his territory from attack, and the human female was protecting a friend. Bear is the leader of all bear shifters, and if you try him, the entire shifter community will declare war on the Coven Nine. I believe we're under enough attack already right now?"

Nessa leaned and whispered something to Peter, who then nodded. "Good point. The record reflects that the shifter didn't actually attack anybody before the guards shot him. He is so released," Peter said.

Simone nodded. "Good. The human is a friend of mine, and she saw me unconscious and being taken. She acted accordingly. In addition, she has no idea the immortal world even exists or that she attacked a witch soldier. Finally, her sister is mated to Kellach Dunne, one of the Enforcers. If you harm her, you'll have to deal with Kell and probably his brothers. Also something we can't afford right now."

"Is that a threat?" Sal asked, his booming voice filling the chambers.

"No. It's a fact," Simone said simply.

Brenna tapped the files in front of her. "The human and the shifter aren't part of Simone's case, and thus, the entire Council would need to be consulted before bringing them to trial. You've already taken care of Bear. Now, dismiss any charges against the human, and we can get on to Simone's case."

Peter didn't look to either side this time. "Did the human female see any evidence of immortal species?"

"No," Simone said.

Peter nodded. "The charges against the human female are dismissed, and she is released. Simone? You're responsible for getting Bear and the female out of Dublin within the night. You, however, are ordered to remain in Ireland until after your trial."

"The prosecution requests a planekite bracelet," the prosecutor said.

"No!" Moira burst out. "We're in a battle against that deadly mineral right now, and putting it on one of our own is ridiculous."

Peter's eyes glowed somber and regretful in the chamber. "The effect of the bracelet is very mild and only inhibits power. It won't harm the accused."

"Bullshit." Brenna pressed both hands on her hips.

Simone jumped and turned in surprise to view her cousin. All three sitting council members gaped.

An angry red flushed up Brenna's pale skin. "I've worn a planekite collar, as you know. There's nothing harmless about it."

Simone reached out and rubbed Brenna's arm. Years ago, the younger witch had been kidnapped and poisoned with planekite. She'd nearly died before mating a vampire to negate the effects. Good thing she'd fallen in love with the wild Kayrs brother. "Bren? It's okay. I can handle it." Her voice cracked at the end.

Peter began to answer, but Nessa leaned forward. "Simone? Do you give your word you'll stay in Ireland without a bracelet?"

"I do." Simone eyed the brunette. "Although I could leave town even wearing the bracelet, as a matter of fact."

"True, but having your powers reduced would make you vulnerable," Peter countered.

Nessa sat back. "I'm against the bracelet. Even though Simone is accused of a terrible crime, right now she's innocent in our eyes and deserves the respect of her Council position. A bracelet is an insult. A dangerous one."

Peter glanced at Sal, who just shrugged.

"Fair enough. No bracelet. See you in trial." Peter banged the gavel one final time. He stood and followed Nessa and Sal through the opening in the wall. It *snick*ed shut.

The prosecutor nodded at Simone. "Good luck." He pivoted and soon disappeared through the side doorway.

"I've never liked him," Moira said, shoving curls out of her eyes.

Nick reached for the stack of files. "Let's get away from here to go through this evidence. I already have investigators on the issue, but this might help them focus their search."

Simone paused in turning. "You have people on this?"

"Of course." He nudged her hip. "Let's go."

Moira reached the wall first and opened the doorway again. "We'll use the penthouses overlooking the Liffey as a case headquarters."

Simone followed as if in a dream, her mind swimming. Shock. Aye. Must be shock. As they moved through the labyrinth, she followed the Kayrs sisters without question. Trust. She had that with them. God, she hoped she wasn't convicted and sentenced to death. Her chest compressed.

"It's okay, little bunny." Nick was a solid force behind her. "Trust me."

She nodded and blinked back tears. Simone Brightston didn't cry.

They finally reached a series of arches that led to a quiet street behind an old church. Night had fallen, and a soft rain pattered down. Bear and Tori sat across the cobbled road on a short rock wall fronting a graveyard.

Tori jumped up, her eyes concerned. She rushed forward to hug her friend, her arms damp. "Simone! You're okay. Where the hell are we?"

Simone cut a look at Bear.

He shrugged and shoved to his feet. "I didn't know what to tell her."

Simone sighed and leaned back. "Tori? I'm part of the government here. There was a skirmish, and you were accidentally taken in. It's my fault, and I'm so sorry. We'll get you back home as soon as possible."

Tori blinked. The purple streaks through her hair glowed in the dim moonlight. When had it become night? Then her gaze narrowed. "What the hell is going on?"

Simone sighed. Many people underestimated Tori because of her youth and wild hair, but the woman was sharp as a blade. "Let's get out of here and away from the graveyard, and I'll try to explain better." During that time, while she was once again lying to her friend, transport back to the States would be arranged for Bear and Tori.

A rumble filled the night.

Simone half-turned just in time to see four motorcycles barreling toward them from the north. Almost in slow motion, she turned to see four more from the right.

Fire flashed.

Chapter 8

Nick grabbed Simone and Tori by the hands, propelling both women toward the wall. "Jump and run," he ordered, gratified when they both launched themselves into motion.

A ball of plasma smashed him square in the back, and pain exploded down his spine. The force threw him over the wall, and he flew face-first into an ancient headstone. Agony burst in his forehead. The stone cracked down the middle, and he kept going, rolling over wet grass. His vision clouded.

His back smacked a tree trunk, and his body folded.

Holy fucking damn it.

Roaring, he stood, turning to face the melee.

Simone and Moira had taken shelter on his side of the rock wall and were hurling fireball after fireball at the eight motorcycle riders. The men had created some sort of plasma shield and were advancing while throwing their own plasma. Their different-colored fire hit another shield hard and then spread. Brenna stood behind the other two, her eyes closed, her hands up.

She must've created and now was controlling their shield. Impressive.

Bear lay over to the side, out cold, his hair smoldering. The human female hunched over him, frantically patting out the fire. Nick hustled over to lean down and feel Bear's pulse. Strong and steady.

"He jumped in front of, ah, fire for me." Tori slapped flames off of Bear's stomach. "I don't understand." Her widened eyes took in the scene. "They're making and throwing fire. Real fire. I really don't understand," she repeated.

Nick winced. He had to get Simone out of there.

The shield wavered, and a plasma ball hit Simone in the stomach. She doubled over with a pained *oof.*

That easily, that quickly, Nicholai Veis lost it. His hands went up, his chin went down, and he strode forward while aiming a devastating blast of mental pain toward the male witches, watching his team through his peripheral vision.

Moira yelped and tackled Brenna out of the way. Simone slowly turned and straightened her body, still holding her abdomen.

The men's shield shattered with an audible blast. The closest man screamed and grabbed his head with both hands, still holding plasma. His own fire bit into his flesh, and he screamed louder.

Nick spread out his attack, basically slicing right down the centers of their brains. He kept an eye on everyone around him, but his internal focus was on the enemy.

"Are you seeing this?" Moira hissed.

"Yes," Brenna murmured. "It's incredible."

Simone moved to the side and out of his way.

Bear growled to the left, and there was a rustling of pine needles. "Status," he barked.

Another two attackers dropped to the ground, one silent, the other keening.

An SUV rounded the far corner down the street on two wheels. Shit. Backup.

"I'll finish with Nick," Simone said urgently. "Moira, get Brenna, Bear, and Tori to a safe house. We'll be in touch."

"My job is to protect you," Moira protested, hauling Bear to his feet.

Simone pushed her toward the headstones. "Nick and I will be fine. Brenna is pregnant, and Tori is human. Go."

Moira grimaced but nodded. "Fine, but you call the second you can. We can't go to the penthouse."

"No. Run, now."

"Human?" Tori said weakly, turning as Moira grabbed her arm and started running. "You're *not* human?"

Nick kept his attack strong, and the remaining four men dropped into unconsciousness in a natural attempt to salvage their brains. The SUV careened closer, and another one came into view.

His hands shook, and something wet came out of his ears. Blood. He was bleeding. Attacking minds held risk.

Simone grabbed his arm. "Nick. We have to run."

She was right. His knees weakened.

Sucking deep, he released the attack just as the SUV roared to a stop. Turning, he grabbed Simone's hand. "Run, baby." Trying to keep his vision somewhat clear, he allowed her to lead the way through the headstones. "Go north," he whispered tersely.

Her steps hesitated, but she turned to the left and cut a path between the dead.

The slam of car doors and somebody barking orders filled the silence behind them. Thunder rolled high above, and lightning flashed down, illuminating grave markers. The rain increased in force. He kept his chin down and his senses tuned in to the men chasing them. There were at least six, and they moved well, spreading out to blanket the cemetery.

He'd told Simone to head north because the men had angled more to the south, but now they advanced quickly. What he wouldn't give for the ability to teleport. Just once, to get Simone out of danger.

The graves turned to large tombs and overgrown trees.

She released his hand to yank open the door to a dilapidated tomb. He clasped her arm to keep going. "We'll be trapped."

"Trust me." She struggled but managed to pull it open. "Come on."

He followed her inside, trying not to step on the colored concrete over the two graves, and turned to shut the door. "Simone, this is a mistake. If they find us—"

She moved a bunch of angels on the far wall into a different configuration, and the floor beyond the graves opened. "Hurry." She ran down steps into the darkness.

He hustled after her, quickly descending until his feet hit dirt. She pushed a lever, and the opening closed. Darkness enfolded them.

"Just a second," she whispered, fumbling around. A flashlight lit up. "Are you all right?"

He shoved wet hair off his forehead and nodded. "I am. The attack weakened me, but I'm regaining strength." He kept his voice soft. "Where are we?"

"Escape route," she whispered back.

He stilled. "If it's a Coven Nine escape route, they may know of it."

"'Tisn't." Her skirts brushed the dirt up as she turned to lead the way. "This is one of my family's routes. We've had members on the Council since the beginning of time."

For once, he appreciated the witches and their love of secrecy and drama. "Where does it lead?"

"It leads several different places, but I know of a safe one for the night. We can regroup there and figure out what to do next." Her voice came back hushed as she hustled down the tunnel, ignoring several forks until finally turning down one.

"Who were the attackers?" he asked, his senses tuned in for any noise or scent that didn't belong.

"I don't know. It wasn't the Guard, obviously. It doesn't make sense that rogue witches would attack me, so maybe it had something to do with you? Or maybe Moira?"

Nick rubbed his chin. "I didn't see the beginning of the fight, but it looked like Bear was a target. They hit him right in the head."

"Perhaps. He did say somebody in Ireland was gunning for him." Simone turned another corner and walked several yards into a dead end.

Nick paused. "You took a wrong turn?"

She patted the stone wall in a series of taps, and it began to glow. "No."

Slowly, the wall parted, revealing a studio apartment of sorts. They walked into a cozy living room complete with leather furniture, next to a utilitarian kitchen. Simone pointed to a doorway off to the right. "The loo is through there. Last I checked, 'twas functional." Now that she was home, apparently her accent was deepening.

He loved that accent. His gaze was caught by a loft beyond the sofas and round table. Five steps led up to the area, and a wide bed took up the entire platform. A plush midnight-blue throw covered the massive bed. His body tightened, and his pulse quickened. "So. What now?" he asked.

Simone gathered her wet skirts, reaching for a basket atop the counter that held several burner cell phones. She grabbed one and dialed, relief bursting from her when Moira answered.

"Are you safe?" Simone asked.

"Aye. We ran west, and the Guard picked us up, having heard the commotion. I believe several of the rogue witches who attacked us are now in custody, but I've heard they're not talking. Are you safe?"

"Yes." Simone wiped rain off her face. "We're in the blue room." Her cousin would know her exact location, but on the unlikely chance anybody had tuned in to the call, they wouldn't have a clue where she'd taken Nick.

Moira breathed out. "Okay, good. That's good. Stay low for a few hours, until we make sure the locale is safe."

Simone nodded, her adrenaline still flowing. "I understand." Some of the attackers might still be searching the cemetery. "The Guard is on the issue?"

"Aye. We'll have all of the attackers in custody by morning." Moira cleared her throat. "Bear is furious his hair was burnt. The man is rather vain."

Simone winced. "It appeared that the attackers were aiming for Bear and not for me."

"I'm not sure. It seemed as if they wanted to take all of us out."

"No. Bear has mentioned other enemies, but he won't tell me who they are. See if you can get the truth from him." Were there rogue shifters in the area after Bear? If so, why wouldn't he ask for help? Even as the thought crossed her mind, Simone mentally shook herself. Bear would never ask for help. "Tell Bear to stop being a dick."

Moira snorted. "I'll tell him, but he's looking rather pissed off right now."

"How is Brenna?" Simone kicked mud from her heels.

"She's fine, but Tori is seriously freaked out."

Simone caught her breath. "Does the Guard know she saw us fight?"

Quiet ticked by for a moment. "I'm not sure they've put it together, and we're being deliberately vague. Hopefully we'll get her back to the States without mishap."

Oh God. Simone exhaled slowly. If the Guard knew Tori had seen them use powers, then she'd be in definite danger. No human could know about the immortals. "We have to protect her."

"Aye. We will. Destroy the burner phone, and call again tomorrow morning. I'll have a plan then." Moira clicked off.

Simone swallowed and dropped the phone, stomping it into several pieces. Finally, she turned to face Nicholai. He leaned against the far wall, his arms crossed, his hair damp. Scruff lined his strong jaw, and a purple bruise marred his right cheekbone. His tie was gone, his dark shirt was in tatters, and his pants were covered in mud. Even so, a tension spiraled from the demon. "We, ah, just have to lie low for a few hours until the cemetery is cleared," she murmured.

He didn't move.

Her hands fluttered together. "I'm sorry to get you all mixed up in this mess."

"Come here, Simone."

She blinked. Heat slid through her like a fine wine. That voice. Sometimes, late at night, she remembered that rough voice. Panic competed with the heat, and she spun around to open a cupboard. "I'm freezing." That's why her voice shook. Aye. She was cold. Regaining her composure, she drew out two glasses and a bottle of decades-old whiskey. Splashing plenty into the glasses, she took one and held it out to Nick.

He crossed the room and accepted the glass. "*Slainte.*"

"*Slainte,*" she returned, *clink*ing her glass with his. Tipping back her head, she shot the entire glass. Fire exploded down her throat and into her stomach, billowing out to warm her limbs. "Better."

"Yes." He refilled their glasses and *clank*ed again.

She tossed back the whiskey. Instead of calming her, as she'd hoped, the alcohol increased her awareness through a heated haze. The demon studied her, his gaze direct and knowing. Her damp clothes suddenly felt restrictive and much too tight.

"You're wet, Simone."

She jerked and then realized he was talking about her hair. Her hand trembled when she brushed the mass away from her face. "I'll dry."

His lip quirked. "Want help?"

Her system went into overdrive, and she sought any bit of normalcy. A low chuckle escaped her, and she gestured around at the intimate apartment. "This is convenient."

"There isn't a damn thing about you that's convenient." He reached out and ran his knuckle down her cheek.

The touch was gentle and reverent, but an uncoiled tension filled the air around them. She cleared her throat. "Did you mean what you said? That you never thought we were over?"

"Yes." His exploration continued down her neck and across her upper chest, that dark gaze following the path of his fingers. "My mission this last century was dangerous, and I figured I didn't have much chance of surviving, even if I succeeded in changing the demon leadership. Letting you go made sense at the time. Now I find out I killed your father. I am sorry for that, Simone."

"You killed him to save me," she whispered, her voice hoarse. "I didn't know him, and those brief moments with him were enough to realize I didn't want to." The first time they met, the bastard had shot her.

"Aye," Nick said.

Emotions, raw and real, ripped through her. Just standing next to Nicholai Veis softened her thighs, hardened her nipples, and created an ache deep inside her only he could satisfy. "My father, like many shifters, was crazy, and you saved me."

Nick tucked two fingers in the neckline of her top and drew her forward. "Then you owe me." He lips met hers, gentle and seeking, all heated power.

She moaned and stepped into him, tilting her head, taking him in. He kissed her, and his rough, unshaven chin rasped against her skin in delicious friction. Finally, he released her. "Is this going to happen?"

Her eyelids slowly opened. One night. Just one night to see whether it was as amazing as she remembered in her dreams. She was facing possible prison time, the loss of her powers, or even death. Why not have one great night of mind-blowing sex? She could keep it casual. "Yes, but it's just physical. I won't risk anything else with you ever again." Sometimes honesty could protect a girl.

Triumph and an intimidating arrogance darkened his eyes. He swung her up and turned toward the bed. Then he paused.

"What?" she breathed.

He turned his head toward the door. "I don't know. Something—"

The entire world rocked, and an explosion roared down the tunnel outside. He dropped her to her feet. Shards of rock pummeled down.

She ducked to avoid losing an eye. "Oh God. They've found the tunnel."

Chapter 9

Nick looked around for weapons and jumped out of the way of a bowling ball–sized boulder dropping from the ceiling. The attackers were using dynamite to blast through the tomb above. They'd be at the tunnel any second. "Tell me you have something here I can use for defense."

Simone gathered her skirt. "We have something better. Escape route." She turned and ran for the bathroom.

Of course. Nick bounded behind her into the room.

She jumped into the narrow shower, tapped a series of tiles in an odd order, and the side opened up into a narrow tunnel. "Run," she whispered.

He followed her, having to duck his head. The door *click*ed shut behind them. Darkness surrounded him, and the walls closed in. His gut rolled, and the inside of his stomach pricked with a thousand needles. "Tell me this goes somewhere and that it's been checked out lately." The breath panted out with his words.

She reached back for his hand. "Trust me."

He had no choice. Even so, the muscles in his back tensed with the need to punch through the too-close walls.

She tugged. "We have to hurry. It's okay. I'd forgotten about your fear of small spaces."

He loped into a jog, hoping she knew the way in the dark. Not that they could turn the wrong way. If they did, they'd hit solid rock. "It's not the space, it's the lack of it." His lame joke fell flat.

She chuckled quietly. "Just think of that nice, big bed back there that you almost got to use."

Even as he was panicking, his cock perked right back up. "That was a nice bed." His toe hit a rock, pain shot through his foot, and he winced.

"I was going to let you do all sorts of nasty things to me," she whispered, increasing her pace.

It was nice of her to try to distract him, but he needed to concentrate. "This tunnel has to end somewhere, right?"

"Just keep moving." She made her way in total darkness without a hitch in her jog. "I know these tunnels well."

He had to hunch to keep from hitting his head, and every once in a while the tunnel would narrow until his arms scraped along the sides. The smell of mold and dirt wafted around. They ran for nearly an hour, at his guess. Finally, after an eternity in the darkness, dim light glimmered up ahead along with the sound of pelting rain hitting cobblestones. His heart rate picked up.

They reached an iron gate, and Simone swung it open.

Rain blew in on a sharp gust of wind. Nick jumped outside, taking several deep breaths as the world righted itself. Simone shut the gate and quickly engaged a lock.

Okay. They were all right. Nick straightened. A building, some kind of warehouse, was directly in front of him, and the gate was behind him, set directly into the rock outcropping. As he watched, a door of solid stone moved to cover the gate. A foghorn moaned through the night, and the slap of water against rocks echoed over the storm. "Where in the hell are we?"

"The docks." She grasped his hand and tugged him around the side of the building. "The edge of the warehouse district. Follow me."

Like he had a choice. He set off at a run, his strength returning with the oxygen around him. They maneuvered between buildings, across several lots, and into the edge of the city. Simone's hair streamed in the rain, which had matted her clothing to the intriguing curves of her body. She moved like a nymph, graceful and fast.

The movement of her fit buttocks kept his attention through several alleyways and back roads.

Finally, she came to a halt and held up her hand. "I need a second."

So did he. His dick was about to punch through his zipper. He discreetly adjusted himself but failed to reduce the pressure.

Brick buildings bracketed them, while the rain slashed down from high above. A series of rickety fire escapes ran up three stories, but they were quiet and empty.

A car drove by the street at the end of the alley, its lights quickly fading into the night.

Simone pressed her butt against the building and leaned over, panting in air. Pressing her hand to her nicely outlined chest, she straightened. "'Tis too bad. I really liked that safe house." Her hair had started curling down her back, and a light pink brightened the feminine angles of her face. Her dark eyes glowed through the dim light, and her scent of wild roses drifted on the breeze.

She was truly the most amazing creature he'd ever seen.

He moved without thought, right into her, and lifted her against the brick. Her sharply indrawn breath opened her mouth, and he dove in, all primal instinct. Drowning in her, going as deep as he could, he unleashed the loneliness he'd felt the last century without her. After he'd tasted her warmth, being alone had been a constant ache in his chest. For a fucking century.

Forgetting all finesse, he cupped her ass, his palms lifting the twin globes and yanking her into his hardness.

She whimpered deep in her throat, and the sound rolled up and into his mouth, lighting him on fire.

Desperate to get closer, he spread one hand across her ass and threaded the other through her hair and tugged, nearly bending her in two as he kissed her with all the pent-up need he'd banished for so long.

She moved against him, the apex of her legs so damn hot he almost went to his knees.

Only Simone. She was the only woman in the entire world who could drop him to his knees. At the moment, he'd go gladly.

The adrenaline from the fight rushed through him, turning into raw passion. Little noises came from her as she returned his kiss, her body rigid and gyrating against him. The friction between them nearly pushed him over the edge.

Rain dropped, and he ignored it. Yanking down her top, he licked his way down her wet neck and sucked a nipple into his mouth. She moaned and shot both hands into his hair, digging her nails into his scalp. The small bite of pain spurred him on, and he licked and sucked the sharp point before moving to the other one.

Her skin was smooth and so soft he almost came in his pants.

Almost frantic, he reached under her skirt and yanked off her panties.

"Nick," she murmured, releasing his hair to grapple with his belt buckle. The damn thing finally came loose, and she released his zipper. Her fingers barely had time to run along his shaft before he'd lifted her and impaled her with such force crumbs of brick rained down.

She stiffened around him with a soft moan of pure pleasure.

The sound licked through his body right to where they were joined.

Her eyes were closed, and her hair cascaded against the wet brick.

He grabbed the back of her neck, strengthened his hold on her butt, and stilled. "Simone. Look at me."

Simone's eyelids fluttered open. Nick Veis was inside her, balls-deep. Cold and hard, the brick behind her helped her to balance against the demon holding her so fiercely. She couldn't move, even if she wanted to.

Which she did not.

Intense hunger darkened his face, edged with a demon's posses-siveness. Slowly, trapping her gaze, he slid out of her and then rammed back in.

Electricity shot from her clit to her breasts. She gasped and stiff-ened, her eyelids closing in pure pleasure.

"Simone."

She opened her eyes again, her insides quaking in devastating tremors. Even so, she kept her mental shields firmly in place. She could have him, could enjoy him, without giving him access to her mind. Her thighs shook. "Nicholai."

At her use of his full name, something snapped in him. His hold somehow tightened, and he pulled out to drive back in. The friction was unbelievable, as was his strength. He hammered into her, shov-ing hard, the slap of his flesh against hers filling the deserted alley.

She kept his gaze as long as she could and then had to shut her eyes to just feel.

An orgasm washed over her out of nowhere, and she gasped. He didn't pause, just kept on fucking her. A second later, she was climbing again, sparks rippling through her, propelling her toward the edge. Heat uncoiled deep inside. She dropped her hands from his hair to his massive shoulders, trying to hold on to any semblance of reality.

He wouldn't let her.

Somehow he drove harder inside her, hitting a spot that detonated stars behind her eyes. She whimpered, her thighs slamming against his hips with enough force to bruise. So close. She was so damn close.

"Please, Nick," she gasped, her body stiffening.

He changed the angle of his thrust and brushed across her clit.

She exploded with a soft cry, biting her lip to keep from screaming. Waves crashed through her, full of fire and sparks. The orgasm tore through her, head to toe, centered around his hard-as-steel cock. Finally, she came down with a soft sigh of pure pleasure.

He tucked her closer, nearly bending over her, ramming hard.

Fangs sliced into her neck.

Her eyelids flipped open, and she cried out, her body going into a multitude of convulsions too powerful to be mere orgasms. Nick released her neck to plant his hand on the brick wall, his body shuddering as he came.

He pulled her close, breathing heavily, using the building for balance.

She dropped her face into the crook of his neck, trying to catch her breath. Her arms slid around his shoulders, and she held on even as her body went limp. Muscle rippled beneath her mouth, so she placed a soft kiss on his neck.

Slowly, reality returned. Rain pummeled them, and a car honked in the distance. She blinked and lifted her head away from his warmth.

He pushed off the brick.

Oh. Hmm. She loosened her thighs, and her legs slid toward the wet cobblestones. Small pains became known. He kept hold of her until she'd gained her balance and tried to step back. One knuckle under her chin lifted her burning face.

"Are you all right?" he asked, his voice a low rumble.

She nodded.

"I—" He glanced around the back alley. "Jesus, Simone. I got carried away. In a fucking alley."

He sounded so bewildered, she had to bite back a laugh. "You should probably zip up."

"Christ." He released her and quickly zipped his pants, wincing at the end. "I meant for this to happen in a bed," he mused, slicking his hair back with rain.

"Oh, did you." She adjusted her sopping wet skirt to try for modesty, although it was probably too late for that. "Sure thing, was I?"

He stilled and moved into her, backing her right into the brick again. "Not in a million years. There is nothing certain about you, little bunny." He tried to yank her bustier up to cover the tops of her breasts and then gave up. "I just knew we weren't finished. Not by a long shot."

But what did that mean? She shivered in the sudden cold and rubbed her aching neck. "You bit me."

"Yes. Plan to do it again, too." His teeth flashed in the darkness.

A shimmer took her abdomen. Sex was one thing, fangs another. A demon mated by biting, sex, and a brand from their hand . . . as did witches. It was a good thing they'd both kept their hands from branding each other. She wasn't one of those women who would end up mated without a lot of thought first. Not that he had offered. She needed time to think about what she wanted, and right now, she mostly wanted to survive the next month or so. "We have to get to a safe house."

"Mine this time, not yours." He took her hand and strode down the alley, leading her around mud puddles and rubbish bins.

"You have a safe house in Ireland?" She hustled beside him.

"Yes."

She shook her head. "Demons aren't exactly welcome in Dublin, as you know."

He turned and lifted her over a sprawling mud puddle. "I know, but Dublin is your home. I have safe houses everywhere you own a home or business."

Humph. Her heart hitched. She blinked against the rain, her mind spinning. "What exactly do you want from me, Nicholai?"

His deep chuckle echoed off the buildings bracketing them. "I want everything, Simone. And this time, I'm going to keep it."

Chapter 10

Nick finished scrambling the eggs in the spacious steel and granite kitchen, feeling more settled than he had in eons. It was well past midnight, but finally, he had Simone in a safe place. He whistled softly, dishing up two plates and placing them in the cozy breakfast nook facing the tumultuous Liffey. As rivers went, he liked this one. Moody and mysterious, it had always called to him.

His phone buzzed again, and he ignored it, but he knew Zane well enough to know that the demon leader would not take the hint and go away. He thought about the past.

Nick had followed fate's plan and helped Felicity escape her brother and demon headquarters. Then when the vampire she'd mated was killed, and she had nowhere else to turn, he'd talked Suri into letting her come home. Sure, Suri had planned to kill Felicity and her three boys, but Nick had manipulated the hell out of him with thoughts of heirs and futures.

Even now, he could remember the day a wounded Felicity had returned home.

She'd sat in the office with Suri, while Nick had remained outside with the three boys. The oldest one, a kid about twelve, had furious green eyes and an already strong build. "I'm Zane."

The name alone sent an awareness through Nick that had to come from fate. "Nick."

The kid's hands had clenched. "My mother is afraid of her brother."

"She should be," Nick said, going on instinct and telling the kid the truth.

"What about you?" Zane studied him, way too much understanding in his young eyes.

"My job is to protect you and your family." The words came out like a vow.

Zane lifted his head, while his younger brothers looked on. "Is that a promise?"

Nick had nodded, his chest filling with a purpose that was no longer so fucking dark. "It isn't going to be easy, kid, but yeah. That's a promise."

Through the years, they'd become friends. Hell. They'd become family.

Nick was jerked back to the present by the appearance of Simone in the doorway wearing a pair of his sweats, rolled up several times, and one of his faded T-shirts. Her thick hair curled down her back after her shower, while her skin glowed from the heat and lack of makeup. She was stunning.

She gestured toward the food. "You're all domesticated now?"

"I can scramble eggs for a late supper." He pointed to her chair while reaching for orange juice. "Sit."

She gave him a look but still sat, grasping her fork to eat a few bites. "Not bad."

"Thanks so much." He poured orange juice along with coffee. "Eat something, and then we'll grab some sleep. I contacted Moira, and she's bringing the evidence against you here; nobody else knows where you are." Keeping his voice as undemanding as he could, he continued, "I'm arranging safe transport for you out of the country. I can fight the case here as your representative, and if we don't win, you'll be safe."

Her fork stopped halfway to her mouth. "No."

He dug deep for patience. "It's the safest course of action. Moira said the evidence is truly damning."

"I don't care. There are several projects I have to conclude while I'm here. I'm a member of the Coven Nine, and as such, I'll follow our laws. Plus, I just gave my word in chambers that I wouldn't leave, remember?" She sipped the coffee, and her cheeks colored. "I have to believe in our system, and I do. The more important question right now is who has gone to such lengths to harm me . . . and why." Her eyes darkened.

It hurt her. That somebody would want to ruin her, maybe see her dead. The woman had been raised by a single mother with a stunning ambition to rule. No father anywhere, and the first man she'd trusted, Nick, had broken her heart. Then she'd finally met her father, and the asshole had shot her.

No wonder Simone had turned to work and power to survive.

Few people fully understood the sweet girl who lived behind Simone's stunning looks and sarcastic wit. That girl had been wounded by such evil being directed at her. Nick saw the kind woman inside her and always had. "Whoever has done this will pay."

She nodded, her eyelashes thick and dark against her pale skin. "I just want to know why."

"My guess is that you're the easiest target."

She straightened. "What do you mean?"

He'd been giving the matter a lot of thought, and if anything, he truly understood strategy. "As a member of the Nine, you live abroad and have many of your own investments and interests, including alliances with other species."

She bit her lip.

"Your business interests are more diverse than those of the other Nine members, and you have accounts to hack." He ate his eggs, his mind working through the issue. "Though I'm curious about motive. The prosecutor said it would be revealed at trial, and there's no legal way to make him give it up now, if there is a possible motive."

"If?"

Nick nodded. "Perhaps they haven't yet figured out a motive and are hoping to find something by trial." Yet something in the way the prosecutor had dangled the carrot was troubling Nick. "Though I think they have something." What, he didn't know.

"I think they have something, too . . . but for the world of me, I can't figure it out." She licked her lips and kept her gaze on the plate. The fact that she was part shifter would hurt her politically, but it certainly wasn't a motive for murder, even if the prosecutor had that information. Perhaps nobody knew about her genetics, anyway.

He stilled, tuning in to her emotions. Ah. "Do we need to talk?"

Her lashes fluttered, and she focused on him. "We are talking."

"About the fact that I fucked you silly in an alley an hour ago." He lifted an eyebrow.

She neither flinched nor turned away, facing him head-on, like the woman she was. "Thanks for the orgasms?"

He barked out a laugh, amusement warming his chest. "I'm sorry if I was too rough." If? Hell, he'd been way too rough, and a woman like Simone deserved a bed, not a brick wall. But she went straight to his head, always had, and that would probably never change.

"I'm fine, Nicholai. Let it go."

"No." The woman wasn't quite understanding him. So he lifted his right hand, palm out.

She swallowed, and her head jerked back. Horror, the real kind, glimmered in her eyes. "The marking. Yours."

"Yes." Man, she didn't have to look so horrified, did she? He flipped his hand over to study the intricate crest with a clear V in the middle, crisscrossed by jagged lines. V for Veis, his family name. The marking itself was buried in their genetics, and it only appeared when a mate was near. Not one ounce of him was surprised it had appeared with Simone again. Last time it had taken nearly five years for the damn thing to disappear after they'd ended their relationship. Something told him this time it wasn't ever going away. The marking wanted to be used. Transferred to her flesh.

She reached for his hand and turned it over, running her finger over the lines as if staring at a bloody train wreck. "Your marking is beautiful. I'd forgotten."

He hadn't. Sometimes just thinking of her made his palm hurt. "How about I use it this time around?" While he didn't want to, he held his breath as he waited for her answer.

Regret twisted her full upper lip. "You're crazy."

"Yes." He slid his hand back. "I let you go once, and you know why. The war is over, Zane is in power, and now I'm free to live my own life. That includes you."

"If I'm convicted?" she whispered, the first hint of fear visible in her dark eyes.

"You won't be."

She reached for her orange juice. "You don't know that. If I'm convicted, I face death. You sure you want to be mated for eternity to a dead woman?" Her throat moved, sexy and strong, as she swallowed. "While a new virus being worked on by the vampire queen might negate a mating bond, it seems silly to put you through that.

Plus, the so-called mating cure has never been tested in a male, as you know."

There wouldn't ever be another woman for him. "If you're convicted, I'm getting you out of here."

"A demon can't get involved, no matter what I decide. The second in command to the demon leader really can't get involved. Publicly, anyway." She shook her head. "These are my people and my laws. I'm fighting until the end." She sighed and sat back. "How about we deal with the current trial and crisis and forget the emotional crap? I need to concentrate, Nick."

That hadn't been a yes, but it wasn't a no, either. He could've easily mated her in the alley, but he wanted more. He wanted her to come to him with her eyes wide open and prepared. Being the mate of a demon strategic leader, the strategic leader of the entire nation, wouldn't be easy. War came too quickly, and he could be one cold bastard when the time called for it. If the witch nation and the demon nation ever went to war again, her allegiance had to be with him. Period. "I agree to concentrate on your trial, but I'm not giving up on us."

She nodded, her gaze thoughtful.

The door burst open, and Moira Kayrs hustled inside, concern blanketing her features.

Simone half-stood.

Nick sighed. "Come on in, Moira." The feisty witch could've waited for him to unlock the door, damn it. He stood and crossed the living room to inspect his door. The Enforcer had used plasma to melt the inner workings. "You owe me a new lock."

"We seriously have problems." Moira crossed the room and filched a piece of bacon from Nick's plate. "Tori and Bear were taken into custody, and the Coven Nine has demanded the demon nation excommunicate you, Nick."

Nick slowly closed the door, energy washing down him. "And?"

"Zane refused." Moira took more bacon, her green eyes somber. "The Nine has given him twenty-four hours to change his mind, and then we declare war." She chewed thoughtfully and then bit her lip. "I mean, the witch nation declares war on the demon nation, which will cause a ruckus because both are now members of the Realm."

The Realm was a coalition of vampires, shifters, witches and now demons. A war between two of the species would tear the newly forged Realm apart.

Simone shoved her plate toward Moira. "Have some eggs." She wiped her mouth delicately with the napkin. "If the Nine declares war on the demons, they'll demand the demon nation be kicked out of the Realm."

Nick felt a growl rising, so he took a moment before speaking. "I spent too much time and energy to making the demon nation part of the Realm. The vampires can't kick out the demons."

"Agreed," Moira said, nodding her head in emphasis.

"So Zane has to excommunicate me, and right now." Nick slipped his cell phone from his back pocket. "Before I call him, what's the status of Bear and Tori Monzelle?"

Moira cleared her throat and reached for Simone's orange juice. "Tori is in containment since she definitely is aware of the witch nation and that immortals exist. Bear went a little nutty trying to defend her and took a beating before escaping into the night."

"Was he all right?" Simone asked quietly.

"Yeah, I'm sure he's fine. Shifters have hard heads." Moira lifted an eyebrow. "Why?"

Simone gave her a hard look. "What? I never express concern for others?"

"No." Moira rubbed her chin. "Not unless you care about them." She leaned forward, her voice hushing. "Is there something between you and Bear?"

"Of course not." Simone reclaimed the remainder of her juice.

Nick leaned against the door, watching the exchange. Simone hadn't even told her cousins about her lineage. Interesting. With Bear hopefully leaving Ireland soon, Simone's secret would be safe.

Witches and shifters rarely mixed, and although there was no requirement for a Coven Nine member to be a full-bred witch, they were definitely preferred. Simone would face opposition if it was discovered she was part-shifter. Even though she'd never shifted and seemed not to have inherited the gene.

Nick flipped his phone around in his hand. "Moira? Where's Brenna?"

Moira sighed. "Jase returned from his hunting trip north, discovered that Brenna had been attacked by those witches, and well . . ."

Simone sighed. "So my other attorney is now not my attorney?"

"She's three months' pregnant." Moira shrugged. "Plus, the group firing planekite darts at witches made an attempt on her life last week, so the Coven Nine Enforcers, including me, agreed to put her into lockdown."

Nick chuckled. "You put her into lockdown?"

"She's a member of the Council of the Coven Nine, sister or no, and my job is to protect council members, although she can still attend regular business meetings if the Guard is around." Moira grinned. "Man, was she pissed."

Simone smiled. "It was nice of you to take the heat for Jase."

"I don't know what you mean," Moira said, her lips curving.

That was nice. With Brenna pregnant and in danger, a vampire like Jase would probably go to the mat to get her to safety, whether she liked it or not. By using her job as an Enforcer and insisting on Brenna's safety, Moira had probably kept peace between Jase and his mate. "You're a good sister, Moira," Nick said.

"I am a peach," Moira agreed. "Although I should tell you that I might be recalled to the States. There's an outbreak of Apollo in the form of planekite darts in Los Angeles, and I have to investigate. Two witches were attacked last night, and one may not make it." Her brow furrowed. "I could disregard orders, if you need me."

Simone covered Moira's hand with hers. "We have enough protection with the Guard here, and you should get back home to your babies."

"I'm a working mom, magic or not. Besides, my mate is bringing the boys to Ireland and should land in about an hour." Moira patted Simone's hand. "Oh, and you have Enforcer protection, just not me. The second cousin Adam discovered Tori was here, he jumped on a plane. Should be here in about five more hours."

Simone leaned back. "Adam? And Tori?"

Moira shrugged. "Don't ask me. I don't see Adam as a guy who'd like a human, you know?"

Simone slowly nodded. "When is Tori's hearing?"

"Hearing?" Nick strode toward the table.

Simone nodded. "She gets a chance to speak."

"Oh great." Sarcasm burned his tongue. The entire situation was getting out of control, and the last thing he could afford was emotion.

Especially since his was way off. "I know you wouldn't harm her. What about the other council members?"

Moira sighed. "Hopefully they're thinking clearly and not running scared because of the planekite attacks. We have to figure out a way to keep Tori safe. Perhaps a simple contract will work in which she promises not to reveal any secrets." Doubt wrinkled her smooth forehead. "It would be better if she had something to use to blackmail the Nine, but I don't have anything up my sleeve."

"Me, either," Simone murmured. "We'll just have to testify as to her trustworthiness."

"You're on the Council," Moira said.

"I know, but I can still testify."

Moira nodded and then sat back, her shoulders relaxing. "All right. Tori's hearing has been scheduled for after your trial."

Simone leaned back, her gaze darkening. "I don't like that."

"Me, either, but she's been sequestered, and I had a hell of a time finding her. She's gotta be scared. I sent you the address for her current location on your cell phone. I know she'll at least be there through the night, so you can drop by and see her tomorrow morning before attending the Coven Nine hearing that was just set." Moira took another sip of Simone's juice. "The Nine has scheduled the hearing to question Nick."

Nick reared up. "Why?"

Moira shrugged. "You were captured in Seattle speeding away from the Guard with a fugitive, Simone, on the back of your bike. They're not arresting you, but they do want to question you, and diplomatically, you should agree to be questioned."

Simone nodded. "I agree. We can explain what happened well enough that you'll be cleared and the demon nation won't fall into disfavor."

"Well, hell. We wouldn't want that," Nick drawled, irritation clawing through him.

Moira frowned. "I haven't figured out who Bear is avoiding in Ireland, but I'll keep working on it." She took a deep breath. Then she stilled. Her eyes widened. She took another deep breath and then lunged up. "Oh my God. You slept with the demon. I smell him on you."

"There wasn't any sleeping involved," Simone said dryly.

Nick grinned. He loved the woman's spunk. The way she owned her life, no matter what. "I'd like another round," he said.

Moira half-turned, delight dancing across her face. "Well, isn't this a nice turn of events?"

Was it? God, he hoped so.

Moira bounded up. "I have to head to the airport to meet my mate, but I'll give him your best."

"Say hello to Connlan." Simone cleared her throat. "Also, last night was a onetime liaison, and I wouldn't mind if you kept this between us." She gestured between Nick and herself.

"Of course." Moira kissed Simone on the cheek and crossed to Nick to do the same. She reached the door. "I'll only tell family." With that and a humorous chuckle, she disappeared into the hallway.

Nick shook his head. "The world is about to know about last night."

"Aye." Simone stood from the table. "All right. We have the hearing tomorrow morning, and I need some sleep. I'll call the Guard and have them meet me at my apartment."

Nick lifted himself to his full height, heat ringing through his ears. "Oh, I don't think so."

Chapter 11

Simone faced the demon, more aware than ever of his power. But she was tapped out. In all her life, she'd never expected to be defending herself against treason charges. She loved her people, and she loved her nation. Leading them on the Council had been the greatest accomplishment of her life.

Now they wanted her head.

Somebody out there hated her enough to work tirelessly manufacturing damning evidence. Good evidence. Now she had a rogue witch group after her, and she'd had sex in an alley with the one male who had the power to shatter her heart.

She was tough, and she was smart, but her emotions needed a break. "Nick——"

"No, Simone." He crossed corded arms. "I understand you require space, and I'm fine with that. Take the master bedroom, get some sleep, and we'll attend my hearing together tomorrow. I'll sleep on the couch." He glanced at the damaged door. "After I fix my damn lock."

She didn't have the energy to argue, and this way, she wouldn't have to deal with the Guard. "All right."

If he was surprised by her acquiescence, he didn't show it.

"Thank you for the eggs." She moved by him toward the bedroom, ridiculously pleased when he stopped her with a hand around her arm.

He leaned down and brushed her lips with his. "Sweet dreams, little bunny."

Desire tingled through her, but if she didn't sleep, she'd be of little use tomorrow at the hearing. "Good night." Turning, she wandered into the masculine bedroom. Dark wood floors, black comforter, oils of Russian landscapes on the walls. The room smelled like Nick— dark and of the forest.

She slid into the bed with a soft sigh and took inventory of small hurts. Bruises and cuts from the run through the cemetery as well as the sex against that brick building. Well worth the slight pain. She turned her face into Nick's pillow.

The dream caught her almost immediately.

Nicholai had just left her after she'd all but begged him to take her with him. So cold and so . . . gone. Even when he had been standing right in front of her, it was as if he no longer saw her. She didn't exist any longer in his world.

She'd sat on the ground near a stone ledge, at a nice picnic spot away from her mother's home. The day was sunny and bright, and all she wanted to do was crawl into a hole and pass out.

Her mother found her sobbing into her knees. In a rare show of maternal compassion, Viv had gathered her close.

"He's gone," Simone had said. "Forever, he said."

"Shhh." Viv ran a hand down Simone's hair, tucking her into her neck. "He hurt you because you let him."

"I know." She'd completely opened her heart as well as her body. Never in her entire life had she felt the weakness now slicing her apart.

"You'll know better next time. This is a tough world for women, and the only way to survive is to gain your own power. You can do that, Simone." Viv had rocked her the way she had as a baby. "You're going to be on the Council, and someday you'll run it. Make your life on your own merits and not with a man who'll leave."

Simone had looked up, tears blurring her vision. "When will it stop hurting?"

Her mother had smiled. "Soon enough. For now, let's get you to work."

They'd both looked up as the eldest Enforcer, Daire Dunne, crossed the meadow, fury on his face.

Simone stood and wiped her tears. "I'm fine, Daire."

"I'll fucking kill him." Daire reached down to assist Viv up. "Right now. I'll go find him."

Simone shook her head. "He's a demon, and I should've known better." Yet her cousin's concern and anger warmed her freezing heart a little. "It's over."

"No." Daire turned to go.

Simone yelled at him, more than prepared to eviscerate the male who'd hurt her so badly all by herself.

Her shout in the dream woke her up to the present.

"What?" Nick rushed into the room, his knife already out.

She gulped in air. Hell. What had she been thinking to have slept with him again? Her mind was mush. "Bad dream. Sorry."

He paused and ran a hand through his thick hair. "Oh." The doorway framed him, so tall and broad. He was wearing a loose pair of sweats; his bare chest spoke of a deadly soldier, one well trained. Yet she knew, without question, that Nicholai Veis's true power lay in his brain, in his massive intelligence and his ability to treat the world as if it were a game of chess.

He declared checkmate every damn time, and he probably always would. Right now, he was on her side, but what about the future?

"You're thinking awfully hard there, Simone." He crossed into the room, all grace and power.

Her lungs compressed in direct proportion to every step he took. So deliberate, as if giving her every chance to stop him.

She straightened her legs, shoving the bedclothes to the end of the bed. "You were right to end us so long ago."

"I know, but that doesn't mean it was easy. It wasn't. Hurt like hell." He studied her, reaching the end of the bed, his eyes glowing with a hunger he did nothing to hide.

That was the first time he'd mentioned his own pain. So there had been pain. She shook her head, trying to stay in the moment and not escape into a fantasyland where everything worked out for her the way it did for her cousins. "Right now, things are looking dismal, Nick. You have to admit that."

Arrogance was stamped hard on his chiseled face. "If you mean the trial, I agree. If you mean that I have one scintilla of a plan to let you be beheaded, you've fucking lost your mind."

She gaped, and not just because she had absolutely no intention of letting anybody kill her, either. But a demon didn't get to negate her people or her laws. She'd do that herself. "Coven law is absolute. You have no say."

He smiled then, and she saw the legend who was whispered about far and wide. "Simone, I've always adored your allegiance to your people, and I've admired your self-possession."

"Ah, okay." Her breath started to come faster. What was he getting at?

"But if you think I'm going to allow you to be taken from this earth, taken from me, by a setup, then you don't know me. Hell, even if you had committed treason, I wouldn't let you pay for it by being executed."

The determination, the absolute conviction of his tone, shot awareness down her back. "What in the world are you saying?"

He took another step, putting his knees flush with the bed, his masculine form towering over her. "I'm saying that you will not die. If I have to kidnap your ass, I will. Fight me or not. I'll win."

Her mouth dropped open. "You're joking."

"Do I look like I'm joking?"

No. He looked like a warrior about to wage war . . . and come out victorious. "I don't think it's your place to make that statement." Her mind was spinning, but she figured logic was the only way to get through to him.

He leaned down, his face an inch from hers, raw determination glinting in his eyes. "It is my place. If you'd like, I'll be happy to cement that place right here and right now."

Nervousness exploded through her. Awareness of her vulnerability arrived second. "What in the hell are you talking about?"

"Lie back, or hell, turn over onto your hands and knees, and I'll mark you like no woman has ever been marked before. The second you become mine, I can protect you from any species out there, including your own."

The sensual threat ticked along her every nerve, centering in an entirely private place. One Nick apparently believed belonged to him. She shook her head. "I'm not that kind of woman."

He lifted one eyebrow. "What kind of woman?"

She plucked at a loose string on the bedspread. "The kind who gets lost in a man. The kind who obeys without question. Hell, Nick. The kind who lets a man shield her." Even if she had been that woman eons ago, he'd changed her by leaving.

He watched her, no expression lightening his face. "Baby, I'm not the kind of man who would give you a choice."

Her chin dropped, and she was fairly certain her eyes bugged out. Even so, a tension, one she barely recognized as intrigue, lit her from within. "Excuse me?"

"If it comes down to life or death, health or injury, I don't give one shit about what type of woman you are beyond the obvious."

Oh, hell no. "What exactly is 'the obvious'?" she asked, anger tingling through her hands.

His shoulders settled. Truth, primal and raw, darkened his eyes to the black of a sky without the moon. Mysterious and powerful. "The obvious? You're mine and have been since the first time I laid you down in that meadow years ago."

She reared back, her heart fluttering. In warning or temptation, she had no clue. "The caveman mentality doesn't work for me, and it sure as hell won't work for you."

He smiled, even while his lids half-lowered. "Caveman? Oh, hell no, baby. This is modern man, modern demon . . . all aboveboard and truthful. I'm not using subterfuge, and I'm not going vampire-ape on you. I'm calmly, very pointedly, telling you how it's going to be. If there's a threat to you, I'll do whatever it takes to get you to safety."

"If it causes war?"

"It won't."

"If it does?"

He lifted a broad shoulder. "So be it."

She shook her head, panic edged with something warm flowing through her. "You can't go to war over me."

"Watch me." He somehow edged even closer, nearly leaning over her. "You're exactly the type of woman to go to war over. How can you not know that?"

"I'm well aware of that fact. Of course, I can wage war on my own if I so choose." There was a time when she had enjoyed the badass side of Nick, but she could fight her own battles. "If I require assistance, I will certainly let you know."

"Do you plan to let them kill you?" Curiosity glimmered along with darkening hunger.

"No." Simone Brightston had little time or patience for martyrs.

"But I'd like to trust the system I've worked within for so long. If it fails me, I'll plan my next move."

He reached out and ran a finger across her upper chest, tracing the path between her breasts. "I'm choosing to back off while we deal with the trial and with finding your enemy. At that point, I'm coming full-force. Prepare."

She didn't like time lines, and she didn't like warnings. Yet she wanted the damn demon with every molecule in her body. Maybe just one more night to get rid of the hunger that wouldn't stop igniting in her. Why deny herself? Slapping mental shields into place, she reared up, wrapped her fingers over his shoulders, and yanked him down on top of her.

Chapter 12

God, Nick loved Simone's sense of self. No pretense, no false modesty, and no coyness. She wanted him, so she grabbed him.

He landed on her, his cock instantly pressed against the vee of her legs. Right where it belonged. "You directing things, little bunny?"

She smiled, all powerful siren. "Don't I usually?"

"No." But that didn't mean he'd deny her.

"Hmmm." She kicked the bedclothes down farther to allow for full-body contact. Her hands splayed across his upper torso. "You have one of the most ripped chests I've ever seen." A soft hum escaped her as she caressed him.

"War requires physical as well as mental preparations." His voice turned demon hoarse, and his lungs burned.

She leaned up and licked along his bottom lip. "Take your sweats off."

He smiled then, grasped her waist, and rolled them over so she lay on top. "You take them off."

Her smile held danger of the most feminine nature. The kind that made a guy either run for the hills or meet the challenge, because she was worth every damn second. He already knew that fact.

She kissed him right behind the ear, and a rapid shiver shot through his body. Humming, she kissed her way down his torso, planting her knees between his thighs before drawing down his pants. His dick sprang free into the cool air.

He dug his fingers into the sheets, trying to restrain himself, when all he wanted to do was toss her onto her back.

"Very nice, Nicholai." She grasped him and licked her way from the base to the tip.

Sparks flew inside him, and his balls drew up tight. He closed his eyes, and his chest expanded. "Remember about payback," he ground out.

She sucked the tip into her mouth and chuckled.

The vibrations ripped through him, and he groaned, flashes lighting behind his eyes. Nails scraped along his balls, and that was it.

Growling, he reared up, manacled her waist, and flipped her onto her stomach.

She yelped and dissolved into laughter, her face buried in a pillow.

He'd forgotten. Somehow, he'd forgotten how the woman could make him hotter than a horny teenager and yet fill him with amusement at the same time. With fun and something lighthearted. No wonder she owned his heart.

Even so, she'd thrown down a challenge. So when he flattened his palm on her backside with a loud *smack*, she shouldn't have been surprised.

She reared up. "What the hell?"

Now he laughed, grabbed the inside of her elbow, and tugged her around. She lost her balance and fell onto her back.

He rolled and effectively pinned her. "I told you about paybacks."

Dare filled her eyes. "You want to play, demon?" With great finesse, she slammed both of her fire-filled palms down on his bare ass.

Heat seared his flesh.

He growled, reached for her elbows, and jerked both arms above her head.

She smiled. More plasma fire cascaded along her wrists, burning him. "You're outmatched, Veis."

"Oh yeah?" His temper pricked at him, even though his dick was hard as rock. "One chance. Snuff the fire and stop burning my hands." Truth be told, it was beginning to hurt.

"Then let go." Arrogance tilted her delicate chin.

He levered himself up, tightened his hold, and gazed directly into her stunning eyes, piercing her mind.

Her pupils widened.

He kept the attack gentle, holding back any pain, sliding friction and erotic images into her consciousness. Every erogenous zone in the body responded to pleasure spots in the brain, and he began to caress each one.

The fire along her arms sputtered and died.

He stimulated the pleasure center of her brain. She arched against him with a soft cry.

Slowly, he reduced his presence, and then let her be.

She gazed up at him, desire flushing her cheeks and her lips a deep pink. Wonder crossed her face. "You shouldn't be able to get past my shields."

"I barely can, so don't worry." The fact that he could, even a little, showed that she trusted him whether she liked it or not.

"Oh, I'm going to get you for that." Her voice went husky. "Using your powers isn't fair."

"You used yours." He grasped the T-shirt covering her, one of his favorites, and ripped it in two. Her pretty pink nipples had sharpened to points, and he drew one into his mouth.

She gasped and tunneled her fingers into his hair, scraping his scalp.

He paid homage to her other breast. She was firm and full bodied, and so damn sexy he had to force himself to slow down and enjoy himself. He traced a path down her abdomen to draw off the borrowed sweats and toss them on the floor. "You shaved." Good Lord, she was bare.

He almost came right then and there against the bed.

She chuckled. "It's the modern thing to do, you know."

Actually, he'd been rather busy planning and fighting a war in modern times. "I didn't know." He leaned down and kissed her before running his tongue through her slit. "I like it."

"Me too," she groaned. "Are you planning to talk me to death?"

He smiled. "No." Then he went at her. No mercy, no gentleness, just pure delight, but not enough pressure to push her over. After several minutes, he had to clamp his hands on her thighs to hold her still.

"Damn it, Nick." She smacked his head, not so lightly. "I will burn the damn hair off your head," she groaned.

He grimaced. The woman didn't make idle threats, and he had probably tortured her enough. "All right." He twisted one finger inside her and snapped his lips against her clit, trapping it.

She arched and cried out, her abdomen vibrating with a set of waves. He prolonged her orgasm until she settled back on the bed with a soft whimper.

He smiled and moved up her, positioning himself right where he wanted to be most in the world. One hard shove had him embedded balls-deep in unreal heat. Minor aftershocks rippled against him, and he closed his eyes, lowering his forehead to hers.

She widened her legs and clasped her feet at the small of his back.

God. She'd always been perfect. He started to thrust, hard and fast, realizing she could take all of him at full force. So he gave it to her.

Her body tightened around him, and he powered into her, knowing the second she broke. Her teeth clamped on his shoulder, and he let himself go, coming so hard he knew he was home.

Finally.

Simone sipped her second cup of coffee as Nick finished getting ready in the other room. She'd had clothes delivered first thing and felt more than prepared for the hearing in a navy dress and high-heeled boots. Her hair was up in an intricate knot, her makeup flawless, and her mind clear.

Phenomenal sex followed by peaceful sleep did that for a woman. Though she did have work to finish after the hearing.

Her phone *ding*ed, and she pulled it out of her bag to see a grumpy Bear staring out at her. She clicked on the video chat. "Bear. Are you back home?"

His dark eyebrows drew down. "No, still in Ireland. I'm visiting friends right now in Kilkenny, and I need to talk to you. We didn't get a chance before my ass was thrown out of Dublin."

She took a drink of her coffee. "First, are you still in danger, and if so, from whom?"

He rolled his eyes. "No, I'm not. What happened was a business deal gone wrong eons ago, and I fixed it earlier, so stop hounding me about it."

She narrowed her gaze. Was he lying? She couldn't tell. "Fine. What's up?"

He growled. "You're not seeing the demon again, are you?"

She blinked, her body stilling. "It's a little late for you to act like an overprotective brother, don't you think?" She adored Bear, but they had a long-distance relationship for many reasons; she didn't need a half-crazy bear shifter butting into her business. "Not that I don't appreciate the concern."

"You can't date him." Bear leaned closer to the camera until only his honey-colored eyes were visible. "It's a mistake that can't lead anywhere."

"I can date anyone I choose." When the hell did the males in her life start seeing her as somebody to push around? She was Simone Brightston, for God's sake. "Butt out."

He shook his head. "You're a witch and are part, um, bear shifter, even though you can't shift. A bear shifter like you, even one who can't shift, certainly can't mate a mind-attacking demon. It's a crazy-bad mix, and you have to know that."

"Don't be silly." She sat back. Nothing in her felt like a bear shifter, so the genes must be seriously latent. She was a witch and a witch only. Besides, what the heck was Bear's problem? "There are demons who have mated shifters, and you know it." Sure, she couldn't think of any right offhand, but it wasn't against the law or anything.

"Bear shifters have, well, sanity issues. You mix that with demon mind control, and you have a serious problem for offspring." Bear shook his shaggy hair. "Trust me."

That just wasn't true. Simone snapped her fingers. "Sally O'Malley, a bear shifter out of Dublin, is mated to a demon. They live in Alaska now."

Bear blinked. "You have a friend named Sally O'Malley?"

Simone rolled her eyes. "Yes. Her great-grandma is a witch. Sally took Byron's last name when they mated."

Bear snorted. "Now, that's love."

"Yes. It's love that has resulted in a whole pack of bear cubs, none of them insane." Well, no more crazy than most bear shifters, anyway. "So your theory doesn't hold water."

Bear shook his head. "Can't you trust me on this? Just this once?"

She frowned. "What aren't you telling me?"

He sighed and rubbed his whiskered chin. "Okay. The bears in our family are a bit more insane than most, and the proof I can offer you is the fact that our bastard of a father shot you, and you had to defend yourself and kill him. Or try to. I mean, before Nick saved your ass."

Simone kept her face stoic. "Just because Roman was nuts doesn't mean my kids will be. No matter what male I mate." Not that she was planning on mating any time soon.

Bear leaned away from the camera, bringing his full face into focus. "Our family can't mate with a demon. Period."

"Why is that?" she asked, trying to read his facial features.

"Listen, Simone. I've never wanted to do this, but in this one instance, I will. I'm the head of our family, and you'll obey me on this."

Humor attacked her, and she laughed so hard tears filled her eyes. "Oh my God, that is so funny. Obey you."

His face hardened to the point that she stopped laughing. "You aren't familiar with our ways, and that's all right, because you chose your path. But you're still a member of my family, I'm the patriarch and the fucking leader of the bear nation."

She cleared her throat, trying very hard not to tell him to stuff it. He was her brother, and apparently she'd stomped on his ego. Damn men and their egos. "I'm sorry to upset you, but I don't obey anybody."

"Either break if off with the demon, or I'll see to it that you do." No amusement showed on Bear's face, for once. She could actually see the predator often hidden beneath Bear's casual attitude. "I'm not messing around here."

There went her temper. "Oh yeah? What exactly are you going to do, big bad bear?" she snapped.

He leaned in again. "First, I'm asking nicely. If that doesn't work, I'll announce to the world that you're a bear shifter with the weakness of not being able to actually shift, which will probably get your ambitious butt kicked off the Coven Nine. And if that doesn't work? I'll put a fucking bounty on the demon's head and collect it myself if need be."

Heat fired through Simone. "Bring it on, Bear, you idiot." She ended the call, her breath heaving through her chest. How dare he?

Nick chose that moment to stalk into the room, dressed in black slacks and a gray shirt, oozing power and intensity. "You okay?"

"Fine. Just family drama." Simone stood. She'd deal with Bear later. "Let's visit with Tori and then go to your hearing."

Nick shook his head. "Something tells me this is going to be one of those days."

Simone nodded. "I think you're right."

Chapter 13

Simone eyed a keypad near the door of the penthouse and then quickly typed in a code. A buzz signaled the lock releasing. She ignored the Guard soldier standing at attention across the hall and swept inside a spacious living room overlooking the Liffey. "Victoria?" she called out as Nick followed her and shut the door.

Tori crossed from what must be the kitchen, munching on a bagel. The purple streaks in her hair caught the morning light from outside. "What the hell are you people?" she asked, her blue eyes wide and more than a little distrustful.

Simone sighed and crossed to the leather sofa to sit. "Nick? Could you give us a moment?"

He nodded. "Are there more bagels?"

"Yes," Tori said, finishing hers and inching away from him to take a chair across from Simone.

Nick disappeared through the kitchen doorway.

Simone cleared her throat and studied her friend. Somebody had found Tori a nice pencil skirt and a gray blouse, which couldn't be further from Tori's usual wardrobe. "Sorry about the clothes."

Tori glanced down. "Yeah, they kinda suck."

This was harder than Simone had imagined. Her stomach hurt. "I want you to know that I'm glad we're friends."

"Me too, considering you're a . . . fairy?" Tori pinned her with a hard look.

Simone coughed out a laugh. "Ah, no. I'm a witch."

"You're a witch." Tori slowly shook her head. "I know some witches. They don't throw fire."

"No, you know people who practice the Wiccan religion. I'm an actual witch—another species on earth." Simone twirled her finger in the air and created a small, swirling ball of fire. "We use quantum physics and a few other sciences humans haven't figured out yet to alter matter—usually into fire."

Tori's eyes widened. "That's crazy."

Simone snuffed out the flame. "I know. But you saw what you saw, and now it's nice to be able to level with you." She hadn't had many friends through the years, and when she and Tori had connected, she'd strongly disliked the necessary subterfuge. "Also, you're an enhanced human, which means you could mate an immortal, if you wanted." Wouldn't that be lovely?

Tori drew back. "Um, mate? What do you mean?"

Heat climbed into Simone's face. "Immortals mate for life. There's biting, maybe marking, and, ah, sex."

Tori leaned back, looking at Simone like she'd lost her mind.

"I know it seems odd, but it's the truth. Immortals can mate enhanced humans, and I know you're enhanced because I can sense it, now." At first somehow both Tori and her sister had unconsciously hidden their enhancements. Now that their status was known, Simone could sense the specialty, even though she didn't know its form. "A human must be enhanced to mate one of us."

Tori paled, skepticism wrinkling her brow. "Enhanced? How so?"

Simone shrugged. "I haven't quite figured it out. You're not psychic or empathic, right?"

"Ah, no." Tori turned to study the river outside.

"You don't have to tell me," Simone said softly. "It's not like I've told you everything up to this point, you know?"

"Yeah. Like you being a witch." Tori craned her neck. "Is the hot blond guy a witch, too?"

Simone grinned. "No. Nick?" she called.

Nick poked his head out the door. "What?"

"Show your fangs."

Nick lifted his eyebrows but allowed his fangs loose.

Tori's mouth dropped open. "He's a vampire? Jesus. Vampires exist?"

Nick disappeared back into the kitchen.

"Well, vampires do exist, but Nick is a demon. They're another species." Simone wrinkled her nose. "This has to be weird for you."

"You could say that." Tori clutched her neck, tension rolling off her. She shook her head, no doubt trying to deny it all. After several moments of thinking quietly, she sighed. "Wait a minute. If you're a witch, and your cousins are witches, that means that my sister is dating a witch. Does she know?"

Simone crossed her legs. "Well, she should be the one to tell you, but I'm finished keeping secrets from you. Alexandra and Kellach are mated, which means that your sister will be pretty much immortal now."

Tori stilled. "Pretty much?"

"Well, we *can* be killed by beheading or burning up, you know." Simone glanced at the grandfather clock in the corner. "I have a hearing to get to, but I wanted to drop by to see if I could do anything to help you."

"Get me the hell out of here." Tori leaned forward, fear all but ricocheting from her.

Simone grimaced. "I would, but I can't right now. There's a hearing set for you in a few days, after my trial, where you'll have to agree not to tell anybody about us. There will be documents and contracts." She hoped. After Simone was found not guilty, she could then be on the Council and help Tori. "This will all work out. For now, enjoy the lovely view and the penthouse hospitality."

"My sister will be looking for me," Tori said, anger glowing over her smooth skin.

"Aye, and we'll let her know what's going on." Hell, the woman probably already knew. "I think Adam Dunne is heading over here to help you."

Tori breathed out and rolled her eyes. "Great. Is there anybody other than Adam who could help?"

Simone bit back a smile. "Why?"

"He's a chauvinistic, arrogant, narcissistic asshole," Tori said evenly.

Interesting. Fascinating, really. Adam was definitely arrogant, but not the other adjectives. Was Tori blushing? Simone kept her face stoic. "I'm afraid he's the one who's been assigned to help you." Not exactly true, but Simone could make that happen. She hadn't considered the two together before, but with Tori's wild ways and

Adam's logical precision, they just might be the opposites that would combust. "When he finds you, be nice to him."

Tori scoffed. "Every time I try to be nice, he says something that makes me want to kick him in the face."

Maybe it was attraction. Maybe not. Simone stood and gathered her skirts. "I have to get to work, but I hope to make it back here tonight and answer any further questions you may have." She'd also love to figure out what kind of enhanced ability Tori had. "Any chance you can move things with your mind?"

"No." Tori also stood and walked over by the tall windows. "If I get the opportunity, I'm out of here."

Simone paused. "Oh. You should know that the Guards are all witches, and they can burn you with plasma. If you insist on making a break for it, please wait until I've concluded my business, and then I'll help you. I promise." If she was found guilty, they could both go on the run. If not, she'd use her position to get Tori to safety.

"No promises."

Simone tried to keep a positive look on her face, but her concern was real. The Guard would never let a human go. "We'll get you out of this. I promise."

Tori didn't answer this time.

Nick exited the kitchen. "We have to get going." He smiled at Tori. "I'm Nick, and it was nice to meet you."

Her chin lifted. "You're my first demon."

His smile widened. "That you know of."

"Good point," she said rather grimly.

Nick opened the door, and Simone followed him into the hallway. "She's mad at me."

"She'll get over it." He reached down and took her hand, his gaze scouting the hallways and stairs for any threats. "This is a big knock to her sense of equilibrium, but since her sister is mated to a witch, it's a good thing. Secrets between sisters can't be good."

That was a wonderful point. Simone brightened. Even so, her stomach rolled again. What in the world was wrong with her?

Her phone *ding*ed, and she glanced down to read the face. "A couple of investigators I have in Seattle have tracked down two dealers of the planekite drug. They're small fish, but they may be able to lead us to the main distributor in Seattle. We're also closing in on the Los Angeles distributors." She glanced up at Nick. "We have got to find out who's behind the manufacture of that poison."

"We will." He pivoted at the base of the steps and put her against the wall.

The breath swished out of her lungs. "What are you doing?"

He leaned in, all male animal. "You've been so preoccupied all morning, you haven't given me a decent kiss."

Ah, she knew what he was doing, trying to distract her from Tori's unhappiness as well as banish any fear of the upcoming hearing. "Who says you deserve a morning kiss?"

His eyes darkened at the challenge.

A slow shiver wound down her back.

"After the things I let you do to me last night, you could at least give me a kiss." He leaned in, amusement quirking his lip.

"The things *I* did?" she gasped. "You were a, well, a demon last night in bed." Humor bubbled through her, and she leaned up to press a hard kiss against his lips.

"Good one."

Aye, it was. Even with the world disintegrating around them, there was something fun about teasing Nick. Temporarily, of course. Yet, for the first time, Simone wondered whether she could have it all. Could she have an important leadership position with the Nine and be with a demon, one of the most powerful in his nation? What if their peoples did go to war again? What then?

He rubbed her forehead. "Stop worrying about undesirable scenarios. The worst is behind us."

Was it? "You mean, except for my trial with the prosecution seeking the death penalty?" She licked her lips. "You can't distract me."

"Can't I?" he murmured. His nostrils flared, and he leaned down to run his tongue where hers had just been. Desire blasted through her, and she had to concentrate not to tackle him and start destroying clothing. His chuckle brushed her mouth, and then he settled his lips against hers, just exploring.

Her breath caught, and she fell into his kiss, her hands grasping his dress shirt.

With a low growl, he encircled her waist and drew her tighter, his mouth becoming more forceful as he bent her back. She would've fallen had he not kept her pressed so tightly against the wall, his heat all but surrounding her. Exhilarating, drugging, his touch was fire and lightning. Breathing became secondary to the feeling of the demon against her.

She whimpered at the demanding thrust of his tongue. The taste of him would be with her forever. Dark and sinful, deadly and tempting, it lured her with the promise of passion and the thrill of lust. A growl emerged from him then, a primal sound that beat within her own body, spearing through her womb.

He pressed his knee up between her thighs and rocked against her. She gasped into his mouth and rubbed against him, needing more pressure.

Sometimes she forgot. For all of Nick's humor, for all of his brilliance, at his core he was *this*. Fire and power and desire, all rolled into a devastatingly demanding male package. Many immortals were more animalistic than human, and demons were no exception.

Demons were in a class of their own.

His fingers tangled in her hair and angled her head to the side, controlling her. No mercy tinged his kiss; only raw male possession. There was no question he was making a claim, right then and right there.

She moaned into him, taking whatever he wanted to give.

Finally, he gentled his kiss, his lips whispering over hers before he released her.

She dug her nails into his forearms, her legs shaking as she regained her balance.

He placed a quick kiss on her nose. "Consider yourself distracted."

Chapter 14

In the underground hearing chambers, sitting by himself at the defense table, Nick gave Vivienne Northcutt, Simone's mother, a hard look as the questioning into his actions continued. She sat at the power position on the Council, surrounded by the other healthy members, including Simone.

"Again, Mr. Veis, who alerted you to Simone's presence in the Seattle penthouse?" Peter Gallagher asked.

Nick bit back a sharp retort. "Again, Mr. Gallagher, I know where Simone is at all times, and I have since the war ended."

She turned a lovely shade of pink at that, but her eyes appeared anything but delighted.

Peter shook his head. "Did the Enforcers ask you to get Simone to safety?"

"The Enforcers did not ask a thing of me." Nick kept his gaze stoic and his expression irritated.

"Why the hell have you been stalking my daughter?" Vivienne asked, her lips set in a flat line.

Because she's fucking mine. "I'd say 'stalking' is a little harsh," he drawled.

They'd been at it for over an hour, and he was growing bored in general and pissed at Viv in particular. While he'd known for a century the woman didn't think him good enough for her daughter, the time for waiting had ended. He would not stay away from his woman.

Vivienne glared back from her position in the center of the Nine.

He was the strategic leader for the entire demon nation, damn it. Simone could do worse. He kept his face in harsh lines to mask the minor hissy fit he seemed to be having in his head. His lips twitched with the humor of the entire damn situation.

Simone lifted an eyebrow from where she was seated next to her mother.

He shrugged. "What exactly is this hearing about anyway?" he demanded finally.

Viv flashed her teeth. "We're here to discover if your actions amount to a declaration of war, or if you just broke our laws. In that case, we can just behead you."

He rolled his eyes. "I've already explained that Simone and I were just going for a ride." The more irritated he became, the ruder his answers. At some point, Simone had started glaring at him, as well, and if she didn't stop it, he was going to cross the chamber and drag her over the desk to show her just whom she belonged to. Challenging him, especially in front of the other witches, was a dangerous idea, and she needed to learn that lesson and fast.

"We have more questions," Viv said grimly.

"Great. Are we finished with the death threats for the day?" Nick asked.

"The day is young," Simone shot back.

Oh, hell no. "If you don't mind, I'd rather our foreplay took place in private, little bunny."

She drew back, and he fought a full-on smile. Too many people had either bowed to her beauty and intelligence or judged her for it; somebody needed to show the spirited witch that the world had some limits, even for her.

He was just the guy for the job.

"You're out of order," Viv bellowed.

"I thought this wasn't a United States courtroom," he said calmly.

Tension spiraled through the room, and he settled, more than prepared to battle the row of irritated witches. There had been enough polite talk about death, and it was time to get serious, whether they liked it or not. "Simone, let's go. We need to go through the silly documents handed over by the prosecutor before your ridiculous trial begins."

More tension. What? Had he insulted them with the "silly" and "ridiculous"? Good.

Viv tapped her fingers on the stone. "I don't think you take us very seriously, Mr. Veis."

"I don't." Why hide it? "Every one of you knows that Simone would never commit treason, and yet you go forward with this farce."

"The evidence is damning," Peter what's-his-name said.

"It's bullshit," Nick replied.

Viv cleared her throat, and for the briefest of seconds, fear glimmered in her eyes before she masked it. "I'm sure the evidence will prove Simone innocent."

What the fuck was she afraid of? Nick narrowed his gaze, gently probing into Viv's head. She clamped shields into place so quickly his frontal lobe ached, but in that one second, he had seen real fear for her daughter—and not because of the trial. What the hell?

She glared at him, no doubt pissed as hell with his attempted intrusion into her brain.

He glared back. "Councilwoman Northcutt? I'd like to interview you as part of my investigation."

"My statement is in the files," Viv said calmly, all but daring him to call her on the fear.

Simone's eyebrows arched down, and she tilted her head to the side. "What's going on?"

The remainder of the Coven Nine looked on, a couple of them seeming to realize that something was up.

"Nothing," Nick said, turning toward the smooth wall. "I'm finished with this place for now."

The gavel smashed down. "Adjourned," Viv all but spat.

The present members of the Coven Nine all left with varied looks of irritation and amusement on their faces.

Simone swept down toward him, her skirts brushing the floor. "What the hell is wrong with you?" she hissed.

"They just wanted to rattle either you or me, and I'm not in the mood for it." He shrugged and grasped her arm. "Let's go through the files. Your stupid trial starts tomorrow."

"Stop with the sarcasm." Fire flashed from her shoulder and burned his hand.

He released her and gave a low growl of warning. "I wasn't kidding about the foreplay."

She huffed and opened the wall, hustling down the carpeted tunnel. "Do me a favor and take a step or two off the red, would you?"

Funny. He followed her, taking measure, memorizing the tunnel and its alcoves. They reached the rear of the ancient church where the motorcycle attack had taken place, and he wasn't surprised to see Guard soldiers fanning out from the area.

He had several bikes stored in Ireland, and he'd ridden with Simone on the back of one to the hearing. Not for a second had he thought the bike wouldn't be right where he'd left it, considering the Guard soldiers all around. He reached the bike and held a hand out for Simone to jump on behind him. She did, her arms wrapping around his waist.

Now, didn't that feel good.

He glanced over his shoulder. "Why does your mom dislike me so?"

Simone leaned her chin on his shoulder, putting their lips in very nice proximity. "I think she wants me with a purebred witch, considering my lineage. She also knows I want to lead the Nine, and ambition is everything to her. And, well, our last breakup left me a bit bereft, I'm afraid. As a mother, she probably doesn't want to see that happen again."

Bereft? If Simone was willing to reveal that much vulnerability, she had to have been much more than bereft. Suddenly, his chest ached, and his earlier humor dissipated. "I'm sorry I hurt you."

"The past is over, and so long as you understand I'm not going back, we're good." She leaned in and brushed a kiss across his mouth. "There's no reason we can't enjoy each other right now."

"I know that you're not the same girl you were, and to be honest, I like the badass woman even better." He smiled against her, surprised by how little she knew him. "I plan to enjoy you to the fullest, but if you think this is casual, think again."

She drew back. "Nick, I——"

He half-turned and captured her mouth, not caring whether the soldiers saw. The kiss was hard and forceful, because he was done holding back. Finally, he raised his head, gratified to see her eyes cloudy and her lips a pretty pink. "Simone. In case you need it spelled out, I'm making a claim."

Her eyes darkened to a mysterious midnight he couldn't read. "I'm not the type of woman who is claimed, Veis."

"Ah, bunny. You're exactly the kind of woman who needs to be claimed, and anybody not up to the task would bore you immediately. Let me be perfectly clear that I'm up to the task." Hell. He was probably the only male on earth who could claim her, the only one with the necessary power, spirit, and brains. "Look at it as an adventure, or look at it as something you want, but either way, you will be claimed."

The flush across her face deepened with anger and something more. Need.

He understood her. She was fiercely independent and had never been able to rely on a male before, which made his path not only more difficult but entirely worth it in the end. She wanted to trust and belong . . . and only late at night, under the covers, did she let that craving slip with him. He'd bet his last stock market fund that she'd never even hinted at her vulnerability with another male.

Whether she knew it or not, she'd made her choice.

Turning around, he gunned the motor and roared out of the quiet parking area, speeding across Dublin. Rain pummeled down, leaving the cobblestones quiet and wet.

They really should invest in helmets at some point.

A silver Escalade kept pace, no doubt the Guard. He didn't require their assistance, and he sure as hell didn't want them knowing the location of his safe house. He angled a command over his shoulder. "Hold on."

She nodded and tucked herself into his body in a display of trust she probably didn't realize she'd shown. Something in him, an awareness deep and dark, roared in a sense of possession.

He was tired of quashing part of himself; the second he'd taken her in the alley, he'd unleashed his true nature, and there was no bottling it up again. Even if he wanted to, which he did not.

Years ago, he'd memorized the layout of the Dublin streets, and he'd kept updated through construction and modernization. All the same, the Coven Nine had resources even he couldn't penetrate with his intel, but hopefully they hadn't found all of his routes, either.

So he took it easy through several streets and back alleys, gradually increasing his speed, and eventually ducking into an alcove he'd had created just a year ago. Set into a century-old brick building that housed antique books and maps, he'd found peace there many a time while keeping watch over Simone.

His duties for Zane hadn't allowed for much vacation time, but every once in a while, he'd found himself in Ireland keeping an eye on her.

"Where are we?" she asked.

"Alcove. They'll pass us, and we can maneuver around to my apartment. It's only a couple of blocks away."

She nodded, her face resting against his shoulder blades, her long hair plastered to his left arm from the rain. They waited several minutes until the traffic sounds behind them faded.

Then he slowly pulled out of the alley and took quiet back streets until they reached the front of his apartment building. "We're here. Let me pull underground to parking, and then we go at full speed for the elevator." He didn't expect anybody to be waiting, but it didn't hurt to be careful.

Simone nodded against his back without saying a word. The woman must be exhausted.

He began to drive down when instinct tickled his neck. Simone stiffened behind him as if sensing danger, as well.

Nick clutched the brake and swung the bike around, trusting her to hold on.

A woman ran out of the underground garage, gun out and shooting. Darts impacted his arm from his elbow to his neck, and a sharp pain attacked his nerves. Shit. Planekite. He swung again, trying to keep his body between Simone and the darts.

He opened the throttle, and the bike jumped out of the garage, careening into the street.

More darts hit his other arm, and Simone gave a low cry of pain.

Hell. She'd been hit. How many darts, he couldn't be sure. Too many could be deadly.

"Hold on, baby," he muttered, opening the throttle wide open.

Simone's vision wavered, but she held on to Nick, her fingers curling into his abdomen. At least one dart had hit her arm, and from the instant numbness, there might be more.

Nick swung the bike around and shot directly into an alley behind a florist's shop. He cut the engine and jumped off, instantly taking inventory and yanking a dart out of her shoulder. "Hell." Quick motions had her shirtsleeve ripped open to reveal a puncture wound already turning reddish purple. "It didn't hit a vein."

Was that good? She swayed, her mind fuzzing.

"Hell, Simone. This is going to hurt." His fangs dropped low and sharp, glinting in the soft light, even through the rain.

She frowned and tried to focus. "Huh?"

He grabbed her arm, tight, and she realized his plan. "No—" Panic had her trying to yank free, but he held firm. A quick pull forward, and a ducking of his head, and his fangs pierced her skin.

Raw pain, almost agony, exploded in her bicep. "Nick—"

He gave no quarter, biting until his fangs met and scraped against bone.

She struggled against him, reality shutting down and only survival instinct remaining. Her strength was no match for his, and she cried out, tears flowing down her face.

He jerked back, ripping away a chunk of flesh, and she screamed. Darkness wavered around her, and she blinked, using every ounce of stubborn will to remain conscious.

"I'm sorry." He swung a leg over the bike behind her and ignited the engine, pulling her back against his body. "Just hold on to the bars until we get to a different safe house." His hoarse voice sounded like he'd eaten glass, and the tension emanating from him pricked against her skin until she shivered.

Having no choice, she leaned back against him and let him take her weight with one arm banded around her waist. Her thighs tightened on the seat, and she tried to keep her balance, but she needed his strength. He drove with one hand, jerking too hard a couple of times, but keeping the bike moving.

Finally, they reached the outskirts of Dublin and drove through several hills, reaching a tidy hut barely visible through trees. He drove along an overgrown path and drew to a fast halt by a front door. He jumped from the bike and lifted her, hustling through the storm and into a quaint one-bedroom cottage.

"Simone?" He laid her down on a plush bed covered with a wedding band quilt.

Her arm bled profusely, and he ran to the kitchen to grab towels to bring back and press over the wound.

She gasped and reared up, the pain almost unbearable. Tears slid down her face and across her lips.

He kept one hand tight against the wound and gently wiped off her cheeks, his gaze intense. "Sweetheart? Talk to me."

It was the "*sweetheart*" that did it. Simone Brightston, the Coven witch known far and wide for being tough to the point of bitchy, lost it. Completely. She sat up and fell against his chest, face-first, and bawled like a newborn.

The pain was excruciating, but the fact that somebody had fired kill darts at her hurt as much as the fact that somebody had set her up for trial. That person really wanted her dead.

Now she had a gaping hole in her arm, one that had probably saved her life, and she wasn't sure she was strong enough to heal it.

So she cried harder into the body of the one man she'd sworn never to be vulnerable with again.

Chapter 15

Nick held the sobbing woman against his chest, his other hand banded around the wound to keep her from bleeding out. Frustration edged into fury within him, and it was all he could do not to bellow a battle cry. Oh, whoever had shot her would die, and painfully at that. For now, his focus had to be on Simone and getting her to heal herself.

He'd never seen her cry before.

Not once, and not after her own father had shot her. Not when he'd said good-bye to her. Sure, he'd figured she'd at least shed a few tears privately afterward, but never in front of him.

"I'm sorry," he whispered, his free hand smoothing down her hair. "I'm so sorry."

She hiccupped and then slowly lifted her face.

Her eyes glowed like onyx jewels, and tear tracks marred her porcelain skin. Vulnerability clung to her lashes and all but oozed from her.

That quickly, he went from a man who'd fight for her to one who'd die for her. "It's okay, baby," he murmured, smoothing damp hair from her face. "I need you to concentrate now." If she didn't heal her shoulder soon, it might scar and never be quite as strong. "I had to bite the planekite from you. How much got into your bloodstream?"

"I don't know." In front of his eyes, she changed. She shook off the pain, and her eyes focused. Healing tingles filled the air around them.

"That's my girl." He caressed down her back.

Even with the healing, pain filled the oxygen around them. So strong and so deep. He'd bitten her all the way to the bone before tearing the poisoned flesh free. "Simone? I need you to open your mind to me."

She stiffened.

"I promise I won't pry, but you need to lower your mental shields." He kept his voice low and soothing. While he could actually pierce her shields since her defenses were so far down, he wouldn't do so without her acquiescence. No way would he violate her like that, even though their combined powers would be something to see. Dangerous and unbeatable. "Come on. Let me help you."

She nodded and shut her eyes, leaning her head onto his shoulder.

He tamped down the wild edges of his thoughts, smoothing them over, before sliding inside her head to the pain centers. Sucking deep for gentleness, he slowly spread a balm better than any narcotic around the pain.

She sighed and relaxed against him. The sense of healing and tingling strengthened.

He gingerly removed the towel from her flesh and tried not to grimace. "You can heal. Rebuild the muscle first."

While she mentally stitched flesh together, he shielded and numbed the pain centers, concentrating on the pain sections and keeping his waves mild. At his age and experience, he could destroy a mind accidentally, and it took more concentration to be gentle and unobtrusive than it did to rip a cerebellum to tatters. He also had to work hard to keep from intruding into other areas of her brain. With her defenses down, he could actually glean images and thoughts if he wanted.

But a promise was a promise.

Her pain neurons flared again, and he wrapped balm around them to provide numbness. Once he again controlled the receptors, he stimulated the base of her brain just a little, promoting power so she could heal faster. It was believed the ability to heal the body was centered in the base of the brain.

She gasped, and her chest swelled.

"Just accept the help and use the power to heal," he murmured. Even though she'd allowed him into her mind, defensive shields hovered all around, showing her strength.

He needed a woman with such strength, no question. At the

thought that somebody had dared attack her while she was on the back of his bike, he growled low.

She sucked in air, and pain slid back into her mind.

Damn it. He needed to concentrate. Slowly, he covered the area again and glanced down to see the hole in her arm nearly healed. Very impressive.

Finally, she leaned back. "I need to call this in." Dark circles marred the skin under her eyes, and even sitting, she swayed.

"I'll call it in to the Guard," Nick said. "You lie down and get some sleep."

"Wait. Where are we?" she whispered.

He breathed out, and his chest settled. "I bought this cottage when I was going to ask you to be mine forever."

Her eyelashes fluttered, but she visibly struggled to focus. "Wh-what?"

He kissed her nose. "I thought we'd live here, but fate had another plan, and I said good-bye instead." The woman was too pale, damn it. "I don't know how the attackers found my other place, but this one is safe. I promise."

She opened her mouth to protest even as her eyelids completely closed. He tossed back the covers and lifted her with one arm, setting her beneath the sheet. First, he'd call the Guard and report the attack. Then it was time for him to start maneuvering chess pieces into place.

Though he'd wanted to allow the Coven Nine to prove their honor and do the right thing, he'd never been one to sit back and see where the chips would fall. Simone needed protection, whether she liked it or not.

The question was whether she would forgive him for taking over, and he truly didn't know the answer. But he could live with her hating him for eternity so long as she *had* an eternity.

He leaned down and brushed his lips across her forehead, noting she still had a slight fever from the wound. Never in his life, no longer how many years he lived, would he forget the pain he'd caused her. It had been the only way to save her life, but it had hurt him somewhere deep inside.

She moved restlessly, and he felt her forehead again. Warm. Definitely warm. Perhaps more of the planekite had slipped into her flesh than he'd thought before he'd removed the poison. There was no cure, so there was nobody to call for help.

For now, he just needed to watch her and make sure she didn't fall into a coma. He'd allow her a couple of hours to fight the fever; if that didn't work, he'd invade her brain again to help if need be.

For now, he had phone calls to make. He stood, strode over to the fireplace, and yanked loose a round stone at the bottom. Gingerly, he reached in and drew out the Alexandrite ring.

Right where he'd left it.

Simone came awake with a strangled gasp, sitting upright in bed.

A gentle arm tugged her back down, and she settled, curling into Nick's side. "You helped to heal me," she said.

"I did, but you did most of the work." He opened one eye to study her. A lock of hair had fallen onto his forehead, and she indulged herself by pushing it out of the way. "You had a fever most of the night from the planekite, but it broke about an hour ago. How are you feeling?"

Weak. Her body felt heavy, as if weighed down by a boulder or three. "I'm feeling much better, thank you."

"Humph." The demon rolled over, revealing the sinewed muscle of his chest.

She swallowed. The mineral had knocked her on her butt, and yet she could still feel desire just being near him? Nick had always messed with her sanity.

Right now, she had to keep him from catapulting his people into a war with hers, which seemed more and more likely. But if Zane excommunicated Nick, it would hurt him in ways that she didn't even think he understood. It also would leave him vulnerable, with no backup should a rogue witch or band of them try to take him out. The protection of one's people was paramount in the immortal world.

She rolled over and set her chin on his shoulder. The cottage, the one he'd purchased for them, surrounded her. He'd loved her. She'd wondered, and now she knew. "Nick—"

"No."

She blinked. "What?"

"I'm not listening to you push me away or say it's too dangerous for us to be together. If you don't want to be together, that's your choice, but don't give me bullshit reasons."

Anger pricked the back of her neck, intensifying the raging headache still pounding in her temples. "My reasons are not bullshit, and I can protect you as well as you can protect me."

"I like your strength." He gently rubbed his thumbs against her temples, and she fought the urge to moan and beg for more. "But I shield you, not the other way around. I'm sorry, Simone, but you're the one in danger, and I'm not stepping aside while it's so prominent."

"You have no right."

"So give me the right."

She shook her head. "Did you call and report the attack?"

"Yes, but the soldier I talked to got pissed when I wouldn't reveal your location, so the conversation was short."

"The Guard doesn't like you, and they're dangerous. Please listen to me about not letting Zane excommunicate you."

"No."

He really wasn't listening to her or watching out for himself at all. There was only one thing she could do. So she scrambled out of the bed. "I need to take a shower and try to regain my strength. Alone."

He lifted an eyebrow and stretched, elongating smooth, hard muscle. "All right. Call me if you require assistance at any point while you're naked."

She rolled her eyes and turned away, her chest feeling compressed as she palmed Nick's phone. The planekite had impacted her entire system, and her knees felt like jelly as she pretty much limped to the bathroom. Once inside, she turned on the shower and then opened up a chat with the ruler of the entire demon nation.

"It's about fucking time you called in," Zane growled, his green eyes ablaze. The demon leader was one long line of muscle and strength in a black shirt with dark jeans. A scar lined his jaw, and faded bruises covered his temple into his black hair. He took one look at Simone and sobered. "Where's Nick? Is he all right?"

The concern was a good sign.

"No, he isn't. In fact, he's about to get himself killed by the Coven Nine, or my enemies, or somebody after Bear, and all he's worried about is me. You can't excommunicate him, Zane. If you do, he'll be a target for way too many people." Not just witches, either. There were plenty of enemies out there who'd like to take down Nicholai Veis.

Zane studied her. "I have no intention of excommunicating my best friend."

"That's a fucking mistake," came a very pissed-off voice from the doorway.

Hell. Simone's senses were dulled and way off, and she hadn't even heard the door open. When Nick strode forward and confiscated the phone from her hand, she didn't have an ounce of strength with which to fight him. She sat on the edge of the claw-footed tub, her hands trembling.

"Nick. Where the hell are you?" Zane asked, once again sounding angry.

"None of your fucking business," Nick returned, sounding twice as pissed. "I didn't protect you for years to have you just throw away the nation because of one soldier. Do your damn job."

"You did more than protect me. You trained me, and you became my friend, damn it. I never wanted to lead, but you drummed duty and destiny into my head," Zane bellowed.

Simone winced. Maybe the call had been a bad idea.

"Then do your duty," Nick said, his voice lowering and the anger dissipating. "We've both worked too hard for you to do anything but that."

Silence ticked by for the briefest of moments, and Simone's heart sank. The smart move for Zane, for the entire demon nation, was to condemn Nick and his actions.

Finally, Zane spoke. "Nope."

Nick reared back. "Excuse me?"

"You taught me more than military strategy and survival, Nicholai. You taught me that friends and family are what matters, and that the people who have your back are more essential to life than political allies. I've thought this out from every angle."

"Have you now?" Lines cut into the sides of Nick's mouth.

"Yes. I could step down and come help you, while allowing my brother to lead. You and I would certainly put up a good fight against these witches."

"Hell, no." Nick's knuckles turned white from his grip on the phone.

"I agree. Sam doesn't want to lead, and the demon nation isn't quite settled yet from my taking over, so I couldn't do that to my brother," Zane said.

Nick's shoulders relaxed. "Good. I'm glad you're seeing reason."

"So I remain as leader, and the entire demon nation fully supports your actions to date and in the future. As far as the world is concerned, you're acting under official orders."

Relief slid through Simone.

"Damn it, Zane," Nick growled.

"Do you think I don't understand the risks you took for years, trying to protect me?" Zane growled right back. "We're the same as family, so deal with it. In the vernacular of the day, Zane out." The line went dead.

Nick stared at the quiet phone, his brows furrowing.

Simone bit back a laugh.

"Did he just say 'Zane out,' and throw an imaginary microphone?" Nick asked slowly.

Simone pursed her lips. "Well. It is the vernacular of the day."

He turned toward her. "I don't think I've ever fully appreciated your difficulties working with family."

She nodded. "It's a pain in the arse, it is."

Nick's phone buzzed, and he lifted it. "Veis." He listened and then handed the phone to Simone. "Your cousin."

Simone took the phone. "Hello?"

"It's Moira. There were multiple attacks on Coven members last night."

Simone closed her eyes. "I know. I took a dart to the shoulder, but I'm all right now. Who else was hit?"

Moira cleared her throat. "Your mother, my mother, and Peter were hit with darts, while Brenna was attacked but not hit. The Guards covered Nessa and Sal, so they're okay. The entire Council was targeted."

Simone shoved to her feet. "How bad are our moms?"

"Our mothers are in intensive care, and Peter is recuperating. The Guards with him kept all darts but one from nicking him." Moira's voice held fear.

Simone drew in air. "Are they at the hospital?"

"No. They're with Doc Pelandrone at your mom's secondary safe house."

Simone tried to keep from throwing up and had to swallow several times. "We'll be there in ten minutes." Everything in her panicked to the point she could barely think. She hung up.

Nick opened the door; obviously he'd heard the conversation. Demons had excellent hearing, even better than witches. "Keep to my six till we're on the bike, and if you feel any sense of a threat, you let me know immediately."

She nodded numbly. Whoever was after the Council had excellent resources and intel. Chances were, they were waiting for her at some point. "Let's go."

Chapter 16

What kind of world were they still living in that the leader of the Coven Nine had multiple safe houses? Simone walked wearily up the stairs to her mother's bedroom in a plush home overlooking green and rolling hills. Truth be told, she'd always loved this home.

Her aunt, Moira's mother, had been moved to a different location. The Coven Nine members had to be separated for their own safety and to make it more difficult to take them out all at once.

A consult with the doctor had revealed that Viv was conscious, which was an excellent sign.

Simone pushed open the door to see her mother in the large bed, her dark hair spread out on the pillow. Her skin was pale, and for once, she didn't appear larger than life. The room smelled like spicy oranges, her mother's scent. Antique oak furniture and priceless watercolors lined the wall, giving the room a sense of sanctuary and peace. "Mother?"

Viv's eyelids fluttered open. "Simone. What in the world?"

Simone inched across the room, dizziness swamping her. She sat on the brocade bedspread and smoothed her mother's hair off her damp forehead. "The doctor said you'll be all right. It was only two darts, and you'll be weak for months, but your body should purge the poison." Another dart, and it would have been another story.

Viv nodded. "The Guard soldier protecting me took several darts. How is he?"

"Coma." Simone sighed. "He's getting the best care possible."

"Are you all right?" Viv's eyes, although bloodshot, were sharp and probing.

Simone nodded. "Aye. Nick reacted quickly."

"I heard." Viv grimaced. "That had to have hurt."

Simone nodded. "Yeah. Remind me never to mess with a pissed-off demon. This was one trying to help me." Sometimes she forgot how dangerous Nick's people were and how deadly their powers.

Viv tried to shove herself into a sitting position, and Simone leaned over to place pillows behind her mother's back. "Thank you," Viv said. "While I appreciate Nicholai's assistance, as I have on other occasions, he is not right for you. Break it off, Simone."

An ache pulsed through Simone's chest. "Why?"

"You know why."

"Mother, we have more immediate issues to deal with, right?"

Viv's head rolled back on the pillow. "You just don't understand, and you need to trust me. Someday, you want to lead the Council. You can't have any blights in your past for that."

"Am I a blight?" Simone voiced the one question she'd never had the courage to ask. But with the possibility of being kicked off the Council with a death sentence on her head, it was time.

"Of course not." Viv reached out and held Simone's hand, her own skin as smooth as it had been centuries ago. "You're the best thing that ever happened to me." She sighed, and her gaze turned to the silver brocade. "I know I'm not the softest of people, or the most nurturing, but I've always been so proud of you."

"I know, and I've also understood why you never told me about my father." It had taken several decades, but she'd reached peace with the secret. "Although I still don't know why you won't talk about him now." No matter how many times Simone had asked, Viv had kept tight-lipped.

Viv blinked. "I didn't know him well, Simone." She coughed, and slight color filled her cheeks. "Those were different times, even for witches, and one didn't just get knocked up in a one-night stand."

Simone snorted. "I guess that's true. You knew he was a bear shifter?"

Viv looked away again. "I suspected, but it was just a single crazy night at a Solstice party, one with witches, shifters, and fairies, and I got carried away. It was and still is so rare to become pregnant without a mating that I didn't even consider the consequences."

"Once you were pregnant, why didn't you tell him?"

Vivienne, even weakened and sick, arched one dark eyebrow.

"Well, the second he learned of your existence, he tried to kidnap you and keep you away from me. So I believe my decision was a wise one."

"True." Simone leaned toward her mother. "You've never said what led you to that decision. Why did you decide he was a threat?"

Vivienne's eyes closed, and she settled into the pillows.

"Mother?" Simone tucked the bedclothes up.

Viv opened her eyes. "I knew you kept in touch with your brother. Through the years, I knew."

"I wanted to know him," Simone said gently. "He's the only sibling I have." All those years, growing up with the Dunne kids and all of their siblings, she'd known exactly what she was missing. Sure, they included her, but no matter how hard they tried, it just wasn't the same. "I didn't mean to betray you."

"Oh, you didn't," Viv said weakly, waving her hand. "But you have to understand, with the blood in your veins, you can't mate a demon. You're part shifter, and Nick's a demon . . . it's a dangerous match for the children. Insanity runs in Bear's people, your father's people, and with a demon like Nick, one so powerful with the mind, the offspring would be too deadly to exist."

Viv rested again, the color leaving her skin. Dots of perspiration marred her smooth forehead.

Simone felt her face. "Your fever is back. The doctor said it would come and go. Just sleep now." She kept her voice calm and not full of the fear now coursing through her.

"Danger," Viv whispered, her focus no longer seeming to be in the room.

Simone stood and finished tucking in her mother. "I still don't understand why you knew, with such certainty, that my father would try to harm me." Maybe if she'd known him as a child, he wouldn't have shot her on sight. Or perhaps if she'd known him before he'd succumbed to insanity, she would've been able to help. "It doesn't make sense." She muttered the question to herself as her mother dropped into the fever.

Viv sighed and breathed deep, her voice going groggy and into a whisper. "Ah, Simone. I saw him shift."

Simone blinked. Was her mother trying to talk or just giving away secrets? Finally? She leaned down again to hear better. "So? Many bears shift. What was wrong?"

"Wasn't . . . just . . . a . . . bear." Viv coughed. "Evil there. So much evil. Must protect my baby."

Simone leaned back, awareness crashing through her along with curiosity. "Mother?"

"Protect Simone. She can never know," Viv whispered. "God help me, the world can never know." With those last words, Vivienne succumbed to the illness and became quiet.

Simone felt her mother's pulse, gratified it was slow but steady. Her mind flared with possibilities, and her breath quickened. Evil? What in the world had Viv been hiding for so many years?

It was time to find out.

Nick finished carting in the manila files pertaining to Simone's trial, more than happy to be staying at Viv's secondary location. Simone had emerged from meeting with her mother pale and distracted, and she'd gone to shower in the guest bedroom after making an odd and frantic call to Bear, who hadn't answered.

The Guards stationed around the house were placed well, and Nick had called in favors from a couple of friends who were also standing watch. Nobody was getting through him to harm either woman, so now he could concentrate on the trial and determining who wanted the Nine brought down so badly. The plan had taken decades to put into motion, so it could be anybody.

For now, his woman had brooded long enough, and it was past supper time. She needed to eat to regain her strength.

He left the files in the spacious kitchen and wandered through the bedroom, stopping at hearing a splash from the guest bathroom. A nudge to the bathroom door opened it enough to see Simone up to her neck in bubbles, her eyes closed.

Worry pinched her mouth, and her cheeks weren't nearly pink enough for someone enjoying a heated bath. While she might not wish to share her concerns with him, he could at the very least take her out of her head for a moment.

The fact that she hadn't heard him enter when she should be on full alert also concerned him. They'd work on that issue next.

He crossed into the room, slowly unbuttoning his shirt.

Her eyelids opened halfway. "What are you doing?"

He held her gaze and dropped his shirt to the ground, reaching for his belt buckle.

Awareness filled her eyes. There it was. Protest came next.

Ah. The woman was feeling vulnerable, was she? He knew her, and he knew her well. The second she turned vulnerable, she shut everyone out. Or at least she tried to do so. It wasn't easy with family, and it sure as hell wasn't going to be easy with him.

Not any longer.

"Nick, I'm not in the mood." Her voice came out woodenly and so forcibly calm it made him grit his teeth.

"I am." He shucked his pants.

"Too bad." She shut her eyes again.

Not the response he wanted to see. Not at all. "Well then. There are a couple of different ways this could happen."

"Just a couple?" Sarcasm laced her tone.

Good. Sarcasm was a start. "Yes."

She opened her eyes again, those dark orbs starting to glimmer a little with emotion. Curiosity or irritation, he couldn't tell. "Go away."

"I'm done doing that."

"Excuse me?"

"I went away for a century, and now I'm done doing that. I truly don't like repeating myself, Simone." He allowed his own frustration to echo in his tone.

"Then go talk to your damn self in the other room." She slid farther down into the rose-scented bubbles.

Oh, he needed to be gentle when all he wanted was to plaster her ass with his handprint. But the lesson she need to learn, at least this time, was that she couldn't push him away. Not again. "What upset you so when you spoke with your mother?"

"Nothing."

"You sound like a spoiled teenager. Stop pouting and tell me the truth." He was rapidly losing his hold on both his good intentions and his temper.

"My life is none of your business." Her breath blew bubbles away.

A hurt, surprising in its sharpness, bladed through his chest. "Do you really mean that?"

She didn't answer.

Damn it all to hell. If she really didn't want him, he'd leave. But she not only wanted him, she needed him, and that was the fucking problem. Simone Brightston, because of the odd way she was raised, wouldn't allow herself to need anybody. It was a good damn thing he was such an expert in strategy, now, wasn't it? "You are the biggest brat I've ever met," he said slowly.

She gasped and sat up. "You just called me a brat?"

"Yes. You're not even at bitch level at the moment, Simone. You're a whiny, pouty, sarcastic brat."

Fire lit her eyes. Finally. She glanced around, somewhat frantically, for anything to throw.

"Only brats throw things." He reached for the waist of his boxers.

"You take those off, and I'll burn your cock right from your body."

He paused. She wasn't kidding. "You create one ounce of a flame, and I'll be in your head forcing you to orgasm before you can throw." He dropped the cotton to the ground.

She stood then, splashing water. Bubbles slid down her fit body in a scene so erotic he'd remember the picture forever. Too bad she was furious.

Fire crackled on her hands.

He lunged, wrapping an arm around her waist and tossing her to the carpet, landing square on top of her.

She gaped at him, looking up, her body a slippery mass against his. "What in the world is wrong with you?"

"You." He grasped her arms and pulled them above her head. His surprise move had snuffed her fire for now. "From day one, you are my only damn weakness, and nowadays I have more worries than I can count." Maybe if he admitted his, she'd do the same.

"There is nothing weak about you, and you worry about nothing." She rolled her eyes.

"Oh yeah? I worry every day about where you are, what you're doing, and what harm might come your way. I worry that you won't call me when you need help." He settled his raging cock between her legs. "I worry about Zane, about the nation, about his baby, and about his mate. I worry about the king, the Realm, and even the damn Coven Nine." He leaned in until his lips hovered just above hers. "More than all of that, I worry that I'll never get to taste you again. Each time I do, it hurts because I know it might be the last time."

Then he lowered his head, and his lips took hers.

Chapter 17

Simone didn't have time to answer, even if she had a reply, before Nick kissed her. He took her deep in a sensual assault that was all the more dangerous for the gentleness behind it.

She wanted fast and hard, and she wanted to forget reality. But as he kissed her, sweeping her mouth with his tongue, she could do nothing but accept him—all of him. His hard body against hers, pressing her into the carpet. His dick at her core, straining against her, wanting inside so badly.

Of their own volition, her thighs widened to make room for him. Now, with him over her, she felt alive in a way she'd forgotten.

Even with danger all around them, for the moment, only he existed.

He reared back, stretched across her, keeping her hands captive. "Your beauty, as stunning as it is, barely compares with the wonder inside you. The absolute sweetness and spirit at your core." He threaded his fingers through hers. "The brilliance and the kindness."

She blinked, tears suddenly pricking her eyes. Most men stopped at her face or her body and never looked deeper. Nick had always seen her in a way that exposed too much. "Nick—"

"No, baby." He licked across her bottom lip, sending sparks of pleasure through her mouth to zing down to her breasts. "No retreating and no hiding. Not tonight."

The struggle inside her, the one motivated by self-preservation, stilled. She settled into the thick carpet, her fingers curling between his. She didn't have the strength or energy to fight his demand, and frankly, she didn't want to. The memory of the little cottage he'd bought for her so long ago wouldn't leave her mind or her heart. Not yet, anyway. "I've missed you, Nicholai."

His eyes darkened in the way they did when she used his full name. "My dreams have been filled with you, even in the worst of times. You gave me hope."

How the hell was she supposed to shield herself from that kind of truth? She stretched up and took his mouth, not surprised when he pressed her back down, taking over the kiss with heat and a demon's fire. She tried to focus. "I have something to tell you. We need to talk."

"We will." He licked down her neck, kissed her collarbone, and moved to her breasts. His hands pressed hers to the ground. "Stay where I put you." Releasing her, he caressed across her chest.

"No." She wanted to touch every inch of him, just in case the world turned south again. Memories and dreams mattered in her world. She lifted her hands—

"Stop." His head rose, and demand glittered in his eyes. "Hands. Back. Down."

She faltered and then stiffened. "Bossy doesn't work for me."

The air changed, grew heated. "Put your hands back down, or I will." He clasped her hips, his fingers digging in.

She grinned. "Your hands are busy."

"Who says I need my hands?" he asked silkily.

She paused. Challenge and curiosity rose in her, hard and fast. "I do."

That quickly, her hands slammed back down on either side of her head, invisible ropes winding around her wrists. Invisible ties much stronger than she was. Her mouth dropped open, and heat flashed through her. "Nick."

He lowered his head and sucked a nipple into his mouth. Lava engulfed her, and she arched against him, even while trying to think. Mind control? Very few demons had the ability, and it usually took eons to develop. "Wait," she whispered. Could he use her powers? Was she vulnerable?

His tongue lashed her nipple and then he released her to pin her with a hungry gaze. "I can't force you to do anything you don't want to do, and I can't control your mind or even combine powers with you unless you let me. However, with you aroused, apparently I can have some effect on your body." His slow smile held more threat than amusement. "Agree to behave."

That was it. Fire flashed along her wrists, and she broke free of the mental ropes.

He laughed out loud. "Beautiful. You really want to play?"

She lifted her chin. "Bring it on."

His gaze pinned hers, and heat slid through her brain, inside her skull. A force, one she fought, slowly lowered her hands back to the carpet. Her breath caught, and she tried to fight the bonds, but they held fast this time.

His power intrigued the hell out of her.

She breathed out, unable to look away.

Ice, the strong sense of it, washed along her torso. She tilted her head, her eyes widening. "How?"

He didn't answer, but the ice slid lower, along her abdomen,

She tried to move, caught in the moment, but the ice didn't stop. If she was able to look, she wouldn't see anything, but the cube felt as real as any ice cube invented. The second the chill moved over her clit, she moaned and pushed hard against him. The ice slid inside her, and she bit her lip to keep from orgasming.

He grinned then, his nostrils flaring.

Her breath panted out. Then the ice turned to heat, and a flame flicked her clit.

She detonated, shutting her eyes, crying out. As the waves pummeled her, shooting through her, he lifted her hips and powered inside her with one strong stroke.

The second he filled her, she went off into another climax. He was so big, so hard, her flesh stretched around him with a sizzling burn that shut down her brain. She tried to jerk her hands free, to touch him, but those invisible bonds held tight. She came harder at the thought.

Finally she drifted down, even while he powered inside her, pumping hard and fast. She bit his shoulder, trying to find any sense of an anchor in the wildness.

As her teeth broke his flesh, her palms ached with a solid burn. The marking of the witch. If she marked him, she'd mate him. But she couldn't move, so she released his shoulder from the bite of her teeth.

Sudden, fierce ecstasy bowed her back, and she arched against him. Hot and wild spasms vibrated through her, throwing her into pure pleasure. He held her, hammered harder, and dropped his head to the crook of her neck as he came with a shudder.

They lay against each other, both panting, their ragged breaths echoing through the room. It took her a moment to realize her hands were free. She lowered them, caressing over the hard sinew of his shoulders and down his damp back.

He lifted up, gaze searching.

She smiled, lightness filtering through her. "Let's do that again."

Nick stacked another pile of papers at the edge of the long kitchen table, rapidly clicking facts into place. He hadn't forgotten her mention that she had something to tell him, but gut instinct warned him to proceed slowly. "Those bank records hold your signature."

"I know." She twisted her lip and glanced out the wide window toward the green rolling hills.

What the hell? He reached for several documents that showed money being transferred through accounts from a deceased witch named Trevan Demidov to Trivet Corporation, an entity that he'd traced through several shell corporations that seemed to own mines producing planekite. The transfers had taken place after Trevan's death, which apparently had been nearly twenty years ago. "Tell me about Trevan," Nick said.

Simone cleared her throat and fidgeted. "He was a member of the Coven Nine, we dated, and he tried to kill me."

Nick stilled. "Excuse me?"

She shrugged a delicate shoulder in a pretty lavender silk blouse. "Well, to be honest, I tried to kill him first."

The reins he kept on his temper began to fray. "Start explaining now."

Defiance crossed her features, and she tossed her head.

"I mean it, Simone." He was done playing nice. The woman needed a good defense, and he was starting to wonder whether he'd be able to offer one. "Talk."

She rolled her eyes. "Trevan was a complete dick who was trying to take over the Coven Nine with the love of his life, Grace Sadler. Oddly enough, she had been mated eons ago and had lost her mate, so she and Trevan couldn't do more than spend time together. They never touched, or the mating allergy would've killed them. He was killed by a vampire, and cousin Moira challenged Grace to a power fight, winning Grace's place on the Coven Nine."

Nick frowned. "Moira isn't on the Nine."

"No. She won but she wanted to remain an Enforcer, so she nominated her sister, Brenna."

Damn witches and their secrets. "Grace died?"

"No. She's probably licking her wounds somewhere, and it should take another couple hundred years for her to regain her power. We've kept tabs on her. From her earlier mating, she has two grown children. They're outlaws, and Phillipe Sadler has been known to speak out against the Nine. He's weak but loud."

Nick tapped the papers, his instincts humming. "Grace and her adult kids are still alive. Do you think she's the one who set you up?"

"No." Simone reached for more papers to study. She should probably tell him the full truth about her activities throughout the century. "I don't think Grace has any contacts or power, but we should probably double-check with the Guard. Whoever has targeted the Nine has also set me up. We have many enemies, you know."

He rubbed the shadow along his jaw. "That does seem odd. Everyone has been targeted with darts, even you, but you've also been targeted with these allegations."

She paled. "What are you thinking?"

He hated to say it out loud. "I think you have more than one enemy making a move right now. It doesn't make sense for somebody to spend all this time and resources on creating darts filled with planekite to harm the Nine and also put together this elaborate case against you."

"Oh." Her lips trembled when she gave him the weakest smile he'd ever seen.

"Don't shut me out." He tried to soften the order, but his temper emerged with bite. "Not now. Work with me."

"I'm not shutting you out. It's just a surprise that I need to look over both shoulders and not just one." She reached behind her to the pale yellow counter to grasp the coffeepot so she could pour two more cups.

"Simone?"

"Yes?" she asked, her gaze on the cups, but not fooling him a bit.

"Why is your signature on these documents?"

She carefully, very carefully, turned to replace the pot. "Well, if you must know, I may have committed theft, fraud, and possibly treason."

"That doesn't sound like you." He kept his voice level when all he wanted to do was shout for her to get to the damn point and explain herself.

A blush colored her high cheekbones. "Trevan and I were close."

Nick snorted. "I'm well aware of your relationship, and any relationships you have had during the last one hundred years." He held up a hand when she started to speak. "I don't want details, believe me. However, it's time to explain."

Her hands wrapped around her mug. "Trevan and I made several investments, and they all were consolidated before his death. Since he was tried and convicted posthumously of treason, all of his holdings were to be transferred to the Nine. I, ah, didn't transfer all of them."

Nick sat back, trying to keep his mouth from gaping. "Why?"

She shrugged. "The Nine used all his money for security and increasing the wealth of the coven, which is important, I admit. I used it for what I believed was a better cause."

He wasn't going to like her explanation. He just knew it. "Wait a minute."

She hunched forward. "I don't want to talk about it."

Ah, hell. "It was you. You were the one who kept the weapons stocked on the islands for my people. For the demons." He and Zane had fought hard against Suri, Zane's uncle, often finding surprising caches of weapons and money to fund their underground war. "I thought the help came from the King of the Realm."

Her blush turned into a fiery red. "I may have filtered funds through Dage."

"Jesus, Simone. I know you dated him, too."

"It wasn't serious."

"I know that." Even though it had been Nick's idea in the first place, to keep her safe, he couldn't deny the absolute relief that had filled him when he'd heard they'd broken things off so long ago. "Dage can corroborate your story?"

"No. Dage can affirm I funneled money to him, but only that he received it. He can't dispute these records."

Well, hell. He'd had no clue Simone had been risking herself to help him all those years. She'd never stop surprising him, now would she? His chest shifted and settled. What a sweetheart. That was a side of herself she didn't show many people. "These records show that you funneled money into planekite mining."

"I know."

Somebody had done a hell of a job setting her up. "Who did you work with?"

She grimaced. "A witch by the name of Paul, who showed up dead a few months ago. He's the only one who knew what was happening."

"How did he find you?"

She swallowed. "We worked together on a Dublin city project a few years back, one that secured the city against, well, demons, and he cut a few corners. Our plan flowed naturally from there, since I'd saved Trevan's money, waiting for a chance to help you."

The fact that she'd helped him warmed him and pissed him off simultaneously. "So we have no way to prove what you did."

She smiled then, the expression sad and accepting. "That doesn't really matter, now, does it? Even if we could prove it, all we'd be proving is that I committed treason by taking money from the Nine and funding the demon nation, which was our enemy at the time."

Holy shit, she was right. He tried to think of a way out for her and came up empty. "You'll have to run."

She shook her head. "The earth isn't big enough to hide from the Coven Nine forever, even if I could hide for years."

He slowly nodded, his gut sinking. "Maybe." The best plan was to win within the Coven laws. "We have to win your trial."

"How? I'm guilty either way."

He hadn't spent his entire life planning strategy to fail now. "Don't worry. I'll figure it out." As he gave the promise, he tried to give her a reassuring smile.

Somehow, he was pretty sure he'd failed.

Chapter 18

Her trial started the next day, and her mother was getting worse. Simone smoothed hair back from her mother's head, her heart hurting. For days, she and Nick had worked around the clock to find a way to win the trial, and they'd come up empty.

Moira sat over in the corner, her green eyes sizzling. "You feel better, Aunt Viv?"

"Yes," Viv said weakly.

Simone tried to hold back the fear, but flames still flashed down her arm. She snuffed them out.

"What the hell?" Moira whispered.

Simone blushed. "I'm upset."

"Yeah, but . . ." Moira stood, so many thoughts scattering across her face it was impossible to read. "I have a meeting with the Guard. Walk me out."

Simone patted her mother's bedclothes and followed her cousin to the hall, closing the door quietly. "When you return, will you bring her some of that beef broth she likes from Bromby's?"

"Yes." Moira leaned in, her chin lowering. "The flames on your arms?"

Irritation swept through Simone, and heat filled her chest. "Nobody is perfect." In fact, she felt very imperfect and a little out of control. As if mirroring her thoughts, another dash of fire swept across her hands. Pink fire. She gasped.

"That's what I mean. It's fucking pink," Moira hissed.

Simone shook her head. "This is just a fluke. I'm really upset." Her mind spun and then just went blank.

"Simone?" Vivienne called weakly.

Moira gripped her arm. "Go sit with your mother. I have a meeting, and then I'll bring the soup. Just stay here and calm down."

Simone nodded and moved woodenly into the other room. Perhaps the planekite poisoning had messed with her fire? She crossed to sit by her mother, her brain flashing to Nick.

He wanted her to run, and she was considering it. But she couldn't leave her mother right now.

"Stop fretting," her mother said weakly. She lay against the down pillows, small purple veins crossing her delicate eyelids. "This is part of the illness."

Viv had been hit with two darts, and her initial strength had ebbed as the poison tunneled into deep tissue and organs. "You'll be all right, Mother."

"I know." Viv opened bloodshot eyes.

Simone reached for a cup of milk, and her mother shook her head. "God. No more milk."

"You need your strength," Simone murmured, trying not to tear up at how quickly her mother was losing weight.

"No." Viv struggled to sit up and accepted help with the pillows this time without protest. "What's going on with your trial?"

Simone bit her lip. "We have it all figured out."

Viv's gaze sharpened. "You've always been a terrible liar."

Simone frowned. "I have not. I'm an excellent liar."

"Obviously not. Now, tell me the truth."

Simone debated the issue for all of two seconds before she poured the whole sordid story out for her mother.

When Simone finished, Viv's mouth opened and closed several times before she could speak. "You are bloody well kidding me."

"No."

Fire lanced across Viv's arms to be quickly snuffed. "I told you that demon was bad for you. I told you, and yet you committed treason to help him in a war against our allies."

Simone nodded, her chest aching. "I know. I'm sorry to disappoint you."

Viv patted her arm. "What's done is done." She wiped the back of her mouth with a shaking hand. "Either way, you're guilty of treason."

"I know," Simone whispered. "We're trying to figure out some sort of defense, but everything we come up with is weak." Hope filled her that her mother, a political genius, would figure something out.

"You're screwed."

Simone sat back, her hopes sinking like a balloon losing air. "Not what I was hoping for."

"You have to run, sweetheart." Viv's eyes opened wide. "You don't have a chance here."

"Run where?" Simone asked. "There's nowhere to go."

Viv swayed and dropped back to the pillows. "The demon could hide you, but eventually, the Guard would find you. The witches would go to war with the demons, and at some point . . ."

"Too many people would die," Simone finished for her. No matter how the war ended, she'd be the cause of too many deaths, maybe even of her loved ones. "I can't take that chance."

Viv nodded, her eyelids fluttering. She grabbed Simone's arm and dug in sharp nails. "Call Bear."

Simone shook her head. "No. The shifter nation can't get involved in this, either."

"Promise me. Call Bear." Her mother's voice grew weaker.

"I've tried." Simone tucked the covers up around her mom, her body feeling heavy with foreboding. "He won't answer or return my calls." When Bear disappeared, he did it right. Always had.

Viv's nails bit harder. "Then call Desmond. Bear must've met with him while he was here." Her voice trailed off.

Simone leaned in. "Desmond? Who's Desmond?"

"I'm sorry, Simone," Viv murmured. "I should've told you. Or protected you. But you have to call him. It's your only chance, if he doesn't kill you."

"Mother?" Simone leaned in, feeling her mother's hot forehead. A chill clacked down her spine. "Who's Desmond?"

Viv's breathing turned shallow, and her eyelids flipped open again. "My phone."

Almost in a daze, Simone reached for the smartphone by the bed and handed it over. Viv's hand shook, but she dialed a number and pressed the phone to her ear.

"This is Vivienne," she whispered. Two seconds went by. Then another. "Are you there?"

Somebody must've answered. "Simone is going to be killed if

you don't come get her, Desmond. It's time for you to protect her."
She clicked off.

Simone sat back. "Desmond?"

Viv pressed one number this time and held the phone to her ear.
A *beep* echoed loudly enough for Simone to hear it. "Bear? Damn
it, check your phone. I called Desmond to help Simone, and he's on
the way. Get here." Vivienne dropped the phone.

Simone reached over to pick it up from the floor and placed it on
the bedside table. Her mother's eyes were closed, and her breathing
turned shallow.

Sleep caught Viv, and a very slight tingle of healing wove through
the air. Oh, when her mother awoke, she was going to start answering
some questions. Simone glanced at the phone and memorized the
mysterious Desmond's phone number. She'd have it traced later.
Giving in to exhaustion, Simone stretched out next to her mother
and fell into a dreamless sleep.

Hours later, a rap on the door had her sitting right up.

"Yoo-hoo?" The door was nudged open, and Moira Dunne-Kayrs
poked her head inside. "I put the soup in the fridge downstairs." She
stepped gingerly inside and walked over to place a hand on Viv's
head. "She's feverish."

"I know. She's getting worse." Simone pushed to her feet, feeling
thousands of years old. She glanced at the brown bag in Moira's
hands. "What do you have?"

Moira grasped her arm and led her into the master bath. "I started
thinking about the pink fire on your arms earlier." She drew out a
pregnancy test. "Just to make sure. You know it's nearly impossible,
right? There's nothing to worry about."

Simone shook her head, tension flying through her on wicked
wings. "You're crazy. Just crazy. We're not mated, so no way."

"But, well, your mom got pregnant with you without being
mated." Moira's worried green eyes sizzled in the muted colors of
the marble bathroom. "And you've never created pink fire. Ever.
Brenna has been creating purple because of her pregnancy, so I
figured . . ."

"Aye." No. Simone could not be pregnant. Immortal females produced enough of the pregnancy hormone to be able to confirm a
pregnancy within hours of conception, and she'd had a couple of

days since having wild sex with Nick. She'd take the test and soothe Moira's nerves. "The pink fire instead of my usual blue is either just stress or because of the planekite attack, right?"

"Right." Moira nodded vigorously.

Simone ripped open the package, her hands shaking, and her pulse racing. "I'll pee on this, and we'll see I'm fine."

"By the way, Conn is downstairs," Moira said.

Simone stilled. "Your mate is here? Did he see this pregnancy test?"

"Aye. Sorry."

Well, hell. "That's okay." Simone dropped her drawers and peed on the stick. Her cousin had seen her naked enough times in her life that she really didn't give a damn for modesty. "Do you know anybody named Desmond?"

"No, why?" Moira asked.

"Because my mother called him to rescue me. I thought she might be delirious, but she knew the number to call."

"Hmmm. Maybe an old ally she can count on? There are witches who live far in the hills and don't like modern life." Moira frowned. "Man. When was the last time you peed?"

Simone stopped peeing and rolled her eyes. "I just want to make sure I got it."

"Oh, you got it."

Simone finished up and placed the test on the counter before washing her hands. "Takes three minutes."

"Girl, if you're knocked up by a demon, you won't need three minutes." Moira stood next to her, half a foot shorter in the mirror, and peered at the test. "Oh."

Simone dried her hands and glanced down. "Oh."

Moira slipped an arm around Simone's waist. "Um. Congratulations?"

Simone swayed. Blooming bollocks. She was pregnant.

Nick practiced his legal argument in his head, all the while eyeing the vampire sprawled in the feminine chair. If Conn Kayrs moved an inch, he might just split the floral high-back.

"So. How are things?" Conn asked, his green eyes curious, his face hard and set.

Nick frowned. The vampire soldier wanted to make small talk? As the war had ended and demon headquarters were moved next to the Realm headquarters, he'd gotten to know and genuinely like the Kayrs men. Not one of them ever engaged in small talk. "Just fucking dandy. How about you?"

Conn lifted a massive shoulder. "Eh." He tapped his fingers on his worn jeans. His gaze darted around, and tension rolled off him like steam on a lake.

"What is wrong with you?" Nick growled.

"Nothin'." Conn leaned forward, and the chair groaned in protest. "You and Simone, huh?"

Nick dropped the paper he'd been trying to memorize. "Are you gossiping with me?"

"No. Geez." Conn leaned an elbow on the armrest, and the thing crashed to the ground. "Ah, hell. Viv isn't going to like that." He grabbed the damaged arm and tried to shove it back into place. Fabric and wood went flying.

"Stop trying to fix it." Nick frowned. If anything, Conn seemed nervous. "I'll get Simone out of this mess, I promise." Perhaps the vampire was worried about his mate, Moira, since she was Simone's cousin. "Don't worry."

"Oh, I'm not." Conn cleared his throat. "It's just that sometimes life takes unexpected turns, you know?" He gave Nick a hard look.

"Um, yeah. Turns." Puzzlement filled Nick.

"Good. Because Simone is family, and well, family is family. Right?"

Had the vampire sustained a head injury lately? "Are you all right, Connlan?" Nick asked.

"I'm fine. Just wanted to get things straight."

Nick rubbed his chin. "Is this about Simone having dated your brother decades ago?" The king was happily mated to Emma Kayrs with a child on the way, so that didn't make sense.

"Of course not. Nobody remembers that, not even Simone. In fact, she and Emma are good friends these days." Conn leaned forward again, and one of the chair legs gave out. He tipped and jumped to his feet. "The furniture here is not good."

Nick searched for words but couldn't find any. "Uh-huh."

"Like I said, the queen of the Realm really likes Simone." Conn placed both hands on his hips. "You don't want to piss off the queen. Ever. Emma has a mean sense of revenge, if you ask me." He nodded. "If you piss off Emma, you piss off the Realm, and if you piss off the Realm, you piss off pretty much everybody."

Dear Lord, Conn had lost his mind. Maybe having twin boys did that to a vampire. "When was the last time you slept?" Nick sputtered.

Conn shrugged. "Dunno. Why?"

"Perhaps you should catch up on the plane ride home. You are heading back to the States, right?" Nick asked.

"Yeah, but Moira is worried about Simone and the trial." Conn scratched a light bruise beneath his jawline.

"Take her home, Conn. If things go south, you want to be far away from here."

Conn's gaze sharpened. "You have a plan?"

"Of course." Hell, he was the ultimate planner, now wasn't he? "I'll need you and especially your mate, the Enforcer, out of Dublin just in case. Moira can't get caught up in the turmoil if things go the way I think they might."

Conn nodded. "Understood." He cleared his throat. "Anyway, I was thinking about life, you know?"

No. Hell no. Nick frowned and tried to find evidence of a brain injury. Conn's pupils looked fine. "Why?"

"Well, it's just that kids bring a lot to your life, and I think everyone should get a few. I mean, start with one. I started with two, and they're hellions." He grinned.

"Uh-huh."

"They'll change your life, but it's for the good." His canines glinted when he smiled. "You have to roll with the punches."

Was Conn going to punch him? Nick tensed just in case. Conn was the Realm's ultimate soldier, and the guy knew how to hit. So did Nick. "I don't think we should bust up any more of Viv's furniture."

Conn's green eyes widened. "Totally agree. Especially you, because you really want to keep her happy now, you know? Family unity without strife. She's Simone's mom."

Nick nodded. Should he call Conn's brothers and have them make sure he was all right? Something was definitely off with the hulking vampire. "Strife is bad."

"Exactly." Satisfaction lifted Conn's full lips, and his face lost the intense *about to lunge* look. "Glad we're on the same page."

They weren't even reading the same fucking book. "Me too. Are you sure you're all right?" Nick asked.

"I am now." Conn cracked his knuckles. "Good talk, Veis."

Nick leaned back and forgot about the papers in front of him. "Um, yeah. Good talk. Glad we had these moments together."

Conn either disregarded or didn't catch the obvious sarcasm. "Family is family, buddy. Our mates are cousins."

Well, he hadn't exactly mated Simone, but Nick definitely had a plan there. "I guess that's true."

Moira jogged down the steps, her red hair bobbing wildly. "Viv is not doing well, and I want to check on my mom. She was better this morning, but I'd like to see her." Moira grabbed Conn's hand and all but dragged him toward the door. "'Bye, Nick. It was nice seeing you." She threw open the door and disappeared. It closed with a sharp *snap*.

Nick stood and stared at the broken furniture. What in the hell was wrong with Moira and Conn?

If that's what having babies did to two normally brilliant people, he wanted no part of it. Ever.

Chapter 19

Simone inched down the stairs, her mind buzzing and her heart hurting. Pregnant. Of all the impossible things, she was with child. Could there be any worse timing?

Her hands settled over her abdomen in a purely protective gesture. Pregnant.

She coughed out a laugh. Her heart lifted. A baby. Nick's baby.

The idea, as unthinkable as it was, filled her with a joy she hadn't thought possible. Perhaps it made an odd kind of sense, considering her mother had become pregnant without a mating, and her father apparently had a gift in that department. Even so, something so rare had to be part of fate. Right?

How in the world was she going to tell Nicholai?

More important, how in the world was she going to get him to back off and let her go to trial? With a bairn on the way, she couldn't go into hiding. They had to figure out a decent defense. If the law didn't work for her, which it certainly did not, she needed to find a political reason for the Coven Nine to find her not guilty. There had to be something.

But first she had to convince an over-the-top, protective, posses-sive male demon to quell every natural instinct he owned and follow her lead.

Aye. That was going to be easy. Not.

She reached the living room to find Nick moving her mother's favorite chair into the corner of the room. "What happened?"

"Connlan Kayrs happened," Nick muttered. "We'll have to get the

chair repaired when we have time. For now, let's put it in the corner
so nobody sits on it and damages it further."

Simone nodded. "We, ah, need to talk." Her hands fluttered together. Fluttered! For the love of the Liffey. She was Simone Brightston, and she did not flutter. Ever.

He straightened and turned to face her. "Last time you wanted to
talk, I believe you wanted to confess to committing treason. Please
tell me this is less of a surprise."

She chuckled, and even her laugh sounded nervous. "I can't tell
you that."

He sighed. "All right. What now?"

She opened her mouth to tell him, and a car screeched to a stop
outside. A second later, the front door burst open, banging against
the wall.

Nick leaped across the room to cover her, landing squarely between her and the threat. "Bear?" he roared.

Simone looked around Nick. "Bear? What in the world are you
doing in Dublin?"

Bear ran into the room, his gaze frantic. His T-shirt was inside
out as if he'd hurriedly thrown it on, and his threadbare jeans were
unbuttoned. "We have to go. Right now, we have to get the hell out
of here."

Nick didn't hesitate to run over and stuff his papers into a back-
pack. "What kind of threat?"

"You wouldn't believe me." Bear ran toward Simone to grab her
arm. "Let's go. God. I can't believe your mom called him."

Simone jerked free. "Desmond?"

Bear paused and reared back. "She told you about him?"

"Yes," Simone said smoothly, her heart thundering in her chest.
"All about him. So let's wait here."

Bear growled and sounded like the beast he really was. "Bullshit,
sister. If she'd told you about him, you wouldn't want to stay here
and wait."

Nick reached them, anger swelling from him. "Who the hell is
Desmond?"

"Later." Bear pushed Simone toward the door. "I'll explain

everything once we're the hell away from here. Hurry. God, we have to hurry."

His urgency and panic took hold of Simone. "I can't leave my mother."

"You have to. She's safe, I promise." Bear pushed her harder, and she fell against Nick. "Go. Geez. Just go. I'll have your mom brought to safety in no time. She's not the one in danger. I promise."

"Who is Desmond?" Simone asked, turning on Bear. If she didn't get some answers, she was going to go crazy.

Bear looked over her head at Nick. "If she stays here, she dies. I give you my word, she's in mortal danger, and neither of you have a clue as to what is coming. For once in your life, trust me, Nick. Go on faith."

Simone hissed. "I'm not moving an inch——*eek.*"

Nick swung her up and started for the front door. She struggled, panic engulfing her. If danger was coming, the type that could frighten Bear so, she couldn't leave her mother here in such a weakened state. "My mother."

"I'll bring her," Bear yelled. "Text me where to meet you once you're safe. Just go. Fucking go, Simone."

Nick ran for the front door and leaped down the three steps, heading straight for his motorcycle, which was parked near the porch.

A dark shadow covered the sun for a second. Then something else.

Simone glanced up. Nothing. She shivered. "What in the hell?"

Nick reached the bike. "I don't know. Something is here." He frowned and glanced around the quiet area. "Get on the bike."

Her legs wobbled, but she managed to get one over the seat before Nick jumped in front of her and started the engine. The bike roared to life. Hope filled her, and she tucked her hands around Nick's waist.

He twisted the throttle, and the bike leaped forward and onto the dirt drive.

Simone held on, her heart racing. The shadow crossed again.

Strong arms grabbed her. The force jerked her off the motorcycle and into the air. She screamed, reaching for Nick, but within seconds, she rose high above him. The air chilled and seemed to swirl around.

He swung the bike around and cut the engine, looking up with shock and a darkening rage across his face.

Simone froze in place. If she struggled, whatever held her might drop her. What the blooming hell had her?

Whatever it was tucked her up, and warmth shielded her back. The hold felt strong, and the ground rushed by below as they flew with immeasurable speed. She didn't know of any immortal creature that could fly, but something was whisking her away. Her and her baby.

She bit back another scream and tried to concentrate. Wisps of cloud surrounded them, but she could make out land below. Green and rolling countryside turned to churning water. If she struggled free, how hard would she hit the ocean?

Probably too hard. Falling from such a height would be like hitting stone instead of water.

"What are you?" she whispered.

No answer. It barely breathed against her, using wind currents to rise and fall easily.

At some point, whatever it was would have to put her down. It would have to land. The second it did, she'd fight. She dug deep, accepted the reality of what was happening, and prepared to kill.

Wind whistled through her hair, tossing it around.

The air chilled her, even through her jeans and sweater. They had to be heading toward Iceland. An air pocket surrounded them, and they dropped several meters. She screamed and clutched the band around her.

"Sorry." The voice was gravelly, kind of like a demon's but raspier.

She dug her nails into what felt like tight leather over, well, arms. "What are you? I know you can speak."

"Shh. I need to concentrate or we'll end up diving for sharks." Humor laced the deep voice this time, and his breath brushed her hair with warmth.

The truth hit her. Whatever had her had to be a shifter. Shifters were either feline, canine, or multi, although everyone thought multis had evolved into bears, if they ever existed in the first place. This had to be a multi-shifter. Some kind of weird bird? "Are you a dinosaur?"

He laughed then, and there was no doubt the voice was male. "God, no."

"Bird?"

"Nope."

The creature holding her had said "*nope*." How bizarre. "Are you going to kill me?"

The bubble of humor surrounding her popped. "I am not."

Fear clutched her throat. That made sense. If he wanted her dead, he could just drop her. "Is somebody else going to kill me?"

"We'll talk about it when we land."

Her stomach dropped. "The Coven Nine won't allow this to happen."

"The Coven Nine has no clue where you're going."

Neither did Nick. God, he'd be furious. She hadn't gotten a chance to tell him about the baby. "Anybody threatens me and I'll end them."

Her captor chuckled. "Fair enough, Simone."

There went the hopeful thought that he'd just kidnapped a random woman to take back to his lair. Or nest. Or whatever the hell he had. "Your name?" Maybe she could forge some sort of connection with the creature.

"Flynn."

"So, not Desmond." This was getting more and more confusing.

"Desmond sent me."

An island dotted the sea below, but they flew right over it. "Who's Desmond?"

"You'll meet him soon enough."

Another island, a fishing boat, a luxury cruiser, and then just open, gray sea. Dark, churning, and freezing. If he dropped her, she might not make it to safety without drowning, which actually could kill a witch.

The air grew misty and thick around them.

Simone sucked in air, trying to keep from screaming her head off. Her head spun, and adrenaline flowed way too strongly through her veins. She gagged.

"Whoa. No barfing."

What kind of kidnapping, freaky creature used the word *barf*? Simone swallowed down bile. Fear combined with morning sickness? Great. Just what she needed. "I'm fine."

"We're almost there. Don't puke until we land," he said.

"Where?" She couldn't see through the mist.

They started to slowly descend, revealing the ocean below. Simone began to struggle. "There's only water."

"Wait for it." He went lower, and suddenly, jagged cliffs began to appear, and then a monstrous island.

"What the hell?"

"Shielded and veiled." The ground rushed up to meet them, and they landed on a massive breezeway made of something sparkly next to some sort of building set into the cliffs. As they landed, he shifted her in his grip, and ended up running on two legs with her in his arms until he came to a stop.

She gasped for air and glanced up into a male face. A normal male face with dark eyes, even darker hair, and symmetrical features. "Who are you?"

He gently set her on her feet, standing there buck-assed naked. "Flynn."

"I know that." She grasped his arms until her knees stopped shaking, looking down as the sparkly ground and trying not to vomit. The sparkles caught her eye. "Are those diamonds?"

"Of course."

They walked on crushed diamonds set into marble tiles. She looked up and then pushed away from him. He seemed unconcerned by his nudity, and considering he was one long line of ripped muscle, she couldn't quite blame him.

The sea crashed far below them across a marble balcony, while velvet curtains billowed out from several tall doorways. She edged toward the balcony to see a sheer drop with absolutely no handholds.

"The only way in or out is flying." Flynn took a step back, obviously giving her some room. "Are you going to throw up?"

Her stomach still churned, but she shook her head. "No." She pressed both hands on her hips and tried to center herself in case she needed to create fire. "Now, how about you tell me what the fuck you are."

A figure stepped out from the entrance. Tall and broad with sandy brown hair, blue eyes, and designer clothing. He tossed a towel to Flynn, who wrapped it loosely around his hips. "Simone. Welcome to Fire Island."

She fought the urge to sidle closer to the now decent Flynn. "You must be Desmond."

He smiled, flashing extremely white teeth. "Yes. So good to make your acquaintance."

"Who are you people, and what do you want?" Her fingers itched with the desire to burn the hell out of them both.

Desmond took a deep breath. "I'm the leader of our people, and you, my friend, are my cousin."

She blinked. "You're a bear shifter?"

"No."

"Multi-shifter?"

He winced. "Well, there have never been multi-shifters, to be frank. There have been feline, canine, bear, and us."

She frowned. "Bear shifters have always existed?"

"Sure. We perpetrated a legend that they were part of the multi-species in case we were ever seen, which we have been. Everyone bought it. We're no more related to the bears than you are to the vampires." Desmond eyed Flynn.

Simone kept her gaze on both men. There was a tension between them, one she couldn't quite decipher. They weren't witches, which only meant . . . "My father was one of you."

"Aye," Desmond said. "He was also father to Flynn."

Her mouth gaped open. She had another brother? "Wait. So you and Bear?"

"Half-brothers," Flynn confirmed. "He, you, and I share a father but different mothers. Our father was a rare immortal to be sure."

Emotion whirled through her with the force of a hurricane, and she tried to center herself and not freak out in front of the males. "Did my mother know? About you?"

"Probably not about me, but she certainly knew about our father and our species," Flynn said. "And she, of course, knows that Desmond is the leader of our people."

"But I'm not one of you. I can't fly or turn into anything that does fly," Simone whispered.

Flynn smiled. "No. Immortals take one form only, usually, and you're a witch. However, you should have had some experiences as a child. Any chance you have early memories of being, something, well . . . else?"

Heat climbed into her face. No way would she confess that one. "No."

Flynn lifted an eyebrow. "I can smell a lie."

So could she.

He cleared his throat. "Any chance you, ah, remember being a small rabbit?"

Holy blooming crap. The only person she'd ever revealed those odd childhood dreams to was Nicholai, which was how she'd gotten the nickname. She'd thought those were just dreams with no basis in reality. "How did you know?"

He glanced down at the sparkling diamonds. "So wrong. We all have bunny moments as toddlers. To think that our magnificent forms start out as bunnies." He sadly shook his head.

Simone backed away two steps down the railing. "You're freakin' bunnies? Rabbits that fly?"

Desmond barked out a laugh. "Ah, no. It's an unfortunate child-hood phase we all go through, even if we end up taking different forms, like you as a witch."

She allowed plasma to crackle down her arms and form fireballs in her hands. "I'm done asking. Explain."

Desmond eyed the blue flames with interest and then gave a short nod. "Flynn?"

Flynn sighed and dropped the towel. The air popped the same way as when a bear shifted. He growled low, stretched out, and within seconds stood on four long legs, tail up in the air. His eyes remained the same, but his face elongated, he turned deep black, and scales sparkled down his back and legs.

Simone coughed, her feet frozen solid in place. She blinked several times, just in case she was hallucinating. Flynn stared calmly back at her, a huge beast. "Holy shite. You're a dragon," she whispered.

Chapter 20

Nick jumped off his bike and squinted up into the now empty clouds. What the fuck was that thing? He hadn't seen anything but a dark shadow before he'd stopped the motorcycle. His blood rushed through his head, and he tried to shoot a mind attack up, if that thing had a brain. But it was already gone.

With Simone.

Rage rippled through him, and he turned to run toward the car Bear had just jumped into. The feel of the door handle beneath his hand spurred Nick on, and he ripped the entire door away from the car, throwing it across the driveway.

Bear's mouth dropped open, and he jumped out, pushing Nick away. "This is a rental," he snapped.

Nick grabbed the shifter by the T-shirt with both hands and slammed him against the car. "What the fuck just took Simone?"

Bear winced. "I told you to run, but no, you wouldn't hurry." He kept his body relaxed, but tension cascaded from him. "You stay here with Vivienne, and I'll go secure Simone's release. Or at least help her."

"Who are they?" Nick drew Bear back and smashed him into the car again.

Bear shook his shaggy head, his brown eyes somber. "It's none of your business. Just stay here and for once, keep out of the way."

Nick shook his head. "I'm going to kill you if you don't talk."

Bear rolled his eyes. "You couldn't kill me, but if you really must know—because I'm sure Simone will tell you anyway, if she lives—you've never seen anything like the guys who took her."

"Bear," Nick growled.

Bear shrugged. "Fine, but you have to know that hearing this might put a bull's-eye on your damn demon head. I warned you, and you didn't listen, but that's your own damn problem. The guys who took her are dragons. Dragons."

Oh, he was going to kill the smart-ass bear. "Do I look like I'm fucking around right now? Give me a straight answer, or I swear to God, I'm going to peel your brain like a damn avocado."

Bear coughed. "Avocado? Weird choice there. I'd have gone with melon or onion, or even cucumber. Avocado shows some really odd childhood issues, demon." His sarcasm failed to mask the very real concern glowing in his brown eyes.

That was it. Nick lowered his chin and shot a piercing blade into Bear's head along with images of death and destruction.

Bear's bourbon-colored eyes stared back. He blinked.

Nick frowned. There was no reaction from the bear. Shifters were usually overly susceptible to mind attacks. Sucking deep, he shoved harder and sharpened the imaginary blade.

Bear growled, and then his pupils widened until his eyes were a glimmering black.

"What the hell?" Nick asked, releasing him, staring deep. Bear's pupils had changed shape to oblong, while a lighter black colored the iris. Eyes could change colors, not shapes.

Bear shrugged. Pain radiated from him. His face elongated. "You wanted to know." Somehow, his voice had gone raspy.

Nick stepped back several feet, ready to drop into a fighting stance.

The oxygen popped around them, and sparkles glimmered through the molecules. Bear shifted, going from human to an eight-foot-tall grizzly. Stretching his neck, he let out a monstrous roar. His coat thickened down his body into a brownish-gold fur, and a small tail emerged.

Nick tried for another mind attack, honing his aim for the base of Bear's skull. The bear clapped its huge paws, allowing the claws to clang together. He eyed Nick and snorted.

The mind attack still hadn't worked. Nick's temples began to ache with the pain of shooting the powerful blades, but no reasons for the failure came to mind.

Then Bear stilled. The air continued to shimmer and pop, and he stretched out, dropped to all fours, and morphed into something else.

Agony vibrated on the breeze from him. Black with scales, a long snout, longer tail . . . holy crap, it was a dragon.

Nick breathed out. A real, breathing, moving dragon stood in front of him. The thing of legends and fairy tales. "Holy fuck."

The beast nodded. "Yeah, I know. It's a shocker." The voice was Bear's but deeper and kind of hoarse. He glanced down at the ripped clothing on the ground. "You owe me new jeans."

Nick shook his head. "You don't exist."

Bear stretched weird-looking arms and then stood upright, bigger than any animal on earth, about twice the length of the car.

Nick frowned. "I would've thought a dragon would be bigger."

Bear blinked, his eyelids moving sideways and not top to bottom. Flames danced along his mouth like the embers of a dying fire. Hot and ready to ignite at any time. "That's not nice."

Nick rubbed his chin, not sure whether to stab Bear or study him. "I guess it's like shifting into a bear—you have to be roughly the same size, if a little bigger in animal form." He'd grown up with shifters, so seeing a dragon wasn't exactly a far stretch of the imagination. The surprise was in their ability to keep themselves a secret. "Dragons. Interesting."

Bear stretched his back, and scales rippled. "Dragons have kept to themselves, mainly, and the headquarters is in the middle of the North Atlantic, not far from Ireland. That's where they probably took Simone."

"Who took her?" Nick growled, accepting the new reality because he didn't have time for denial. If he was going to go after her, he needed intel and fast.

Bear slowly shifted back to a grizzly and then a man. With a sigh, he reached down and hopped into the ripped jeans, his lips turning down. "Maybe I can fix these." Then he fell back against the car, his body shuddering.

"Bear?" Nick narrowed his gaze. "What's wrong?"

Bear shoved off the driver's side door. "Nothin'. It has just been a while." He staggered in place for a moment and then seemed to gain his balance, but his coloring remained wan.

Nick settled his stance. "Bear? Who took my . . . Simone? Who took Simone?"

Bear sighed and shoved a hand through his shaggy hair. "Okay.

The dragons are led by our cousin, Desmond, who probably ordered my half-brother, Flynn, to take her. She was taken because Vivienne called Desmond for help, and Desmond wouldn't let his own flesh and blood be killed by the witches."

"She's safe?" Not that Nick was going to take any chances.

"Well, maybe. If she says that she had anything to do with the death of our father, then she's not safe." Bear scratched his arm.

Nick opened his mouth and then shut it. "She didn't kill Roman."

"I know that." Bear shook his head. "But she will cover for you or me, I'm afraid."

Urgency tightened Nick's shoulders. "Who the hell do they think killed Roman?"

Bear shuffled his bare feet. "Well, they actually think I killed him."

Nick stilled. "You took the rap for Simone?"

"Yeah. She's my sister."

Nick shook his head. "Wait a minute. If they didn't punish you, what makes you think they'll punish Simone?"

Bear tugged his ripped jeans up. "Who says they didn't punish me?"

"What do you mean?"

"I've been exiled from the dragon community, and if they catch up with me, they're gonna put me to death." He shrugged. "That's why I moved to the States and have stayed under the radar."

Nick heaved out a breath. "That's fucking crazy. You were just a kid."

Bear slowly nodded. "Yeah, well, insanity is a staple with dragons. Sometimes they go too far over the deep end, like my father did when he tried to kidnap Simone."

"So why the hell are you here and not preparing to save your own life?"

Bear lowered his chin. "Since the damn witches kidnapped me to Ireland, I chanced one last meeting with my half-brother to see if there was any way to stop the execution. When that failed, I was heading home to get ready for a fight because they will come after me. Then Vivienne called me and Desmond, and I was afraid Simone would end up in the wrong place and confess to the wrong thing. I haven't spent a century in exile for her to go and get herself killed now."

Nick coughed out heat and tried to retain focus when all he

wanted to do was hit something. Hard. "You're telling me that if Simone confesses to killing her father, she'll be murdered."

"Yes."

Nick scrubbed both hands down his face. "Simone didn't kill your father. I did."

Bear winced. "I know, but she'll probably try to protect you."

"She'd better not." She wouldn't, would she? "You should've told Simone the truth about her being a dragon and not a bear shifter," Nick said.

"Maybe, or maybe not. Either way, I wanted to protect her."

Nick eyed the setting sun. "So a century ago, you lost your father, lost the sister you'd just found, and returned to dragon land to be sentenced to death." Against his will, empathy slid through Nick's mental armor.

"Pretty much. After, I'd headed to the States, joined the bear shifter nation, and never let anybody know about dragons." Bear's voice remained level, but Nick could sense the loneliness he must've felt as a kid.

"I'm sorry for any pain I caused you when I killed Roman." Nick would do it again, to save Simone. "But now, we have to let the dragons know that neither you nor Simone killed Roman."

Bear scratched his arm. "You have to understand that the second you confess, you're a dead man, right? They definitely won't let you leave."

Nick nodded. "Unless you have a better idea, I say we go in and fight our way out."

Bear winced. "You've noticed that demon mind attacks don't work on dragon shifters, right?"

"Right."

"You'll be up against shifting beasts that can burn you to a crisp, and you won't have any of your natural abilities. Can you teleport?" Bear asked.

Nick shook his head.

Bear sighed. "Then it's crazy for you to even think of taking on the dragons. You don't stand a chance."

Nick mentally counted the weapons he'd stored in his temporary Dublin home. "I have more than my mind to use in battle. I couldn't attack your mind, but I've been inside Simone's, so there must be a way in."

Bear shook his head. "The only way you got into Simone's head was because she let you. On some level, she must really trust you."

Nick tried to banish his fear as to what was happening to Simone. If she did confess to protect both Bear and Nick, would the dragons really kill her?

Nick had to save her, if it was the last thing he ever did. From the sound of things, there was a good chance it would turn out that way. "I want a layout of the dragon lair." He turned and headed into the house.

Bear followed him inside. "It's not a lair. It's a mansion set into a cliff several thousand feet above jagged rocks and churning water."

Nick paused. "So flying is the only way in or out?"

"Yep."

"Are you sure you can become a dragon and get me in? You're still not looking too good." Bear's normally bronze color hadn't returned.

"I'm fine. Just takes practice."

Okay, then. "Well then, shifter. Get ready to take a passenger right in."

Chapter 21

The surreal night took an even more bizarre turn as Simone sat down to an opulent dinner, complete with servants, hosted by her newly discovered half-brother and cousin. The servants were deferential, or perhaps just plain fearful, and Simone's teeth began to ache.

Everything in the room glittered with gold accents, including the utensils. "The legends about dragons and gold are true," she said, taking a sip of an excellent Bordeaux and then leaving it alone for the baby's sake.

Desmond nodded. He'd changed for dinner into a silver Armani suit complete with red power tie. With his brown hair and dark eyes, he could be a model. "Aye. Haven't you felt the pull of gold and jewels?"

Hell yeah. She loved baubles and pretty things. Curiosity filled her about these new relatives. She'd been alone for so long, and now, suddenly she had more family members than she'd ever dreamed of, including Bear. "Sure, but no more than anybody else."

"So you've never stolen money or hidden cash for pet projects or something only you approve of?" Flynn asked, cutting into a steak. While he'd also changed, there was something rough and untamed about him, even in a black suit that matched his hair.

Simone lifted an eyebrow, quite liking the roughness about him. It made him more approachable. Did he know about her trial? Was he hinting at the accusations against her? "That's different."

"Not really," her brother said. "Don't tell me you didn't get a rush out of taking that money and hiding it from the Coven Nine, even if your purpose was honorable and your ends just. The taking and manipulating of riches is like a drug to us."

She shifted in her chair and glared at him through antique candlesticks. So he knew all about her current situation. Made sense. "I have no idea what you're talking about." Yet she understood completely. "Why haven't you contacted me before?" Yeah, it kind of hurt.

He sighed, his black eyes softening. "We didn't know you existed until you joined the Coven Nine Council, which, of course, we keep dossiers on. Then our father put two and two together, and as you know . . ."

"Aye. He tried to take me and was willing to kill me if he failed." Although bewilderment filled her, she kept her voice calm and factual.

"Well, yes." Desmond poured more wine into the glasses. "He ruled our nation, and some say he had been slipping mentally for years."

"I didn't know," Flynn broke in, his eyes burning with an emotion she couldn't read. "I was on a mission on the other side of the planet, and I was unaware of your existence or his plan to take you. Beauregard only found out the day they visited you, and it was too late for him to contact me."

Beauregard. Simone nodded. "I believe he goes by Bear now."

Desmond snorted. "That name is silly, and he will be referred to by his given name here."

Simone squinted at her brother. "What if you had known about me and the threat?"

Flynn paused and studied her. "I would've protected your life."

"Really." Surprise filled her at how badly she wanted to believe that.

"Aye. You're my sister, and I'd do anything to protect you." Flynn's eyes morphed to reptilian and back. "I've lived nearly five hundred years on this earth without a sister, and I'd very much like to change that."

Five hundred years? Man, that was as old as Nick. Simone nodded, almost afraid to believe she could be close to a sibling. Maybe she, Bear, and Flynn could get to know each other. Perhaps the baby would love having uncles. A bear and a dragon uncle. How fascinating. "I would like to know you," Simone murmured.

Flynn smiled, the corners of his eyes crinkling. "Good." He moved to allow a small blond woman to refill his water glass, giving her a gentle smile. She smiled back, no fear showing.

Yet she changed as she neared Desmond, her shoulders hunching and her steps slowing. When she'd refilled his glass, she scurried out the door.

Simone watched the exchange, her instincts kicking in along with an unnerving sense of nausea. Morning sickness? At night? "How many dragons are here?" she asked mildly.

"We go deep into the cliffs, and about a hundred or so live here permanently," Desmond said. "In addition, only about twenty percent of shifters with dragon genetics can actually shift into dragons. We have another hundred of our people spread throughout the world, most of whom can't shift. Immortals can only have one true nature."

"So I won't be able to shift," she breathed, her eyes widening.

Flynn nodded. "Only male dragons shift, anyway."

Oh. Well, that bit. "Bear can shift into a dragon?"

"Yes, shifters can sometimes take different forms, but his true nature is a bear, so it harms him," Flynn said quietly.

No more shifting into scales for Bear. "Why are there only two hundred immortals with dragon genetics across the globe? That number seems really minute," she said.

"Dragon offspring are rare, even rarer than vampires or demons. It's possible for a mated dragon to live thousands of years and not procreate," Flynn said.

"Yet our father had three kids and was unmated," she said.

Desmond shook his head. "Believe me, Roman was an anomaly. One we can't explain and haven't seen the likes of before or since. It was a shock that he'd procreated with a shifter, let me tell you."

Poor Bear. How alone he must've felt. For so many years, she'd wanted to be close to Bear, but they hadn't had a chance. Now she understood better why. Bear kept secrets, especially about his having dragon genetics, and that needed to end right now. "Are you and Bear close, Flynn?"

Flynn's nostrils flared, and a veil dropped down over his eyes.

"We were close when he was young, but I was on mission quite a bit, and then he was excommunicated."

Simone frowned. "Why?"

Desmond shook his head. "Let's not go into tragedy, shall we?"

Simone glanced from one man to the other. There were undercurrents she couldn't quite grasp. "He's in Ireland now."

"Yes, I know," Desmond said smoothly. "In fact, I've sent our soldiers to fetch him. He will join us soon."

Tension emanated from Flynn as the men waged a silence-filled war, not quite glaring at each other but coming damn close.

Finally, Simone couldn't stand the swelling atmosphere. It probably wasn't good for the new babe she carried, right? "If you don't mind my asking, why is Desmond the leader and not you, Flynn? Considering your father was the ruler. Our father, that is."

Flynn grinned. "We use elections here and not order of succession." Flecks of green glowed in his eyes. "When Father died, Desmond threw his hat in the proverbial ring of fire, and I did not."

Desmond nodded. "Your brother prefers the front line and being a soldier. Said he'd rather have to eat his own fire than run for office."

"Amen to that." Flynn eyed his cousin. "Although I may have to take a run for it if the current administration doesn't change a law or two." He glanced at Simone and then back. "You understand what I'm saying, Desmond?"

Desmond stilled. For the first time, the predator lurking inside his handsome body became visible. "If you want to challenge me, do so."

"I don't want to lead. You know what I want." Flynn held Desmond's gaze, no give on his hard face.

"Our laws are our laws," Desmond countered. "I'm not changing them for you or anybody else, and even if I wanted to, the nation wouldn't agree and you know it." He smiled at Simone, all charm again. "Our people need to approve changes to ancient law by a two-thirds vote."

"How democratic." She shivered at the definite chill in the air, and wondered what the hell they were arguing about without arguing about. Either way, she needed to change the subject before she threw up from the tension. "What about your mother or other siblings, Flynn?"

"My mother is a dragon who is currently on a cruise in the Bahamas, and she hasn't mated anyone. You and Bear are my only siblings." Flynn took a healthy drink of his water.

Simone coughed. Dragons on cruise ships. Who knew? She might as well try to understand as much as possible about these new relatives of hers. "I still don't understand why Roman decided to kidnap me." Her instincts focused on the problem.

"He most likely would've left you alone after meeting you initially." Desmond nodded. "But when Roman investigated you, he discovered you were seriously dating a demon, and that pretty much was that, as they say."

Simone frowned. "Excuse me?"

Flynn finished chewing. "Even though our father had lost his hold on reality, his fear was well founded. At the time, of course."

Simone sat back, her nape tickling. "How so?"

"Well, dragons and demons can't mix." Desmond nodded at Flynn. "Right?"

So that was what Bear had been talking about when he'd insisted Simone break it off with Nick. It wasn't demons and bears that couldn't mix, but demons and dragons. "I've heard rumors," Simone murmured.

Desmond laughed, the sound a little too loud. "Think about it. Demons attack minds, but dragon minds can't be attacked."

She studied him. Serious. "That's a nice gift." Damn, she wished Nick was there to prove the theory. With his age and powers, if anybody could slice into a dragon brain, it'd be Nicholai Veis. "So?"

Flynn sighed. "So, imagine if you, a witch-dragon, mated a demon and produced offspring. That child would possibly be the most powerful and deadly being on the planet. The biggest threat to dragons, for sure, because it would be able to mind attack."

Simone shook her head. "You don't know that."

"Unfortunately, we do," Flynn breathed.

"It has happened before?" Simone whispered.

"Yes. Where do you think the human legends about dragons come from?" Desmond said, pushing back his plate. "A millennium ago, such a creature actually existed, and it took out half of the dragon and witch races."

She frowned. "There was a legend, one I didn't believe, about a fire-breathing shifter that harmed my people."

"Yes." Desmond nodded. "There was a cross breed, a crazy being, and it killed for sport. With its skills, it was nearly infallible, and that can't happen again. The Coven Nine and the Guard hunted all dragons down at that time, believing them to be mutated multis. We had to create this island just to survive and protect ourselves from the witch nation."

"Witches and demons are now allies. Why don't dragons come back into the world and do the same?" Simone asked.

Flynn leaned back. "I think it's time we stopped hiding, but Desmond doesn't agree."

"No. Hidden we stay safe," Desmond countered. "We can counter witch fire, avoid demon mind attacks, and fight as well as vampires or other shifters. We're too dangerous to be allowed to live, and the other species will combine to take us out. Again."

Simone swallowed. Perhaps the world had been that way before, but now peace reigned. "I think you're wrong."

Desmond studied her. "Maybe, but look at the bright side. Fate obviously stepped in with you, Simone."

She tilted her head to the side. "How so?"

Desmond smiled. "You see, it's a good thing you didn't mate the demon and procreate our worst nightmare. The second you were with child, we'd have had to kill you."

Chapter 22

Nick had faced death before, several times, and yet this was the worst. Guided by moonlight, a bear-dragon hybrid mix held him high above the churning sea, flying in what could only be described as a turbulent mission. He strengthened his hold on the pack holding clothes and weapons.

Bear dropped several meters again, and bile shot up Nick's throat. He swallowed it ruthlessly down. "Would you please stop doing that?"

"You weigh a fucking ton," Bear complained, flying high above the ocean, his hold on Nick not at all secure. Pain tingled from the scales all around Nick. They dropped again, and Bear grunted, trying to gain altitude. "I haven't practiced flying in a long time."

"Why the fuck not?" Nick shut his eyes as the sea rose up to meet them again.

They lifted higher, and cool air slammed into them.

"It's not my thing," Bear groaned. His wings made audible flaps through the night. Bear's hold slipped, and Nick fell into rushing air.

He bellowed, his arms and legs windmilling.

Fast and hard, Bear pummeled into him, slamming his weird arms through Nick's and rapidly flapping his wings. Pain ripped through Nick's abdomen.

He held perfectly still, his heart pounding against his rib cage as they rose again. He was upright, his legs catching the wind, his blood rushing through his veins. "What the hell?"

"Sorry." Bear tucked him up against his belly again. "You shouldn't have brought so many weapons. They're really heavy."

"Just don't drop me again," Nick ordered, his entire body already in serious pain. He took a deep breath and sent healing cells to three of his ribs, which Bear had broken when he'd caught Nick up. "How much farther?" Nick asked, gritting his teeth from the pain of healing.

"A ways." Bear seemed to find an air current, because his body relaxed, and he began to soar better.

Clouds wafted around them, and the moon glinted off the wild ocean below. "What's up with all the secrecy about dragons? I mean, who cares?" Nick asked.

"Dragons can counter any attack, and the smartest move for other immortals is to take us out. The witches and demons combined years ago to make it happen, and they could do so again," Bear said.

Nick forced his eyes to remain open on not on the earth spinning by. The shifter had a point, and it was something they could figure out at a later date. For now, he had a job to do. "Are you all right with the plan?" Nick asked, aiming his question for the beast's long neck.

"Yes. I'll do anything for Simone," Bear returned, his body moving as his wings went back to work. "The plan sucks."

"I know, but at the very worst, they'll kill me and not Simone, so you're on board, right?"

"Yep. I don't want to see you die, but if it comes down to you or Simone, I'm all right with you taking the sword to the throat."

Nick coughed. "Thanks, Bear." He meant the words.

"You're welcome." Bear sounded as if he was sincere, too.

Simone was all that mattered, and as long as she walked away unscathed, Nick would gladly give up his head. Of course, that was his last option. He'd be happy to fight first. "We try to battle our way out before I take the sword, right?"

Bear gave the equivalent of a dragon shrug, which felt like a whole body roll from under his massive body. "Eh."

Hell. Not the right answer. "If I die, Simone is going to be upset." Nick kept his voice level. Just how crazy and nonchalant was Bear? Nick had never been able to get a grasp on the shifter. "You don't want your only sister upset."

"I think you're basically a hitch in her life, demon." Bear's voice sounded like Bear but with a raspiness that carried on the breeze. "Any alliance with you ultimately will hinder her plans."

A bird flew into them, and Nick ducked his head, taking a mouthful of feathers. The bird flapped away, clacking in anger. He spit out feathers. "Would you watch where you're going?" What the hell had he been thinking to work with Bear instead of working around the damn shifter?

"Sorry." He didn't sound sorry.

"What do you mean, I hinder her plans?"

"Geez, man. Simone is as ambitious as they get, and she wants to run the Coven Nine. You just get in the way."

Nick sneezed out another feather. "I could make her happy." He gingerly reached up and picked more feathers off his face.

Bear dropped a meter.

"Bear!"

"Don't wriggle so much," the shifter muttered.

Nick shook his head. "You're one crazy bastard. Simone is already established in the Coven Nine, assuming they don't order her death." Which they wouldn't, because he had a decent defense planned finally. Well, kind of. All right, he could still lose, and then he'd have to put her in hiding, which would be a disaster.

"No way would a witch mated to a non-witch ever lead the Council. Hell. Why do you think Viv never mated my dad? I mean, besides the fact that he was a real dick." Bear snorted, his massive dragon body shuddering.

Nick opened his mouth but couldn't find any words of comfort. "Simone makes her own path."

Bear coughed. "Those witches are big on tradition, allies, and war. The demons might be allies right now, but you know that can change on a sneeze."

True. Definitely true. Nick struggled to argue his position, even while his chest ached at the possibility of Simone choosing duty over him. "If I mate her, then her alliance will be to me."

Bear chuckled. "You're fooling yourself, demon."

There was a better than slim chance that Bear would let Nick be killed and then just go happily on with his life. Nick restrategized his plan in case Bear turned against him. He wanted to trust Simone's brother to have his back, but he just didn't know the guy.

The air changed, thickening and warming. Nick peered down at the sea, trying to find the difference in the night. Magic and veils whispered on the air currents. A chill clacked down his back, and his fangs elongated.

"We're almost there. Get ready for a fast landing." Bear pointed his reptilian face toward the waves, and all of his muscles bunched.

Nick tensed, trying to see anything but water. He shoved his fangs up tight. "I can't find the land."

"Unless you're a dragon, you can't see it until you're on it." Bear descended rapidly, and the ocean came closer. Suddenly, they impacted something hard, and Bear dropped Nick.

The air flew from Nick's lungs. He tucked in his head and extremities, sliding across a smooth surface. He rolled several times and crashed into a stone wall, shoulders first.

The earth stopped moving. He blinked and then slowly opened his eyes fully, glancing around. Pain ripped through his back and down one leg, and he took a quick inventory, shoving healing cells into place. Bruised and ripped but not broken. Good enough.

He shoved to his feet and wavered.

The dragon stared at him. Its eyes morphed from black to brown, and he shifted into a grizzly bear. The air shimmered and popped, and soon Bear was back to human form, standing against a white railing overlooking a cliff. He heaved in huge gulps of air, and his entire body shuddered with the movement. "Clothes," he groaned.

Nick reached into his pack and tossed Bear a pair of jeans that had once probably been blue and a T-shirt blacker than the night. Bear quickly dressed. "Are you all right?" Nick whispered.

Bear held his stomach and then nodded. "Yes."

Oh, something was wrong, but Nick would have to figure it out later. "All right."

"Are you ready?" Bear rumbled.

Just as Nick nodded, bright lights illuminated the entire balcony. He stiffened.

Several men moved out of the shadows and the building, all holding weapons. Then another man, tall with blondish-brown hair and dressed impeccably, strode out.

Bear sighed. "Desmond."

"Beauregard. We spotted you several miles out, and your landing was the loudest we've had in centuries." Desmond nodded regally toward Nick. "You must be Nicholai Veis."

"I must be," Nick murmured, edging his leg back in case he needed to go for the gun in his boot.

"I wouldn't," Desmond said smoothly, casually sliding his hands into the pockets of his perfectly pressed pants. "There are about twenty barrels on you right now, and even if you were able to somehow dismantle all of them, I have Simone under guard and gun, as well. You move the wrong way, and I'll have her shot and beheaded."

The blood in Nick's veins froze, and energy popped through his mind. "Threatening Simone was a bad idea, dragon." It was only fair to warn the bastard, and allowing his voice to go demon hoarse worked for him.

Another man walked out, this one with hair darker than night. "Bear, what the holy fuck? Are you trying to kill yourself?"

Bear nodded, and his upper lip curled. "Nick, this is my brother, Flynn."

How odd that Bear, of all people, had a half-brother who was a dragon. A real dragon. Nick studied the guy, probing deep for any sense that he was family or ally. He tried to move into the dragon's brain, but shields stronger than any metal created kept him out.

Damn dragons. They really could block mind attacks. On to plan B, then.

Flynn edged himself between Desmond and Bear, his hard gaze on his brother. "Why the hell are you here?" he asked, fire flashing in his black eyes.

"To get Simone," Bear said easily. "Fetch her, and we'll be on our way."

Desmond laughed, the sound throaty and rich. "I've always liked your humor, and now you've made it so easy for us to carry out your sentence. I appreciate it."

Flynn growled low. "I'd like to revisit the sentence. Bear was acting in self-defense, I'm sure, and now that Simone is here, we can have another hearing, get to the bottom of this. We didn't have the benefit of talking to her last time."

Desmond shook his head. "The laws are the laws, and the sentence has been declared." He looked soberly at Bear. "I'm sorry, but you need to say your good-byes tonight. We will allow you some time with your sister."

Ah, shit. Nick stepped forward. "Bear didn't kill Roman. I did."

"Liar," Desmond said, his gaze narrowing.

"It's true. Ask Simone." Nick gestured toward Bear. "He was tossed out a window, I came in, and I battled to protect Simone. I ran a sword through Roman, and then I sliced off his head."

Flynn looked from Nick to Bear and then back again.

Nick waited patiently. If dragons were half as powerful as demons, they could smell a lie and discern the truth.

Finally, Desmond frowned and studied Bear. "I never had an inkling that you weren't being truthful before."

Bear lifted a shoulder. "I'm half-bear. We lie well."

"Why?" Flynn asked, his gaze hardening. "I know we've never been close, but why would you lie to your own brother?"

"I thought Simone had done it," Bear said simply.

"I see." Flynn's gaze softened. "You're still trying to sacrifice yourself for her, apparently. With the shift."

Nick pressed his hands to his hips. "Shifting into a dragon harms you?"

"No," Bear said just as Flynn nodded.

Flynn growled. "Stop lying. Bear's true nature is that of a bear and not of a dragon, so when he shifts into a dragon, he's pretty much flaying his soul open."

Nick winced. Bear hadn't said a word and had insisted on saving Simone. "You're a good brother to her," he said.

Bear nodded. "I surely am. So, let's get out of here, shall we?"

Desmond eyed the interchange and then turned his focus on Nick. "I believe you about killing Roman."

Bear breathed out. "Good. So, I guess we need to have another trial or whatever, right? Should take some time to suss out the truth."

"No." Desmond shook his head. "Pursuant to dragon law, Nicholai Veis, tomorrow you will die for the death of Roman."

Nick tried to sense Simone, but he couldn't find her signature nearby. Without knowing where she was, he didn't dare start a fight. "My people will declare war."

Desmond smiled. "Your people don't know we exist, so I'm not concerned." He gestured toward two of the armed men. "Please escort Mr. Veis to the dungeon. I assure you that it's nicer than most five-star hotels."

One of the soldiers grabbed Nick and pushed him toward the open doorway. He went ahead, hoping to catch either sight or scent of Simone, but they turned quickly into a stairwell made of stone. He could hear Bear talking as he began to descend.

"We have a dungeon? Cool," Bear said. "Are there wall racks and shit?"

Chapter 23

Simone paced the palatial private suite, calculating her odds of taking down the three guards outside her door.

A quick knock sounded, and she stood back, allowing fire to dance down her arms.

Bear poked his head in, and his eyes widened. "Whoa. What's up with the pink fire?" He slipped inside and shut the door.

She gasped and quickly doused the flames. "What in the hell are you doing here?"

"Me and Nick decided to recue you." Bear stretched his neck.

She studied him. His normally bronze face had lost quite a bit of color, and for some reason, his chest didn't seem as broad as usual. "You shifted into a dragon."

"Yep." He grinned, but his honey-brown eyes didn't sparkle.

"Damn it, Bear." She slammed both hands on her hips. "Flynn told me what shifting into a dragon does to you. Under no circumstances will you do it again." She couldn't lose him now that she finally had him in her life.

He rolled his eyes. "It's fine. Flynn exaggerates."

Her temper, born of fear, flashed through her. Pink flames cascaded along her fingers.

"More pink. What in the world?" Bear asked, his gaze on her hands.

"I can make different colors." There was no reason to tell Bear about the baby before she told Nick.

"Okay. Wanna go to the dungeon? We have a real dungeon. Can you believe it?" Bear asked.

Simone narrowed her focus. Bear was usually a little off, but this was more than normal. Was he acting simple for a reason? Or had he finally lost his damn mind? Either way, she didn't have time for it. "Knock it off."

His gaze flickered from amused to dangerously focused and then back again. "Knock what off?"

She shook her head. "Why would I want to visit the dungeon?"

"That's where Nick is, awaiting death for killing our dad."

Oh God. She nodded. "Yes. Is he okay?"

"He's fine." Bear opened the door. "Just follow me."

She nodded and completely ignored the guards while following Bear's long stride through rooms carrying enough riches to bankroll several countries. They finally reached a huge stairwell that tunneled into the earth.

She jogged down the stone steps, her mind whirling. Oddly enough, she felt less powerful in the jeans and sweater she was wearing than she did in a full dress, but right now, she had other things to worry about.

They climbed down for what seemed like hours. "These guys ever think of an elevator?" she muttered.

"No kidding," Bear snorted.

"Seriously. It's a new century and all. Put in a pulley or something." Her calves were actually beginning to ache.

Finally, they reached the bottom, and the sound of the sea could be heard outside. Well, above them. How deep under the ocean's surface were they? She tried to tune in her sense of hearing, but the stone was thick and solid around her.

Bear shoved open an iron door out of an era long past, and it creaked as it moved.

Simone shuddered. "There had better not be rats down here." Could rats get onto an island? Dragons ought to be powerful enough to banish rodents, right?

Bear turned and handed her the lantern. "Don't trip."

She kept her head high, accepted the lantern, and swept through the doorway. The door clanged shut behind her, and she stood in a long hallway with several metal doors set into the rock.

The nearest door opened, and both Flynn and Desmond walked out.

Desmond smiled. "I like your demon. He threatened to kill me at

least twenty different ways in less than five minutes. Too bad I'll
have to chop off his head."

Flynn nodded toward her, gave Bear a look, and then turned for
the exit door.

Simone reared up into Desmond's face, allowing fire to cascade
down her arm. "You kill him, and I'm going to kill you."

Desmond's smile widened. "Yet another death threat. This really
isn't my day, is it?" He nodded at Bear. "Beauregard. When you're
finished here, we need to talk."

Bear didn't respond. He waited until Desmond had disappeared
behind the heavy door before turning back to Simone, his usual
humor gone. "You have the night with Nicholai." Then he lifted his
nose and scanned the hallway, his head moving before his gaze
landed back on her. He sniffed the air several times. His eyes
widened. "You're with child."

Simone gasped and stepped back. It was way too early for anybody
to be able to sense a baby. "Barely. How in the hell?"

Bear lowered his chin, his gaze dropping to her abdomen. "I'm a
bear shifter. Our senses are better than any others out there. You
smell like baby powder and pure honey. Pregnancy smell."

Simone placed a hand against her stomach. "We can't let Desmond
or Flynn know about the babe. They'll try to kill me."

"I know." Bear shook his head, and he straightened, looking in-
tently over her shoulder. "This changes the plan for tomorrow. You
have to tell Nick about the babe, and we need to figure out a different
way to get out of here."

Simone frowned and stepped toward her brother. "Why?"

"Because you can't fight," Bear snapped.

Simone stiffened. In the century she'd known her brother, she
had never once heard him snap. "Why the hell can't I fight?" She
slammed both hands on her hips.

His mouth opened and then closed. Red spiraled across his rugged
cheekbones. "Because you're knocked up," he hissed.

"So what?" Anger rippled through her, yet she kept her voice low.

Bear shook his head vigorously. "Listen up, sister, and listen
good. You go take the next several hours with that demon, say what
you have to say, do what you have to do, and then tell him the truth
about the baby. Then you get your sweet ass out of the way while we

fight to get out of here. If anybody dies, which is likely, it ain't gonna be you or that babe."

She glared and moved right up into his face. "You listen up. I'm pregnant, not an invalid. My fire-throwing ability is better than any other witch's, and you're going to need my assistance in getting out of here. Besides, after you shifted into a dragon, you lost strength. What's the plan?"

"Oh, hell no. As of now, there is no plan." Bear grabbed her shoulders and set her away from him. "Tell Nick the truth, or I will."

Simone shoved him back a foot, somewhat surprised when he let her. "This is my baby, and I'll tell Nicholai when I'm ready. You keep your furry snout out of it."

Bear growled. "You're crazier than I'll ever be." He turned on his bare feet and stomped down the corridor, slamming the heavy metal door shut behind himself.

Oh, she would not let her brother sacrifice himself for her. Already, after apparently shifting once into a dragon, he was losing muscle mass. A lot of it.

Simone took several deep breaths and then pushed open the door to the cell. She walked inside and stopped short. A fully appointed bed with velvet bedclothes took up the left part of the cell, and a doorway showed a complete bathroom. Whoa. The dragons had a seriously fancy dungeon. But the wall opposite her was definitely the focus of the room.

Nicholai stood in front of a floor-to-ceiling glass wall that revealed the depths of the ocean. Fish sparkled, and green stuff floated around. "I think it was originally designed to mentally torture people with being under the sea . . . to show them how impossible rescue and freedom really is," he said.

Simone nodded, watching a yellow and blue fish swim by. "It's beautiful."

"Yes, it is." Nick's gaze caressed her face. "The most beautiful thing I've ever seen."

Heat climbed into her face, and she fought the urge to pat her abdomen again. Knowing about the babe would certainly distract Nick, and she needed him focused. Plus, he required her fighting abilities, and if he put her on the bench, he might be killed. Even so, not telling him grated on her.

"What's going through that head of yours?" he murmured, black eyes thoughtful.

"Just wondering what the plan is," she returned quietly. At the very least, she needed to know the plan before telling him the truth. That way he couldn't alter it without her knowing. "Bear mentioned you had a plan."

"We're still working on it, and much of it depends on Bear. I should know by tomorrow morning." Nick angled to the side and glanced out at the fathomless sea.

"So, what is it?"

Nick sighed. "I need you to get close to Flynn. See if he'll work with us instead of against us."

Simone leaned back against the door. "Okay."

Nick studied her. "I know you're an *in your face* type of fighter, but strategy and subtlety are what matter right now. Can you do that?"

"Sure. What are you and Bear planning?"

"If I tell you, and Flynn asks, he'll know you're lying when you deny we have a plan." Nick moved forward and grasped her hands in his. "I'd rather you could honestly tell him you don't know what Bear and I have in mind for tomorrow."

"So long as Bear isn't going to shift into dragon form again. It hurts him, Nick."

"I know. Don't worry—the second I discovered the weakness, I altered any plan that had him shifting into anything but a badass bear."

"Good." She smiled. "Thanks. Now, what's the plan?"

"I'd rather you stayed in the dark."

Simone breathed out. "You're asking for a lot of faith there, demon."

"If you want me to tell you the entire plan, I will without hesitation." Nick leaned down and brushed her forehead with a kiss. "But the strategy works better if Flynn, and especially Desmond, believe that we've left you in the dark or that we don't even have a good plan."

Simone winced. "My approach with Flynn is hysterical, scared female? One going to a newly found brother for help when there doesn't seem to be any plan." As much as she hated it, and she really did, she could see the wisdom of the approach.

"Yes. Bear was excommunicated at a young age and never really got to know Flynn, but he believes that Flynn is fairly decent with a strong proclivity for protecting women. Takes good care of his mother, I guess."

"I'd rather just burn him into submission," Simone muttered.

"Now that I'd like to see." Nick smiled, transforming his face from deadly to stunning. "Again, I'm not keeping secrets from you, little bunny. If you want me to detail our entire rather hopeless, crazy plan, I'm happy to do so."

She swallowed. Secrets, huh? Well then. "No. I understand the strategy behind my being clueless with Flynn. But I will know the entire plan before I have to start throwing fireballs, right?"

"Of course." Nick ducked his head and pressed a hard kiss to her mouth, remaining a breath away. "Thank you for having faith."

She kissed him. No matter what, she knew she could count on Nick. "Of course." She paused. "The door isn't locked, you know."

"I know, but Desmond warned me that there would be guards lined up the entire stairwell."

"What about the other cells or down the tunnel?"

"Apparently the other cells are empty, and I had Bear double-check, so that's true. The tunnel ends without another exit." Nick shrugged.

Simone angled slightly to the right and examined the glass wall.

"Nope. According to Desmond, the helpful bastard, if we break the glass, an alarm goes out that sends thousands of volts of electricity into the water. We'd fry."

"All bases are covered," she muttered. "Smart dickheads."

"Your relatives," Nick said smoothly.

She punched him in his iron-hard stomach. "Not nice."

He lunged for her and swept her up. "I have never been nice, my little bunny." Moving slowly, he wandered over to the large bed.

She struggled against him, heat climbing through her. "What in the world are you doing?"

He smiled. "It might be my last night on earth. I've given everybody orders to stay the hell away for a few hours while we say our good-byes, and just in case, I think we should do so."

"No." Pain rippled through her at the very thought, and she reached up to cup the side of his whiskered jaw. For so long, she'd tried to ignore her feelings for him, but they'd never gone away. Nick Veis had stolen her heart a century ago, and he'd never really given it back. She couldn't lose him now. "Whatever your plan is, we'll make it work."

He sat her on the bed, her legs dangling over. Both hands threaded through her thick hair, and he tipped back her head. Slowly, so deliberately, he leaned down, and his mouth took hers.

Fire and heat and energy flowed through her like a drug.

Her chest exploded with emotion, and she planted one hand on his chest, moving him back. He was giving her trust, and she had to do the same for him.

He studied her, one eyebrow rising.

"I have to tell you something." The man deserved to know about the baby; she couldn't keep a secret like that. They both needed to make decisions with all the information. "I'm——"

The door blew open, and Nick jumped up, spinning to place his body between hers and the door. "Bear?"

Bear grimaced. "Sorry, dude, but the big guy has called for a family dinner. I offered to come and get Simone."

Nick growled low. "I said no interruptions for the next several hours."

Bear lifted a massive shoulder. "Apparently prisoners don't get special time to get laid. I'm sorry. This way, Simone can have a nice chat with Flynn during drinks or the appetizers or whatever these fancy dudes do. It's time she got to know our older brother, don't you think?"

A guard became visible beyond Bear.

Simone got up from the bed and tried to banish the desire still humming within her. Time to play the game. "I would very much like to dine with family." And get to know Flynn and hopefully bring him over to their side.

"That's the attitude," Bear said.

Nick subtly adjusted his jeans. "Bear, if time wasn't so damn short for me right now, I'd kill you."

Bear slowly nodded. "I get that a lot."

Simone patted Nicholai on the chest, her heart beating so hard her ribs ached. "I'll be back after dinner, and then we'll have a nice chat." She had no problem manipulating a man, but since Flynn was her brother, she couldn't use her usual arsenal. "Trust me. I can do this," she whispered.

"I do." Nick pulled her back around and pressed his mouth against hers, urgency and emotion in his kiss. "Be careful."

She kissed him back and then sidled around him, not meeting Bear's eyes. It wasn't as if there had been any time to tell Nick about the baby, and now she couldn't do so with the guard listening. He'd probably report right back to Desmond, and that prick could never know about her pregnancy.

Bear moved past her and exchanged a few words with Nick, quickly turning to grasp Simone's arm and follow her into the hall. She kept her face stoic for the guard's sake. Bear shut the door and looked down at her, his honey-brown eyes burning.

"I didn't have a chance to tell him, ah, about my feelings. We looked at the room, then we started kissing, and then you were there." Simone kept her voice quiet as Bear grabbed a lantern off the ground.

"He deserves to know, about um, how you feel," Bear rumbled.

"I know." There was no way to elaborate with the guard trailing them, so she just nodded. "The night is young." And there was so much to do, damn it.

A sense of urgency pressed in on her as she moved up the stairwell and tried to center herself. Nick was alone in the dungeon, and while he was a hell of a fighter, he couldn't use his abilities against dragons.

She could control fire, but so could dragons.

The enemy for once actually seemed to have more power than the side she was trying to fight for. She rubbed her belly, fully cognizant of how much she had to lose. Her shoulders went back, and she drew on the fire of her people.

Time to manipulate her brother and hope it didn't backfire in her face.

Chapter 24

Simone smoothed down the wispy green dress. The fine silk drew in over the bodice and smoothed down her hips, ending right above the knee. The color suited her, and with calfskin boots, she felt feminine power course through her.

Not once in her entire life had she apologized for enjoying her femininity. As a witch, she was a badass, and she could dress however she liked.

"Thank you for the clothes," she murmured to Flynn as they sat in a drawing room.

"You're lovely," he returned, lifting his glass of aged whiskey in the air.

"Thank you." She held her glass, enjoying the scent of the potent brew. "Will Desmond be joining us?"

"Soon. He's taking care of business right now."

Perfect. Simone looked around the room. Antique chairs, probably handcrafted, had been placed in several individual groupings, a couple with game tables. Priceless oil paintings lined two of the walls, and an enormous bookcase took up the third, while the final wall was actually a doorway to the dining room. "This is a nice room."

"There's a much better library farther into the cliffs. I'll take you after dinner, if you'd like." Flynn sipped his drink, his gaze thoughtful. For dinner, he'd thrown on slightly wrinkled black slacks and a white button-down shirt open at the collar.

She forced a smile. "I need to know. How much danger is Bear in if he shifts into a dragon again?"

Flynn's eyes darkened. "Terrible danger. It's like forcing a square peg into a wood chipper. His soul is shredded, as is his body. A bear can't be a dragon, and at some point, his organs will just blow up and kill him."

"Then he needs to knock it off." She wouldn't let Bear harm himself.

"Agreed." Flynn sighed. "Get to it, Simone. Please."

She set down her glass. "Get to what?"

"Come on. I wasn't born yesterday, and Desmond is going to be here soon. Say what you need to say, I'll say what I need to say, and we'll move forward from there." His voice remained low and rough, reminding her of his dragon lineage.

She took a deep breath. "You're my brother."

"I surely am." Although his eyes were black, there was a shimmer, a bluish shimmer in them that was all dragon.

Would she someday have that shimmer? "So help me."

"I am helping you."

"How is that?" She lifted her chin.

He leaned forward. "By keeping you from committing treason and getting yourself killed. Well, treason here. You've already committed it in the witch nation."

She ground her back teeth together. "Not really."

"Yes, really. So here's the deal. You refrain from attempting any silly rescue of the demon, and we'll grant you sanctuary on Fire Island for the rest of eternity, if you so desire."

Fire Island. Catchy name. She sat back. "Sanctuary?"

"Yes. Our sources inform us you're likely to be found guilty of treason by the Coven Nine, and you'll be sentenced to death. If you run anywhere on earth, they will find you. However, if you stay here, a place the Nine doesn't know exists, you will remain safe." Flynn kept her gaze, no give on his angled face. "Someday you might even be allowed back into the witch nation, once enough time has passed."

"I can handle my own people and my own future, thank you." She subtly looked around for any type of weapon, but even the crystal on the bar appeared harmless. "I will not allow Nicholai to be killed for protecting me."

Flynn shook his head. "The demon killed Roman, and I can't change that."

"Sure you could, or maybe Desmond could, since he's the leader.

Your cousin is a bad guy, and you know it." Simone was going on instinct.

"Desmond is your cousin, too." Flynn didn't blink. "I don't know what you mean disparaging him."

"Aye. Aye, you do." She pressed harder. "The servants are afraid of him, and even the soldiers seem nervous when he's around."

"Desmond is a tough leader, but he's fair, and he follows the laws."

"You need to change the damn laws." Fire danced down Simone's arms, and she cradled a plasma ball in her right hand.

Flynn's lip curved. "Impressive."

"Thank you. Now, act like a brother and help me." She abandoned any thought of pretending to be helpless and acted from a position of strength. "You don't want me for an enemy."

He smiled full-out then. "Are you threatening me, little sister?"

The condescension got her. She tossed the ball, and it landed on his leg.

He yelped and patted it out, leaving a perfectly round hole in his pants. His flesh glowed a burned red. "Damn it."

She smiled. "That was a love tap."

He looked up, his gaze narrowing. "You're not the only one with fire." Opening his mouth, he looked up, and fire flew out of his mouth to singe the ceiling.

Simone watched, more than a little impressed. "Okay. We both have fire. But Flynn, you know Desmond isn't fair."

The blond servant, the one from the other night, entered the room with a tray of canapes to place on the table. She glanced around, saw it was only the two of them, and visibly relaxed.

Simone took a chance. "You're afraid of Desmond, aren't you?"

The blonde's dark eyes widened. "No. No, not at all." She backed away, her hands wringing together.

"Stop," Flynn said quietly.

The woman froze.

"What has he done?" Flynn asked.

"Nothing, sir." The woman gave a half curtsy and all but ran from the room.

Anger rippled through Simone so fast she swayed. "What the hell is going on here?"

"I've only been back a short while after being away for the war." Flynn's jaw worked, and a muscle ticked down his neck. "Whatever is going on, I will handle. For now, you need to promise to stay out of the way until Nicholai meets his fate."

So much for help. Simone stood and towered over her brother. "That woman was scared to death. How have you let this happen?"

Flynn stood so suddenly, she had to step back. Anger etched into the fine lines of his face. Now he towered over her by at least a foot. "I've been away since Desmond took over, working overseas, and I've only been back a week. You can trust me that I'll find out what's going on."

"I don't trust you worth rubbish," she spat, jumping up.

"In this matter, you don't really have a choice." He ran a hand through his dark hair. "I don't want to contain you in the family private suite, but I will if you don't agree to stay out of the way tomorrow morning."

Simone gaped at him. "You want me to just stand by and watch you kill my, my, well, Nick?"

Flynn nodded.

"Who will do it? You?" she asked, her hands clenching with the need to throw more fire.

"Aye. I'm the one who will ultimately carry out the sentence," Flynn said, his gaze somber but no less intense.

"He'll fight you," Simone said, her chin lifting.

"I hope so." Flynn's shoulders drew back. "It wouldn't be fair to just cut off his head. But you know that demons can't mind attack dragons, right?"

Simone froze. "Maybe that has changed."

"I doubt it. Dragon minds are impregnable. Well, except by mates."

Nick had played in her brain, hadn't he? And they weren't mated. "What if you open your mental shields?" She'd always been able to visualize shields in her head. Must be her dragon side.

"Sure. You can always open yourself up for attack." Flynn frowned. "I don't plan to do so with your lover."

"So dragons can defend against a mind attack but truly can't perpetrate one," she said slowly.

"No. Which is why a dragon can never mate with a demon. The hybrid that was born years ago was able to destroy minds without even meaning to do so." Flynn glanced at a worn watch around his wrist. "Desmond should be here soon."

Simone's throat closed. "Flynn, you have to help me. Nick was just protecting me when Roman tried to harm me. You can't follow through with a death sentence. Excommunicate me instead."

"But you didn't kill our father."

"No, but if there needs to be punishment, let me take it." As long as they didn't try to cut off her head. If they tried, she'd fight and burn their asses.

"No."

"Surely it's okay to kill a dragon in self-defense." She reached out and grasped his hand. "That's what really happened."

Sympathy twisted his lip. "It's too late to matter, sister. I'm sorry." He flipped his hand around to grasp hers. "Now, tell me what the plan is. I know there has to be one."

She looked him right in the eye. "If there is an escape plan, I have no clue what it is."

He studied her, his eyes darkening. "You really don't know."

"No." She allowed her shoulders to slump. "I'm afraid there isn't a good plan." Hell, that was the truth, so it should convince him. "I need your help, and you know it. Please."

His dark eyebrows slashed down. "Nicholai Veis is a demon, and if you want to someday rule the Nine, even if it's centuries from now, then you can't be mated to a demon. I'm trying to save you from yourself here."

"Fuck you," Simone said evenly. "I'm a grown woman who can save herself, you asshat." It was a good insult she'd learned from the queen of the Realm. "I require your assistance in saving Nicholai only."

Desmond strolled into the room from the dining area. "That is not going to happen." He took Simone's glass and tipped back the whiskey. "Well? What's the plan?"

Flynn sighed. "If there is a plan, she doesn't know it."

Betrayal coated her throat like acid. She swallowed bile and tried not to throw up. "You bastard," she muttered.

"Actually a true statement," Flynn said.

So Flynn had been trying to get information from her while she had been trying to manipulate him into helping her. They were quite a pair, weren't they? "I hope I don't have to kill you," she said to her brother.

He nodded. "I hope so, too."

The unconcerned note in his voice made her want to burn him from head to toe, right then and there. Then she'd have to take on Desmond, too, and first she needed to find Bear. "I'm suddenly not hungry."

"Too bad," Desmond said, looking around. "Where in the world is Beau—"

"I'm here and starving." Bear loped into the room.

Desmond looked his way and grimaced. "You could've changed for supper."

Bear glanced down at his faded jeans and worn T-shirt. "These are clean. What's wrong with them?"

Desmond rolled his eyes. "There are several suits in your size in the closet of the rooms you were assigned an hour ago, and I know this because I put them there."

"Dude. Do I look like I wear suits?" Bear asked, sniffing the air. "Is that aged whiskey?"

"Those who don't wear suits don't get the good whiskey," Desmond said.

Bear frowned. "That sucks."

Simone shoved down a scream of frustration. They were chatting about booze and clothes while still intending to murder Nicholai the next day? She had to figure out a way to save him.

Simone frowned at Bear, wondering what the plan would be without Flynn. In fact, Flynn had set her up, expressing the same sentiment about her future with a demon that Bear had earlier. Her frown deepened, and she squinted her eyes. Could she really trust Bear?

"What?" Bear asked, rubbing his square jawline. "Is there something on my face?"

There was about to be a ball of fire in his hair. She'd never really been able to count on a man, and now was probably a bad time to try. "No. Shall we eat?" she murmured. At least in the dining room there would be knives.

"Not yet," Desmond said, turning to face Bear. "I'd like to know where you've been the last hour."

Bear shrugged. "Exploring the fortress. I haven't been here for a hundred years, as you know. It's totally the same."

"Hmmm. Exploring?" Desmond asked.

"Yep." Bear tucked his thumbs in his jean pockets, his stance casual. "You could use an update here and there, cousin."

"I'll keep that in mind." Desmond gave Flynn some weird head bob. "I'd like to know what you and the demon have planned for your pointless resistance to the law."

Bear snorted. "You think I'm planning something with the demon?"

Flynn drew out a double-edged blade. "We know you're planning something with the demon. You risked your life to turn into a dragon and bring him here, Bear."

"Yeah. I brought him here because you had Simone, and I was afraid she'd confess to killing our father, which I thought she had." Bear scratched his chin, eyeing the knife. "So I pretty much delivered the real killer to you. You're welcome."

Flynn twirled the knife. "Don't you want to avenge our father's death?" Emotion darkened his voice.

Bear shrugged. "I would've killed Roman myself in a few years, anyway. The guy was a prick."

"He was an excellent ruler," Desmond shouted, his face turning red.

Simone took a step back in case she needed to throw fire to protect Bear.

He mirrored her movement. "If you say so. All I remember is people being scared to death of the guy. And he hit a lot."

Desmond growled. "That's because you're a moron."

"Think so?" Bear asked silkily.

"Yes." Desmond apparently missed the threat that had just surfaced in his cousin.

Simone did not. She tensed in preparation for a fight.

Desmond reached inside his jacket and drew out a green gun. "I know Flynn wants to slice you open, but I'd rather just shoot you in the head."

Bear growled. "Now, that's just not nice, cousin."

"Last time," Desmond said. "Tell me what your plan with the demon is, or I start with the kneecaps and work my way up to your brain."

Simone gathered the fire inside her and prepared to strike.

Chapter 25

Nick unfolded the cell phone that Bear had passed him before escorting Simone to dinner. He peered at the face. Seriously. Where had Bear found the ancient device? Who still used phones that actually folded? Taking a deep breath, wondering whether his emotions had taken over for his logic, he stood close to the glass wall and quickly dialed the number.

"What?" Zane Kyllwood growled into the phone.

"Zane? It's Nick." Maybe the older phone actually worked better in these crappy conditions than a new one, but there was still a crackling along the line.

"Nick? Where the hell are you?"

Nick shut his eyes and tried to focus. "I need you to send help, but I'll understand if you refuse." What the hell was he doing, asking Zane to risk himself and the demon nation? But it was for Simone, so he didn't have a choice. If he was on the other end advising Zane, he'd tell him to say hell no.

Static echoed for several moments. "I said, tell me where you are."

They were losing the connection, damn it. "I'm going to type in coordinates to the best of my knowledge, but they could be off. We're on an island in the middle of the Northern Atlantic Sea that isn't noticeable until you're actually on it." Man, this was a terrible idea.

"The fucking witches have a secret island?" Zane barked.

"No." Nick cleared his throat. "Dragons."

Static and silence. Then Zane, "Dragons."

"Yep. Simone and Bear are half dragon—long story—but the dragons are going to try to kill me tomorrow. Simone is here and I need to get her away." Nick leaned against the chilled glass. "Send a demon who can teleport to get her."

"Send the coordinates."

"It's dangerous, and it's unfair of me to ask." But for Simone, he'd do it.

Static overcame whatever Zane said.

Hell. The line went dead.

Nick hurriedly typed in the coordinates he and Bear had figured out and said a quick prayer that they would reach Zane and not put the demon soldiers he sent into the rock. The text seemed to load.

Then he waited.

Two figures suddenly appeared in the freezing sea outside.

He bellowed and hurried toward the glass.

Zane's eyes widened, and suddenly, the two were inside the room, gasping for air. "Close coordinates, my ass." Water sluiced off him. His green eyes sizzled, and water slicked back his thick, black hair. The wet clothes revealed a hard line of muscle and strength.

Nick gaped at him and at Adam Dunne, the Coven Nine Enforcer. "What in holy hell are the two of you doing here?"

Zane coughed. "It's good to see you, too."

Nick shook his head. "I wanted you to send a couple of soldiers, not come yourself. Jesus, Zane. You can't be here." He glared at Adam. "Neither can you. The Enforcers can't know about this place."

Adam Dunne was a Coven Enforcer and one of the smartest people on the planet, but right now, his face was turning blue and water dripped out of his nose. "You said Simone was in trouble, and as an Enforcer, it's my fucking job to know where she is." He wiped sea-weed out of his shorter brown hair. "She's also my cousin."

Nick looked from one hulking man to the other. "What were you two doing together?"

"We were trying to find you and Simone, obviously." Zane rolled his eyes. "When your call came in, the witch here wouldn't let me teleport without him. So you get two for the price of one."

"And if you teleport Simone out of here?" Nick asked, stepping back from the spreading pool of water.

"I'll come back for Adam and for you." Zane lifted a shoulder. "Unless there's another way off this weird place."

"There is." But he would not ask Bear to shift into dragon form ever again. "You get Simone and Adam out of here, and I'll figure out the other way." If he survived the fight, and if Bear survived, then they'd find a boat or something. "Sorry about the coordinates."

"That's all right. You are in the middle of nowhere," Zane said.

Nick held up a hand. "This isn't right. It's my job to protect you, not put you into danger." He couldn't sacrifice Zane, the leader of the entire fucking demon nation, like this.

"He *is* a pain in the ass," Adam said to Zane, as if agreeing to an earlier comment.

Zane grabbed Nick's hand and sliced a knife across the palm. Pain rippled.

"Hey." Nick tried to yank back, but surprise gave Zane the advantage.

Zane quickly ripped the blade across his own hand and smashed it against Nick's palm. "There. I've always considered us family, but if you need to share blood, now we do." He released Nick and wiped the blade off on his wet T-shirt before turning to Adam. "Why does everything always have to be such a pain?"

"Dunno." Adam shrugged and leaned over to sneeze. "Shouldn't we be fighting somebody?"

Nick gritted his teeth and sent healing cells to his palm, more touched than he wanted to admit. "Thank you."

Zane nodded, his green eyes deadly serious. "Family, Nick."

"Family," Nick repeated, his chest warming. He stepped over the puddle toward the door. "We have four hundred and twenty-three steps up, and there are probably soldiers set every ten steps or so."

Adam looked at the depth of the sea out the glass. "I hate to think it, but could we go through there and swim up?"

Nick shook his head. "If we break the glass, an electrical jolt is sent out."

Zane winced. "Thank goodness it only happens if the glass breaks and isn't on a motion sensor."

Nick nodded as a pit dropped into his gut. "Plus, the living quarters are far above sea level, and swimming won't get us there." He eyed his friend. "Our other option is for you to teleport us up, but then will you be strong enough to get Simone and Adam out of here?"

"I won't be able to fight right away, but I can get Simone to safety." Zane winced. "Not sure I can make a jump back here and then cart

Adam out, though." He took out a smartphone and glanced at the face. "I think we're screwed for service."

Nick flipped open his phone and saw no bars. "Shit." They couldn't call in anybody else. "It's just us."

Adam cleared his throat. "I say we teleport up, and then Zane gets Simone to safety."

"What about you?" Zane asked.

Adam shrugged. "Nick and I will have to figure another way off the island. My job is to protect my cousin, and her life is paramount, even if it wasn't my job. Does everyone agree?"

"Yes," Nick and Zane said in unison.

"Good." Adam shook seawater out of his shirt. "Any chance we could get better coordinates for wherever Simone is?"

Nick tried to clear his head. "I think straight up should do it."

"You think?" Zane asked, stepping toward him while also grabbing on to Adam's arm. "All right, then. Let's all give a quick prayer I don't put us into a stone cliff somewhere."

Nick nodded and wished that weapons could teleport and that Zane had brought some. "Let's do this," he muttered, closing his eyes and sucking in air to hold his breath.

Zane clamped onto his arm, and the earth fell away.

Simone calculated the distance from her position to the dining room. There wasn't time to grab a weapon for Bear. "Desmond, you need to stop this right now. Bear hasn't done anything wrong."

Desmond shook his head. "Last chance. What do you and the demon have planned?"

"Why don't you ask the demon?" came a low voice from the doorway.

Simone gasped as Nick entered the room, followed by a dripping wet Zane Kyllwood and her cousin, Adam Dunne, who had seaweed in his wet hair. How in the world? Her eyes widened, and she turned toward Bear.

He grinned. "'Bout time you guys got here."

Desmond pulled the trigger. Green lasers shot from the barrel, striking Bear's thigh and turning into metal. Blood spurted from his artery.

Bear roared and jumped forward at Desmond, throwing them both into the bookcase. Books and candlesticks rained down.

Soldiers, at least five of them, poured in from the shadows outside.

"Cover Zane," Nick ordered Adam, running forward to plant his body between Simone and the attackers.

Adam shoved a pale Zane into the wall and held his hands out. Fire, dark and blue, billowed down his arms to form balls, which he started hurling toward the soldiers. One hit a man in the face, and he screamed, turning for the doorway.

The other soldiers ducked, grabbing swords and coming out swinging.

Nick grabbed a three-pronged candleholder and defended himself against a sword that was so sharp its edge glinted in the dim light. He moved and parried, keeping the metal between him and the blade.

A soldier made it past Adam, and Zane punched him in the face, kicking the sword from his hand. They dropped to the ground, grappling and punching.

Simone jumped back onto a chair, formed fire, and belted it at Flynn.

"Hey," Flynn yelped, jumping back. "I'm on your side." Without waiting for an answer, he pivoted and took down a soldier running toward Nick.

Simone halted her next attack, her mind spinning. "Bear? Is he on our side?" she yelled.

"Yes," Bear bellowed, punching Desmond in the face and sending him into a backflip.

"Oh. Sorry." Simone winced. From her perch on the chair, she looked around for somebody to help. They were all fighting man to man, punches landing and swords parrying.

If she threw fire, she might hit the wrong person.

A ruckus sounded from the dining room, and pounding footsteps echoed through the night.

Excellent.

Her heart thundered, and her breath burst out of her, but she set her feet against the arms of the chair for balance. Fireballs formed on her hands, and she threw them with all her might into the other room.

Yells of pain came back.

She teetered on the chair and formed more fire, quickly lobbing ball after ball through the entryway. While she couldn't see her targets, she could sure as hell keep the doorway clear. Anybody who stepped near would be burned.

The air shimmered.

"No!" Flynn yelled, leaping across the fray and tackling Simone off the chair. He flattened her with his body. "Everybody get down," he bellowed.

More *pop*s filled the air.

Simone struggled against her brother, but he held her fast, tucking her under him so that not one part of her was exposed.

A flash of light exploded, and a static boom reverberated.

Even safe under Flynn, Simone winced as her brain concussed.

Flynn jumped up and brought her with him, shoving her behind his back.

She gulped in air and peered around him.

A huge brown dragon took up most of the room, its beady eyes surveying the men trying to get up off the ground, most bleeding from the ears.

She swallowed. "Shifting isn't fair, Desmond," she yelled.

He turned her way, opened his mouth, and blew fire.

She grabbed Flynn and yanked him down behind the chair. Flames flew over their heads to ignite the curtains.

The dragon moved his head, spreading fire toward Nick and Zane. Both men rolled out of the way as the room caught fire.

Simone stood.

Flynn leaped up and tried to push her behind him.

"Knock it off." She shoved him in the ribs and centered herself, calling on her own fire. Taking a deep breath of the smoke-filled air, she waited until Desmond had inhaled and started blowing fire again.

Simone threw plasma balls at his face. The second her fire hit his, sparks ignited and an explosion ripped the atmosphere. He screeched.

Nick grabbed a fallen sword, rolled, and came up quickly, jabbing the blade into the dragon's belly. He ripped up.

Desmond roared in pain.

"The neck," Flynn yelled. "The base of the neck."

Nick used both hands to yank the blade free and then shoved up again, this time below Desmond's dragon chin. Then he wrenched the blade to the left and the right, cutting the tendons.

The dragon hissed and dropped to the ground.

Nick jumped onto its back with the blade and cut from the other side. Within seconds, the dragon's head rolled away from the body right before the entire room went up in flames.

Chapter 26

Nick slid off the dead dragon and ran for Simone, lifting her up and racing toward the dining room. A quick glance showed everyone on his heels. They reached the dining room and plowed through more soldiers than he could count.

One grabbed his arm.

Flynn jumped onto the dining room table. "Cordon off this area, immediately." He kicked a glass full of water onto a flame about to ignite the tablecloth.

"Where is Desmond?" a soldier asked.

Flynn stilled. He looked at Nick and then at Bear. Finally, he coughed out smoke. "Desmond confessed to killing Roman a hundred years ago, and he took Bear's place in rightful death. Your leader died following our laws."

Nick kept his gaze stoic and returned Flynn's short nod.

"Get out of here," Flynn ordered. "I need to shift to counter the fire with my own flames, and if I do so with you here, you'll all be on the ground again."

Nick nodded and ran with Simone out onto the balcony. There was a more than fair chance the soldiers wouldn't accept Flynn's explanation, but for the moment, he had to protect Simone. He waited for Zane. "Get her out of here."

Bear hurried over to them and jumped over the railing and into the wild breeze.

Nick stopped breathing.

Simone started struggling. "Let me down." When he did so, she ran over to the railing and looked down. "Bear?" she yelled.

Bear in dragon form flapped his massive wings and came into view.

"That wasn't funny, Bear," Nick yelled, wanting nothing more than to mind attack the damn shifter. Maybe the reason he couldn't was because Bear didn't have a fucking brain.

Bear laughed, the sound raspy and full of pain. "Zane? Get Adam out of here." Without waiting for an answer, Bear scooped up both Nick and Simone, tucked them into his belly, and flew over the railing and into the lightening sky.

Simone screamed.

Nick grabbed her hand, trying to keep his legs from dropping and causing wind resistance. His heart beat rapidly, and his lungs filled with more panic than air. "Don't move, Simone. The less you move, the better he flies."

She turned wide eyes on Nick.

He glanced down at the bulging arm around her midsection. "Bear? If you drop anybody, make it be me," he bellowed.

"No problem," Bear said clearly.

"This wasn't the plan," Nick couldn't help muttering.

Bear lost altitude, and Simone screamed.

Nick tightened his hold on her hand as whitecaps flew by below. Water sprayed across his face. Bear flapped, and they rose into the air again. "Jesus."

"I had to go with a new plan because you killed Desmond," Bear intoned in his dragon voice. "The soldiers saw, and I'm not sure Flynn will be able to keep them from coming for your head. You need to go somewhere safe until I figure out what to do next."

Nick wanted to struggle, but that would just end up with him in the ocean freezing his ass off. "I don't need your help."

"We're family, dude," Bear said cheerfully.

"No, we are not." Why in the world did everyone suddenly want to be his family? If Bear tried to cut him and create a blood bond, Nick would have to shoot him. For now, he had to worry about his woman. He eyed a very pale Simone. "You okay?"

She shook her head, and her skin turned a light green. "I don't like flying."

"It's all right." He tried to reassure her, but her color got worse. She gagged.

"No," Bear muttered. "Do not puke."

Simone breathed in. "I'm trying. Stop being so bumpy."

"Do you have any idea how hard it is to fly the two of you?" Bear asked, sounding wounded. "I'm doing my best." They dropped again.

"I'm going to kick your ass when you feel better," Simone hissed. "I told you not to shift like this ever again."

"God, you're bossy," Bear muttered.

The air chilled and blew into them. Simone's hair billowed all around and plastered to Bear's dragon belly. She shut her eyes and visibly drew in several deep breaths.

Dark clouds rolled around, right at them.

"Ah, hell," Bear muttered. "They're too thick to go above them." Rain slashed them.

A small dot came into view surrounded by tumultuous waves crashing against rock walls. Bear changed his angle of flight to straight down.

"Oh God," Simone moaned, her free hand going to her belly.

"It's okay," Nick whispered. "Slow the hell down, Bear."

"I'm getting wet," the shifter complained.

The island appeared to be about a kilometer across, surrounded by jagged rocks. Trees dotted most of the landmass. They approached the island at breakneck speed. Nick slid his arm between Simone and Bear, so he could wrap himself around her if they landed hard. "Get ready for impact," he whispered to her.

She gave a strangled sound.

Bear landed and flipped over onto his back, tossing Simone and Nick into the air. Nick tucked her close and rolled through rain, getting them in the right position before landing on his feet and falling to his knees in sopping wet sand.

The dragon slid along the sand and impacted a pine tree. It cracked with a loud protest.

"Duck!" Nick yelled, holding Simone tight and throwing them both out of the way. The tree fell and bounced twice, right where they'd been a second ago.

Bear rolled over, his reptilian eyes blinking. White sand covered his scales and his nose. "Sorry." He sneezed.

"Jesus Christ, Bear." Nick set a trembling Simone on her feet, and she sank in the sand. Wind smashed sand and pine needles into them, while the waves crashed higher as the storm gained force. Nick looked around to see a stone cabin set just beyond the odd beach. "What in the world?"

Bear's dragon ears twitched. "I can't fly you guys through that storm, and I need to go back up Flynn in case he needs help."

"No," Simone snapped. "You need to change back to yourself and let us help you to heal."

"Nope."

"What is this place?" Simone asked. "Are there medical supplies? Will any help you?"

Bear shrugged. "My island. Sometimes when I wanted to see either you or Flynn, I'd sneak here and try to get glimpses, you know." A sadness filled the dragon's voice that he failed to mask. "I have to take a boat and not fly, obviously. Right now, nothing can help me but sleep and protein, so stop hovering."

Nick winced as thunder rolled across the sea. "Is this place safe?"

"Pretty much, unless there's a huge storm surge, and then it might flood. There's a generator behind the cabin full of gas, and there's food in the pantry. Stay here, and I'll be back as soon as I can." Bear squinted toward the dark clouds.

"No—" Nick started, but Bear bunched his legs and shot into the sky, doing a funny flip as he rose.

"I am so going to kick his butt when he gets back," Simone murmured, her gaze on the rapidly disappearing dragon. "If he gets back."

If not, they were screwed. "Tell me you have a phone." He'd lost his in the fight.

She shook her head. "They took my phone away when I landed in dragon land."

"Fire Island," Nick said absently, scanning the area for threats. Nothing. They were alone in the middle of the ocean with nothing but a storm coming their way. "Let's check out the cabin."

"I can't believe we survived that," Simone murmured.

Neither could he. He turned and studied her. Her silk clothing clung to a fit and feminine body with curves, an abundance of them, in all the right places. The wind whipped her thick hair around her face, but those eyes. The unique hue of them had never been duplicated by man or nature. Deep and mysterious, and so damn powerful.

His entire body hardened to the point of pain.

She lifted her chin, and her full lips, pink now, curved. "Nicholai?"

The way she said his name shot to his heart every damn time. As if his name was a secret, and she alone held the code to opening him. Which she probably did. "You're beyond beautiful, Simone." The word didn't come close to doing her justice.

She smiled then. A confident woman with a storm raging around her. "So are you." Slowly, deliberately, she kicked off her flats. Her bare feet sank into the sand, and she moved toward him, her hips swaying.

He almost stepped back. "What are you doing?"

"Enjoying the oncoming storm."

The words held multiple meanings, but before he'd considered each one, she'd reached him. Her hands moved up his chest to his neck, and she gave a happy hum, tracing the line of his jaw.

"We should go inside the cabin," he whispered, his voice hoarse.

"I like the storm." She stepped into him, a siren dressed in silk as the wind whipped her dress.

His dick tried to punch through his jeans, and his hands, of their own volition, gripped her damp hair. The mass trapped his fingers. "Simone." He had to get her to safety, and the incoming storm might hit before he could do so. Rain pelted down around them, all over them.

She chuckled, and the sound licked right down his torso to his balls. She hooked a foot through his leg and shoved. He chuckled and allowed her to drop him, landing on his ass and taking her weight. The woman sprawled above him, pulling her knees up to sit on his groin.

Sand cushioned his head and was shoved up the back of his shirt. "This is crazy." He no longer really cared.

"I know." She smiled then through the rain, and his heart turned over just for her. Her hands cradled his jaw, and she chuckled as roughness met her palms. "I like your uncivilized side as much as your smooth and cultured one."

"The smooth and cultured is part of the job." Deep down, where he lived, Nick fought to find civility.

"Aye," she whispered, leaning over, her mouth a bare inch away. "Come on, Nicholai. Do you really want to go inside when you can do anything you want right here and now?"

She'd always been a temptress, but he'd never pushed her. Years ago, she was young and vulnerable. Now, after her success in life and business, she could handle all he had to give. The idea caused a growl to rumble up from deep in his chest.

Her eyes widened in surprise and then feminine anticipation. "I do love that sound."

"You're going to hear it again," he said, jerking down the top of her dress to reveal her round, high breasts.

She gasped, and he reached out, cupping both. With that simple touch, he forgot all about the dragons, the witches, and even the demons. Only Simone and the storm existed, and the storm came in a far second. He tweaked her nipples, enjoying how she shoved herself down right on his cock.

She moaned and pressed into his palms, more than filling them.

Every damn time with her was new. He could spend the next five centuries exploring her, every facet of her, and he'd never know all.

She leaned down and licked the rain off his lips, her face protecting his from the drops. Everything in him wanted to flip them over and drive into her hard and fast, but he didn't want sand irritating her skin. Besides, the woman seemed to enjoy being on top.

For now.

Her dress slid up, revealing her smooth thighs bracketing his hips. She kissed him, a wild force, stronger than nature. His hold tightened on her hair, and she moaned into his mouth, making little movements against him.

He tweaked her nipples with enough bite to force a shudder down her back that he could feel. So damn perfect.

Her nails scratching, she reached down and plunged her hands up his shirt to his pecs.

The rain sharpened, hitting them both. Sand and water popped up all around them.

He allowed her to play, sweeping his mouth with her tongue, caressing his chest. Finally, she bit down on his neck, her hands sliding down his body at the same time. Her nimble fingers reached his jeans, and she freed each button, scooting farther down his legs.

He caught his breath and released the hold on her hair. She had to struggle with his wet and sandy jeans, but Simone was nothing but determined, thank God. She pulled them down enough to release him. He sprang free, straining for her.

She chuckled again, the hoarse sound filtering through the pouring rain.

He closed his eyes against the deluge, wondering when he'd lost the sense of self-preservation he'd always held so dear. Then her lips closed over his cock, and he no longer gave a shit.

Heat edged with fire engulfed him, making him jerk hard inside her mouth. She tickled him with her tongue, running it down his length and back up, once again enclosing the tip with her hot mouth.

He arched against her, his fingers now digging into the sand.

Electricity and raw hunger ripped through him, radiating from her talented mouth.

Thunder cracked.

Lightning struck, the sound a sonic boom. His eyelids flipped open to see a nearby tree smoldering. Holy shit. In one smooth motion, he sat up, yanked Simone off him, and leaped onto his feet with her in his arms. He shuffled, as fast as he could, with his pants caught between his thighs and feet.

They reached the dark cabin in mere seconds, and he put his shoulder to the door, shoving it open. A pause and cursory check of the interior revealed no threats.

He crossed the threshold and kicked the door closed.

She laughed. "That was fun."

Was? Oh, hell no. "We're just getting started, little bunny."

Chapter 27

Simone caught her breath at the carnal hunger Nick did nothing to hide. Maybe she'd taken on a bit more than she should've on the beach, but the man had always challenged her. Seeing him lose control, even briefly, was a rush she couldn't deny.

"Fire," he said, pointing at an already equipped fireplace.

She turned, saw the piled logs, and formed a fireball. The flame arced across the room, hit the logs, and ignited. Soon the crackling inside competed with the storm outside.

Cozy was too generous a term for the cabin. Wide bed in the corner, utilitarian kitchen to the right, and a small living area complete with stone fireplace. No rugs were on the floor, and no paintings were on the wall. Rustic, hidden, and perfect.

Nick immediately turned for the bed.

Simone smiled. "The bed, huh? How traditional, Veis. I at least came up with sand, beach, and storm."

"So true," he murmured, pivoting and heading for the rough, handcrafted table near the kitchen. Round with uneven boards, it appeared as if Bear had created it in his spare time.

Simone opened her mouth to comment and found herself facedown over it. "Hey."

Rough hands tore her dress down the back. "You wanted something different."

Surprise mixed with a wary humor inside her. "Nick."

"Too late, bunny." Her dress hit the floor. The sound of jeans dropping whispered through night, and then he was behind her, all heated male. Both hands gripped her shoulders and caressed down, strength and power in the massage.

She groaned and relaxed against the table.

He reached her butt and squeezed.

"Hey," she said, laughing. She wanted one more wild night with him before telling him about the babe.

A quick smack to her right cheek had her rearing up on her elbows. She flipped hair from her face and looked over her shoulder. "Have you lost your mind?"

"Yes. A century ago." He slapped her other cheek. Erotic pain vibrated through her rear to her pounding clit.

Her mouth gaped open.

He shot a hand between her legs, his arm extending to her belly, the movement caressing her clit. One twist of his wrist, and she was turned over, on her back. Exposed and breathless.

Darker-than-midnight eyes kept her gaze as he curled his fingers against her abdomen, scraping down her flesh with precision and a bite of pressure that merely hinted at pain.

"Spread your legs," he ordered softly.

Vulnerability flowed through her right before she accepted his dare. "Gladly." She widened her thighs. "You remember what to do down there?"

He smiled then, lopsided and sure. "I think I can find my way." Dropping to his knees, he palmed her thighs and leaned in.

His hands were warm, his breath hot. Slowly, he blew against her aching clit.

Her knees trembled, and muscle spasms tried to close her legs. His hold easily kept her open for him. Fangs dipped into her thigh in an erotic burn, and she drew up, a gasp escaping. His tongue, rough and firm, lashed the small wound closed.

"I didn't know we were biting tonight." She tried to remain calm, but her voice emerged shaky and breathless.

For answer, he nipped her clit.

She cried out, her back bowing. It took her a second to realized he'd just used his lips and not his teeth or fangs. Even so, a tingling started deep inside her, wanting friction to explode. "Nick, please," she groaned.

"Shhh, baby." He licked her entire slit and swirled his tongue around the tingling bundle of nerves. "I'll tell you to beg later. For now, just enjoy."

She wanted to argue, to punch him for his arrogance, but he gently and slowly sucked her clit into his mouth.

The whimper that escaped her would've embarrassed her if she hadn't been right on the edge of falling into ecstasy. Wet heat from his mouth surrounded her tender flesh, but she couldn't get any friction.

He kept her trapped and ran two fingers on either side of her labia, sliding one and then two inside her. Her entire body tightened with need, but there was nowhere to move. The fingers inside her twisted, slowly moving in and out, fucking her with enough pressure to drive her crazy but not to orgasm. She gyrated against his hand, but he continued to play.

His free hand—man, he still had a free hand—wandered up her torso and pinched a nipple. Fire lanced down her torso to her clit, sparking and zinging on the way. She was so close. Right there. She could go over with just a hint of pressure. So close.

A growl, deep with frustration, fell from her mouth.

He chuckled around her clit. The vibrations were light but almost enough. So close.

Then he released her. Fingers, mouth, hands . . . he let go.

"Nooooooo." She sat straight up, her hair flying, and grabbed for his chest.

He smiled, grasped her hips, and fell backward to the floor, his butt and shoulders taking the impact. She landed on top of him, groin to groin, her knees bracketing his thighs.

"Finish what you started on the beach earlier," he commanded.

She didn't need to be told twice. Rising over him, impossibly wet, she positioned him at her entrance and shoved down. Firm hands on her hips stopped her when just the tip was inside her. "What are you doing?" she breathed, her nails cutting right into his chest, trying to wriggle her way down.

"Slow." He allowed her to drop another inch.

The delicious stretch made her groan. "Let go, or I swear to the goddess, I will burn your balls from your body," she hissed, her thighs tightening against his hips.

"I see." Hunger glowed in his devastating eyes, and he moved his hands to her breasts. "I've let go."

She rose up, using his ripped chest for balance, and shoved down using all of her weight. Even as ready as she was, she gasped as his cock rammed inside her, so big and full. She quivered around him, nerves shooting, pain melting with pleasure.

He gripped her hips again, preventing her from moving. "Take a second."

"No." She tried to lift herself, but he held firm. "Nicholai."

Somehow, he swelled even bigger inside her. "I said to wait." A vein bulged in his neck, and perspiration dotted his forehead. "Adjust so I don't hurt you."

"I'm adapted," she ground out. If she didn't move, she was going to freakin' pass out. "Let. Go. Of. Me."

"For now." He squeezed hard; just another sensation piled on all the rest. Then he reached up and grabbed the back of her nape, drawing her down to his face. His kiss was carnal and shot through her like a jolt of lightning. She bit his bottom lip and then sat up, gaining balance with her knees. Her thighs bunched, and she lifted up, pounding down, her body out of control.

She rode him hard, almost too desperate to reach the finish line. Every time she came down, her clit hit his groin, but then she was up again. She couldn't stop pounding. Leaning forward, she changed her angle and almost gave herself enough friction. So bloody close, damn it.

With a low chuckle, Nick abandoned her tits, reached down, and pinched her clit between two fingers. The impact was localized in a sharp detonation that spiraled out rapidly. The cabin went white, she threw back her head, and exploded. She increased her pace, pushing down hard, prolonging the pleasure.

Finally, with a muffled sigh, she fell forward onto him.

He ran both hands down her back to cup her butt.

Her heart raced, and no doubt he could feel it. She sucked in air, her body tingling. Slowly, awareness crept back in. He was still inside her, still fully erect. She shoved herself up high enough to see his face. "Um."

Sin coated his smile. "My turn."

"Ah," she said, unable to form a complete word.

"Hmmm." He released her clit.

Blood rushed back into the bundle of nerves, and she gasped, leaning over him. Her body was one long, electrical wire with pulses still pounding through every inch. Even so, there was no way she could go again. "I need a reprieve." She chuckled.

"No." He sat up and lifted her right off him, the muscles bunching in his arms. Demon strength was beyond cool and caused a surprising flutter in her abdomen. Standing, he took her with him, and placed her on her feet. He reached out and ran a hand across the edge of the table. "Too rough." Looking around her, he scowled at the sofa. "Too grungy." He turned her toward the bed. "The best choice."

She eyed the clean-looking linen bedspread. "I agree."

"Good." He leaned down, and his lips brushed the back of her ear.

She shivered and started for the bed, only to be stopped by his hand around her bicep. "On the bed, hands and knees," he whispered.

The sexy, raspy tone licked straight through her. She pulled away and turned to face him, standing there so proud and strong. And erect. Very. "Hands and knees?"

His gaze swept her bare body. "You rode your way, now it's my turn to ride my way."

Even as she became quickly aroused again, she felt a quick bite of amusement. "Ride? I'm no horse."

"No. You're all woman. Now, get over there before I put you there."

Oh, he knew her way too well to even think she'd obey blindly, and by the anticipation glinting in his eyes, he was counting on a show of spirit. "You wanna fight, Veis?" she asked, her legs tensing.

"No, I wanna fuck, Simone." He took a threatening step toward her, the intensity on his face almost giving her pause. "Last chance, baby. It's too late for gentle, but I'm not too rough . . . yet."

A tremble rolled through her, toes to head, pausing in her center to heat. Desire ignited inside her like a flash fire. Oh, he'd never hurt her, that she knew. Yet pushing him when he was in such a state of arousal held enough danger to make her think twice. She certainly wouldn't crawl on over and get in position. But she could take the safer route, chuck a pillow at him, and jump on the bed, or she could take a risk and challenge him full-out.

Nicholai Veis would meet any challenge.

She chose danger.

The second a flash of fire showed on her arm, he was on her.

She yelped, half-laughing, as he took her down to the floor. He wrapped himself around her, so when her hands and knees landed on the sanded pine, the impact was feather light. One strong arm banded around her waist, his front to her back, her gaze down on the floor. Laughing, impossibly turned on, she tried to shove back against him to free herself.

She didn't move an inch. His strength heated her lungs and drew a haze over her eyes.

A hard slap to her inner thigh stopped her breath in her throat.

"Spread your legs."

She shut her eyes, so turned on she couldn't see straight. As one of the most powerful women in the world, this should not be turning her on.

He bit her earlobe, and his erection pressed against her sex. "You want up, burn me, and I'll let you up. If not, spread your damn legs."

She shivered, not ready to call it quits, but not ready to submit, even in play. "I'm not into the whole domination thing, demon," she breathed.

He reached between her legs and slid his palm over her very wet core. "Liar." His tongue swirled in her ear, and without warning, he slapped her other thigh. "Spread."

She wanted him inside her so badly, small tremors shook her core.

"Burn me or spread your thighs, Simone. You've already earned the spanking of a lifetime, so now you get to decide if it's before or after sex." He tapped two fingers across her clit.

She arched against him, biting her lip against the excruciating need. Later she could deal with his threat. Right now, she hungered, so she slowly widened her knees.

"Better." He lifted up behind her, grabbed her hips, and powered inside her.

Nerves sparked and jumped as he filled her. She whimpered and lowered her head to her arms, letting go of the fight.

He swelled bigger inside her, pulled out, and powered back in. From his position, he could go impossibly deep, filling her to unreal pleasure. She relaxed her body, going soft, and slightly angled her knees in.

His groan echoed through her body, and then he started pounding. Fast and strong, he hammered into her, each strike shooting sparks of need throughout her. His grip tightened, and she couldn't move even if she wanted to.

Tension uncoiled inside her. Fierce and hot, the mass detonated and exploded out, hurtling her into an orgasm so wild all she could do was hold her breath and ride out the waves. The second she came down, he clutched her harder, shoved deeper than before, and came inside her. His voice was a hoarse whisper against the back of her neck.

They both breathed heavily, and she groaned when he pulled out.

Gentle and firm, he lifted her off the ground and turned toward the bed. She placed a soft kiss on his damp chest. He grinned, looking no less intense but definitely more relaxed. "Oh, you're still getting that spanking."

Her eyebrows lifted, and her haze dissipated. A spanking wouldn't hurt the baby, probably, but she wasn't sure. Plus, if he tried, she'd burn him badly, and they just didn't have time for a full-out fight or a burn unit. She reached up and let his whiskers tickle her palm. "There's something I need to tell you."

He dropped to the bed, legs over, cradling her against his ripped chest. "You're procrastinating."

"Actually, I'm not." She took a deep breath.

His gaze focused and narrowed, no doubt caught by her obvious concern. "What is it?"

"First promise me that you won't go all caveman-crazy on me. That we're in this together, because I still need to face the Nine."

That quickly, any postcoital glow deserted him, leaving the hardcore warrior ready for battle. "I'm not negotiating with you, Simone. If you have something to tell me, do it now."

Well, it had been worth a try. She nodded and cleared her throat. The man definitely had the right to know about the baby, and no matter what, she couldn't keep that kind of secret from him. "Um, I'm pregnant."

Chapter 28

Nick was fairly certain he might have blinked, and then reality set in. "You can't be pregnant."

Simone's cheek creased. "I am."

"But. But how?"

The woman laughed out loud. "Well, I could draw you stick figures, but I'm thinkin' you should be able ta figure it out."

Her eyes sparkled, but her slip into brogue showed her nervousness. Everything inside him shifted and settled. He breathed out. "You're all right?"

"Fine." She shrugged. "I'm only a few days along." Then her fine eyebrows arched down. "You believe me?"

"Yes." Of course he believed her. Simone would never lie about something so important. "I'm just surprised, but considering your parents, maybe I shouldn't be?"

She shivered, and he reached for a blanket at the end of the bed to wrap around her. "It's still incredibly rare, and it's not like we coulda used birth control, right?"

He nodded. Birth control didn't work for immortals, but that wasn't a big deal because most immortals took eons to procreate. Not Simone, apparently. So many thoughts assailed him, he couldn't grasp just one. "I was too rough."

She rolled her eyes. "You were fine. The babe is well protected, Nicholai."

Relief coursed through him. Even so, he'd be much more careful in the future. "Okay. Wow. This is a big deal." How lame were those words?

She patted his chest. "I've had a little time to get used to the idea, and I'm still kind of freaking out."

A babe. Simone with child. Nick tightened his hold on them both. "We need to get you somewhere safe." A small island in the middle of a stormy ocean didn't count. They also needed to mate and soon.

"I need to face the Nine, but I'm more worried about the dragons." Her jaw firmed, but real fear swirled in her eyes. "They said they'd kill any dragon-demon child because of its potential mind attack ability. There was a hybrid years ago, and it sounds like he was an evil monster with powers nobody could overcome."

Heat and power jerked Nick's spine into a straight line. "That's ridiculous. Our child will know love and security. That's not an environment to create evil." He leaned down and rubbed his nose over hers. "We'll make sure he's a good person."

"She," Simone murmured. "I'm betting on she."

"Even better." He smiled to mask the furious need to protect slamming through him with more force than the storm hammering the small cottage. "Nobody is going to harm this baby. You have my word." He'd kill every last dragon on earth if they were a threat to his child. His hands shook, and his voice lowered to glass in a cement mixer. So he stood and carefully placed her back on the bed as if she were something infinitely fragile, which suddenly, she was.

He leaned down and pressed a soft kiss on her upturned nose. "I'm happy about this, Simone." There were so many damn emotions battering him that *happy* had to be in there somewhere. "Give me a minute to gather more firewood from outside, and we'll create a plan. All right?"

She nodded, understanding filling her dark eyes. "Take your time."

He turned to the doorway and had just reached it when she called out.

"You might want to put on your jeans." The laughter in her voice warmed him throughout.

Giving her a grin, he leaned down and tugged up his jeans before stepping back into his boots. Then he paused and stalked over to the cupboards to open several. Simple utensils and plates. He glanced around the small room.

"What?" Simone asked.

"Weapons. Where would Bear hide weapons?" Nick looked up and around the ceiling.

"Somewhere simple. Probably under the bed." Simone moved to get up.

Nick stalled her with a hand. "Stay wrapped up." He crossed to the bed and crouched down to find a flat metal chest. He pulled it out and flipped open the lid to reveal several guns, swords, knives, throwing stars, and even explosives. "Whoa."

Simone leaned over the edge of the bed. "He's got an arsenal in there."

Nick grabbed two green guns and handed them to her. "Until I get back." Preferring a blade, he took two and tucked one in his boot and the other in his pocket. "Shoot anybody that's not me. Including Bear."

"Funny." Simone set the guns down. "If you need backup, call me."

He eyed her. If she thought she was going into any sort of battle now, she truly didn't know him. "We'll talk when I get back."

"You're damn right we will." She met his gaze levelly.

He gave a short nod and turned for the storm outside, which would probably be easier to tame than the woman behind him. Once outside, he shut the door and leaned back against it, taking several deep breaths. A baby. The world suddenly felt both heavier and lighter, scarier and more beautiful.

Lightning arced across the water, flashing silver and purple. Waves crashed, high and angry, and rain barreled down to attack the earth. The wind blew sand into his legs and over the front porch. He stepped off the porch, shielding his eyes from the sand, and walked the perimeter of the cabin to find the generator in a stone outbuilding connected to the house. Then he patrolled farther out, keeping the cabin in sight at all times and strategizing his next move with Simone and the rest of the world. Finally, deciding the weather was the biggest threat to them at the moment, he gathered more wood from a shed and stomped back inside.

The fire had died down to small crackles, and Simone lay asleep on the bed, still in the blanket he'd wrapped around her. Her thick hair had dried splayed over the pillow. Soft firelight caressed her delicate cheekbones and pursed lips. In sleep she was just as beautiful as when fully animated.

He studied her, and something inside him, something deep, down, and hidden . . . relaxed. Everything he'd ever want or need lay sleeping on that bed.

For years, he'd wondered. Would he be whole again? Would he feel love again?

He did. With her, a wild witch of a woman, and now their babe. It was more than he deserved, but he'd hold on with both hands. Nothing and nobody would harm them. Ever.

He kicked off his boots and padded to place the wood near the fire. Carefully, he piled on a few more logs and then removed his clothing to dry over the table before finding a pair of old sweats in the dresser and yanking them on. Gently, he took the two guns off the bed and pressed a kiss to Simone's forehead before stalking over to the couch to keep watch for the night.

His short spell of sleeping peacefully was over.

Simone came slowly awake, and her stomach rumbled. She had to shove wild hair out of her face before sitting to find Nick cooking something that smelled delicious. "Nick?"

He turned. "Hungry?"

She swallowed. The demon stood in old sweats, his broad chest bare, muscles rippling with simple movements. "Yes."

One eyebrow rose. "For food."

"That, too." She swung her legs over the bed and gathered the blanket around herself. "Tell me there's a loo."

He wrinkled his nose. "There's an outhouse of sorts."

"Wonderful." She pushed off the bed and swayed as dizziness swamped her.

He was there in an instant, holding her elbows. "What's wrong?"

"Nothing." She took several deep breaths. "Just a little off, that's all."

He picked her up, and the room whirled around. "I'll take you outside."

She planted a hand against his chest with a solid *thump*. "I am all right now, and I can certainly take myself to the loo." They had to nip this nonsense in the bud and now.

He ignored her and stomped across the cottage to open the door.

"Oh," she breathed at the enchanting view. The storm had fled, leaving sparkling water as far as the eye could see. The sun shone down, and the waves caressed the shore. "It's beautiful."

"Yes." He walked across the porch and set her gently down on a stone walkway. "There's the outhouse."

She nodded and gingerly stepped from stone to stone to the outhouse, which had a bear carved into the door. "Funny." After taking care of business, she returned to find Nick waiting on the porch for her. "We need to get this overprotectiveness taken care of and now—*eek*." He swept her up, and her hair flew all around. "I can walk."

Again, he didn't answer. So he thought by just ignoring her that he'd get his way, did he? "Don't make me burn you," she muttered, snuggling into his neck just for a moment. She was so tired, and she'd just slept the entire night away. "What did you cook?"

"Dried eggs with a bunch of spices but nothing too hot."

"I like hot."

"Not when you're pregnant." He set her on the couch as if she were a porcelain doll, fetched her clothes, and helped her into them.

Her mouth dropped open as he gently zipped her jeans. "You have never tried to get me into clothes before."

He chuckled and turned to the stove.

She grabbed his arm and jerked him toward her. His eyebrows rose and he leaned in, his eyes right above hers. "Yes?"

"Stop it." There was absolutely no need to expand on the statement.

"No." Apparently he saw no need, either.

The door burst open, and he spun around so quickly the momentum tossed her against the back of the couch.

"Howdy, all." Bear stomped off his feet, his dick swaying. He gestured with a smoldering book that shook in his trembling hands. "Hey. Those are my sweats."

Nick looked up at the ceiling. "There has to be another pair. Find some."

Bear frowned, and blood leaked from his nose. He wiped it off.

"Clothes don't make the shift, you know. It's not like I enjoy being naked all the time."

"Are you all right? Please tell me you're okay." Simone tossed her discarded blanket his way, concern chilling through her.

"I will be. Just need rest and good food," Bear said, snagging the blanket in his hand.

"What happened?" She scrutinized him. Pale, shaky, but standing all right.

"It looks like the soldiers who saw Nick kill Desmond are willing to back Flynn's totally untrue version of events." Bear threw the book to land next to Simone on the sofa.

"What's this?" Simone carefully picked up the volume.

"It's about Traxton, who was an evil dragon-demon hybrid way back when." Bear wiggled his eyebrows, his gaze suddenly piercing.

Could he be any more obvious? Simone turned the book over in her hands. "I told Nick about the baby."

"Whew." Bear moved forward and clapped Nick on the back. "Congratulations and welcome to the family."

"Get. Dressed. Bear." Nick spoke through clenched teeth, his gaze remaining on the shifter's face.

Bear guffawed. "Why? We're family, or we will be. You two are getting mated, right?"

"Yes," Nick said at the same time Simone said, "No."

Nick turned around to face her fully. "Yes."

Bear leaned around Nick and shook out his shaggy hair. "I'm with the demon. You gotta get mated."

That was it. Simone stood and glared at her brother. "Would you cut the shit with the dumbass good-ol'-boy routine? I'm sick and tired of it."

Bear blinked. Once and then twice. His face hardened, and his eyes sharpened. "All right. You and that baby boy need the protection of a mate, whether you like it or not. Add in the protection of an entire race of demons loyal to your mate, plus the entire Realm, which is allied to that demon nation, and you are going to mate him if I have to bring the proverbial shotgun to the ceremony."

Nick grinned. "I knew I liked you."

Bear turned his full focus on Nick. "You hurt my sister or that boy, and I'll do things to you not even a mind-attacking demon could imagine."

Nick's smile widened. "Could be a girl, you know."

Bear paled. "Jesus. A demon, dragon, witch hybrid female. God help us all."

Nick lost the smile. "Yeah."

Bear cleared his throat. "So. Where should I take you two?"

"Nowhere. Go get us a boat." Nick rubbed his chin.

Bear shook his head. "Boats can't get close enough because the ocean is still way too wild from the storm. Rocks. And before you ask about helicopters, there's nowhere to land."

"Then find a dragon whose true nature is that of a dragon to come get us," Simone hissed. "Get Flynn. Wait a minute. Call Flynn."

"No phone." Bear shrugged. "I'm gonna shift into a dragon, so you might as well tell me where to go."

Nick shook his head. "Just to land so we can grab transport somewhere safe."

Simone glared at them both. "You're forgetting my trial starts tomorrow. I have to show up, or I'll have a bounty on my head for the rest of my life."

Nick growled low. "If you're found guilty?"

"Then we'll deal with the situation at that time." She rubbed her belly. "I can't have this child be a wanted person from birth. We have to somehow win at trial." She leaned in and pressed a kiss to Nick's chin. "It's our best chance for a normal life for him or her. I have to face the Nine." She stepped back, trusting he'd make the right decision and not fight her.

"Absolutely not," Bear snapped. "Stay away from those crazy witches and go somewhere safe."

Simone ignored him and focused on Nick.

Nick lowered his chin. "I agree it's the smart thing to do, but if things go badly, you have to promise to let me get you out of there. No matter what it takes."

She nodded, her hands still over her abdomen. "I promise." Her lips trembled, but she tried to force a smile for her brother. "Promise me this won't hurt you too badly."

He rolled his eyes. "It won't. Geez. I can shift a few times every century or so without losing my spleen."

God, she hoped he was telling the truth. "Any chance you can keep the ride smooth this time?" she asked.

Bear sighed. "Nothing else is going smooth, so why start with the ride?"

Chapter 29

Nick shook sand out of his boots and stomped up the beach in Port-Donegal, balancing easily while moving over the rocky terrain. His stomach still lurched a little from Bear's flight across the ocean, and from the green tinge of Simone's skin, she was also still trying to keep from hurling. Bear had dropped them off and turned right back around for Fire Island to back up Flynn. "You all right?" Nick asked.

Simone nodded and struggled against the wind. "Aye, but I wish we could've talked Bear into staying here."

"Maybe he'll rest with Flynn. I'm sure Flynn will take good care of him."

"I hope so." She led the way up the rocks to a peaceful-looking cottage overlooking the ocean. "You have no' been here."

"No." Even with his impressive intel, he had no records of the cottage. There was no way a dragon could fly over the landmass to Dublin without being spotted, so Simone had asked Bear to drop them off in Donegal, where she could arrange for a flight home. "I'm taking it that this place is more than a nice vacation cottage?" Nick asked.

She smiled and reached the front stoop. Cheerful yellow paint covered the slightly warped front door. Wide windows made up the front, surrounded by heavy stone walls that rose to what appeared to be a dark blue metal roof. Interesting. She placed her hand in the middle of the door, several *clicks* echoed, and then it slid inward.

Nick took a deep breath and followed her inside a quaint gathering room with a sofa, chairs, end tables, and a lovely stone fireplace.

Quiet filled the space, but he could sense signatures of energy. "Who's here?" he asked, his voice dropping to a whisper.

"I am." Adam Dunne moved around the wall from what was apparently a kitchen, a large ham sandwich in his hand. "Where the hell have you been?"

Simone opened her mouth and then closed it again. "Long story. What in the world are you doing here?"

Adam blew out, tension vibrating from him. "I had Zane drop me a few miles south before he headed back to his Dublin safe zone. I've been trying to locate Victoria Monzelle by hitting each and every local safe house, but the Guard has her locked down somewhere and good. They moved her from the Liffey penthouse right after you visited her the other morning, apparently."

Nick winced. "Is Kellach fit to be tied?" The woman was Kell's sister-in-law, and his mate had to be going crazy, which would lead Kellach to war, probably.

"Aye. He and Alexandra are checking all of the known houses from Dublin to the south of Ireland, while I came north. So far, we haven't found Tori. You'd think an American with purple streaks in her hair would be easy to spot." Lines cut into the sides of Adam's mouth.

Simone scrubbed both hands down her face. "The good news is that Tori won't go on trial until mine is over." Even so, concern darkened Simone's already dark eyes. "Since her sister is mated to a Coven Nine Enforcer, surely they'll just have her sign a nondisclosure agreement and let her go."

Nick paused and turned to study his woman. "You sound . . . unsure."

"I am." She sighed. "The Coven Nine is drawing inward in protection since we have such a powerful enemy out there with the planekite. News of our existence can't get out right now."

"They'll let her go, or they won't like the result," Adam said darkly.

Nick paused. "You sound like you have a personal stake."

"She's family," Adam said. He surveyed Simone's ragtag appearance. "Now it's time you told your cousin the Enforcer where the hell you've been."

Nick stepped in front of her. "Watch your tone."

Adam lifted one dark eyebrow. "You're on my land now, demon."

Simone edged Nick to the side and shook her head at Adam. "Knock it off. Now isn't the time to measure your manhood, boys." She shoved unruly hair away from her face. "I'll explain everything, but for now, what's the status of the Nine?"

Adam's expression softened. "Your mother is doing better but is still recuperating. She won't be able to resume her job for some time, the doctors said."

Simone's relief was palpable. "But she'll be all right?"

"Aye." Adam reached out and wiped grime off her face.

Nick kept still. They were related, and the gesture was brotherly, so he didn't have to kill Adam. Win-win for them both. "The rest?" he asked.

"Our aunt is recuperating, as well, but the other two council-members are still in comas. Not sure if they'll make it." Adam turned back to the kitchen. "If you want updates on the planekite, come into the control room."

Simone followed him, while Nick took a good look around and then went after them a bit more slowly. Adam reached a small green refrigerator before turning to look over his shoulder at Simone.

She nodded. "As a Coven Nine member, I grant access to Nicholai Veis."

Adam gave Nick a hard look and then slammed his hand dead-center on the fridge. The thing rolled to the side as if it was made of feathers, revealing stone steps leading down.

Nick sighed. Why did the damn witches always have stones, steps, and darkness? He sensed they all just loved the drama. "For Pete's sake," he muttered. "Must we always descend? Why can't you have secret chambers in high-rises?"

Simone snorted and followed Adam down a surprisingly well-lit stairwell. "Our chambers were created before skyscrapers, and you know it." Her voice echoed off the rounded stone walls. She picked her way carefully, her steps sure, water squishing from her boots. Her hair was a wild mass of curls down her back, and even without makeup, the woman was magnificent.

Nick kept close in case she stumbled.

The sound of the ocean still rumbled through the stone, and no sense of creepy magic followed him down. They reached a wide cavern cut into the rocks. More weapons than he wished to count lined lockers at the far end. "Planning a war?" he asked dryly.

Adam glanced over his shoulder as he reached a round table in the center of the room surrounded by chairs. "Aren't you?"

Yes. In fact, Nick had several stash houses spread across the world just like this one. "Of course not. Demons believe in peace."

Simone snorted and leaned over to study a bunch of papers. "Is this the most current research on planekite?"

"Yes. More specifically, the research is on Apollo, which is the weaponized drug using the planekite mineral." Adam pointed to a couple of spreadsheets. "What we've gathered from different sources. Ten darts *was* the number needed to cause death, but whoever is creating them has become more efficient lately."

Nick rocked back on his heels. "How so?"

"They've managed to multiply the deadly effects, so now we think three darts at the same time could cause death." Adam rubbed his bloodshot eyes. "We've been very lucky so far, but I'm fairly certain our luck has run out."

Nick stepped closer to Simone, wanting her within reach. "Any luck finding the manufacturer?"

Adam growled. "No. We haven't found the mastermind behind the attacks, but we're closing in on the distributors in Seattle as well as Dublin. From there, we'll trace the drug up to the source."

Nick surveyed the many stacks of research on the table. "Is Titans of Fire still the main distributor in Seattle?" The motorcycle club had been infiltrated by the Dunne boys as part of the investigation, but they had so far been unable to find the manufacturer.

"Yes, and Bear's club has been contacted several times about distributing," Adam said. "We're coming up with a plan for him to do so undercover. Hopefully between his men and our Fire contacts, we'll finally get a break in this fucking mess." He walked over to the weapons and took several knives to slide into his boots and pockets. "For now, what's your plan?" He turned back around and crossed his arms.

Nick grabbed a chair. "Simone, you need to sit down."

She lifted both eyebrows. "I'm just fine with standing."

"Sit."

"Stand."

Adam looked from one to the other of them. "What's wrong with you two?"

"I'm standing right now, and tomorrow I'm facing trial," Simone said. "It's better than going on the run."

"Are you prepared to defend her?" Adam asked, his gaze hard on Nick.

"Sit down before I sit you down, bunny." Nick turned toward Adam. "I am, and I'm prepared to get her the hell out of there if things go south."

"The Enforcers have been banned from the chambers," Adam said quietly.

Simone gasped and sat in the damn chair.

Nick took a deep breath. "Considering the Enforcers are all cousins to Simone, that doesn't surprise me." While forcing her underground held appeal, it would put her on the run from the Guard, and that wouldn't be healthy for her or the baby. "Do you have any insight as to how the trial will go?"

"She's innocent, so it has to go her way," Adam said simply.

"Agreed." Nick forced confidence into his tone.

Adam cleared his throat. "I have to get on the road shortly, but first, time for the two of you to report in."

Simone took a deep breath. "Well, let's see. Bear is my half-brother, I'm part dragon, and guess what? Nick and I are going to have a baby."

Silence reigned in the underground room for a moment. Then, "You're pregnant?" Adam took one look at Nick and charged.

Simone finished drying the dishes, her gaze out the kitchen window at the jagged rocks leading down to the sea. "How's your face?"

"Better than Adam's," Nick said cheerfully from the small table in the corner.

Simone shook her head. The men had gone at it, throwing punches, both working out stress more than anger. In fact, they'd seemed to enjoy the silly skirmish, and then Adam had taken off to search for

Tori even farther north. The man's razor-sharp focus would lead him to the human female, without question. "He seemed fine about the whole dragon issue."

"Why wouldn't he be?"

"I don't know." Maybe she'd been a little worried that the Enforcers would think less of her, or at least be pissed she hadn't told them about her connection to Bear. But they understood the need for secrecy, and frankly, her silence had probably protected Bear through the years. Especially since his other secret, that dragons existed, was far too dangerous to get out. Or at least, it had been. She understood the reason for it, but now was a time for peace, and the dragons should reenter the world.

Nick stood and reached her in seconds, drawing her back into him and wrapping an arm around her waist. "They're family, sweetheart. They love you no matter what."

She smiled and smacked his arm. "You are such a pain in the ass."

"Of course." He leaned in and nuzzled her ear.

The heat of his mouth sent desire through her body, zinging at several important stops on the way. They did have the night before a helicopter arrived the next day to take her to the trial. She wiggled until his hold loosened and then turned to face him, safely within the circle of his arms.

The door blew open on its hinges, flying past the kitchen and into the table Nick had just vacated.

He pivoted instantly and shoved her toward the refrigerator. "Downstairs. Now."

She'd barely made it a step when Guard soldiers ran into the room, fully armed and wearing battle gear, including night scopes. She paused and straightened, refusing to run or cower. "This is quite a show for little ol' me."

Their flak boots crunched debris on the floor, and their weapons remained centered on her and Nick's chest. He stepped to the side, partially covering her. "Lower your weapons, now."

The soldiers didn't flinch.

The muscles in Nick's back vibrated, and the room filled with the swell of his fury. "You have guns pointed at a member of the Coven Nine. You will lower those weapons."

Slowly, the weapons lowered a couple of inches.

One of the soldiers cleared his throat. "By the power of the Nine, we're to escort you to Dublin, Miss Brightston."

"My trial starts tomorrow," she said clearly, showing no fear, even though her insides were absolutely quaking.

He nodded. "I understand, but you've been out of contact, and the Nine sent a warrant."

Well, she couldn't exactly tell them where she'd been, now, could she? "How did you find me?"

The soldier shrugged. "I don't know the details, ma'am. Just that we have a force of twenty surrounding the area to take you in."

Twenty? Jesus. As pissed as Nick was, he could probably fry all their brains, but one or two of them would get off a shot first. Simone couldn't risk the baby, and since she was headed to Dublin anyway, why not cooperate? She reached out and clasped Nick's arm. "We'd appreciate the ride, gentlemen."

Nick's arm was steel beneath her fingers.

She tightened her hold. "There's no reason not to go." Although one more night with him had held a lot more appeal.

"I had plans for the evening," he rumbled, his gaze not leaving the soldiers.

As did she. She paused. "What kind of plans?"

"The kind involving markings, bitings, and coming hard," he returned, keeping his body between her and the weapons.

Oh. Heat climbed up her neck to her face. The soldiers didn't react to the words, but her entire body did. The markings should probably wait until they'd had a good discussion . . . and she had her freedom. "I'll have to take a rain check," she said, stepping to his side and nodding at the lead soldier. "Let's go."

Chapter 30

The skies opened up and poured furious rain the morning of the trial. Nick had slept in a hotel near the Nine headquarters, while Simone had been sequestered somewhere else. As his escort delivered him to the innocuous building at the edge of Dublin, he tried to rein in his temper. Clear and cool thinking would win the day. Should he choose to mind attack everyone, there would be no coming back from that.

The silent guard took him through the labyrinth of hallways that turned to secret tunnels and finally led deep into the earth to the chambers surrounded by rock.

Simone was waiting for him at what he considered the defense table, while the prosecutor was busily laying out manila folders in perfect order on his table. Several guards had been stationed at points around the perimeter, fully armed. Nick leaned down and brushed Simone's head for a kiss before dropping his tablets and manila files onto their table. "Are you all right?" he asked.

She turned and lifted an eyebrow. "Of course."

He smiled. The woman was all grit and class. For the trial, she'd worn a deep blue skirt and bodice-style dress that made her eyes sparkle. Her thick hair was piled atop her head in a fancy chignon, her lips were red, and her skin flawless. A Celtic knot pendant settled between her breasts and matched her earrings. "Nice necklace."

She fingered the silver design and smiled. "Kellach bought a bunch of them one year and gave them to all the female cousins for their birthdays. It's my good luck charm."

Sweet. Here she was wearing her beauty as a shield, and she'd thought to bring family with her. "We'll win this."

"Of course we will." Determination hardened her chin. There was the woman he adored.

The wall slid open behind the raised dais, and Peter Gallagher, Nessa Lansa, and Sal Donny walked in, all taking the same seats as before. Apparently Peter was sitting in for Viv as the head of the Council until she returned. The door closed.

Peter banged a gavel, deep lines cutting into the sides of his mouth. "Council members Louise Fronts and Frances Murphy have both succumbed to planekite attacks."

Simone gasped, and her body shuddered as if a physical blow had been delivered. "They died?"

"Aye." Stress fanned out from his bloodshot eyes. "Vivienne Northcutt and Dr. Dunne are expected to reach a slow but complete recovery." He cleared his throat. "With the death penalty on the table, Brenna Dunne has been excused from serving, as well."

"So my future is up to the three of you," Simone said clearly.

Nick's mouth twitched. Coming out fighting, was she? Good.

"Yes," Peter said. "Let's get started. Colman Foley, is the prosecution ready to present its case for treason, murder, and attempted murder against Simone Brightston?"

"I am," Colman said.

"Good. Let me remind everyone that the defendant is a member of the Council of the Coven Nine and has given service to this institution for over a century. She will be accorded all respect due to her. The Council can detect falsehoods, so the witnesses are forewarned." Peter set down the gavel and leaned back in his leather chair. "And, Mr. Veis?"

"Yes?" Nick asked.

"We've deployed certain aspects of the veil here, so your powers, as well as the defendant's, have been minimized."

Nick instantly shot a mind attack toward Peter, who didn't so much as blink. "Understood," Nick said. Well, shit.

"Good. There's no need for opening arguments, as the sitting Council is more than up to speed here. In addition, we do not require character witnesses since so many have sent in letters supporting Ms. Brightston. Mr. Coleman, please call your first witness," Peter said, gesturing to a witness stand to the right of the dais made of smooth, round stones.

Colman nodded and called a forensic accountant named Berry Pine, who was a thousand-year-old witch with wild gray hair, even wilder gray eyes, and terrible taste in clothing. His plaid suit had seen better days, and his paisley tie held more mustard stains than design. He droned on about all the money, the location of the mines, and the banking transfers bearing Simone's signature.

Finally, Nick had had enough. He stood. "Begging the Council's pardon, but we're happy to stipulate about the money transfers, land transfers, and the transfer and usage of the mineral rights that may or may not have mined planekite."

Peter's mouth gaped open. "You're stipulating to these facts?"

Nick shrugged. "Sure. We're not arguing any of the transfers, or whether or not planekite was mined. Even if we're not sure, we're fine stipulating that planekite was mined, it was used to create Apollo, and it was then weaponized against witches and humans."

Peter cleared his throat. "You're on Simone's side, right?"

"Yes," Nick said.

Peter looked at Simone. "You're on board with the stipulations?"

"Aye," she said without hesitation.

Nick's chest warmed. The woman trusted him.

"Very well," Peter said, turning his focus to Colman. "In light of the stipulations, do you have any further questions for this witness?"

Colman coughed and shuffled papers, obviously caught off guard. "Ah, no. I tender the witness."

Nick stood and buttoned his suit jacket. "Mr. Pine, do you know who ordered all of the transfers?"

Pine slightly turned his large bulk in the witness box. "Simone Brightston's name is at the bottom of all the transfers."

"Are you an expert in handwriting analysis?" Nick asked.

"No."

"Is there a chance that somebody else could have forged Ms. Brightston's signature on all the documents?"

Pine shrugged. "I'm not an expert, so I have no clue. My job was to trace the money and land transfers, which I've done."

Nick paused. "Mr. Pine, do you know Simone Brightston?"

"Aye, I do. We've met at many functions and have served on different organizations together," Pine said.

"Is she smart?"

"Excuse me?" Pine asked.

"Simone. In your opinion, do you think she's an intelligent woman?" Nick asked.

Pine nodded, his gaze serious. "Yes. I do think she's very bright."

"Ah. How bright is it to sign your own name to a bunch of illegal land and money transfers?" Nick asked smoothly.

"That would actually be either arrogant or stupid," Pine said.

"Thank you," Nick said, keeping his face calm. He'd made the point, but Pine's mention of "arrogance" didn't help. Simone was more than confident, and Pine had just given the prosecution material to use that against her. "I tender this witness."

Colman cleared his throat. "Next I call Orrin Forsent, who is a handwriting analysis expert."

Nick sat down and watched Orrin take the stand. Tall and whipcord thin, the witch had thick red hair and more freckles than sand at the beach. Colman ran him through all the documents and had him compare the signatures on them to ones he'd had Simone submit right in chambers. He spent an inordinate amount of time on the shipping transfers that had brought the planekite from Russia to Seattle in the last couple of weeks. Orrin concluded, based on his expert opinion, that the signatures were authentic.

Nick stood when it was his turn to question. "You're a witch, right?"

Orrin nodded. "I am."

"Witches alter matter using quantum physics as well as a myriad of other sciences, right?"

"Yes." Orrin shoved light-refracting glasses up his nose.

"Isn't it possible that a very talented witch could easily copy another witch's signature? I mean, with all the power witches hold?" Nick asked, his eyebrows rising.

Orrin's nostrils flared. "I do not believe that's what happened here."

"Answer the question," Nick returned evenly.

Orrin lifted a shoulder. "I guess it could happen."

"Could you do it?" Nick challenged.

"I would not." Orrin leaned forward in the box.

"That's not what I asked you," Nick said silkily. "Do you have the talent or skill to forge a signature well enough that it couldn't be detected?"

Orrin cleared his throat. "I could."

"Then it's possible." Nick turned away from the shithead. "This guy can go." He eyed the Council. Peter and Sal remained stern, but Nessa had definitely mellowed. He figured she'd find Simone not guilty anyway, considering she was known to be not only fair but brilliant. She'd know Simone wouldn't do such a thing. However, the other two men were both vying for political position, and he couldn't read where they'd come down.

Colman gestured for the guard to escort Orrin out the side wall. "The prosecution calls Phillipe Sadler."

Nick stood. "We object. Mr. Sadler offers nothing but his vendetta against Simone, her family, and the Coven Nine as a whole."

"We'll allow the testimony while keeping the past in mind," Peter said.

The wall opened, and Phillipe Sadler strode in wearing Armani. He had vivid blue eyes and a shaggy mane of brown hair, but he strode like the fighter he was rumored to be. He took his seat, and his gaze landed on Simone, hardening instantly.

Nick fought the urge to step between her and the witness.

Colman reached for a notepad and read quickly. "Mr. Sadler, is it true you have a vendetta against the Nine?"

"Yes," Sadler said.

Nick lifted his chin. Interesting strategy.

"Why?" Colman asked.

"They hurt my mother," Sadler said simply.

Colman nodded. "I understand, but your mother was accused of treason based on her relationship with Trevan Demidov, right?"

"Aye, but my mother had been mated to my father, who died centuries ago, so she and Trevan obviously couldn't have had a physical relationship. This was before the time of viruses and the ability to negate mating bonds." Sadler snapped the words out. "On the other hand, Simone Brightston had a relationship with him that I do believe included all sorts of terribly kinky sex."

Nick bit back a snarl, sorry that he couldn't kill Trevan all over again. One of the Kayrs men had taken care of the rogue witch ages ago. Trevan had hidden his agenda to take down the Nine from

Simone but had shared it with his partner in crime, Grace Sadler, Phillipe's mother.

"Where is your brother?" Colman asked, as if right in tune with Nick's thoughts.

Phillipe looked down at his hands. "I don't know. We've been investigating Simone Brightston, and my brother has disappeared. I have no doubt he met his death at her hands." He looked up, his gaze piercing Nick. "Or at her lover's hands."

Nick allowed his fangs to drop just a bit. "You have any proof of that ridiculous accusation?"

Peter banged his gavel on the desk. "Mr. Veis, wait your turn."

Colman continued, "Tell us about your vendetta."

"My mother hired several investigators the second she was forced off the Council, and we've spent years watching and compiling evidence against all of the Coven Nine members." He turned toward the three sitting members. "We know all of your secrets, and we're willing to make them public."

Was that a threat or what? Nick watched the council members, who looked back at Sadler without revealing a thing.

Sadler turned back toward Colman. "We've watched Simone for years, and we've compiled evidence against her. The second we saw she was behind the planekite mining and manufacture of Apollo, we turned over the proof to you."

Colman nodded, took a remote control, and started a film on the stone wall. "Is this one of the recordings?"

"Yes. This one shows Simone at the Boltucli Bank in Switzerland, where the documents prove the planekite funding originally came from." The recording showed Simone in the bank, signing papers, and putting cash in safety deposit boxes.

Nick glanced her way. She grasped a pen and a notepad. THAT'S ME, AND I DO BANK THERE.

Wonderful. Nick nodded.

BUT I DIDN'T MOVE PLANEKITE.

He nodded again. It sure as shit looked like she had when the camera zoomed in on one of the land transfers.

She sighed. MY FINANCIAL ADVISORS HAD ME BUY AND SELL LAND AS PART OF MY PORTFOLIO. I DIDN'T KNOW.

Made sense. Whoever had set her up had spent years doing it. It was entirely possible she had signed some of the documents, but definitely not any of the shipping manifests. Those were the key, but so far, his experts hadn't been able to prove the signatures were falsified.

Colman went through recording after recording of Simone conducting business in the bank. Finally, he shut off the film. "Mr. Sadler, you have compiled a lot of evidence here, and even though your motivations aren't exactly pure, I appreciate the hard work. I do have to ask you one more question, one we're all wondering about."

"What's that?" Phillipe asked, triumph darkening his eyes.

Nick tensed.

"Why in the world, based on all of your research, would Simone Brightston want to take down the Coven Nine as well as the witch nation?"

Phillipe smiled. "Because she's not a witch."

Peter coughed. "Of course she's a witch."

"No, sir. Her father was known as Roman, a shifter who deeply hated the Coven Nine. He contacted Simone a hundred years ago, and they've been planning this atrocity ever since."

Peter shook his head. "I don't understand. Why would a shifter want to harm the Nine?"

"He's not your ordinary shifter." Phillipe lowered his chin to look straight at Simone. "He's the father of Traxton, whom the Nine put to death a millennium ago."

Colman stepped around the table. "I've lived long enough that I remember Traxton. He was an anomaly. A multi-shifter that could defend against any species and even fly. He was a sociopath, and the immortal world banded together to take him down."

"Well, now. Turns out multi-shifters don't exist, but . . . dragons do." Phillipe pointed at Simone. "Just ask Simone Brightston. She's a dragon, and she's been plotting against you all along, my friends. You killed her brother, Traxton, a long time ago."

Chapter 31

Simone paced the conference room, trying to count the energy signatures of the guards outside. Many, many guards. "Can you believe that? Is there a chance that Traxton was actually Roman's kid, too?" Did the dragon have some great gift of spreading his seed or what?

"Could be," Nick said, poring over documents, an untouched roast beef sandwich next to him on the table. "That testimony killed us. Well, after the council got over the shock about dragons." He sat back, fury sizzling in his dark eyes.

True. Sadler had even had pictures to prove that dragons existed. By the time he was finished testifying, everyone had believed him.

Nick shoved the sandwich away. "What's the Nine's position on pregnant defendants? I mean, say they do sentence you to death? Will they agree to wait to carry out the sentence until after the babe is born?"

Simone dropped into a chair, her curiosity about Roman deflating. "Uh, I don't know. God. Do you think I'm going to be executed?"

Nick started and then reached out and covered her hand with his. "Not a fucking chance, sweetheart. I'm just looking at all scenarios. Worst case, if you're found guilty, how much time do I have to get you to safety? With the babe, could be nine months."

She nodded and took several deep breaths to keep from throwing up. "I'd say they'd normally wait, but . . ."

"But what?"

She shrugged. "Witch, dragon, demon mix here. What if they decide he's a danger to society like the dragons believe him to be?"

"Shit." Nick reached for the book Bear had given them on the beach. "According to this, he's not. Traxton was an aberration, probably created because Roman was such a prick. Any kid can be good or bad, and environment matters. Our kid will be as good as a loving home can make him."

Simone swallowed. "Good. Any proof of that?"

"No. Just conjecture." Nick set down the book. "The only proof will be our child."

"If he's allowed to live a normal life and not be on the run," Simone said woodenly, tears pricking the back of her eyes.

Nick shoved his chair back, reached over, plucked her out of her chair, and set her on his lap facing him. "I know you're feeling vulnerable and tired, little bunny. But it's time to get pissed instead."

She nodded and took another deep breath. "I know." Not in a million years would she give up, but it still hurt that her own people might order her death. "I'm also worried about Flynn and the dragons. Their secret is definitely out now, and since they can counter any immortal attack, they're dangerous" If she stayed in her position, she could help them and arrange a treaty. The dragons needed allies.

"That's their problem." Nick grasped her chin and lifted her face to his gaze. "Your only concern is your health and the baby. I'll take care of the rest."

How badly she wanted to snuggle into his chest and let him save her. But she could damn well save herself. Time to snap out of it and grow a pair. "Our powers don't work in the chambers, but take one step outside, and we're both at full battery charge." She wiggled her butt to get more comfortable on his firm thighs.

He made a sound that was a cross between a groan and a growl. "Hold still."

Her lips twitched, and she did it again, sliding forward until her core met his. "Why?"

His erection immediately rubbed against her clit. "That's why." His voice was hoarse.

She ran her fingers through his thick hair and bit back a moan at the pure heat now between her thighs. His energy, all Nick Veis, surrounded her in comfort and security.

His dark eyes promised everything she could ever want. Her heart thumped. For so long, she'd been afraid of getting hurt again. Afraid to take a chance.

Everything in the demon holding her promised he'd catch her if she leaped. She settled into that reality and smiled at the only man she'd every truly love. "You're as prepared as you're going to get for my testimony. Stop looking through documents you've already memorized." Her thighs tightened against his.

"We have fifteen minutes to kill, then. What should we do?" He caressed her arms, one hand sliding to her nape to knead it.

Delicious tingles cascaded across her neck and down her spine. "I'll have to be inventive." Her body ached for him, so she reached down and released his zipper before opening his pants as much as she could. His cock, fully erect, jumped against her palm. "Very nice, Veis."

"I aim to please." He reached under her skirt with his free hand and snapped her panties in two. "I'll buy you new ones."

Her breath panted out, and she got up on her knees, allowing him to position himself right where she wanted him. Grabbing his shoulders, she lowered herself slowly, inch by inch, her body stretching decadently around him. Finally, her butt hit his thighs.

He filled her completely, and she had to breathe out for a moment. Her head fell forward to the crook of his neck, so she could just feel.

His arms vibrated. "Simone?"

"Hmmm." Her body rioted with the need to move, but she felt so damn good in this moment, she wanted to hold on to it forever. "Nicholai."

He snapped. She sensed his loss of control a second before the hand at her nape yanked her back, and his mouth crashed down on hers. He kissed her hard, his tongue taking charge, his lips molding against hers.

One hand grabbed her ass, and he stood, laying her on the table. The cool maple soothed her heated back.

Papers and pens scattered in every direction. He leaned over her, his mouth still working hers, and started to pound.

The friction fired sparks through her, and she shut her eyes, overcome. He hammered into her so hard, for a moment she thought she'd go over the other side of the table, but his hands at her nape and rear kept her in place for him. For whatever he wanted to do. He gripped her hard enough to bruise, and he angled her to the side, pounding so forcefully inside her the sound of flesh against flesh was all she could hear.

"More," she moaned, her nails digging into his chest.

He obliged her, completely letting go. Each pound battered her clit, and she held her breath, crying out when she went over. Waves upon waves of raw pleasure cascaded through her, taking her breath, taking her will to do anything but ride them out. She came down with a sigh, her eyelids opening.

Nick leaned over her, his gaze beyond intense, power embodied in his form. He stopped moving, still fully erect and embedded in her. His hand lifted to reveal his family crest with the intricate *V* in the middle, across his right palm. "Where do you want it?" he growled.

Her eyes widened. "We, ah . . ."

"Where, Simone?" All male, all intent, there was absolutely no denying him, and she knew it. The uncertainty of the future was no reason not to grab all the good she could get.

She breathed out, having imagined his marking on her skin more times than she could count through the years. Her heart pounded so hard her breath caught. God, she wanted this. She really wanted to wear his mark . . . wanted to make him hers forever. "Right shoulder blade."

He withdrew, yanked her up, and turned her around. "Down."

She leaned over the table, her cheek to the smooth mahogany, her heart thundering.

He grasped her hip and powered inside her with one strong stroke, lifting her up on her toes. She gasped and tried to rear up, but a hand at her nape stopped her. He tightened his hold. *A warning.*

She settled back down, her mind spinning. He pulled out and shoved back in, setting up a hard rhythm that kept her on her toes. She closed her eyes again as electricity uncoiled inside her. He slammed against her G-spot, and her internal walls clenched down, sending her into an orgasm so intense she stopped breathing. Fangs sliced into her left shoulder while a piercing hot pain burned into her right.

She cried out and reached back with her right hand to grab any part of him, finding the side of his butt. Her nails dug in, and fire roared between their flesh.

His forearm moved in front of her vision and she latched on, her teeth digging in to taste blood.

He growled close to her ear, his fangs sliced deeper to connect, and he stopped moving, jerking hard inside her.

Tears spiked the back of her eyes. Pain pounded at several points of her body, and she couldn't get a mental handle on any of them. The fangs retracted, and she bit back a sob. A lazy swipe of his tongue sealed the wound, and a healing balm covered the pain. She released him and slapped her hands against the table, glancing over her shoulder to see the edge of the marking. Man, she needed a mirror to see the whole thing. If it looked anything like his palm had, it would be beautiful.

Nick withdrew and gently put her skirt back to rights before helping her up and turning her into his embrace. "Are you all right?"

Tears clouded her eyes. "Yes." It had been much more intense than she'd thought. What in the hell had they been thinking, mating each other with everything around them so unsettled?

"I meant to do that tonight in a bed with candles and flowers," he murmured against her hair, one hand sweeping down her back.

She allowed his heat to surround her with protection and security. "This is more us. I mean, in the middle of a trial for my life. You know." But had it been a mistake? God. They hadn't even really discussed mating, and now it was a done deal.

He chuckled and pulled her away, looking down into her face. "I vow to protect you with all that I have and all that I'll ever be. You and the babe."

She smiled and tried to will the tears away.

He frowned.

"What?" she asked.

"I'm not sure." He glanced down his side and then stilled. "Jesus, Simone."

"What?" She angled over and followed his gaze to see a perfect Celtic knot, her marking, askew on his buttock.

He coughed. "You marked my ass. And it's not even straight."

Humor bubbled up through her, and she threw back her head,

laughing long and hard. She'd marked his butt. "Oh, Nick. I got carried away."

He grinned. "I guess that's good."

With his powers, he could probably heal the burn until it was barely noticeable, but he didn't move to change a thing. His obvious acceptance of her crazy marking warmed her throughout. "I'll protect you and the babe, too." Her vow was just as heartfelt as his, and just as powerful. They were talking protection and not love, but at the moment, her emotions were so jumbled she couldn't find the right words.

Maybe he couldn't, either.

Or maybe in Nick's world, the offer of protection meant more to a warrior than the offer of love. She opened her mouth to say something, anything, about emotion, but a sharp rap sounded on the door. "One minute," a guard called.

Nick jumped back and jerked up his pants, quickly straightening his shirt.

Simone pushed back her hair, having no doubt it'd be obvious what they'd been doing to prepare for her testimony. Her mind clouded, and she couldn't grasp just one thought. She had just mated Nicholai Veis, one of the most powerful demons on the planet.

He grasped her hands and captured her gaze. "Several deep breaths. On the stand, I want you to be all you. Confident, honest, and strong. Don't let them see one iota of concern, emotion, or doubt."

She nodded, grabbing on to his directions like a lifeline. "I can do it."

"I know. And Simone, if I tell you to run, you obey me without question." He leaned in, his gaze so intent she could feel it in her abdomen. "Promise me."

"Nick, I—"

His hold tightened. "Promise me."

"What have you done?" she breathed, trying to back away.

He held her in place and ran a knuckle down the side of her cheek. The animal in him, the one he kept so carefully caged, stretched beneath the surface. She could *see* him. "What did you think would happen when you became pregnant with my child?" he asked, his voice even deeper than usual.

A tremble shook her spine. "Nothing. I mean, I figured we'd go on and work things out."

"We will." His hold gentled, but his gaze sharpened. "Your safety and protection are mine, Simone, as are you."

What the hell? "Listen—"

"No." He leaned down and kissed her. Hard. "No negotiation on that one, little bunny."

The door opened, and two guards waited.

Nick turned to her. "Let's do this."

Chapter 32

Nick tried to readjust his pants and will down his hard-on as they wound through the tunnels. What the holy fuck had he just done? He'd mated Simone in a conference room right before she gave the most important testimony of her life. Oh, he'd had every intention of mating her that night as they waited until the Council announced a decision the following morning, but he'd wanted to romance her a little. It was crucial that she carry his mark before the sentencing, but he could've been gentle when mating her.

Instead he'd bent her over a table and fucked her hard with the guards no doubt hearing every sound.

Not that he gave a shit about the guards, but even so, he would've liked to have charmed her.

They entered the courtroom, where more guards had been stationed around the perimeter. Peter watched Simone walk in, his gaze darkening. Nick kept his expression bland, but it was fairly obvious how he and Simone had spent their lunchtime.

Simone swept to the witness stand and took a seat. "Let's begin," she ordered the prosecutor.

Nick hid a smile and took his seat.

Colman stood. "Ms. Brightston, please tell the Council how long you've known you were part shifter."

"For about a century," she said evenly.

The Council kept it together, but Nick could see evidence of surprise.

"The Nine thought they'd exterminated multis, but it turns out the enemy were dragons. The proof offered by Phillipe Sadler confirms the existence of dragons, as unbelievable as it seems." Colman clasped his hands behind his back. "For one hundred years you've known you're an enemy the Coven Nine had thought was exterminated?"

"No. I thought I was part bear shifter," Simone said, her hands resting easily in her lap. "I just found out two days ago that dragons even existed, much less that I have dragon genes." She turned toward the Council.

Colman cleared his throat. "Surely you must have had an inkling."

Her eyebrows rose. "That dragons actually existed? Ah, no. I had no clue." The ring of truth definitely echoed in her tone. "Frankly, I don't think they're enemies of the Coven Nine or the witch nation. They've been hiding out to avoid persecution."

"Where is your father now?" Colman asked.

"Dead," Simone said.

"Did you kill him?" Colman shot back.

"No, and it's irrelevant who killed him, so we're moving on." Simone shifted her weight in the seat.

Peter sat forward. "We'll determine relevance. Who killed him?"

Her jaw firmed, and she met the Council's stares.

"I killed him," Nick spoke up. "Walked in, saw the bastard trying to kidnap Simone, and took him out." She glared at him, and he shrugged. If she thought to piss off the Council by protecting him, she was sorely mistaken. "I don't care who knows it."

Peter narrowed his gaze, probably scenting for truth. "All right. Did Vivienne Northcutt know about dragons? About your father? Since she procreated with him, surely she knew he was a dragon."

Simone laughed outright at that. "That's your plan, Peter? To take my mother's place on the Coven Nine by using rumor and dragons?" Simone shook her head, real mirth in her dark eyes. "Oh, my friend. You do *not* want to take her on."

Peter's ears turned red. "Continue, Colman."

Nick gave her a look. She did not need to tick off Peter right at the moment.

Colman resumed questioning, going through the videos as well as all of the banking statements. Simone kept to the truth, admitted she wasn't sure about a few, and vehemently denied signing several. Colman was good, but Simone was spectacular.

Nick clarified a couple of questions when he got the chance, and then he released her. She stood, all grace, and made her way to his side, right where she belonged.

Colman then gave a passionate closing about betrayal, country, and of course, dragons. Nick tuned him out halfway through his speech, his brain putting all of the facts into order. There was a lot of evidence against Simone, but she'd done a good job on the stand. The verdict would boil down to what the meager three-person Council wanted to do with her politically.

Finally, he stood. "You know Simone did not intentionally do any of these things. You know it." He walked around the table to be closer to them. "This was a setup, albeit a good one. The man providing evidence admitted to a vendetta against all of you, and especially against Simone. How can you trust one iota of what he offered to the prosecutor?"

Nessa nodded as he spoke.

Good. One down for sure.

"In addition, dragons are now out. They're not your enemies, and their connection to Simone is a good one. You do want a liaison there, right?"

Peter's face settled into thoughtful lines.

"Finally, and please listen closely. Even if you wrongly, and I mean very wrongly, decide to convict Simone Brightston, you can't sentence her to death."

"Why not?" Peter asked.

"I am Nicholai Veis, second in command of the demon nation, and Simone Brightston is my mate and the mother of my unborn child." He pierced each one of them with a hard look. "The demon nation will not accept one of our own being killed by you. Such an action would be tantamount to war." Yeah, he had no problem making it clear that the easy choice for them was to find Simone not guilty.

Peter's mouth dropped open. "You *mated* during lunch?"

Nick didn't turn to see Simone's expression. "The timing is hardly relevant. But it is done, so heed my warning."

"War," Sal said grimly.

"War between our nations." Nick flashed his teeth. "In addition, there is nowhere any of you can hide if you put a bounty on my mate's head. I will find you, and I will make you wish you'd never heard my name."

Peter banged the gavel. "You will not threaten the Council."

Nick lifted a shoulder. "The defense rests."

Simone swept into the guest quarters at the rear end of Coven Nine headquarters, her temper simmering. The studio apartment was sparse with bed, table, and couch . . . and nothing good to throw. "What in the holy hell were you doing today?" She whirled on Nick, who'd walked calmly in behind her. "You confess to killing my father, inform everyone that we've mated, and then threaten the three sitting council members?" She set her hands firmly on her hips.

Nick shut the door. "Pretty much."

She shook her head, and her hair tumbled out of its knot. "Do you really think that was smart?"

"Yes."

Her breath heated enough to burn her lungs. "Did you mate me because of the trial?" A hollow feeling emptied her stomach. "To win, I mean? To make the claim that the demon nation would avenge me?"

His gaze softened. "I mated you because I've loved you from the first time I set eyes on you. A century ago."

She blinked and drew up short. "Wh-what?"

He gestured, palms up. "Many soldiers who've fought in wars, who've killed like I have, wonder if they have a heart. I've never wondered."

"Why not?" she whispered.

"Because you're in it and always have been." He reached her in three long strides. "My heart is yours and always will be. Everything I've done in this life from the good to the truly terrible has been to make the world a better place for you and any children we may have." His hand flattened over her abdomen. "Everything I am or will ever be belongs solely to you."

Tears filled her eyes. "Nicholai."

His chin lifted. "No woman has ever been loved more than you are right now, Simone. It's impossible. I promise you."

Geez. When he brought out the good words, he did so with a vengeance. "I—"

"Let me finish." He kissed her forehead. "I'm difficult, I'm sure. Possessive, protective, and downright bossy."

"You're not that bad." She reached up and ran her palm across the stubble on his chin.

"Good, because I'm not going to change."

She paused. "Huh."

"You stay safe, period. Whatever I have to do to ensure your safety, I'll do it." He leaned in, his face an inch above hers. "Fight me all you want, but I don't recommend it."

Fire cracked on her hand, and he jerked his face away from the burn.

"There's more where that came from," she said, keeping his gaze. "We'll protect this baby together, and I love you, too. Always have and always will."

He smiled then, his face taking on a stark, masculine beauty. "We're going to have some fun through this life."

Aye, if they didn't kill each other.

He kissed her, going deep, using gentleness in a way that stole her breath. Before she knew it, she was undressed and on the bed. He stood over her, so large and powerful, and definitely hers. He removed his clothing, piece by piece, and her mouth was watering by the time he stretched over her, all hard male.

She ran her fingers through his thick hair and traced his eyebrows, nose, and mouth. "I hope she looks like you."

"He." Nick leaned down and nibbled on her mouth. "The first one has to be a boy, just to help me with the next one, which will probably be a girl."

"Maybe you'll need help with the boy," she whispered against his lips.

He grinned, his mouth tickling hers. "I have no doubt your children, boys and girls, will be absolute hellions."

God, she hoped so.

He kissed down her neck and across her collarbone to her breasts, licking and sucking until she was a writhing mass of need beneath him. Nick's tenderness brought on a slow burn that was no less intense than the heated desire they'd shared in the conference room. But somehow, the sweetness went right beyond her body to her heart.

When he slowly slid inside her, it truly felt like she was home. Finally.

He moved out and then back in, setting up a rhythm he matched with his teeth and tongue on her breasts and up her neck as he kissed her deeply. The first orgasm rolled through her, taking her worry. The second caught her unaware, and she sighed his name. The third sparked her on fire, and she held on so hard she burned his shoulder.

They made love again near dawn, laughing and loving like they had the first time, so many years ago. Finally, the sun came up.

Together, they showered and then got dressed. For her sentencing, Simone wore a crimson red skirt with flowing top and her hair up. She slipped her hand into Nick's as the guards arrived to lead them through the labyrinth of tunnels to the Chambers. At least eight guards stood at attention around the inside perimeter of the room.

Simone and Nick sat, their fingers entwined, and waited until Peter, Sal, and Nessa took their seats, no expression on their faces.

Colman had dressed in a pin-striped gray suit for the occasion and looked like he needed a vacation.

Peter reached for the gavel.

Simone and Nick stood.

Peter cleared his throat. "We looked at all the facts and the law in addition to the evidence. We took into account all matters, and by a vote of two to one, we hereby find Simone Brightston guilty of treason and murder . . . and thus sentence her to death."

The gavel crashed down.

Chapter 33

Simone's knees gave out, and she fell onto her chair. Her mouth dropped open, and an odd buzzing sound echoed throughout her head.

"Guards, please take Simone to a cell to await punishment," Peter said.

Nessa stood and vehemently shook her head. "I again object to this sentence."

"So noted," Peter said. "It is being posted to our top officials right now, and death will be carried out within the hour." His gavel crashed again.

Simone coughed and looked up at Nick. Fury darkened his face, yet he hadn't moved an inch.

She hadn't thought, not once, that she could die. At least eight guards stood armed and ready to take her down if she fought them, and one hour wasn't long enough to plan anything. Taking a deep breath, she slowly stood to face the Council. "I request an appeal."

"Denied." No give showed on Peter's face.

Simone gave him a look and turned, stretching up on her toes to whisper into Nick's ear. "The cells aren't as secure as this room. Five minutes after I'm in, I have a team coming in through a weak spot. I'll meet you in Seattle in exactly one week." From day one of the investigation, she'd set the plan in motion just in case, although she never thought she'd need to use it. She pressed a kiss to his cheek and dropped back down.

He looked down at her. "I really wish you'd shared that information with me earlier."

She blinked. "I know. You've been worried. Sorry," she whispered.

He winced. "That's not why."

"Oh?" She frowned.

The side wall, the one without the veil, blew completely open. Smoke and debris rained across the chamber.

"That's why," Nick muttered, pivoting to put Simone behind him.

She coughed out dust and tried to peer through the haze to the opening. Zane Kyllwood marched inside, fully armed, a powerful squad of demon soldiers behind him.

Peter stood and pounded his gavel. "This is unthinkable," he yelled.

Zane cocked a large gun of a type Simone had never seen before. "Simone Brightston is a member of the demon nation, and she will come with us now."

Simone looked up at Nick.

He lifted a shoulder, eyeing the Irish guards who now had guns trained on Zane and his men. "I called Zane," Nick said unnecessarily.

"No shit," Simone said. "Everyone please take a moment," she called out. If there was a way to reduce bloodshed, she had to do it. "We can work this out."

A rumble echoed on the side of the veil. Slowly, Simone turned. The world seemed to hold its breath.

The cloaked door crashed open, and Kellach Dunne, Daire Dunne, Moira Dunne-Kayrs, and then Connlan Kayrs marched inside, guns out, battle gear covering them boots to hats.

"Oh God," Simone whispered. A rock fell from the ceiling, and she jumped out of the way as it smashed into the table.

Peter's face turned a motley red. "Why are three of our four Enforcers and a vampire holding guns in this chamber?" he bellowed.

Daire stepped forward, his green eyes sizzling and threat all but pouring off of him. "By the order of the Enforcers of the Coven Nine, we disagree with this travesty and will protect Simone Brightston with our last breath. She will come with us now."

The Coven Guards swung their weapons, half facing Zane and his crew, and the other half facing the Enforcers.

Peter lifted his head. "You cannot do this. I'm ordering you to take her into custody and defend the Nine from the demons, who have just declared war."

"No." Moira stepped up, her red hair curling wildly around her shoulders.

Peter's lip twisted.

Sal stood next to him.

"Everyone stand down," Nessa said. "Let's talk."

"No." Peter stood even taller. "Last chance. Enforcers, do your job."

Kellach shook his head. "This is wrong, and you all know it. Simone, come here. We have an escape route prepared."

Peter banged the gavel. "You've given me no choice. By executive order, Kellach, Daire, and Moira Dunne, you are hereby removed from the Coven Nine and your positions as Enforcers." His gavel rapped furiously on the stone table, even as smaller rocks fell from the ceiling. "We consider Connlan Kayrs's presence a declaration of war by the vampire nation if not the entire Realm."

Simone gasped. "Wait a minute—" She tried to stem the disaster. One woman wasn't worth an all-out war. Her plan had been so much neater—she really should've shared it with everyone. But she truly hadn't thought she'd need the plan. "Let's take a moment before anybody gets hurt." The guards settled their stances, preparing to attack.

The earth shook.

"What the hell?" Nick looked around and leaped to Simone's side.

Peter glanced up, his jaw working. "In addition, only Council members have the codes to get weapons through the veil. An investigation will instantly be launched into Vivienne Northcutt, Brenna Dunne-Kayrs, and Brigit Dunne to see who relinquished the codes. Until that is concluded, they are also relieved of duty."

Simone's mouth dropped open, and temper finally exploded within her. "You bastard." So Peter's political agenda was finally out in the open. He'd just cleared the Council of pretty much everybody.

He smiled, his canines glinting.

The ceiling shimmered.

Earthquake? No way.

The world rocked, and explosives ripped through the ceiling, dropping rocks. A second later, a squad of five men jumped from above and down into the chamber between Simone and the Council.

She frowned, trying to see through the debris. "Bear?"

Her brother turned, relief sliding across his rugged features. "You're not dead."

"Not yet," she said slowly, looking at the man to his left. "Flynn."
Her other brother smiled. "Hi."

The men behind them were armed and more than prepared for battle, based on the sheer number of weapons they carried. They'd gone through layers and layers of floors and rock to reach the chamber, and it was damn impressive they'd made it. Even with disaster surrounding her, Simone's heart warmed.

Bear turned to face the Council. "Hi, assholes. We're here on behalf of the dragon and the shifter nations . . . let our sister go or you're not gonna see another sunrise."

Nick's entire body vibrated, no doubt from the myriad of threats in every direction. "It appears you have a lot of family and friends, little bunny."

She stilled and looked around. Three different groups had infiltrated the mystical chambers in order to free her. Her entire body settled, and she placed a protective hand over her belly. Her little one would be well loved and protected in this life. "How can we get out of here without anybody being harmed?"

Nick slowly shook his head. "Peter won't back down."

Neither could the guards. Running footsteps came from every direction. "More guards are coming," she hissed.

Zane Kyllwood cleared his throat. "What's it going to be here?"

"Attack," Peter bellowed.

Nick instantly moved, grabbing Simone and running full-bore toward Zane.

She screamed and clutched his chest. "Put me down."

The firefight erupted behind them with a snap of gunfire. Bullets whizzed by them.

Nick took a gun from Zane, leaped behind the demons, and kept going.

"Nick, we can fight." Simone ducked as shards of rock continued to fall from the ceiling.

"Not with the baby," Nick yelled back, zigzagging through another tunnel, which had been marked with fluorescent green paint. "Thank God Zane remembered the paint," he muttered.

Nausea rose up Simone's throat from all the running and jostling. She gasped in dusty air, trying to calm her stomach. Her head swam. Morning sickness sucked.

Nick took a sharp left, and the world spun. She coughed.

"You okay?" he asked, his speed increasing.

"I may throw up." She settled her face into his neck, smelling salt, wild forest, and man. Every inch of her wanted to go back and fight, but Nick was right. The baby had to be protected at all costs. "We need to work on our communication skills," she muttered against his skin.

"I should've told you, but I didn't want you to worry." Nick ran down a narrow tunnel, his boots splashing water up to her legs. "Sorry."

She swallowed several times, her eyelids remaining closed. The air became lighter. Lifting her head, she gasped at the gaping hole in the exterior wall of the building, leading to a nearly empty parking area. "The demons weren't messing around."

"No." Nick ran through the opening to a drizzly Irish day, where a quiet street led away from the green rolling hills. A car waiting by the curb exploded, and fire flashed out. "Shit. That was our transport." Guards shouted and came around the far corner. At least six of them. "Hell." He dropped Simone to her feet and turned, gun already firing.

A car careened around the corner, fishtailing and then flipping around. The passenger side door opened. "Get in," Vivienne North-cutt ordered from the driver's seat, her knuckles white on the steering wheel.

Simone gaped. "Mother?"

"Now, Simone. More guards are on the way." Vivienne shoved a gun onto the dash. Dressed in pressed jeans and a flannel shirt, she couldn't look less like the ruler of the witch nation. "Now. Get in."

Two guards plowed into Nick, knocking him back inside the building. He half-rose, throwing punches. "Go, Simone. Protect the baby." A guard took him down to be immediately put into a headlock. Nick kicked the other guard in the face, and blood sprayed. Zane came into view and tackled two more of the guards.

"Now, Simone," Vivienne ordered.

Dizziness swamped Simone. She couldn't fight when she needed to throw up. Nick and Zane could handle themselves, and she had a baby to protect.

"Go, now!" Nick bellowed, punching through a guard's neck.

Simone leaped into the car, grabbed the gun, and shut the door. "Go, Mom."

Vivienne punched the gas, and the small compact leaped forward and onto the street. She dovetailed and swung around, increasing the speed until buildings flew by outside. "You all right?"

Simone tried to breathe evenly, her hand on her stomach. "Yes. Just a little nauseated."

Viv nodded. "I was sick for nine whole months with you."

"You know about the babe?" Simone asked.

"Yes. Your testimony and Nicholai's closing went live to the witch nation yesterday." Viv's pale lips trembled. "Congratulations."

"Thank you." Simone frowned and studied her mother. "You should be in bed."

Viv's lips twitched. "I couldn't exactly stay in bed when my only daughter was facing a death sentence, now, could I?"

"No." But Viv had just sacrificed her position on the Council. "What have you done? The Council is everything to you."

Viv turned, her dark eyes soft. "No. It's a job, and one I was good at. You're everything to me. Don't make the mistakes I did and let ambition warm you at night. You can have love as well as power." She turned back to the street ahead of them. "I'm going ta be a grandmother." She chuckled.

"I love you, too." Simone kept watch out the window in case she needed to shoot, when all she wanted to do was lay back her head and calm her stomach. "But you've just committed treason." God, how could she help her mother?

"Eh. It's only treason if they catch you and prove it." Viv turned onto a narrow road heading into the hills. "I have enough political clout and blackmail materials on everybody on the Council that I should be all right. Of course, I fully intend to retake my position on the Nine as soon as we get this mess with you straightened out."

There was the mother she knew and loved. "Thank goodness." Although Viv would make an excellent grandmother, the idea of her hanging around and directing everything added to Simone's nausea. "We will figure this all out."

"Of course we will." Viv cleared her throat. "Do you, ah, ever wish I had been more maternal? You know? With all the mushy stuff?"

Simone laughed. "No. I always felt loved and like I was a priority.

And you gave me a lot to aspire to, seeing how hard you worked and how successful you are." She bit her lip. "But you did try to cook many times, remember?"

Viv winced. "I never quite got it right."

No. She was a terrible cook. "You'll make an excellent grandmother." It was true.

"Yes. Yes, I shall." Viv slowed down to cross a narrow bridge.

"Did you, ah, give the codes to the veil to the Enforcers?"

"Nope, and if I did, I would not tell you and make you an accomplice after the fact." She drove the car over several warped pieces of wood, causing them both to jump in their seats. "So don't ask again."

That's what Simone had thought.

Vivienne looked in the rearview mirror. "We have company."

Simone jerked and looked around to see a red pickup truck zooming closer. "Punch it."

"Shit." Vivienne slammed on the brakes. "I had to make the arrangements so quickly——but I used secure lines. How did they find us? Damn it. I should've known we'd have trouble."

Simone turned and clutched the dash to keep from hitting it. "What——" A black SUV had driven across the other end of the bridge, blocking it. "We're trapped."

"Is it the Guard?" Vivienne clutched the steering wheel and leaned forward to stare through the rain.

"I don't think so." The red truck behind them wasn't Guard issue, and the SUV in front of them had several dents along the side. The Guard wouldn't allow a vehicle to remain in such disrepair.

Three men stepped out of the SUV, all armed with laser assault rifles.

"Bloody hell," Vivienne said, looking through the rearview mirror.

Simone tightened her hold on the gun and glanced in the side mirror. Four more men, similarly armed, set up behind them. "Who——" Her breath caught as Phillipe Sadler stretched his legs out of the SUV in front of them. "Oh." Her arms trembled as she tried to figure a way out. "We're outgunned, and if Phillipe is a witch with powers, I'd assume several of his men are, as well." She stuck the gun in her right boot.

Vivienne kicked open her door. "In the name of the Coven Nine, back away."

Phillipe smiled and lifted a green laser gun. "Simone? Get out of the car, or I'll plug your mother so full of holes she'll never be complete again. Although she did make it ridiculously easy to find you. By the way, I have a world-class hacker on my payroll now. Everything from phones to computers to satellites."

Simone's hand trembled, but she shoved open the door. "You're making the biggest mistake of your life, Phillipe." She wasn't talking about Nick, either. If Phillipe thought to put Simone's child in harm's way, she'd burn him inside out the first second she got. "Take the reprieve and run."

Rain dotted his blond hair and slid down his face. "Get in the SUV, or we kill your mother."

Simone slammed the door shut. "You're garna regret this." She lifted a hand when Vivienne tried to protest. "It's our only chance. Get back in the car."

Vivienne, her face pale, looked around and then nodded. "I'll come find you," she whispered.

"Bring backup," Simone whispered back. Then she walked casually through the rain, stopping when halfway to Phillipe. "Tell the red truck to move."

Phillipe sighed and gestured. The sound of a truck moving filled the day.

Simone turned and motioned for her mother to get the hell out of there. Vivienne frowned but gunned the car in reverse, swinging 'round when she was clear of the bridge. Seconds later, she sped out of sight.

Simone turned back around to face Phillipe's arrogant smile. She'd saved her mother. Now she had to save her child.

Chapter 34

Nick paced the wide windows of the demon safe house, his body aching from the fight, his head pounding. "Where the hell is Vivienne?" he growled for the tenth time, his gaze on Dublin Bay across the road.

Sprawled in one of the two leather chairs, Zane shrugged and shoved several bullets out of his right arm. "Daire said he'd call with an update as soon as he knew anything."

After the battle, the various species had all retreated to safe houses they controlled, and he was pretty sure the dragons had headed out to sea. If Nick called Bear and Flynn, they'd return, but for now, he didn't have anything to tell them. Although once they'd declared they'd protect Simone and her child with their lives, he felt a lot more secure having them as relatives. "It makes sense that Vivienne took her daughter somewhere underground that not even the Enforcers know about, right?"

"Sure." Zane kept his voice level, but Nick had known his friend a long time. Zane was doubting her safety, as well.

"Shit." Nick glanced around the utilitarian living room. Two chairs, one sofa, and a wall of communications equipment in front of a table littered with computers. "If the Guard had them, we'd know." Simone had to be underground just waiting to get word to him. That had to be it.

Zane rubbed his arm. "You've mated, right? Can you reach her telepathically?"

Nick tried to reach out mentally again, but nothing. Not even static. "Simone has stronger mental shields than anybody I've ever met. She'd probably have to concentrate to let me in." He hated failing, but breaching her mind was nearly impossible. They'd only been mated for a matter of hours. "The computer guys haven't spotted anything via satellite?"

"Not yet," Zane returned. "We had to hack into a Soviet spy satellite and haven't turned up anything." A darkening bruise swelled under his right eye. "If you want, I can call the squad back."

"No." Getting their men out of Dublin had been important for their survival, considering several Guard soldiers were no longer standing at the end of the skirmish. "You need to get home to headquarters, as well." Nick tried to look stoic and remember the importance of protecting Zane and the demon nation, but only Simone and their child filled his mind. "Now."

Zane smiled around a fat lip. "Would you leave me if my mate or my child was in trouble?"

"Of course not." Nick gingerly poked at a burning bruise on his chin. "But you're the leader of the entire demon nation and can't put yourself in danger just for a friend."

"Brother." Zane held up his perfectly smooth palm. "Remember?"

"We're not Boy Scouts in junior high, Kyllwood." Nick glared out at the storm building outside. "You have to worry about the nation and not me."

Zane stretched his neck, his green eyes flashing. "Yet here I am." He stood and tugged a knife out of his left boot. "We can argue as long as you want, but I'm not going anywhere until I see that your mate and child are perfectly safe. In fact, if you don't mind, I think you should all come to headquarters until we get this Coven Nine mess figured out."

Nick nodded. "That's the plan." Simone and the babe would be safe at demon headquarters in the States, and that was all that mattered right now. "I need to arrange transport out of Dublin."

"Already taken care of. I have a plane ready to go the second we arrive at the airport," Zane said.

"Thank you." Nick turned and studied his best friend. "You know you have to denounce me and what happened today, even if you do grant us sanctuary at headquarters."

Zane snorted. "Dude. I was with you, remember?" He flexed his right hand, visibly mending two broken fingers. "How can I denounce it when I was there?"

Nick shook his head. "It doesn't matter if you were there. Publicly, you have to condemn my actions. The three remaining members of the Coven Nine will accept your condemnation with some very strong words of warning, thus saving face and avoiding war." He scrubbed his bruised hands through his hair. "We need to avoid war."

Then, true to his fucking nature, Zane Kyllwood lifted a shoulder. "If the bastards want a war, they've got one."

Jesus. "Why do I always have to be the damn voice of reason?" Nick shouted.

"You like reason," Zane said calmly.

Right now it felt like reason had fled, and he needed to hit something very hard. "Where is she, Zane?" Something was wrong. He just knew it.

"We'll find her." Zane moved over to the computer console and started to type. "I have people ripping through Vivienne's financials right now for records of any safe houses or other property."

The far right computer *ding*ed.

Nick's breath caught. He hustled over and brought up his secured email. Within seconds, Moira Kayrs-Dunne appeared.

"Moira," Nick said. "News?"

Her pale skin was almost translucent across the screen. "We have Vivienne and are getting her to a safe location. Simone was taken by Phillipe Sadler and a bunch of soldiers." Concern sizzled in her green eyes. "I'm tracking down everything I can find out about him, and we'll be ready to go in the second we find her."

Nick eyed the woman Simone loved like a sister. "You have two babes at home, Moira. Send me the location the second you have it. Zane and I will bring her back."

Moira lowered her chin. "She's family, Nicholai. When we find her, we all go in." The screen went black.

"I've always liked that witch," Zane said, his fingers tapping quickly over a keyboard. "I'll know everything there is to know about Sadler within a few moments."

Nick tried to keep his anger in check. "Why did Phillipe take her? I mean, if he wants revenge, he could've just killed her."

Zane nodded. "My guess? He wants intel on the Nine for the last few decades since his mother was removed. That means we have time to find her."

"Right. So you, the three Enforcers, four if Adam makes it back, and me." Nick rapidly calculated the odds. "This is going to be bloody."

"She'll be all right," Zane said. "We'll get her back."

They had to get her back. Nick rubbed his chest, which suddenly felt hollow. "When I find Phillipe, I'm ripping out his heart."

Simone sat on the folding chair with metal cuffs securing her hands behind her back. They'd confiscated the gun from her boot, so she was currently without weapons or the ability to throw fire. Oh, she could create fire, but setting the small shack aflame would just end with her burned to a crisp. There had been a hood over her head for most of the drive, so she had no idea where they'd taken her. All she knew was that the place smelled like fuel, and the outside was silent.

Phillipe had carried her into the empty shack before yanking off the hood.

The walls, ceiling, and floors were made up of exposed beams of wood. It was some type of storage area, but everything except her one chair had been removed. If she had to guess, they were at one of the small airports outside of Dublin that catered only to private planes or helicopters.

Whistling eerily, the wind competed with the sound of pounding rain. In the distance, thunder clashed across the sky. Night had fallen, and the air had cooled with the storm.

She calmed herself, trying to send reassuring feelings through her body to the baby. Fear couldn't be good for the little guy or girl, so she took several deep breaths and kept her thoughts gentle. For now.

The door burst open, and Phillipe dodged inside, dripping from rain. He had to fight the wind to get the door closed, and once he had, he turned to face her. "The pilot is late, but we'll be in the air very soon."

"Where are we going?" Simone asked as if discussing the weather.

His lip twisted. "You're a mellow one, now, aren't you?"

"For the moment." She allowed power to glow in her eyes. "The second I decide not to be mellow, believe me, you'll know."

He smiled then. "Oh, I can't wait to see you try. I'm going to burn you in ways you can't even imagine."

"Shouldn't you be rubbing your hands together or twirling an imaginary mustache?" she asked.

"Funny. You won't be so smart after a couple of hours with me."

"I doubt anybody would be," Simone said sweetly.

His nostrils flared. "My mother would like a turn with you first."

Now Simone smiled full-on. "I would truly enjoy that, as well, but since Moira took her powers, it might be a short match." She pretended to think about the situation. For now, she needed more information. "Will your twin brother be there, as well?"

Sorrow and anger darkened his eyes. "My brother was killed by a business partner."

She frowned. That was intel she hadn't had. "Maybe you should get out of such a dangerous business."

"I don't think so."

"Is this just about revenge for your mother?" Simone asked. "The manufacture and distribution of Apollo is a deadly game."

He tucked the gun at the back of his waist. "Deadly for humans and enemy witches, you mean. There's a lot of money to be made from the humans, and once we control the Coven Nine, we'll continue to rake that money into the family coffers."

Money and power. "Your motivations bore me." Simone listened to the storm pummeling the world outside. "Are you the one who sent witch soldiers to attack us at the cemetery?"

"Aye."

"It seems like you were really targeting Bear, considering your soldiers aimed for his head and barely shot at the rest of us until we ran." Simone tried to free her wrists without success.

Phillipe nodded. "Yes. Bear has been reluctant to help us out in Seattle, and we thought if he was killed, we could then get the grizzlies to distribute Apollo for us."

"You missed Bear, and you have to know, I'm not planning on helping you."

"That's where you're wrong. You'll give us all current intel from the Coven Nine. Passwords, land holdings, enemy files." He shrugged. "That's pretty much all we want."

That didn't make sense. "So I give you the information, and you kill me? I don't think so."

"No. You give the information, and then I trade you to the demon nation for a shitload of money and land holdings." Phillipe smiled. "Win-win all around."

"The demon nation won't give anything up for me." She kept his gaze. "Sorry."

"Sure, they will. You went ahead and mated Nicholai Veis for us, and everybody knows Zane Kyllwood would lay down his very life for Veis. Giving up riches won't mean anything to Kyllwood." Phillipe grasped a knife from his back pocket and twirled it around. "I appreciate your ensuring this part of our plan with the mating."

Simone kept an eye on the knife just in case he wanted to plunge it into her neck. While he seemed logical, an odd gleam showed in his eyes. "You expect me to believe you'll just turn me over to the demon nation?" What was she missing?

"Well, after my mother and I strip you of all powers." He smiled and moved closer, the knife glinting in the soft light. "Your cousin ripped my mother's powers away, and I plan to do the same to you. Then you can go back to your demon as weak as any other human." He leaned in, his breath brushing her ear. "Payback is a bitch."

Simone shot her knee up, solidly connecting with his groin.

He gave a muffled *oof* and stumbled back, still bent at the waist. "You . . . bitch," he breathed, his eyes bugging out, tears filling them. "You fucking bitch."

She smiled to mask the raw terror coursing through her. While she might be able to successfully fight Phillipe and Grace Sadler, if they had any other allies joining in, she'd lose her powers. A fight like that would certainly harm the baby if not kill him. His chances of survival would diminish even with one witch attack, much less several. "How did you find out about dragons, anyway?" she asked, already having suspicions.

He sighed. "Research and more research. My mother and yours were good friends at one point, and my mother knew your father wasn't normal. It was matter of tugging threads from that point."

"This is your last chance to let me go," she said, infusing her voice with power.

He slowly straightened up, pain etched into his face. "Oh, I'm going to enjoy destroying you."

An airplane droned outside.

Simone caught her breath and tried to remain calm.

Phillipe smiled. "Our ride has arrived."

Chapter 35

Nick tucked the communicator in his ear before tugging down his bulletproof vest outside of the small airport. The intel from Moira had come in, and he'd immediately organized a rescue force. He and Zane faced the tarmac from the north, and the Enforcers from the south. He hadn't been able to reach Bear or Flynn, so they'd have to work without air support. By tacit agreement, the Enforcers had adopted his plan, not that he'd given them much choice.

Simone and the babe were his, and he was the strategic planner for a nation, if not the world now.

He patted the tactic balaclava ski mask over his features. If there was a satellite observing through the clouds, he didn't want anybody to be identified, so they were all masked.

Adam Dunne had made it back to Dublin in time to join the attack. Right now, he was the only Enforcer still working for the Coven Nine. While he'd probably be fired soon, for the moment, he still had an in, which Simone needed.

"Adam, you clearheaded?" Nick asked over the comm line. He hadn't liked the witch's grim expression and tired eyes.

"Aye," Adam replied. "I'm good on go."

Nick glanced over at Zane, who nodded. Even though Adam had been unable to find Victoria Monzelle, he'd hold up for the mission. The guy knew how to fight with brutal, logical precision. "Eyes."

Moira came online first. "Seven men outside the plane with one more guarding what looks like a storage shack. Probably two pilots, but I can't see inside. Confirmed sighting of Phillipe Sadler, and

I recognize two soldiers as witches who washed out of Guard training."

"You know any of the others?" Nick asked.

"Negative," she said. "I study all field and training reports from the Guard, and I never forget a face."

Impressive, that. Nick kept low behind a row of barrels. "Nobody move until we get a visual on Simone."

A chorus of "affirmatives" came through the line.

He covered his mic and turned toward Zane. "You clear on our plan?"

"Yes." Zane bellied up next to him, his gaze on the tarmac. Only the lights from the plane illuminated the area. "If I have the chance, I'll grab Simone and teleport her to headquarters in Idaho."

"Good." Nick flexed his hands in the thick leather gloves. "The Enforcers have some damn good equipment."

Zane nodded, his gaze remaining on the targets. "The weapons are new to me. You'll have to filch a couple since I can't teleport with them."

"Copy that." Nick stared at the small shack as if the walls would somehow part and let him see inside. "She has to be in there. Right?"

"Oh, she's in there." Zane reached for his gun. "They wouldn't be guarding the shack for the hell of it. Now, clear your mind for battle and push emotion away."

"I taught you how to do that," Nick returned.

Zane released the safety on his laser gun. "Then you should know how to do it right."

Nick grinned, and adrenaline flooded his system. While he enjoyed a good strategy, there was nothing like the final conclusion, which often meant battle. "If anything happens to me . . ."

"Ditto." Zane crouched up on his knees. "Mates and kids taken care of, no matter what. But we'll live to fight another day."

"Yes." Nick sobered. The door to the shack opened, and Phillipe Sadler drew Simone from inside. She walked sedately, her hands behind her back, her head held high. Without seeming to move, her eyes scanned the surrounding area. Whatever she saw or sensed had a small smile tickling her lips.

"Your woman is impressive," Zane said, rocking back on his heels while remaining in a crouch.

Yeah, yeah she was. "All teams on ready and keep your masks in place," Nick said evenly, counting the steps between the shack and the plane. "Prepare for my go." He wanted to wait until Simone was close enough to jump into the plane, where she would be better protected. "If Zane and I give the sign, everybody clear out of the way for a massive mind attack."

"Hell," Kellach Dunne said through the earpieces.

Nick nodded. "We'll try to focus the energy, but you need to be clear." The attack would be focused on one or two people—if he and Zane tried to take out everybody, there was a good chance they'd accidentally include the Enforcers and Simone. "First we have to take a few of these guys out." If he and Zane scattered an attack, it wouldn't be nearly as effective as a concentrated mind offensive, and with powerful witches, it might not even work.

He turned his focus back to Simone.

Her movements slowed as she reached the steps to the plane.

"Go!" Nick yelled, charging forward and clipping Phillipe in the neck with his first shot. The bastard leaped behind the wing of the plane, returning fire wildly.

Simone dropped and rolled under the plane's belly, doing some weird shimmy with her arms down her legs. She jumped to her feet, her hands now in front of her, and raised her arms high with her hands spread as far apart as the cuffs would allow. With her hair blowing wildly in the blustering wind, she looked like an avenging angel.

Nick paused, took aim, and fired between her hands.

The laser beam turned to metal the second it connected with the chain securing her cuffs, blowing it apart.

Flames instantly shot down her arms to form plasma balls. She turned and fired hard at the men guarding the shack. Several of them jumped out of the way, and plasma hit the shack, instantly engulfing it in flames. The wind and rain were no match for the otherworldly fire, and it consumed each inch of wood with a rapid *hiss*.

A soldier ran straight for Zane, who paused and lowered his chin in an obvious mind attack. The witch soldier grabbed his head, screaming in pain, and dropped to his knees.

Nick ran in a zigzag pattern, dodging bullets, heading straight for Simone.

The woman was throwing fire like a master, hitting several soldiers before they could return fire. A witch over to the north battled fire with fire against the Enforcers, who were certainly gaining ground.

A pilot jumped out of the plane, throwing plasma balls.

Nick roared and leaped toward Simone, tossing her aside and taking a ball to the chest. The plasma threw him several yards, and he landed hard, shoulders first.

No pain. He refused to acknowledge pain until he saved his woman.

He backflipped to his feet and lowered his chin to send out an attack when the world lit up.

Two helicopters hovered into view, shining spotlights on the ground. Several Humvees came from all four directions, heavy guns mounted on top.

Hell.

"We're surrounded," Zane said, pressing his back against Nick's. "Any ideas?"

Phillipe Sadler moved around the wing, one hand pressed to a bleeding hole in his upper arm. Blood and dirt matted his face. He smiled. "Looks like backup just arrived. Oh. I called the Guard."

Shit. Good plan. Without their attack, Phillipe would have had Simone safely away from the airport before the Guard arrived. But just in case, he'd hedged his bet.

Simone was a fugitive. If the Guard took her, she'd be dead by morning.

Kellach Dunne came into view, pivoting and firing a ball of plasma up at a helicopter. Bullets rained down, piercing him, and he dropped to the ground, spraying blood on the way down.

Simone cried out and started to move, but the cocking of more guns stopped her cold.

Nick eyed her and tried to motion her inside the plane. She stood in the rain, breathing heavily, her hair cascading down her back. She turned just as another pilot slipped into view on the top step, his gun pointed at her head.

Simone shoved wet hair from her eyes and tried to focus. The spotlights lit up the small tarmac with a brightness that hurt. The Enforcers stood still over to the left, muscles tensed, weapons down. Daire grabbed his fallen brother and jerked him upright. Blood trickled from above Kellach's bulletproof vest, so at least one bullet had found its way through the protection. He wavered but managed to remain standing, fury on his broad face.

Nick's vest smoldered, but he stood steadfast, with Zane at his back.

They were outnumbered by far. If she didn't surrender, somebody would surely die.

The pilot of the small plane kept his gun pointed at her.

Slowly, she raised her hands, palms out in surrender.

Phillipe Sadler was instantly by her side, a gun pointed at her ribs. "There's a hefty reward for your capture. Did you know that?"

"No." That was fast. But it wasn't like the Coven Nine to mess around. "So, this was your plan?"

"This was plan B in case of attack." Phillipe leaned in to whisper. "I told you plan A with my mother taking your powers. Now, because your friends have tried to intervene, you'll go with the Guard and be killed. You would've been better off with my plan."

Being powerless for a couple of centuries certainly did trump death. "I woulda taken your mother's powers as well as yours," Simone said, her gaze on one Humvee slowly making its way onto the tarmac. Perhaps if she ended up in a prison cell, she could employ her original plan. Were the people she'd hired still in place? Somehow, she doubted it.

Nick took a step toward her, and lasers *ping*ed the ground in front of him. He halted and looked up.

"Nick!" She waited until he'd focused back on her before shaking her head. If he employed a mind attack at the helicopter pilot, everyone around him would start firing.

Tension rode the wind and swirled around. One wrong move on anybody's part, and the Guard would blow most of them up.

She kept her hands up and waited.

The Humvee rolled to a stop mere yards from her, the door opened, and Peter Gallagher stepped out.

She tilted her head. "This isn't Coven Nine territory," she yelled at the current Coven Nine leader through the gathering storm.

He nodded. "I understand, but we've been attacked on our own ground by demons and rogue Enforcers." Taking a deep breath, he slowly looked around and then grabbed a communicator to press to his mouth. "These are enemies of the Nine. Take them out."

A missile impacted the ground near the Enforcers, sending them all flying through the air along with concrete and debris.

Simone screamed.

Nick and Zane leapt into motion, heading for her, their faces intent. A missile slammed into the concrete before them. Fire flashed into the sky.

The world slowed.

Simone partially turned, her gaze narrowing to peer through the smoke and falling concrete. Nothing. "Nick!" she yelled, panic rippling through her.

Nothing.

The helicopter above her shimmered and turned. They were going to shoot again.

She couldn't lose him. Not now.

"Let me in, Simone," he bellowed. "Let me in your head. We can do it."

It was the only way. She loved him. He was worthy of that, and he'd protect her brain. Trust. They needed such trust to protect their babe. She nodded and settled herself, mentally shattering every shield around her brain. Energy resonated through her, filling her veins. Emotion, raw and pure, pulsed inside her chest, filling her to overflowing. Her muscles snapped. A burning sensation spiked just beneath her skin, flaring out with sharp barbs.

Nicholai Veis was in her brain.

Panic attacked her liked heated knives. What the hell?

Pain. Raw, desperate, complete pain torched her nerves. Wait a minute. It was Nick. She relaxed. Suddenly, the sensations stopped.

Fire danced along her skin.

A mind attack shot out with the power of Nick's brain as well as her complex genetics. God. The rush was fucking amazing. She turned her head to find Phillipe staring at her, his face stark-white and his mouth wide open with blood welling from his lips. He backpedaled away.

"Kill her," Phillipe yelled as he kept running.

Rage filled her, and she swung out, throwing bright pink fire with Nick's power to hit Phillipe in the back. He flew through the air and landed hard on the Humvee, glass slicing his neck and his head rolling away. She'd killed the bastard. Gunfire erupted all around them.

Nick shot up at the nearest helicopter while Zane hit the other one with a series of green blasts from his gun. Metal burst in every direction.

Shouts sounded from the Humvees, and the glow of lasers filled the now-darkened tarmac. A cry of pain echoed up from Moira.

Simone hissed and turned around, aiming the deadly fire toward the Humvees. She'd had no idea she could combine her powers with Nick's in such a devastating way. So this was trust. True trust. The wind whipped against her body, and she shifted slightly, removing resistance, throwing fire.

Men screamed, and one of the Humvees blew up, throwing glass into the air. Two other Humvees careened in reverse, flames erupting from their windows.

A bullet impacted her side. Pain ripped through her.

She screamed, and the ground rushed up to meet her.

Chapter 36

Nick stumbled to his feet and jumped for Simone. He'd been concentrating so hard on combining their powers that he felt the bullet slash into her side. Panic seized his lungs. He jumped across the burning tarmac and caught her a second before she reached the ground. The force threw him back.

He wrapped his body around her, leaping up, and let them both spin through the smoke.

His shoulders hit the still-burning shack, and he rolled, taking her with him.

He impacted the cement hard. Pain exploded in his hip. His fangs dropped low, and he levered himself up on his good leg. "Plane," he bellowed through the still-working comms, carrying the woman across the rubble.

She lay limp in his arms, out cold.

Zane reached his side, bloody and bruised. "I'll take her."

"No. You cover." Nothing in Nick could release her at this point. He grimly made his way across the battlefield, reaching the steps to the plane.

Zane sprayed bullets into the abyss behind them.

The Enforcers hustled toward him, Daire carrying Kellach over his shoulder, and Conn carrying Moira against his chest while Adam covered their backs. They ran up the stairs, and Nick followed with Zane bringing up the rear.

Adam stood on the tarmac and waved them off. "Go. I need to find Tori, and I'm still an Enforcer for now." His mask hid his face, but part of the material was smoldering. He covered them, firing at the Humvees, until they'd all gotten safely inside. Then, like the strategic soldier he was, he disappeared completely into the smoke.

The plane had several leather chairs, two tables, and a long sofa along one side. Daire dumped Kell on the sofa and hurried for the pilot's seat, sitting down and igniting the engines. "Everyone take a seat," he yelled.

Zane yanked the door shut and stretched into the copilot's seat. Within seconds, he and Daire were working the controls together as if they'd done so for decades. Considering Daire had just mated Zane's mother, it was a good sign. They drove the plane across fire and ripped concrete toward a smoldering runway. Nick dropped into a chair cradling Simone, his gaze focused through the windshield.

A Humvee careened across the runway, smoke billowing from it, guns firing furiously out the windows.

"Hold on," Zane yelled.

The plane gathered speed, roaring down the airstrip, aiming right for the firing Humvee.

Bullets *ping*ed against the windshield.

"Fuck," Daire muttered, swerving to the left. "Faster. Go."

Zane nodded, and the plane jumped forward, speeding up almost too fast.

Nick could make out the eyes of the men in the Humvee. He tightened his body around Simone, who hadn't moved an inch.

Daire yanked up on the stick, and the plane slowly lifted.

More. God, go up more, more, more. Nick chanted in his head, leaning forward as if that would help.

The plane rose into the air, its belly barely missing the Humvee.

Good. His lungs compressed, and he frantically ran his hands over Simone. "Wake up, baby." God. The baby. Was the baby okay? Calm. He needed to calm the hell down and help her.

He leaned down and nuzzled Simone's neck. "Little bunny?" Her pulse was strong against his mouth.

She moved in his arms, and he leaned back.

Her eyelids fluttered open, and sparkling black eyes took his measure. "Did you see that?" she whispered, her voice hoarse. She winced.

He nodded. "We can combine powers and each get stronger than before."

She coughed. "My side hurts," she croaked.

"Okay. I need you to take several breaths to heal it. Relax and focus. You can do it." His voice shook.

She pushed against his chest to sit up. Cuts and bruises marred her stunning body.

He allowed her to swivel her legs around to face him on his lap. "Simone?" The sense of tingling and healing came from her.

"How do you feel?" Kell asked.

She bit her lip. "Weird. I mean, I feel like me again, but I have to tell you, letting a powerful demon into your brain is just awesome."

Nick leaned in and calmed himself with her scent. "Is the babe all right?" His chest hurt, and doubt assailed him.

She closed her eyelids and took several deep breaths, obviously working through her body. Finally, she nodded. "Aye. I feel fine, and I can sense the little person."

Everything inside Nick released and relaxed. "Boy," he drawled, his body shutting down as it healed itself. Relief was a balm to him. His family was all right, and he'd make sure they stayed that way.

"Girl," she countered, snuggling right into his neck, her lips against his jugular. "Is everybody else all right?" she asked.

"Yes," he said, running a hand down her back.

"Aye." Moira sat in Conn's lap, blood pouring from her temple. "We just cleared cloud cover. Take that, Guard."

Conn winced and ran a finger over a cut above her eye. "Heal that or I will," the vampire muttered.

Moira nodded and closed her eyes. The tingles of healing filtered through the air.

The plane went silent as everyone set to healing themselves, and the *pop* of energy coursed through the oxygen. Nick closed his eyes and laid his head back, allowing his hip to pop back into place and the bones to knit together.

His woman patted his heart. "Thank you for catching me."

"I'll always catch you, little bunny." He turned his head and kissed her smooth forehead.

"What now?" She yawned against him, and her jaw popped.

He tried to focus, but his skull was repairing itself. "Ah, now? We get to safety and come up with a plan." They had created a shit-storm of ridiculous proportions, and thank God they had Adam on the inside of the Coven Nine for now. "My nation might be at war with the Coven Nine, you're a fugitive, the Enforcers are fired, and your family has been taken off the Council." But none of that mattered. Not really.

He and Simone had found each other, and they had a baby on the way. The present was more than he could've ever dreamed about, and the future was dazzling. They'd figure it all out.

Conn cleared his throat. "Not to mention there's still Apollo on the streets and somebody masterminding this whole mess against Simone and the witches. We have to find that bastard and rip off his head."

"Yes." Nick appreciated the vampire's way of getting to the heart of things. It was good to have a plan as well as allies. Hell. Family was all around him. It was a good place to be. "Our first step is to find Grace Sadler."

"She's not behind the whole scheme," Moira said slowly. "She's part of it, I'm sure, but Grace isn't smart enough or strong enough to create this much of a mess. She's a follower and always has been."

Nick nodded. "I've studied her and I agree. We'll find the mastermind, and while we're at it, we'll find proof that Phillipe and Grace set up Simone."

"We need to make sure Bear is okay," Simone said.

"Agreed," Nick said.

"We're safe, and life is good. I know we're going to fix it all . . . tomorrow." Simone kissed his neck. "At least we won't be bored."

Nicholai chuckled. "There is that."

"I love you, you know," she murmured, her hand now flattened over his heart, which she'd owned for centuries.

"Yes, I know." He drew out the ring he'd bought for her so long ago and slipped it on her finger. Finally.

After several plane rides, Simone settled into the sofa of a very nice apartment outside of Seattle that was definitely off the grid. Lake Washington glimmered outside in the early morning light, sparkling and beautiful. "I'm starting to think that a long term relationship with a demon will be quite luxurious." She patted the chenille pillow next to her.

Nicholai stalked into the peaceful living room and slid his phone into his pocket. The demon had showered before donning faded jeans and a black silk shirt that made him look like a predator barely hidden. "The Nine is sticking to the results of the trial, and Peter has put a bounty on your head." Irritation etched into the lines of Nick's face. "I'm thinking of just taking him out and then deciding about Sal and Nessa." He rubbed his chin and moved closer, eyeing the lake outside for any threats.

Simone sat up. "You can't just kill a member of the Nine."

"Sure I can." He turned, a deadly man with determination stamped on his hard face. "If you're in danger, they die."

So calm and so assured.

"I'd rather clear my good name, if you don't mind." She took a deep breath to keep the morning sickness at bay.

He reached her in two long strides and crouched on his haunches. "We'll try it your way first, but then my way if necessary." Two of his knuckles ran across a bruise she hadn't been able to heal on her cheekbone. Another day and she'd regain all of her strength. "But you're not going to be doing anything, sweetheart."

She smiled then. Truth be told, when he got all demon possessive and bossy, it turned her on a little. "I'm a witch with some dragon genetics thrown in, remember? I don't need shielding."

"Yet shield you I will." Concern darkened his eyes. "I'm sorry about your removal from the Council. I know how much your position means to you."

That quickly, she realized her ambitions had changed. Well, maybe not changed, but definitely expanded. "You and this babe are more important than anything else out there." She cupped his whiskered jaw with her palm.

His gaze softened.

There he was.

She smiled. "Oh, I'm definitely ambitious, and I will rule that Council someday, I promise you that." But that was what she chose to do for a living and not who she chose to be. She'd be a good mate to this amazing male, and she'd make an excellent mother, even if she couldn't cook or sew. She could teach the little person inside her how to throw fire and maybe even blow fire. That was beyond cool.

"Did you talk to Bear?" Nick asked.

Simone nodded. "Aye. He's healing and eating tons of protein. Told me to stop smothering him." She smiled. "Bear and Flynn both agree that the babe inside me isn't evil and that we can teach him or her to use demon, dragon, or witch powers for good and not evil. Or rather, not too evil." It wasn't possible to believe that their kid wouldn't have a little bit of bad in him, considering his parents. Or her parents.

"Good. I'd kind of hate to kill either Bear or Flynn." Nick smiled.

Funny that he was only kind of kidding. If anybody threatened his child, he'd take them out; that much Simone knew. Of course, he'd only get to an enemy if she didn't get there first. "My brothers are working on a plan dealing with the fact that dragons are now public. We'll need treaties."

"Not a problem. We'll take care of it." He smiled. "I figured part of the problem with the dragons was that Desmond was a paranoid lunatic."

"Aye." She couldn't help but return the grin. "I know there's a lot going on right now, but I can't help but be happy." He meant so much to her, and finally, they were together. So much stronger together.

"We'll figure it all out. I promise." Nick's shoulders straightened, so strong and sure. "We're going to be happy, Simone."

She nodded. Aye, aye, they were. "I love you, Veis."

He leaned in and whispered a kiss across her mouth. "I've loved you from the first second I saw you, and you've definitely been worth the wait. My little bunny."

Please read on for a special Dark Protectors novella from Rebecca Zanetti.

Dear Reader,

I wanted to write a novella and tie the Dark Protectors to the Realm Enforcers, so I put out the question to my Facebook Street team, Rebecca's Rebels, on who they'd like to see in a novella to be included with *Wicked Burn*.

There was one pair they overwhelmingly said they'd like to catch up with—so here's *Talen*, an adventure for Talen and Cara. I hope you like it!

Chapter 1

Cara Paulsen Kayrs hummed as she finished watering the plants in her spacious kitchen and sprawling living room. She'd settled nicely into the new neighborhood fronting an Idaho lake with her family and friends all around.

Her mate strode in from the back porch. "There's another letter from that university across the country."

She stilled. "I haven't given them an answer yet."

He growled low then . . . six and a half feet of pure male, stubborn vampire. "The answer to your teaching botany glasses at a human university is . . . no."

She forced a smile. As an empath, she could feel his concern for her down to her bones, but it was time for them to enjoy being alive. "The war is over, and I'd like to get back to work. There are so many uses for simple plants, and it's time we used our advanced technology to help humans."

He lowered his chin in what could only be described as a warning. He'd nearly died not too long ago, but only a thin strip of gray in his thick dark hair showed he'd ever been vulnerable. Corded muscle and masculine strength lined his body, and his rugged face held health and a warrior's experience. Those golden eyes could go as hard as death in an instant if his family was threatened.

He was the biggest, strongest, toughest badass of them all . . . and he was all hers. Although he'd lived more than three centuries, the man looked thirty-two. He'd been tense lately—bossier than usual— and she'd had enough. "You can work here, privately and not go public," he said calmly.

Oh, her temper wanted loose and now. "The war is over, and we can't stay shacked up forever." While she appreciated his driving need to keep her safe, she had a lot to contribute to this world, and it was time for her to get started. She was finally healthy. "Why don't you get the car ready and stop bossing me around."

One eyebrow rose in an oddly sexual way. Oh, she'd pay for the comment later, but as long as the night ended in multiple orgasms, it was difficult to really care. "Watch yourself, mate," he rumbled.

Her body quivered head to toe. They'd been mated for more than twenty-five years, and he still had the ability to make her breath catch in her throat. "*You* can watch me all you want on the road. Go get the car."

He cocked his head then, his gaze thoughtful. "All right. You asked for it." Turning on one combat boot, he loped through the house and out the front door.

She tried to calm her raging hormones. When he got all dominant and sexy, she could barely stand still. But it was time the man stopped treating her like the fragile invalid she'd been for over two decades. She was cured . . . and she was healthy. Life was great.

The front door opened, and her daughter, Janie, moved aside as a bundle of energy toddled past her.

"Hope!" Cara set the watering can on the floor and leaned down so the little girl could waddle into her arms. At fourteen months old, the child never stopped moving.

"Cara." Hope patted Cara's cheeks with chubby hands, her deep blue eyes sparkling. "Pretty Cara."

Cara tucked the girl close. No matter how hard any of them tried to get the girl to call them Nana, Papa, Aunt . . . she used first names only. "Did Kane have any luck getting her to call him by the right name?"

Janie snorted and shut the door, pushing light brown hair away from her classic face. "No, and he tried with every trick he had. Even gave her cookies."

Cara stood and took Hope with her. "That's hilarious." Kane was Hope's great-uncle and the smartest person on the planet, so when his brother had called him "Fucking Einstein" a month before, Hope had caught on and now called the poor guy "*Funkin Eeeenstine.*" It shouldn't tickle Cara so, but she couldn't help it. "Well, I hope it teaches those guys not to swear around her. She picks everything up."

Janie nodded and set a bag by the door. "I brought that sundress you wanted to borrow for your trip. You packed yet?"

"Yes." Warmth slid through Cara as she sat with the baby on her lap. Hope's brown hair was tied up in pretty green ribbons that matched her sweater. Flowers decorated her jeans, and little sparkly shoes covered her feet. The blue marking winding up her neck showed her to be a prophet declared by fate, but for now, fate could stay out of her life. All of their lives, actually. "Maybe I shouldn't go."

Hope faced her and tapped her cheeks again. "Cara on trip with Tayen. Water."

Cara smiled, her heart full. "Yes. We'll see water."

"You'll only be gone two weeks." Janie ran her hand down faded jeans and crossed to sit on the couch. "The war is over, everyone is healthy, and you and Dad deserve some fun. I promise nothing interesting will happen while you're gone. Plus, it's crucial we get those samples to the lab in Seattle. They have nuclear equipment we don't have here."

"I know." Cara ran through the checklist of the research materials she'd included with the tissue samples. "I'm quite curious what they'll be able to find out about the virus and the cure. I mean, how the cure for the vampire virus might be used to help humans with so many diseases." She studied her daughter. Janie's blue eyes were clear, and a happy glow covered her cheeks. "You're happy."

"I am." Janie returned the smile. She ran her hand down her daughter's back, studying her mother. "How weird is it that we look about the same age?"

"It's like a sci-fi movie." Cara shook her head. She'd mated a vampire, and Janie had mated a demon-vampire, which had changed their human chromosomal pairs to something more . . . something immortal. "I freely admit I love not aging. Never understood those old movies where the vampires were all sad and full of self-hatred."

Janie chuckled. "Maybe they were alone and didn't have immortal family all around."

"Good point." Cara leaned in and nuzzled Hope's neck, tickling until the girl giggled. "Plus, in those movies, the vamps sucked blood to survive and couldn't go outside or they'd melt."

"How goofy is that?" Janie stretched her neck. "But the legends have to be built on some reality."

The door opened again, and Talen Kayrs stalked into the room.

"Tayen!" Hope pushed off Cara and toddled toward the massive warrior.

He caught her before she rammed into his legs and lifted her high, his hard eyes softening in a way that just melted Cara's heart. "There's my girl." He tucked her close and rubbed her back.

Delight glowed from her, and she wiggled enthusiastically, patting his chest. "Tayen. Yaaaaaay, Tayen."

Cara started laughing. "Traitor."

Janie grinned and shook her head. "She sure doesn't hide the love, does she?"

"Why should she?" Talen easily held her with one muscled arm and tugged on her hair, not looking anything like a grandfather. "The kid has excellent taste."

"Tayen!" Hope agreed with a vigorous head nod. "Water and Tayen. Lotsa water." She gurgled. "And fire."

Talen glanced down at her. "The forest fires are just about over, sweetheart. The smoke is finally going away." He swung her around, end over end, and she giggled uncontrollably, her legs kicking as she played.

"Thank goodness." Cara looked at the clear day outside. It was late fall, but summer had been dry, and many forest fires had cropped up in Washington and Idaho. While the fires hadn't come close, the smoke had hung over the lake for weeks. It was time to get out of town for some fun.

She stood and walked over to grab the sundress out of the bag. "I'll toss this in, and we're off."

"The Hummer is having electrical problems." Talen settled Hope again and then frowned. "I called Kane to come fix it, but he's in the middle of something. So I'm borrowing Dage's Jeep."

Cara stretched up and kissed Hope's cheek. "I'm ready."

Janie hurried over and hugged her mother. "Have a good time, and good luck on the adventure."

"Thank you," Cara said, anticipation lighting her veins. "We're driving to Seattle to deliver those medical research samples to the lab, and then we're catching the plane to Hawaii for some fun. I've left all the travel information by the fridge, in case you need it."

Janie nodded. "Definitely check in, but don't worry about us. Everything will be great. Bring some macadamia nuts home."

"I promise." Cara settled her palm over her abdomen. The war was over, life was good . . . so why was her stomach tingling with butterflies?

What could possibly go wrong?

Janie and Hope left, leaving her alone with her overprotective mate. Perhaps on the trip, they could realistically discuss her research and the benefits of teaching the next generation of humans how to look outside the western medicinal box in healing diseases.

She winked. "Lose the frown, or I'm kicking you right in the shin. Maybe higher."

He leaned in. "Kick me. Please."

Her stomach fluttered. "Don't think I won't."

He smiled then . . . all dangerous soldier. "I'm waiting. Kick me, I'll spank you, and then I promise you'll be too damn sore to even think about riding in a car for five hours."

Oh, he wasn't getting his way that easy. She stretched up on her toes and pecked a kiss against his mouth. "Nice try, vampire."

Talen couldn't shake the itch between his shoulder blades. Taking his mate from the safety of their headquarters didn't set well with him, and his muscles tensed in one long line.

"Would you relax?" she whispered from the passenger seat, her head back on the leather and her eyes closed in pleased abandonment. Her legs were up on the dash, her feet in little sandals that showed off bright pink toenails. Sexy and pink. Her long auburn hair cascaded over her shoulders, and he fought the urge to tug on a strand.

The woman was right. The war had ended, and he really did need to relax. He watched the road outside and yet kept a close eye on his woman out of his peripheral vision. "It occurs to me that you think things have changed."

She opened her eyelids then . . . her eyes a stunning blue. "Huh?"

He cleared his throat and made sure her seat belt was firmly around her small body. "The war is over, you're well, and you think things are different." In fact, his woman hadn't been healthy since right after they'd mated, and for years, he'd been more than gentle with her. At the thought that she was whole, finally, his heart started to thrum.

"Of course things are different." She gestured out with one arm. "We're on a road trip, without guards, without death hanging over our heads." Her laugh was throaty and full. "Emma and I are taking a Vegas trip next month for a girls' weekend."

"Absolutely not."

She gaped. "I did not ask permission, Kayrs."

He bit back a wince. Whenever Cara used his last name, he was about to end up in the doghouse. Yet she was no longer vulnerable or weak, and he was finished placating her. "Mate? I have no intention of allowing you to go anywhere for a girls' anything." The second the word *allow* was out of his mouth, the tension in the car ratcheted up several degrees.

"Oh, you did not," she sputtered, her eyes narrowing.

He sighed and turned to pin her with a look. He'd forgotten her stubbornness in the last difficult years when she'd been fighting a deadly virus that had almost taken her life. Now that she was healthy, memories of their first months together, before she had become infected, filtered through his mind. "I was fairly certain I tamed you way back when," he said thoughtfully.

Red infused her face. "I'm about to kick your ass, Kayrs."

Maybe not. Interesting. At the thought, his entire body tightened, and his cock started to throb. "Cara."

Her shiver enticed him. "What?"

"I strongly advise you not to push me." It was only fair to warn her, and he went on instinct. After nearly dying when the war had ended, he'd been restless since. For so many years, he'd treated his mate with more gentleness than he would've thought possible as she'd endured the virus.

Now that she was healthy, a primal part of him, one much closer to the surface than he liked, wanted to claim her again with all the dominance that was inherent to his species. "Okay?"

She breathed out. "Oh, mate. You're the one who needs to stop pushing."

He reached out, catching the long strands of her hair before she could avoid him. Her eyes widened, and he twisted his wrist with enough pressure to tilt back her head, fighting instincts he'd forgotten he had.

Curiosity and desire spilled from her.

His nostrils flared, catching his mate's scent. It had been too long since they'd both been whole and healthy. He'd forgotten her defiant nature and how much she liked to challenge him. "Maybe this trip was a good idea," he said softly, the beast inside him raging as her lids half-lowered.

Chapter 2

Several hours into the trip, Cara's first headache pounded in the middle of Washington State. Monstrous steel windmills, dotting the rocky hills, swung their grand arms in the slight wind. The sight was both alien and lonely somehow.

She rubbed her temples. "I think the smoke from the earlier fires is bugging my head."

"I'll need gas soon. We can buy aspirin." Talen kept an eye on the rearview mirror while passing a school bus. "My head hurts a little, too." He grinned. "Maybe we're getting the flu."

She laughed and wrapped her arms around her shins while resting her chin on her knees. "Very funny." They couldn't catch normal illnesses.

At her laugh, appreciation lit his rugged features. Good. He was finally relaxing.

She cleared her throat. "Maybe this is a good time to discuss this way-overprotective attitude of yours and how you need to tone it down now that the war is over."

Talen slowed down until he could pass a bunch of teenagers with inner tubes in a compact red truck. "I understand your need to work, but why in public? One of our laws is staying off the human radar, you know?"

"Yes, but I could teach for a while publicly." Cara turned to look through the rearview mirror at the teens. It was way too cold for inner-tubing, and they should be in school.

"They're fine. Playing hooky, most likely." Talen sped up until the truck was out of sight, easily reading her concerns, as usual.

Smoke filtered through the trees and soon thickened until the sun was an odd red orb through the mist.

Talen punched a bunch of buttons on the dash. "Dage?" Talen asked. "How close are we to forest fires?"

A crackle sounded, and then the King's face took shape in the center consol. "How's the trip?"

"Great," Talen said, squinting. "I'm getting concerned about the fires, though. What can you see?"

"The ones around you have been contained, according to the news." Dage *clacked* keys in the background.

Talen shook his head. "I don't think the fire is contained. Bring up satellite."

"Just a sec. I have to hack into a different one." More keys clattered. "All right. It appears there are fires to your east and west . . . smaller but gathering speed, I think. Stick to the river road you're on, and stay near the water."

"My head is hurting a little, and so is Cara's. Do you see any threats?" Talen asked grimly, his hands tightening on the wheel until his knuckles appeared white.

"I'm not sure. There are several trucks, vans, and campers going in both directions on your road, and nothing stands out," Dage said.

"I'm sure it's just the smoke," Talen said.

Dage chuckled. "You just don't know how to relax. Give it a shot." The screen went black as the king disconnected the call.

"Everyone keeps telling me to relax," Talen muttered.

Yeah. There was a reason for that. Cara hid a smile. "We can take it easy after we deliver these." She looked in the backseat, where the cooler containing the tissue samples was nestled safely. The samples were from people who had taken a mutated virus to negate the immortal mating bond that bound them to just one lover. "I'm curious about these samples. Is it possible to really negate a mating bond of a living couple?"

"No." Talen grinned then, a flash of white against his bronze face. "I don't see what the big deal is. If somebody is your mate, then they're your mate, bond or not. Besides . . . we have no proof that a mating bond can be negated when both mates are still alive."

True. The only ones that had been negated were ones in which a mate had died some time ago. "I'm sure there will be a test subject soon," she murmured.

"I doubt it."

"Why not? Humans get divorced all the time. Negating a mating bond is the same thing in the immortal world," she mused.

He shook his head. "Matings are forever, or at least during life. I think the bond is too strong to completely break while both parties are alive."

Perhaps. "Maybe I should give it a shot and see," she teased.

His grin widened. "Try it." The warning rumble of the words belied his smile.

She swallowed. There had to be a quick retort that showed her spirit but didn't push the irritated vampire too far. "Bite me." Nope. That wasn't it.

"I fully plan to."

Her abdomen heated, and she instinctively touched the bite mark along her neck——her mating mark. She also wore the Kayrs marking, an intricate design with a *K* in the middle, on her butt from the mating. "Maybe I'll bite you this time."

"Baby, you can bite me any time."

She grinned and tried to enjoy the moment while pretending the tension surrounding them had dissipated. But it hadn't. Not really. Not for the first time, she wondered how much of Talen's true nature he'd had to tamp down the last couple of decades as she'd fought the virus and he'd battled enemies in the war. They had two children together as well as one granddaughter, and sometimes she wasn't sure she really knew him.

He leaned over and rubbed the frown lines between her eyes. "Stop fretting. Everything will be fine."

Hmm. Apparently he knew her pretty damn well. "I love you, you know," she said slowly.

"I know. You're everything to me," he said softly.

She nodded, fully secure of her place in his heart and his life. Yet they were still somehow . . . off.

"My brain has relaxed, so the fires must've died out. Right now, we need fuel." He glanced in all the mirrors and then pulled into a quiet service station built with what appeared to be reclaimed wood. "Stay in the car."

"Need restroom." She opened the door, and he was by her side within a heartbeat. "Geez. We're safe, Talen. No more war."

"I know." He grasped her arm and escorted her from the car to the building, keeping his body between hers and any threat from the road.

She tried—really hard if asked—to keep from rolling her eyes into the back of her head. "You have got to mellow out."

"Humph." He nodded to the elderly woman behind the counter before scanning the tidy store and dropping Cara at the women's bathroom. "I'll fill up the car." He paused and then pushed open the door to quickly scout the one-stall room. "Okay." Then he turned and stalked from the charming store.

Cara shook her head and used the facilities. After drying her hands, she wandered into the store and purchased soda and some potato chips from the wide-eyed woman behind the counter.

"You okay, honey?" The woman pushed back springy gray hair while also shoving up bifocals.

Cara grinned. "I'm fine. He's just a little overprotective."

The woman leaned in, bringing the scent of bottled roses with her. Her gaze swept Cara's faded jeans and light blue sweater. "Are you some superstar or something?"

"No." There was a time when dangerous enemies had had a bounty on her head, but now she was just a normal person. Well, a normal immortal person mated to one of the most powerful vampires in the world. "I used to have a stalker, and my, ah, husband still worries."

"Ah, now. That's sweet." The woman's bright red lipstick cracked as she smiled and placed the items in a bag. "He's a handsome one, that he is."

"Thanks." Cara said, turning for the door and stepping into the slightly smoky air.

"Well, hello there," said a deep voice.

She turned on the wooden porch to see a kid about twenty lounging in an old metal chair, his cowboy boots propped up on a green cooler. Shaggy hair cascaded out of a faded blue cap. He held an energy drink in one hand. "Excuse me?" she murmured.

"You are a sight for tired old eyes," he said, his blond eyebrows wiggling and his eyes sparkling. A smile curved his full lips right above a little goatee.

It took her a second, it really did, for her to figure out he was hitting on her. Sometimes she forgot she only looked twenty-five. "You have got to be kidding me." Geez. Her son was probably older than this kid. "Shouldn't you be in college or at a job?"

He blinked and puffed out his chest. "Maybe I don't have to work."

For goodness' sake. She fought every instinct she had not to grab him by the ear and kick his butt to the road toward the employment office. "Somehow, I think you do." Shaking her head, she started down the porch.

He jumped up and grabbed her arm.

"Oh honey," she breathed just as her mate caught sight of them. "Those boots better be for running."

Talen kept his focus on them while shoving the gas nozzle in place and then screwing on the gas cap. Then he moved through the smoke, his gaze hotter than the fire that seemed to be getting closer.

"Uh," the kid said.

"Let. Go." She should probably try to save the kid's life. Being stupid shouldn't end it.

He dropped her arm like it had shocked him. "That's a big dude," he whispered.

She slowly nodded.

"Is he fast?" the kid asked.

She nodded again. "Unfortunately."

Talen reached the bottom of the steps, definitely the most dangerous thing the kid had ever seen.

"I'm sorry." The kid backed up. "Really, really, really sorry." He tripped and fell back into his chair, his boots swinging.

Talen sighed. "Jesus." He rubbed one broad hand through his hair and studied the kid as if deciding whether or not to take a bite.

The kid audibly held his breath.

Cara gingerly stepped down. "He should probably go to school or get a job, right?"

Talen lifted an eyebrow.

The kid jumped to his feet. "I'll go fill out an application for school right now. My granny's been trying to get me to, but I've been lazy, and that just ended." He was still chattering as he all but ran around the corner of the store and disappeared.

Talen looked down and to the side. "I only left you for two minutes."

She smiled. "Yeah, but we just did a nice thing for his granny. She'll be so proud he's off his butt and going to college."

"The next guy who touches you, I get to hit." Talen took the bag from her and turned them both. "Scratch that. Nobody ever touches you again but me. Yeah. That's the deal." One hand at the small of her back offered constant support and protection. "You are far too beautiful for my own good."

Now, that was sweet, especially since she wore no makeup and was in comfy clothes. Perhaps she should make more of an effort. She was taking immortality and young skin for granted. Good thing she'd brought sexy lingerie for the trip. "Just wait 'til you see what I brought to wear to bed."

His stride hitched. "Can't wait. It'll look lovely on the floor since you won't be wearing it long."

Her nipples peaked. She grinned. "I don't suppose you brought silk boxers or anything."

He laughed and opened her door for her. "I don't suppose I did." Then his head lifted, and his nostrils flared like a wolf catching a scent. "Hell." He grasped her arm and lifted her, shutting the door quickly.

Her head suddenly pounded. "Oh God." She knew the feeling. She just *knew* it.

Fast strides had him around the car and inside, igniting the engine. "There are demons close."

Chapter 3

Talen cursed to himself as he barreled onto the river road and punched the gas. A beat-up yellow Chevy careened around a bend behind him, gaining speed. Pain lanced into his temples a second before Cara cried out.

Demons had the ability to attack minds with both pain and horrible images. Through the years, Talen had gained a few mental shields, but certainly not enough.

He swerved the truck, ruining their line of sight. Even if there were four of them in the truck, all directing the attack, they wouldn't be able to keep it up for long, especially over a distance.

Gunfire pattered into the asphalt, sending shards flying.

"Hell." He swerved again, speeding up while also grabbing Cara's head and shoving her down. She bent at the waist and he kept pushing until her knees were on the floor. "Stay down."

She fought against his hold, drawing a green gun from the side compartment. "I can shoot."

He swerved again, making it too difficult for the demons to continue the mind attack. The pain in his temples receded. "I know, but for now, stay there." If the woman thought she was going to get up and engage in a firefight, she was fucking crazy.

Even now, the scent of her fear filled the SUV, and the animal inside him stretched to life. His fangs lengthened, and his heart rate slowed as his body prepared for battle. There was no more dangerous creature on the earth than a vampire defending his mate, so he allowed his primal instincts to take over.

Smoke billowed from the right, forcing him to take a sharp left turn and barrel over a narrow bridge.

The truck followed in his wake, a shooter half out the passenger-side window. The next round of bullets impacted the rear of the vehicle.

If they hit the tires, he was screwed.

Trees flew by outside, and soon, smoldering grass lined both sides of the road. The fire had swept through but seemed contained. Hopefully.

Talen punched in Dage's number.

"What?" Dage drawled.

"We have demons on our asses. Get our location, and send backup. STAT." Talen swerved again.

Dage instantly tapped in keys. "Shifters nearby to the north. They're sending help. Are you sure it's demons?"

"Yes," Talen snapped.

"I've brought you up on satellite. Shit," Dage said.

Talen nodded. "I know." The demons had certainly chosen their attack spot carefully. They were in one of the few places in the Pacific Northwest where the minerals in the rocks messed with the ability to transport, which Dage had. He couldn't transport there and get Cara out. "The second I'm far enough north, I'll tag you," Talen barked.

"I'll be ready to get there," Dage said. "For now, stay low, and wait for backup."

Cara kept silent on the floor, her blue eyes wide.

While Talen wanted to comfort her, he needed her alert and ready to flee just in case. "If I tell you to run, you do it."

She shook her head. "If you're staying to fight, so am I. It's not like I've spent the last two decades on my butt, Talen."

No. He'd made sure she trained to fight regularly, whenever she had the strength. But she was still an immortal human without any extra strength or speed. Against a cadre of demons, she'd have to be skilled as well as incredibly lucky. "I understand. Do as I tell you to do." As the strategic leader for the entire Realm, his orders were obeyed, damn it.

She sniffed and held the gun on the seat, her entire body bunched to strike. "Can we outrun them?"

Only if the demons stopped shooting. Even as the thought crossed his mind, more bullets sprayed, and the back of the SUV lifted in the air. "Shit." Talen jerked the wheel to the left, trying to keep from tumbling over the bank. "They hit a tire."

The SUV rocked. Talen swerved, and his side of the vehicle crashed into a series of rocks fronting a forest. "Out. Move now." In one smooth motion, he grabbed the cooler, grasped Cara, kicked open her door, and leaped from the vehicle.

Her feet had barely touched the ground when he had her around the hood and running into the smoke-filled forest, shielding her with his body in case the demons kept shooting. "Go, and I'll catch up." He pivoted and dropped to one knee, simultaneously whipping the gun out from his waist. The red truck screeched to a stop on the dirt road, and he plugged the windshield full of holes.

A scream echoed.

His fangs dropped, and he turned to run after his woman. He'd hit at least two targets, because he could smell their blood. But bullets would only slow them down and definitely not stop them.

The ground smoldered, and flames still licked along dead grass. He opened his senses and immediately found his mate moving quickly to the west, her sweet scent overlaid with fear. Every instinct he owned told him to turn around and take the demons out, but her safety came first.

He'd find seclusion and then go hunting.

The smoke impacted his vision, and up ahead, Cara coughed quietly.

He reached her in long strides and quickly ripped a piece off his shirt.

She frowned and leaned against the trunk of a pine tree, her eyes watering, her nose quivering.

There was no immediate heat around them, so hopefully the fires were just smoldering. Leaning forward, he gently tied the material around her head, masking her nose and mouth. "This should help filter a little bit." Making sure it was tight, he leaned back. "You all right?"

She nodded, her eyes red. "Fine. Just don't like smoke."

There was his blue-eyed fighter. Fierce and stubborn, she'd battle furiously to live. He nodded toward a barely discernible trail through several cottonwoods. "Let's head that way." Hopefully the smoke would mask their scents until they reached backup, which should be coming from that direction.

"Okay." She visibly shook out her shoulders and then launched herself into motion.

He strode into a jog, keeping track of her steps, his senses on full alert for any danger around them. The smoke screwed with his perceptions, too.

They ran for nearly an hour, winding along next to the river in case the fire descended upon them. Cara's breath became labored, and her steps slowed until Talen could walk briskly and keep up. He directed her through another series of trails until they came to a cabin set against the hill.

She paused next to a blue spruce and leaned over, hands on her knees, her breath panting out.

He stilled and listened, using all his senses to track the area. Nothing.

Finally, she lifted up and jerked off the material around her face. Her eyes softened, and she eyed the cabin. "Our first time was in a cabin like that," she whispered softly, her voice hoarse.

"I remember." He studied her breathing and frowned at the slight wheeze from her chest. "'Twas the best day of my entire life." And it was. He'd mated her in a cozy cabin after rescuing her from the enemy. The moment she'd become his, he'd become whole.

She nodded and coughed out smoke. "Mine too."

He set the cooler on the ground and pressed a hand against her upper chest. "Are you all right?"

"Yes." She nodded and patted his knuckles. "Just inhaled some smoke."

His own chest burned from her obvious pain. Every hurt she experienced settled deep inside him. "I'm sorry." It was his responsibility to protect her, and he was doing a piss-poor job of it.

She rolled her eyes. "Unless you started the fires, you don't need to apologize for anything."

"Yet I am." He released her.

"You don't control the world, Talen." She straightened and brushed dirt off her jeans.

How many times had she told him that through the years? "We need to get going again."

She glanced with longing at the cabin.

"That cabin isn't secure enough, sweetheart. We'll find a better spot," he said, retrieving the cooler of virus samples.

"All right." She cleared her throat and moved again, edging into a jog.

Talen followed right behind her, his instincts sizzling along with the fire that felt like it was coming closer. But if they stuck to the river, they'd be all right.

Well, until the demons found them. He had to get Cara to a safe place before he fought. She was his only priority.

Cara concentrated on putting one foot in front of the other without tripping and falling onto her face. Tension from Talen all but choked her, competing with the smoke swirling around. The gun lay heavy against her rib cage. She'd use it if she had to, but it had been a while since she'd practiced with a target.

If the demons caught up with them, her husband would take them all on and order her to run. She couldn't leave him to a mind attack, not when she could at least shoot and disrupt the demon brain waves with a bullet to the head.

Her foot slipped on dry leaves, and she stumbled.

He instantly grasped her elbow until she'd regained her balance. "You're doing great," he said.

His heat warmed her from behind as he kept pace with her—so solid and protective.

She ducked away from an overhanging branch. "They must want the samples, right?"

"That'd be my guess," he said.

"How did they find us? I mean, how did they know we were delivering the samples today?" She jumped over a downed tree.

"I'm not sure. Best bet is somebody at the lab in Seattle, because I can't imagine anybody at our headquarters doing it," he said mildly, his footsteps silent in the forest.

The air heated, and she lifted her head, stilling. A crackle filled the afternoon. Slowly, she turned to the right. "Fire," she whispered.

Talen grabbed her hand, looking around.

Cara gulped in smoky air. The demons were behind them, the river to their left, the rock mountain to their right, and fire up ahead.

"Across the river." Talen charged down the grassy bank, heading for the water.

Cara kept pace, her tennis shoes slipping on moss, her gaze on the rushing river. "Looks deep." Even though it was fall and snow hadn't dropped yet, the river rushed as if a full snowpack was feeding it.

"Wet summer and fall," Talen said tersely. They reached the bank, and he glanced down at her shoes. "Is there any traction on those?"

She slowly shook her head. "Not really, but I'll be okay." She tried to peer past the rushing water to see how slippery the rocks looked, but white and frothy bubbles masked the bottom of the river.

"Too risky. Stick to the bank and run." He released her hand. "I'll be right behind you."

She nodded and moved off rocks to the smooth grass, her gaze on the ground. They ran for nearly fifteen minutes, mostly uphill. Her mind was so full of fear that she missed the end of the trail.

Suddenly, she was falling.

"Ack!" she yelped, her hands windmilling, her legs kicking the air.

The rocky mountain blurred by, while the rushing sound of water echoed up. She glanced down.

Holy crap.

The river. The wild, tumultuous rapids below her held more rocks than water. *In a ball, in a ball, in a ball.* She curled tight.

A jagged rock caught her eye, and she tried to angle away. It would split her open.

Just as she was about to hit, a hard body crashed into her, sending them away from the rock and into the water. Freezing cold covered her head, and she shut her eyes. Scrambling, she fought for the surface. A roaring filled her ears. Panic blew out her air.

She broke the surface, immediately going under again.

A rock scraped her arm. She kicked off another boulder, her head emerging into daylight. The current smashed her against a rock and swept her farther downstream. She gulped in oxygen, searching frantically for Talen.

He shouted a warning. Giant, turning waves propelled the massive vampire right at her. He swung the green cooler away from her head. She screamed as they impacted, and she went under again.

Hands under her armpits, he yanked her up. She spit out water, clutching his waterlogged shirt. The cooler bobbed next to them. He tucked her head into his neck, his body bouncing off dangerous rocks as the river battered them downstream.

A rushing sound echoed over even the wild river. A waterfall! It sound huge, long, and deadly.

She struggled against her mate. They needed to get to the riverbank.

He tucked her closer. "Hold still."

Seconds later, he kicked against a looming rock, propelling them out of the middle. Grabbing an overhanging branch, he paused. The water piled up against them, gaining power.

The branch snapped in two.

She cried out. The water swirled them around and around, while bouncing Talen off rocks. He growled low each time he impacted, his body stiffening.

He grabbed another branch, and the bowed wood splintered away from the tree.

"Damn it," he muttered.

The waterfall loomed closer, the river foaming. Oh God. They were going over.

Talen wrapped one arm around her waist, shoved off from a rock, and leaped for a sweeping branch. He connected, swinging in the air. With a harsh grunt, he swung her back and tossed her toward the bank.

She landed in shallow water, splashing mud. Her hands scraped off rough rocks. Turning, she gasped in relief as he maneuvered hand-over-hand along the branch, the cooler hanging off his arm, until he dropped next to her. She blinked water from her eyes.

Grabbing her by the scruff of the neck, he hauled them both out of the river and under a tree.

He lay on his back, eyes closed, chest heaving.

She followed suit.

They were alive. Only his strength had kept them so, and she rolled over to put her head on his thundering chest.

Pain instantly flashed into her brain.

The demons had found them.

Chapter 4

Cara gasped in air and tried to shove imaginary shields all around her mind. Talen stood and brought her up, setting her behind him. A quick glance around found fire to one side, a rushing river to the other, and demons before him.

"I guess we fight, then," he murmured.

The demons walked out of the smoke—three of them looking a little worse for wear. All were blond with black eyes, showing their lineage as purebred demons, and they had dressed in head-to-toe black from shoes to shirts. Blood matted their chests and necks from bullet holes that were still visibly closing. Who were they? Definitely not allies with the demon nation.

Feelings bombarded her from every direction. Anger from Talen, fear and intent from the demons. She drew protective shields into herself to mute her empathic abilities.

Talen's body visibly tensed. "Love the matching outfits, boys."

The guy in front held a green laser gun at his side. A cut marred his left cheekbone, and he rubbed it, his eyes glittering. "You shot me."

"Looks like the bullet barely scraped you," Talen returned. "You're fine, so go away before you end up with the entire Realm on your ass. This is your one chance to avoid a lifetime of pain."

"No." The lead demon lowered his chin, and his pupils overtook his irises. "We have backup on the way, but I don't think we're gonna need it."

Talen held up a hand.

The demon's eyes opened wider, and he tried to move forward, his body shaking.

Whoa. Cara hadn't seen Talen do that in eons. She'd almost forgotten his ability to attack and control the nervous system of an enemy. Apparently the gift halted a demon mind attack—at least temporarily.

The other two demons darted forward, only to also hit that invisible Talen wall. The first guy stopped completely, while the other one managed to twitch his hands.

"Cara? Start running and keep going until you reach the shifters. They should be here soon," Talen said through gritted teeth, his voice a hoarse rumble.

She couldn't leave him there with three furious demons. Even with his talents, at some point, they'd break free. Gingerly reaching into the back of her pants, she drew out a sopping wet laser gun. It probably still worked. "How about I just shoot them?" she whispered.

"Won't work."

Shoot. Immortal laser guns couldn't take a little water? Definite flaw in the design. "I'm not leaving you." The demon twitching his hands slid one foot forward.

"Now." His order held bite this time.

This was one of those moments. She had a gun, and he needed backup, but having her there would complicate things. She calculated the odds in her mind and finally settled her stance. "You need me just in case." She wasn't an idiot plunging headfirst into danger. She was a healthy immortal who wanted to protect her mate.

"Move your ass now," he growled, sweat rolling down the side of his face.

A mate who didn't want her protection. The lead demon broke free.

Cara yelped and pulled the trigger. Her gun sputtered, and no laser came out. Shit.

The demon lunged for Talen, hitting him midcenter, and throwing them both into the sheer rock mountain.

The other two demons slowly broke free of their bonds, moving forward, determination on their smooth faces.

Cara shook out the gun, several times, and water went flying. *Please work, damn it.* She lifted and aimed. Green shot from the gun, the light impacting the nearest demon and turning to metal when it met flesh.

The demon yelled and grabbed his chest. She fired two more

times, aiming for his face. The bullets took out his cheekbone, and he fell to the ground, unconscious.

Pain and brutal images of hell pierced her brain. Her mind exploded, and she dropped the gun, grabbing her ears.

The demon mind attacking her stalked nearer, his gaze hard, his vision focused.

"Stop," she whimpered.

He increased the pressure, and imaginary blades ripped through her cerebellum. Her eyes closed, and blood spurted from her nose. She barely heard the roar of fury from her mate.

Suddenly, the pain stopped. She held perfectly still as her nervous system stopped firing her nerves to life. Her lungs relaxed. Slowly, she lifted her head.

Two demons were prone on the ground, out cold. Talen punched the demon who'd attacked her mind right in the face, and the demon crashed into a tree. He came up swinging, roaring with fury.

Talen caught him and they grappled.

The demon lowered his chin, and Talen's head jerked back.

Oh, hell. Mind attack. Cara's vision was fuzzy, but she patted around her to find the gun. Where was the freaking gun?

Talen growled in pain, his movements slowing. The demon continued the mind assault, his gaze intense, and kicked Talen in the chin.

Cara cried out and tried to scramble to her feet.

The demon turned on her, and pain sliced through her eyes.

She fell, and dizziness swirled around her. "Talen," she whispered.

"Cara," he yelled. His head went back, and his shoulders straightened. Bellowing, he rushed the demon and plunged fingers into the demon's throat, angling just right. A brutal twist of his wrist, and he yanked the demon into his fangs to pierce and cut. The demon's head flopped down its body to roll into the river.

One in a million vampire soldiers could've succeeded in that move.

He turned then, his fangs down, his eyes a glowing gold. Sometimes she forgot the deadly predator that lived inside her mate.

She swallowed and tried to stand.

Instantly, he was at her side, wiping blood off her face. "Are you all right?" he asked.

She nodded, even as tears spilled from her eyes. "Are you?"

"Fine." He took her hand and glanced around. Blood dripped

down his chin. Then he stiffened and pressed her against the rock before covering her.

Several wolves, graceful and brown, ran out of the forest.

Talen's shoulders relaxed. "You're late," he muttered.

After washing the blood off in the river, Talen kept an eye on his mate as they maneuvered through the forest, covered on all sides by a wolf shifter contingent. The shifters remained in wolf form and easily avoided the fires being snuffed out by human fighters.

Finally, they reached an old logging road, where several off-road vehicles waited. The wolves shifted into human form and quickly donned clothing.

Terrent Vilks, the Alpha of the Raze pack, loped toward him. "It's good to see you," he said as they shook hands.

Talen grinned at his old friend. "You, too. Sorry about the unexpected visit."

Terrent shrugged. "You're welcome any time, and I know Maggie would love to see Cara." His eyes darkened with concern as he took in Cara's bedraggled form. "You okay, darlin'?"

She nodded, her body shivering.

Talen slid an arm around her and tucked her close, not liking the pallor of her skin. "She could use dry clothing and some warm food."

"Absolutely." Terrent motioned them into a battered Jeep. "We're a couple of hours out, but I'll blast the heat." He jerked his head toward three of his soldiers. "Go back and clean up the garbage."

Talen lifted Cara into the backseat and slid in next to her, settling her against his body. Fury threatened to consume him, but he kept his hold gentle and murmured a thanks when Terrent tossed back a blanket. He wrapped her close and tried to keep his temper in check.

When he'd seen her, blood pouring down her face, raw agony in her pretty blue eyes from the demon attack, he'd nearly lost his mind. He'd torn the head off a demon, which sure as hell wasn't a normal ability.

Besides anger, confusion swamped him. His order for her to run had been crystal-clear, and she'd disobeyed it completely. While he knew she had her own mind, when it came to battles or fighting, he was the strategic leader of the entire Realm, much less within his little family. Just because the current war had ended didn't mean the danger to them was also gone.

He'd been mated to the woman for over two decades, and he still couldn't figure out how her mind worked.

Before they had family, if anything had happened to her, he would've avenged her slightest pain and then followed her into the unknown. Now they had kids and even a grandchild, and he couldn't leave them alone.

So Cara needed to keep herself safe, damn it.

She murmured and cuddled closer to his side, her eyes closing. He tucked her into his body, holding her close, providing safety and warmth.

Terrent ignited the engine and drove over several bumps. "Sorry."

"It's all right. She's out," Talen said softly.

Somber brown eyes met his in the rearview mirror. "Demon mind attack?"

"Yes."

"Why didn't she run?" Terrent asked, his eyebrows drawing down.

Talen shook his head. "She stayed and fought with the gun."

"Did you tell her to run? We would've caught up with her quickly and then helped you."

"Of course I told her to run," Talen snapped.

Terrent grinned. "How'd she do?"

Talen's lips twitched. "She was magnificent. Kicked ass, actually." He didn't bother to keep the pride from his voice. "Though my heart almost stopped."

Terrent chuckled. "My mate never listens, either."

No. Maggie Malone Vilks was one stubborn little wolf, and Talen knew, because he'd helped to train her years ago. "Is Maggie still as clumsy as ever?"

Terrent's eyes sparkled as he nodded. "I swear she tripped over air the other day. She claims there was something in her way, but, Talen? It was just air."

Talen grinned. "I've seen her in action."

"Oh, and we're having the wedding next spring," Terrent said with a sigh.

Only Maggie would want a real human wedding. She and Terrent had been planning it for years, but the war had kept intruding. "Can't wait," Talen said, biting back another smile.

"Shut up." Terrent shook his head. "She's not even human. I mean, she was never human. The woman is a wolf, for Pete's sake."

And yet, the tough Alpha was going through with a wedding to make her happy. Talen breathed out, his body finally calming after the fight. "Sometimes they want weddings. Cara and I had one."

"Yeah, but not with the white dress, flowers, and all the music," Terrent rumbled, speeding up until trees flew by outside.

"Sometimes they don't make any damn sense," Talen whispered.

Terrent scratched his chin. "You and your mate aren't gonna fight at my place, are you? Because then the women will be on her side, the men on yours, and then I have a bunch of pissed-off wolves to deal with. Including my mate, who has a mean streak."

"Sucks being Alpha."

Terrent sighed. "Well, at least you didn't bring your youngest with you."

Talen winced. "Um."

"Um, what?"

"When the demons started following us, I'm sure Dage gave Garrett a call. He's in Seattle working with the witch Enforcers, and his mama would like to see him." Talen leaned back and rested his head. "He'll behave."

"I'm more worried about a couple of young wolf shifters, crazy cheerleaders, I have to keep a constant eye on," Terrent ground out.

"Then I should probably warn you that Garrett's best friend, Logan Kyllwood, will more than likely be with him if they visit." Talen didn't have time to worry about female wolves.

Terrent tapped impatient fingers against the steering wheel. "Great. Twenty-year-old vampire and demon, two horny kids you sent to work in Seattle because they kept getting in trouble, and they're coming here."

Well, since he put it like that. "I give you my word they will both behave and not deflower anybody."

"Hell."

Yeah, the boys could be a little wild, but they'd be on their best behavior with Cara there. Truth be told, Talen missed both of them and pretty much would jump at the chance to meet up at the wolf headquarters. The work they were doing was important and good training, but his home was kind of quiet without them. Although his kitchen was stocked for once. "I hope you have a lot of food on hand."

"Plenty." Terrent relaxed as the fires dissipated around them. "Also, we're safe. The land around our headquarters is well protected from the fires."

"Good. Cara was having problems breathing." Yet another reason the woman should've listened to him and gotten out of the line of fire.

"It's weird, right?" Terrent asked.

"What?"

"Life without the war. Trying to have normal lives when we've been fighting for so long. It's like everybody is trying on new skin that doesn't quite fit." The Alpha wolf rubbed his chin, his tone thoughtful. "Although, it's nice to have peace."

"Those of us who've lived centuries know that peace is temporary. It's always just *temporary*, my friend." Talen shrugged. "It's not just that. My instincts are flaring and sharp . . . and I don't know why. Danger is near, and I can't quite put my finger on it."

"Living through peace is sometimes the hardest part," Terrent murmured.

Amen to that. Talen looked down at his sleeping mate. Her dark lashes lay against too-pale skin, and even now a dot of blood marred her upper lip. They had to find some sort of way to allow her the freedom she craved without putting her at risk. "The bigger problem is that when peace ends, it's often at the price of losing those we love."

Nothing and nobody could take this woman from him. Not even peace.

No matter what.

Chapter 5

Cara awoke alone in the wide bed, safe and warm under a thick quilt. She blinked several times and partially sat up to see a still-smoldering fire safely contained in a stone fireplace across the spacious room. Exposed beams made up the high ceiling, while tongue-and-groove wood made up the walls. A window set into the nearest wall showed the very dim dawn light peeking through the blinds. It had to be about four in the morning.

The bedroom door opened, and Talen strode in, wearing running sweats and a ripped T-shirt. His thick brown hair had matted to his head, and his muscles strained in his arms and neck. His natural scent of wild pine filled the room.

She blinked. "You went running?"

"Yes." He moved past the bed to an attached bathroom, all male grace, quietly shutting the door.

Wonderful. They'd been attacked by demons, had fought hard, and instead of sleeping, he'd gone for a run in wolf land.

The shower started.

She flopped back down and pulled the covers up to her neck. Talen in a quiet mood was never a good thing, and as terrible as his temper could be, she much preferred it to silence. The man had gotten too used to treating her with kid gloves through the years as she'd battled the deadly virus.

When was he going to see that she was healthy?

Not that he would've been okay with her fighting demons, no matter how strong she became.

The shower shut off, and her heart started to thrum. Seconds later, he opened the door, a towel wrapped around his waist. His hair hung to his shoulders, and a shadow covered his rugged jaw. The muscles in his chest shifted as he moved, so broad and strong.

His golden gaze remained steady as he crossed the room, dropped the towel, and slid into the bed.

She rolled onto her back, keeping some space between them. "Are you mad at me?"

"No."

She didn't believe him. "It's okay if you are." Then they could fight about it.

"I'm not mad."

The stubborn bastard. "I think you are."

"I can't help what you think."

Oh, he did not just go passive-aggressive on her. What happened to the full-on aggressive mate she fell in love with? At this point, she was going to have to kick his ass to get him to lose the attitude and treat her like she wasn't some weak invalid. "You're being a dick." She moved to get out of the bed.

One hand wrapped around her bicep and pulled her across the flannel sheets.

She kicked out, struggling to be free.

He casually and way too easily subdued her by rolling over and flattening his huge body over her. "Calling names isn't nice," he said, his eyes burning.

She narrowed her gaze into a glare and tried to ignore the heat pouring from him. His elbows kept his weight off her, but still, the press of sinew and strength made her breath catch in her lungs. His cock, hard as steel, pressed against her clit.

Desire slid through her, flaring nerve endings to life.

Her body softened and responded to him, as it had since the first night he'd mated her, so long ago. His bite, his mark, had changed her at a chromosomal level. One that responded only to him, and so damn easily. "We need to talk," she murmured, her nipples sharpening against his chest.

"Talking hasn't done us much good lately." Desire poured from him, infusing the room with the masculine scent of pine. "Let's try something else." His head dipped, and his mouth took hers.

Every time was like the first time. Shock, heat, and desire so hot it singed. The kiss was electricity and ice, infused with the dark taste of the man himself. His tongue stroked hers, and his sinewed body pressed hers farther into the bed.

She tunneled her hands through his thick, wet hair, holding tight.

He growled into her mouth, and wetness spilled between her thighs. So easily, and he knew it. His teeth nipped her lips, wandered down her jaw, and scraped along her neck. "You're too beautiful for words," he murmured, his tongue flicking a nipple.

Pleasure, dark and edged, winged through her. She arched against him, her fingers digging in to his scalp. "Talen," she moaned.

He licked her other nipple. "Sometimes I dream about these hard little nipples."

Her body pretty much lit on fire from within.

"But then I realize there's more pleasure to be found." He reached up and removed her hands from his head. Kicking the bedclothes away, he dropped to his knees on the floor and yanked her toward him.

She gasped, her arms flinging out.

His hands pressed her thighs wide, opening her for him. She looked down, her breath catching at the raw hunger on his face. His gaze, brooding and primal, captured hers as he licked his lips.

She fought a groan. "Talen?"

"Mine, Cara. Don't you ever forget it." His heated breath brushed her clit, and her body arched. His mouth covered her, and he sucked her clit into his mouth.

Delicious, decadent, and dangerous. Ecstasy bit into her. She threw back her head and shut her eyes, allowing pleasure to take over her body.

His fingers caressed her, pressing inside her, stretching her tight flesh. He stroked her inner muscles, his tongue lashing her, until she was thrashing and trembling with the need to climax.

He kept her right on the edge. She tried to grab his head, but her hands flailed around her. So close. So damn close. Waves of sensation built inside her, so fast, so intense. Pleasure broke over her, and she cried out, arching into his mouth with an orgasm so powerful sparks flashed behind her eyes.

Talen stood and came over her, fitting his cock at her entrance and working inside her with slow, deliberate thrusts. His teeth raked her shoulder, and one arm banded around her waist, half-lifting her from the bed.

His cock filled her, overtook her, pleasured her. He hammered inside her, and mini-explosions rocked her core, all building up to something that almost scared her. She dug her nails into his chest and tilted her pelvis to take more of him.

He growled low and pounded harder. His teeth latched on to her neck. The erotic pain sent her over, exploding ecstasy inside her. She cried out his name, holding tight.

He dropped his head to her neck and came, his body shuddering.

She released him, drowsiness attacking her. He grasped the bed-clothes and dragged them up, covering them both before drawing her into his arms to wrap his big body around her.

"We still need to talk," she murmured sleepily, wiggling her butt into his groin.

A hand on her hip stopped her. "Go to sleep."

"I'm going to continue to push and work publicly for the humans. You're going to have to let that temper free at some point," she whispered.

He stiffened and then slowly relaxed around her. "You'd better hope not."

She blinked. "Why not?"

"Because if I let this temper free, you won't be able to sit for a month." He kissed her head. "Go to sleep."

She opened her eyes to stare at the dying fire. A month, huh? Well, some things were worth the end result. For now, she needed to sleep. Then she'd push her stubborn, dominant, Alpha mate to the end of his rope so they could move on from this odd place they seemed to be stuck in.

God, she hoped they both survived.

Talen slipped from the cabin out to the misty day, taking note of the wolves stationed around the area. He gave a head nod to one of them before continuing down the worn path to a building set deeper into the territory.

"I wondered when you'd show," Terrent said, leaning against the rough-worn planks, his scuffed boots crossed. Today he'd donned a ripped gray T-shirt along with older-than-old jeans.

"Did you wait for me?" Talen asked, stretching his neck.

Terrent nodded. "Sure. They attacked you and your mate . . . I figure they're yours for now. Then I'll discuss their hunting my friends in my territory." The wolf bared his fangs.

Talen grinned. "Thanks for the guards."

"We always have sentinels roaming the property, but I figured a couple extra around your cabin would be a good idea since your mate was just threatened." Terrent shoved open the door and stalked inside. "Maggie will probably head over there shortly. She misses her friends at Realm headquarters."

"They miss her, too." Talen followed his friend into a storage area complete with ropes, gardening tools, and what looked like a bunch of empty flowerpots.

Terrent kept going and kicked open a trapdoor. His boots clomped as he started to descend.

Talen glanced down, surprised to see wide cement stairs. He followed. The rock walls on either side of the stairs were well lit with mining lights. After minutes of descending, he reached a tunnel cut into the mountain.

Doors to several cells had been secured to rock and cement walls.

"The first one, the guy I think was in charge, is in here." Terrent released several locks on a red steel door before yanking it open.

Talen nodded and stepped inside. He gave a low whistle. "Impressive." While rock made up the floor and walls, a bulletproof-glass wall separated his area from the prisoner's area, which had a cot, a toilet, and a sink. "You've put some time into this."

"I had hoped never to need it," Terrent said, stalking to the northern wall to open a silver panel.

"What's that?" Talen asked, glancing back at the demon staring at him through the glass.

Terrent shrugged. "I have the cell rigged to send electrical shocks through it if your pal there tries a mind attack."

The wolves didn't mess around, now, did they? Of course, the safeguards at Talen's headquarters had plenty of such options.

He stepped closer to the glass, and once there, he could discern small holes for communication. "Who sent you?" he asked.

The demon pushed from the bed and stood, his eyes black, his chin up. "Fuck you."

Terrent flipped a lever, and the cell lit up. The demon hissed, and his fangs dropped, pain emanating from him until Terrent disengaged the lever.

"This is boring for me, and I don't want to see you destroyed," Talen said calmly. The demon was much younger than he had originally thought, and he really didn't want to hurt the kid. "But you threatened my mate, and I want answers. Start talking now."

"Listen. We were hired for a job, and that's it. I don't know or really care about you," the demon gasped, blood flowing from his nose. "We didn't do anything to harm you or your mate and just had a job to do."

"Who hired you to get the samples?" Talen asked. He wasn't surprised that there were immortals out in the world who wanted to end all research into a virus that negated bonds.

The demon blinked. "What samples?"

Everything in Talen stilled, stretched, and then went silent. "Excuse me?"

The demon frowned, wariness settling across his smooth face. "Ah, is that what was in the cooler you wouldn't let go of? We were wondering. What kind of samples?"

Talen stiffened. "If you weren't after the samples, why did you attack us?"

The demon bobbed his head. "We didn't exactly attack you. All right, we kind of did, but we didn't do any harm. It was one little job, man."

"If you don't answer the question, I'm going to rip the wall free and then tear you apart," Talen said through gritted teeth, his stomach roiling. "Once last time. Why did you attack us?"

The demon backed away, the scent of fear rolling from him. He looked toward Terrent. "I'm requesting asylum from the wolf nation."

"Denied," Terrent drawled. "Answer the vampire's question."

The guy paled. "Okay, but remember it was just a job."

"The job?" Talen asked, his voice going hoarse.

"The girl. The job was to take the woman." The demon backed to the wall, his hands out. "Safely. We were supposed to transfer her safely and not injure a hair on her head. I promise."

Rage boiled through Talen, yet he kept his face stoic. "Who hired you?"

"A group of demons out of Alaska known as—"

"The Sadovskys," Talen said, energy rippling through him as the puzzle pieces dropped into place. He had dossiers on the group as a possible enemy to watch. "Why do they want Cara?"

The demon swallowed, and his Adam's apple bobbled. "I don't know all of it."

"Tell me what you do know," Talen said, rapidly losing patience.

"She's called the First One, and they want her for some kind of testing."

"Well, shit," Terrent murmured. "Cara was the first vampire mate infected with Virus-Twenty-seven, wasn't she?"

Talen nodded.

The demon cleared his throat, his need to please obvious. "Plus, I think her granddaughter is the one who cured the virus, right? The baby vampire with an X chromosome? The Sadovskys just want to test Cara."

"To create a serum that counteracts the virus," Talen murmured. The virus was cured, but it had been altered so mated vampires could become unmated . . . maybe.

"The Sadovskys are purists," Terrent said.

The demon nodded. "We were just hired by them because we live local here. We're not part of their group."

"You should be careful who you work for, kid." Talen moved for the door.

"Maybe, but you should be careful who you kill," the demon shot back. When Talen turned around to face him, he paled. "The guy you killed? He was one of the Sadovskys."

Explained why the guy fought better than the rest of them.

"Now they'll be after you as well as your mate," the demon said quietly.

Talen shoved open the door and stomped into the long hallway, his gut on fire.

Terrent followed him. "What about this moron?"

Talen's temples began to pound. "We don't kill morons or young, stupid kids. Beat the hell out of him, scare the shit out of him, and let him go."

"That was my thought, as well." Terrent engaged the locks. "Well, look at the bright side."

Talen stopped and turned to face his friend. "Bright side?"

"Yeah. Your instincts were right on track. Your mate is in danger."

Chapter 6

Cara finished braiding her hair and then walked outside into the crisp morning. Her jeans felt a little tight, but she had just washed them, so she did a couple of leg bends and squats to loosen them up.

"You're exercising?" a soft voice said from her left.

She swung around to see her friend. "Maggie!" Cara hustled down the porch and hugged the wolf shifter. "And no. My jeans are tight." She laughed.

Maggie leaned back, shoving curly brown hair from her face. "You look wonderful as usual."

Cara grinned. "So do you." Her friend looked amazing in a deep green sweater with a brown skirt and very cool leather boots. "Great outfit."

Maggie rolled her eyes. "Somebody has to dress for success around here. I swear, if it fits, Terrent wears it, no matter how old. Last week he actually put on a pair of bell-bottom jeans . . . the kind from the seventies."

Cara winced. "The genuine kind?"

"Oh, yeah. I burned them that night before he could stop me." Maggie's pretty brown eyes lit up. "Then I threw in a cloak from the eighteen hundreds." She frowned. "Looking back, I might've been able to sell that on eBay."

Cara chuckled. Wolves were wicked smart when it came to finances. "You would've made a fortune."

Maggie sighed and tucked her arm through Cara's. "Come with me. I have a surprise for you."

"I love surprises." Cara trooped along next to her friend, fully appreciating the stunning fall foliage all around them. "It's beautiful here." She catalogued a blue spruce, several cottonwoods, many pine trees, and kept going in her head. Finally, they reached a wide clearing in front of a sprawling wooden lodge. "We're at headquarters."

"Yes." Maggie stopped and whistled through her teeth.

The door to the lodge opened, and a large vampire strode through.

"Garrett!" Cara called, releasing Maggie and running for her son.

"Mom." He caught her as she reached him, swinging her up. "I wanted to let you sleep in." Setting her down, he leaned back to study her. "You all right?"

She smacked his chest. "Of course. What are you doing here?"

"Uncle Dage called and said you'd be here." Shocking gray eyes surveyed the area before he concentrated on her again. "Headquarters is secure, and I like it here." He smiled, and lines crinkled at his eyes. "The food is great. Huckleberry pancakes."

Cara winced. "Don't eat them out of headquarters, sweetie."

"I'll try." He looked down at her, so tall and broad. In his early twenties, Garrett was sinewed and fit with Talen's strong build.

She reached out and touched his dark hair, which almost reached his shoulders. "You're growing your hair out?"

He shook his head. "I hadn't noticed. Been busy with the Enforcers."

"Where's—" Just as Cara started to ask the question, Logan Kyllwood loped out the front door, munching on a bagel.

"Mrs. Kayrs," he said, his green eyes lighting in pleasure.

"Cara," she corrected him for the zillionth time. The demon-vampire mix was obvious in his hoarse voice and large build. The boys, both the same age, had quickly bonded when Janie had mated Zane, Logan's brother. Family was family, as they'd both attested. "Are you two behaving?"

"We are," Logan said solemnly, his lips twitching. "Honestly, we don't have much of a choice, you know? The Enforcers are always around." The boys were helping the witch Enforcers on a case in Seattle involving a deadly mineral that harmed witches.

"Ah, I know. How are you feeling about your mother mating Daire Dunne?" Daire was a dangerous Enforcer who had always seemed a little cranky and a lot honorable.

Logan lifted a massive shoulder. "We decided to let him live."

Cara laughed. That was as good as a declaration of love, now, wasn't it? "Smart of you."

"Well, Mom loves him. Plus, she likes to rob banks lately, and Dunne has a talent there." Logan shifted to the side, his gaze narrowing. "I sense a demon near."

Garrett moved faster than she could track, scooping her up and setting her on the porch behind him.

Cara caught her breath as Logan deposited Maggie right next to her. The boys took up defensive positions in front of them.

"Oh, hell no," Cara muttered, planting her hands on her hips. Both she and Maggie knew how to fight. "Garrett Talen Kayrs—"

"The demon?" Garrett asked Logan, visibly scanning the area.

Logan shook his head. "It's muted . . . but I know one is around here. I mean, one besides me."

Garrett glanced over his shoulder. Even though he was two steps down from Cara, his eyes were level with hers. "Mom? Do you mind going inside? Please?"

Her face heated until the tips of her ears burned. "Yes, I do actually mind. I'm trained, and I'm your *mother*. That means *I* protect *you*." She stomped down the steps but then had to tilt back her head to glare at him.

He shuffled his feet.

Cara turned on his friend. "Logan Henry Kyllwood? Why are you angling your body between me and the forest?"

Logan looked over her head at Garrett, a definite *please help* expression in his eyes.

Garrett grasped her arm. "Mom, I'm really sorry, but, well, you know. You're not a vampire."

"Or a demon," Logan whispered.

Maggie tripped down the steps. "I'm a wolf."

Garrett cleared his throat. "Yes, ma'am." Even so, he turned just enough to block both women from the unguarded tree line.

Cara rolled her eyes. "You two are unbelievable."

Two girls wandered out from around the lodge, both with long hair and short skirts. They stopped cold and then smiled.

Garrett frowned. "Where the hell is that demon, Logan?" he muttered.

Logan drew in a breath. "I'm not sure."

One of the girls bounced closer. "Did you say 'demon'? You mean, the ones they have in the cells?"

"Cells?" Garrett asked, remaining ridiculously close to his mother.

"Yeah. The demons that chased Mrs. Kayrs are in the cells being, ah, questioned right now." The girl closest to them smiled. "I'm Shannon, and this is Andrea."

"Hi," Andrea said, her eyes sparkling.

"Well, hello." Logan slid toward the girls, obviously no longer worried about a demon attack.

"Oh, hell no," Terrent Vilks bellowed, emerging from the trees.

Logan sighed.

Cara caught sight of Talen right behind the wolf, and she took a quick inventory. No blood. Whatever questioning had occurred apparently hadn't taken much of a fight. "Did they say who wanted the samples?"

"Kind of." Talen reached them and clasped his son in a hug. Then, for good measure, he hugged Logan, too. "Thanks for coming."

"Sure." Garrett smiled and shifted so that Talen was between him and Cara. "Mom's glad we're here."

Logan nodded solemnly.

Cara shook her head. "I'm really glad you boys are here, but you have to lay off the caveman-protectiveness crap. I have enough to deal with right now with your dad."

Garrett dipped his head toward the girls. "I'm Garrett." He flashed a dimple.

Andrea chuckled.

"No. No, no, no." Terrent pointed at the girls. "Both of you have duties to attend to, and now is the time to get to it."

Andrea pouted. "Somebody has to show the visitors around."

"Not you." Terrent bared his teeth. "Work. Now."

Shannon rolled her eyes. "Fine, but we'll be finished by lunchtime." Her smile lit up the entire clearing. "We'll see you guys then."

"Sure thing," Logan agreed.

Talen waited until the girls had headed across the clearing to a bunch of cabins before speaking. "You two are such complete dorks."

"They didn't think so." Garrett rocked back on his heels. "I kinda liked Andrea."

"Good. Shannon seemed to like me." Logan fist-bumped his buddy.

Terrent growled as only a wolf could do.

Maggie smacked his arm. "Knock it off."

"Their mothers are on that mah-jongg cruise, and we're supposed to watch out for them." Terrent straightened to his full and rather impressive height. "If anybody, and I mean *anybody*, touches either one of them, I will personally rip off his balls and shove them in his ears."

Logan winced. "Geez, man."

"Define *touch*," Garrett murmured.

Cara gasped and slapped her son's arm, while Talen bit his lip, obviously trying not to laugh. "Do not encourage him," she admonished her husband.

Talen clapped Garrett at the base of the neck, and by her son's wince, it wasn't gentle. "We're guests here," Talen said.

Garrett gave a short nod. "Got it."

"Logan?" Talen asked.

"I understand." Logan stuck his hands in his worn jeans.

Talen released Garrett, and by the twisting of his lips, he was still fighting a proud smile. Apparently smart-asses liked that quality in their offspring. "Why don't you guys go make yourselves useful and help the shifters drop the demons off back in town? Logan, as a demon, you should be able to ensure no demon attacks."

"Sure thing." Logan nodded.

Terrent pointed toward a trail into the woods. "Go that way, and you'll meet up with Lock and Ace, who are taking care of the demons. Thanks, guys."

The boys took off.

Talen snorted and repeated his son's words. " 'Define *touch*.' "

Terrent grinned. "Definitely your kid, Kayrs."

Pride glowed in Talen's golden eyes. "Copy that."

"Keep them away from the innocent cheerleaders, all right?" Terrent asked.

Cara hummed. The cheerleaders had seemed more than capable of taking care of themselves.

Maggie snorted. "Those two are more dangerous than Garrett and Logan put together. Assassin cheerleaders who can fight better than any warrior I've ever seen."

Terrent shrugged. "Don't care. No sex on my watch. When their mamas get back, then they can go as wild as they want." He slung an arm over Maggie's shoulder and tugged her into his lean body. "Morning, darlin'."

Maggie smiled and leaned up to kiss his chin. "Did you have fun with the demons?"

"Kind of." Terrent's lips turned down. "Was over quick, though. Not much to do. Demon was barely an adult and gave up the information fast."

Cara's eyebrows lifted. "Did they say who hired them to get the samples?"

Terrent cleared his throat, his gaze going to Talen.

Cara frowned. "Talen?"

He grasped her hand, his palm instantly enclosing her knuckles with warmth. "Let's go for a little walk, and then we can meet back here for breakfast." Without waiting for her agreement, he started down a path toward the mountain and tugged her along at his side.

"I'll get coffee going," Maggie called from behind them.

Cara nodded and tripped alongside him. He slowed down. "Sorry."

"What's wrong?" she asked.

He breathed in, his muscled form blocking out the sun. "The demons were sent to take you by a purist group from Alaska."

Her stride hitched. "What?"

"The group is against any research into negating mating bonds, and since you were the first ever infected, that they know about anyway, they want you for testing." His voice remained low and calm, but tension swelled from him with the heat of anger.

Crap. "So I'm in danger again."

"Apparently so, mate. Sorry about that." He sounded more irritated than sorry.

"I'm not living my life hiding at headquarters," she said, searching deep for both patience and strength. When he started to answer, she held out a hand. "Oh, I'm not going to do anything stupid or put myself in danger, but if we take precautions, we can still live a little." They had the best trained forces in the entire world at their disposal, and once in a while, she needed to explore the world.

"I understand," he said.

But did he? Somehow, she wasn't sure.

Chapter 7

Several hours after leaving wolf territory, Talen had to admit that having the boys in the backseat of the borrowed Escalade eased his mind a little bit. He'd had time to train them since the war had ended, and they both fought well.

Cara relaxed in the passenger seat once again, humming softly to herself. She liked having the boys there as much as he did.

"Are you feeling better?" he asked, taking note of her sparkling eyes and rosy cheeks.

"Much." She rubbed both hands down her dark jeans, her fingers digging into her knees. "Just fine."

Logan leaned forward. "A demon mind attack can leave impressions for a couple of days. You're probably still feeling the aftereffects."

She nodded. "I think so, too. My head still aches a little bit."

Talen frowned and leaned over to brush his fingers against her forehead. A slight pounding, a bit of a pain, echoed in his own brain. He drew out her pain, all of it, and allowed his head to hurt for a second before banishing the ache into nowhere.

She smiled. "Much better."

"Why didn't you say anything?" he asked. One of the greatest pleasures of his life was taking away any pain she had.

She shrugged. "It just started to hurt a little while ago. Not enough to really worry about."

That was his woman—tough and stubborn. Yeah, she was right about exploring the world a bit, and he could understand her desire to do so since she'd been cooped up for so long during the war. She hadn't even had a chance to take immortality out and play with it yet. Although, she could lose her head and her life, so she still needed to be careful.

She glanced at him from the corner of her eye. "You're thinking awfully hard."

"I was thinking of a trip to Africa. That maybe you'd like to visit there." He could show her the world and cover her back at the same time.

Her smile lit up her entire face. "I've never been there and would love to go."

"Sounds good to me," Garrett chimed in from the backseat.

"Me too," Logan agreed.

Talen cut them a look. "You two are heading back to work with the Enforcers until that stupid Apollo drug is taken off the streets. Then we'll talk about you guys doing some traveling." He wouldn't mind having them protect Cara at all times. But first, they needed to see their mission through.

They took the interstate and made several changes until arriving at an innocuous building in downtown Bellevue. Talen parked outside in a no parking area.

"Take the cooler inside to Dr. Brown, get a receipt, and come back out," Talen said to the boys.

They nodded, and Garrett carried the cooler out of the car and swept the vacant sidewalk with his gaze before he and Logan strode through the glass front door, acting like any other messenger service.

"They look so grown-up," Cara said, watching them disappear into the three-story brick building.

"I know." Talen reached out and covered her hand with his. "I called the Enforcers earlier and asked if they could have a few days off, and Kellach said it was fine."

Cara leaned forward, and her eyes sparkled. "They can come to Hawaii?"

"Yes, but they're staying in their own room."

"Totally agree."

They sat there in comfortable silence for a few moments. The misty day hung around them with the promise of rain.

Cara played with a loose string on her jeans. "I feel like we're not getting along."

His hand covered hers. "We're getting along, but for some reason, you're pushing me and hard. I don't understand why."

She turned, and a smile tickled her mouth. "I'm tired of you treating me like I'm still ill. Like I'm fragile."

He studied her, those dark eyes knowing, obviously thinking through his response. "You are fragile, but I know you're not ill." Sighing, he tugged her closer to him and immediately surrounded her with the scent of male and pine. "You're also unsettled, and you're looking for something, and I can't figure out what it is. It's frustrating."

She blinked. *Was* she looking for something? Her life had been on hold for so long, perhaps she need to think things through. But no matter what, she was strong enough to be Talen Kayrs's mate, and he needed to realize that fact. "I have a thought to shake things up," she mused.

He barked out a laugh. "That's all I need."

Perhaps that was exactly what he needed. Cara opened her mouth to say so, when a loud *boom* erupted from the building.

She gasped and scooted over to look out the window.

"Hell." Talen tapped an ear communicator. "Garrett? Logan? Status now."

Smoke billowed out from a second-floor window. "There's fire." She moved to open the door, and Talen stopped her with a hand on her arm. Her head swiveled. "Let go. The boys are in there."

"I know." Talen flipped open the glove box and drew out two green guns, handing her one. "Stay in the car." Indecision darkened his features.

Heat flared through Cara. "Go help the boys. I'll start the engine in case we need to run."

Another explosion rocked the day.

Talen looked at the silent doorway, a muscle ticking in his jaw.

Cara smacked him with the gun. "Go get the boys."

"Can't leave you." His teeth clenched together, and his entire body vibrated. "The boys can fight."

"If you're not going, I am." She reached for the latch on the door.

"No." He pulled her away.

Glass shattered, and Cara twisted to see Garrett fly through the air on top of another man. They landed on the sidewalk with a loud *thump*, and cement flew in every direction.

"Garrett!" she yelled, kicking free of Talen and shoving the door open.

Talen was right behind her, gun out, gaze surveying the broken window on the second floor. "Is he okay?"

"No." Garrett groaned and rolled off the unconscious man. A cut bled above his right eye, and bruises already darkened his chin. "The demons were waiting for the samples." He stood and shook his head, spraying blood, and turned for the front door.

"Wait." Cara grabbed for his arm. "What are you doing?"

"Logan is in there," Garrett said grimly. "Hey. Can I have that gun?"

Cara handed over the weapon, her mind spinning. "Talen? Go with him."

The pattering of gunfire filled the day.

Suddenly, Logan leaped through the glass doors, scattering shards, the green cooler in his hand. Talen swept Cara up and around, shielding her from the glistening sharp projectiles.

"Go, go, go," Logan yelled, dodging into the back of the SUV.

Two men in all black, both bleeding profusely, ran out the door, already firing at the vehicle.

Talen tossed Cara into the passenger side and ran around to the front, firing his gun the entire time. The two men jumped to opposite sides, out of the barrage of bullets.

"Seat belts," Talen said grimly, igniting the engine and hitting DRIVE in one smooth motion.

Garrett leaned out the backseat window, firing at the men still shooting. One bellowed in a shout of pain. "Fucker," Garrett muttered, getting off several more shots before Talen careened around a far corner.

The boys sat back, both breathing heavily.

Cara turned around, her heartbeat roaring through her head and echoing in her ears. "Are you all right?" she gasped.

They both nodded.

"What the hell happened?" Talen whipped the vehicle around a corner and down another street.

"They were waiting for us," Garrett muttered, wiping blood off his chin.

Cara tried to calm her breathing. "What about the lab techs?"

"Tied up in the second-story lab," Logan said. "I tossed my knife at the security guard, so they should be free soon."

"I hit nine-one-one on the phone before tackling that demon out the window," Garrett said, poking at a purple bruise on his left cheekbone.

Sirens trilled in the distance.

"Good job," Talen said. "Cara? Call Emma and ask her where we should send those samples now. This lab has been compromised. How the demons found it, I'd sure as shit like to know."

"Me too." She tugged her cell phone from her back pocket and quickly texted a message to her sister. "We have five more labs in the area that we could use, but that one had the best facility, I think."

"Stupid purists," Logan muttered, resting his head back on the seat. "What's the big deal, anyway?"

Cara swallowed. "Are you two sure you're all right?"

"Yes," they both said.

Talen tensed, looking out the back window as he drove rapidly past high-rise buildings. "Good. We have a problem."

Cara turned to look through the back window to see a black truck eating up the distance between them. Her frontal lobe began to ache. "Demons," she whispered.

Talen kept an eye on the truck as well as upcoming alleys. If the demons had waited for them, then surely the bastards had a trap already set in place. "Everybody armed?"

"I gave my gun to Garrett." Cara fumbled in the glove box and drew out a new purple prototype. "Whoa. What's this?" She turned the sleek gun over in her hand, her finger inching down the barrel.

"New gun the wolves have been working on," Talen said. "It's a laser that turns to bullets upon impacting flesh, but these are supposed to explode at that point. Like a hollow point."

Her eyes widened. "Cool." She hit the button to roll down her window and visibly stiffened in preparation.

"Relax your body, baby," Talen said, jerking the wheel around another high-rise building and almost careening right into a huge crane. Fucking construction. There were several cranes in the area, all surrounding at least three half-finished high-rise buildings. "The more relaxed you are, the better the aim. Deep breaths."

She nodded and blew out air. "I remember."

"Wanna trade guns?" Garrett asked, hope in his voice.

"Not a chance. Purple exploding gun is mine," Cara said with way too much anticipation.

Where was the trap? The truck kept on their ass but didn't make a move to intercept. Talen drove around the construction zone on high alert.

A low-flying black helicopter suddenly zoomed around the nearest crane.

"Shit." Talen yanked the wheel to the left just as the helicopter opened up fire. Bullets impacted the pavement and crane, flashing sparks in every direction. "Hold on," he yelled, turning quickly into the partially finished parking garage at the base of the nearest high-rise.

He slammed the accelerator to the floor. Steel beams, orange traffic cones, and boxes sped by in a blur. The Jeep jumped as he ascended through the parking area and screeched to a stop against the concrete block used for the central stairwell. "Out."

Everyone jumped out of the Jeep, and Talen looked around, quickly finding the door to the block. He grasped Cara's arm and all but carried her inside. "Stay here until I come get you."

Garrett and Logan fanned out, both taking sniper positions toward the two entrances.

Cara shoved against him. "Wait."

"No. Shoot anybody you don't recognize." Talen shut the door on her protest.

He turned back and waited, his senses sweeping out.

Vibrations. The helicopter. He gave hand signals to the boys, ordering them to stay in position and protect Cara. They gave twin nods, both well trained, suddenly looking like killers and not boys.

He ran for the open area outside the concrete ceiling, turned, and jumped to grab the cement floor above. His hands caught and he swung over, rolling to stand. Wood, metal, and cables littered the ground, which was still open to the air. Columns rose in several areas, concrete and round, all with rebar sticking out the tops.

The helicopter went high around the nearest building.

Timing. It was all about timing. He rushed full-bore for the nearest yellow climbing frame to a huge crane, swung inside, and started running up the ladder as fast as he could.

Thunder clamored, and the sun disappeared behind thick clouds. The first drop of rain hit his head as he went up, hand over foot, running up a ladder and trying not to look down. When he was at least fifteen stories up, he paused and set his ass against the heavy metal cage.

Drawing his weapon from his waist, he set it on the opposite metal bar and waited.

Chapter 8

Cara crouched in the stairwell, her ears straining to hear anything. The cool air over her shirt sent chills through her body. While she understood taking cover was a good idea, especially so Talen could fight, the idea of waiting inside while her son was in danger made her fingers itch to shove open the door.

The fact remained that she was human without immortal strength or speed, unlike Garrett, Logan, and Talen. Even so. Sitting and hiding didn't set well with her. Plus, she had trained as much as possible during the last couple of decades.

The weird pattering of gunfire came through the door, and she jumped to her feet.

Slowly, she inched the door open.

Logan and a demon fought hand to hand over by the entrance, their guns already on the floor and spinning away from them.

Garrett ran between stacks of steel beams, firing both in front of and behind him, trying to angle around closer to Logan.

Panic rippled through Cara. She held her breath and slipped from the safety of the stairwell, her gun out and her hand steady. She crept along the edge of the Jeep, letting it shield her. Slowly, she reached the rear bumper, crouched down, and waited.

Garrett barreled out from behind the beams, and a demon leaped out from behind some huge round ducts, tackling him into concrete blocks. They fell hard, and at least two blocks split open. Another demon rounded the corner from behind Garrett, his gun pointed.

Cara closed one eye, aimed, and fired.

A purple beam shot out of her gun, zipped through the air, and slammed into the demon with the gun. He frowned, and his arm lowered. *Pop!* His shoulder exploded.

He screamed, grabbed his arm, and dropped his gun. Blood spurted between his fingers and coated the cement in red. He turned and ran full-bore for the rough cement steps in the center of the area and quickly disappeared while going down.

Garrett rolled the guy on the ground over and punched his face three times, really hard. Blood spurted up. The crunch of cartilage and bone cracking made Cara nauseated.

Logan flipped his attacker over his shoulder and pile-drove him onto the floor. The guy passed out with a muffled roar, his face in the concrete, blood filling the area around his head. He might have twitched a few times.

Cara stood and took inventory of both boys. They were bloody and bruised but both standing.

Garrett shoved hair from his eyes, his chest panting. "Are you all right, Mom?"

She nodded, gulping down bile. "Yes. Where's your dad?"

Garrett shook his head and jogged out from under the concrete, then looked away and up in the air. Rain instantly coated his hair and face, mingling with the blood on his chin.

An arm slid around Cara's neck and yanked her back. Her head instantly hurt, and her eyes stung. She tried to struggle, but the barrel of a gun pressed against her jugular. Where the hell had this guy been hiding?

Logan strode toward her, his hands up, his gaze concentrated above her right shoulder. "You don't want to do this, buddy. Trust me."

Garrett's gaze swung down, and his entire being seemed to still. He moved toward them, his gaze dangerously intense. "Let her go, and I promise you, I won't rip your fucking head off your body today."

Cara shivered. She'd never seen her son in killing mode, and he was almost as frightening as his father. His metallic-gray eyes darkened to flint.

The demon holding her jerked her tighter against his body. He seemed to be holding off on the demon mind attack for the moment, because she could still see. "Back off or I blow a bullet through her pretty neck." Deep and hoarse, definitely a purebred demon voice.

Garrett stalled and held up a hand for Logan to pause. "You have to know we're not letting you take her. So let go, run, and we'll see what happens next." His fangs dropped.

Cara angled her wrist around, trying to keep her grip on the gun. The demon pressed his leg against her hand, trapping it against her thigh. "Drop the weapon, lady."

She didn't have much of a choice with his gun shoved into her neck. "Fine." She relaxed her body, waited until his hold lessened, and then tossed the gun toward Garrett. It clattered across the concrete and finally came to a stop a foot away from him. He smiled.

The demon stiffened. "Move for that gun, and I'll take her out."

Garrett studied him, edging left while Logan went right. "I don't think so. You need her alive, right?"

"Nope. Just need her, period. They can do as many tests on a corpse as on a live chick, if you ask me." The demon dragged her toward the exposed part of the level. The overhead concrete disappeared, and rain dropped down on them.

Cara blinked away rain and tried to find an opening to fight as the boys stalked them, their steps even and in sync. "This is silly," she whispered. "You can't halt progress. The virus may not even negate mating bonds for still-living immortals."

The demon shrugged. "Don't care about halting or progress. You're just a job to me, lady."

Fantastic. Demon mercenaries. She tried again. "You don't understand. There's no new information to be gained from testing me. Just take the samples, and you'll know everything the Realm knows."

"My job is to take you, so I'm taking you." The demon's boots scraped over rocks as he moved.

Logan cleared his throat. "My brother is Zane Kyllwood, the leader of the demon nation. We are now aligned with the Realm, and I can assure you, he takes that seriously."

"So?" the guy hissed.

"So? Well, now. You're a demon, and he takes that kind of thing seriously, as well. He really won't like demons attacking the Realm, especially his mate's mother." Logan shrugged. "You know that you're holding a gun to Zane's mother-in-law, right?"

The demon audibly swallowed. "I don't give a shit."

Logan shook his head, his body tense and ready to strike. "Believe me, you don't want Zane on your ass."

"I'm not afraid of some vampire-demon breed, boy." The demon shoved the gun harder against Cara's neck, and pain lanced through her throat. Tears filled her eyes, and she had to fight to keep from crying out.

Logan's chin lowered, and his green eyes darkened to almost black. "Now, that just isn't nice."

Garrett edged to the side. "Let her go."

The rain increased in force and *ping*ed off the concrete.

"Get back," the demon said, jerking his head toward the enclosed part of the construction. "Get out of the way. The helicopter is going to touch down here."

Cara tried to eye the area. Sure, it was big and flat, but building materials littered the entire ground. There wasn't a decent place to land. She ran through self-defense techniques she'd learned. If the demon would just move the gun a little, she could take her chance.

The hum of the rotors competed with the driving rain, and the black helicopter seemed to glide around the nearest completed building, a hotel with blue windows. She blinked water from her eyes, unable to move her arm to wipe her face. While she couldn't move her head, her gaze caught Garrett's as he looked over and up. His eyebrows rose.

She tried to swallow around the gun at her throat and glanced toward the long ladder part of a yellow crane. A flash caught her eye. She lifted her gaze and bit back a gasp. Talen was halfway to the top, at least ten stories above them, aiming a gun at the helicopter. His concentration was absolute, and his face was set in fierce lines.

He fired.

The green laser ripped through the front windshield of the helicopter and hit the pilot. He fell forward, blood coating the window. The helicopter jerked up and spun around. A man holding a long machine gun fell out the open side door and yelled, plunging stories down to the ground several floors beneath them. The crash when he hit the ground reverberated up.

The helicopter continued to swing around and around, emitting an odd whine. The tail swung toward the yellow crane ladder, and Cara screamed.

Talen's eyes widened, and holding on to the sides, he jumped away from the steps. He pummeled toward the ground like he was attached to some odd zip line, his knees up toward his chest.

Cara's entire body shook, and she gagged.

"Stop it," the demon said, jerking her.

The helicopter's tail smashed into the yellow cage. The impact was deafening, and the entire building seemed to rock.

Talen fell with a loud roar, hitting the cement and rolling. He came up, his fangs flashing.

Thank God. He was okay. Cara's knees wobbled.

The helicopter whirled around and dropped, disappearing from sight. It crashed hard, and fire flew up to flare hot and bright before dropping. Another clatter echoed from down below. Smoke and debris burst up and then cascaded down with the rain.

Talen ran toward them, blood on his face, his eyes swirling with fury. Barrels were tossed out of his way along with several pieces of rebar. He reached Garrett and stopped. His gaze ran over Cara, head to toe, and a muscle ticked in his jaw. Then he turned his attention to the demon. "Looks like you lost your ride."

The demon tightened his hold and backed away. "I have insurance." A wave of pain emanated from him in the form of a mind attack, dark and sharp.

Cara winced, and dots danced across her eyes.

Logan held up a hand, and the demon's head jerked back.

The pain receded from Cara's brain, and her vision cleared. Wow. Logan had completely halted the mind attack. But not without cost. His body was one rigid line, and blood dripped from his nose, but his green eyes focused and didn't blink once.

Cara took a deep breath. "Let me go, and I won't let them kill you."

"No." The demon shuddered and backed away. "Come with me, and I won't kill *you*."

She tried to dig her tennis shoes into the wet concrete, but he easily dragged her toward the rough stairs.

Rain slashed down around them, but his hold didn't weaken.

The three soldiers tracked them, keeping spread out, their gazes intent.

Cara allowed her body to relax. They reached the stairs. The demon moved quickly, sliding an arm beneath her chin and cutting off her air. He then pointed the gun at Talen.

Finally. Cara instantly pivoted into the demon, loosening the hold on her neck. She shoved one knee up into his groin and punched him full-on in the eye.

He howled and stepped back.

She finished with a one-two kick to the chin. His head snapped back, and he fell, rolled, and came up firing.

Garrett tackled her out of the way just as Talen dodged forward and knocked the gun from the demon's hand. With a roar that sounded much more animalistic than vampiric, Talen lifted the demon by the armpits, swung around, and threw him down to the next floor.

Cara lifted her head and then pushed up to sit. She looked over the edge. The demon had landed on several prongs of rebar that now stuck up from his neck and various points of his body. Blood gurgled from his mouth.

Garrett helped her up. "We have to go. Now."

Talen nodded and reached her in long strides. "Are you all right?"

She nodded and tried to shake out her hand. The demon's head had been like rock.

"Good." Talen ran a knuckle down her neck, anger pouring off him.

"Got the guns," Logan said, jogging up with his hands full.

Talen nodded, taking Cara's hand. He turned and led the way, tapping his ear communicator as they ran down the stairs. "Kayrs 45738 calling in. Backup no longer needed, but we require a cleanup crew. With a truck for a downed helicopter." He hustled to the SUV and opened the passenger-side door. "We also need safe haven for the night . . . get me a secured location."

Cara slid inside. "Talen, I—"

"We'll talk later, mate." He ran around to jump into the driver's side and gunned the engine as the boys leaped into the backseat. "Let's get to safety, sweetheart."

Chapter 9

It was supposed to be a time of peace, damn it. Talen finished scrubbing off blood and cement in the dark-tiled shower, his anger nearly splitting open his head. The secured location was the penthouse of an exclusive hotel, and after Cara had showered, he'd taken some time for himself.

When he'd seen the demon with a gun at her head, he'd nearly lost his mind. A gun. At her head.

They hadn't spoken while finding the hotel and reaching the penthouse. He finished his shower and dressed in old jeans and a black T-shirt that he'd had in his bag for Hawaii. Taking a quick inventory, he determined any injuries he'd sustained in the fight had already healed.

Unfortunately, his temper had not.

He stalked out of the bathroom to find his mate on the bed, pale and plucking at a thread on the bedspread. "Are you in pain?" he asked, trying to sense any vibrations from her.

"No." She lifted those stunning blue eyes. "Are you?"

He shook his head. Three sharp raps came from the main door in the other room. Grabbing his gun from the bedside table, he hustled out to the main living room of the penthouse, where Garrett and Logan already waited, guns at the ready. Both boys had showered and thrown on jeans and button-down shirts.

He nodded for Garrett to open the door.

A hulking vampire stood waiting, his stance casual while wearing flak boots, a black jacket, and cargo pants no doubt stuffed with weapons.

"Max," Talen said, gesturing him inside.

Max Petrovsky grinned and half-hugged Garrett before doing the same with Logan. "Heard you guys handled yourselves well."

"Of course." Garrett shut the door behind the Realm soldier.

Max had fought wars side by side with the Kayrs vampires for centuries, worked as a bodyguard, and was pretty much family. "We're scouting the area for additional Sandovskys, and our Intel confirms they're here. I'll have a location for you shortly."

"Excellent." Talen leaned back against the wall. "It's time for a chat."

Max nodded. "In addition, I have six soldiers ready to escort that cooler to a lab in Vegas, if you wouldn't mind turning it over."

"Happy as hell to turn it over," Talen drawled. "Thing's more trouble than any of this is worth."

Max rubbed his square jaw. "Agreed. I don't think anything can negate a mating if the parties are both alive. No way, no how."

Talen nodded. "I'm with you." He looked up as Cara came from the bedroom.

Her entire face lit up when she saw Max. She reached him quickly and leaned up to press a kiss against his cheek. "Is there any chance you brought Sarah?"

"No. My mate is safely at home," Max said, rather pointedly.

Talen barely kept himself from nodding.

Cara rolled her eyes. "The war is over, boys."

"The war is never completely over," Max countered. He patted her awkwardly on the arm with a hand larger than a salad plate. "But you should have a good time in Hawaii anyway."

Her lips pressed together. "I plan to."

Talen frowned. Was it just him, or was there a whole shitload of defiance in her tone of voice? Irritation clawed through him. He strode to the closet and yanked out the offensive green cooler. "I can't tell you how happy I am to get rid of this thing."

Max took it gingerly.

Cara chuckled. "There's nothing dangerous in it, Max. Only tissue and other samples . . . nothing poisonous."

Max nodded but didn't lose his frown. "Do you need me in Hawaii?"

"No. The boys are coming," Talen said, knowing full well Max wanted to get home to Sarah. They'd been trying to conceive for an entire year, but it sometimes took centuries for vampires to procreate. "As soon as you find the Sandovskys here, you need to get home."

"Agreed. You're safe here, too." Max nodded. "I have men stationed at every entrance to this building, and snipers across the way. The residence in Hawaii is similarly secured, and I've sent two extra squads over tonight to prepare for your arrival. Also, we canceled your commercial flights. A Realm airplane will be waiting to fly you across the ocean at your convenience."

Talen flashed his teeth. He'd forgotten how much Max hated to fly. "We'll be fine."

"I'm aware. I'll let you get settled in, and I'll give you a call later today. If that goes well, we'll meet in Anchorage midnight tomorrow."

Cara rocked back on her heels. "We're going to Alaska?"

Talen slowly shook his head. "You'll be staying in Maui with Garrett and Logan. If all goes well, I'll only be gone a day." He had Realm strategists putting together a strike plan that he'd tweak before going in.

Cara frowned. "You're going after the Sadovsky group."

"Most likely. We'll see who we can corner here in Seattle first." Talen glanced at her. "They're after you, and they won't stop, so we're stopping them." Sometimes it was as simple as that. "Sorry you have to fly, Max."

Max shrugged. "I'll make sure I have a parachute on board just in case."

Talen grinned, but Max was probably serious. "How many of my brothers will be joining us?"

"All of them." Max sighed and shook his head. "I think the king should stay safe at headquarters, but when I told him that, Dage hit me in the face." Max rubbed his jaw. "Hard."

Sounded like Dage. "We're all spoiling for a good fight." Talen didn't miss the quick wince Cara gave. Yeah. His first fight was going to be with her.

Max glanced from one to the other. "Maybe the boys should come with me."

"They're staying here," Cara said firmly.

Max shook his head and refocused on Talen. "Did you get your hands on the new wolf prototype?"

"Yeah." Garrett handed over the purple gun. "Thing is awesome."

Max turned the weapon around in his gigantic hand. "I'll have our guys get on duplicating it and then creating defenses. We need updated bulletproof vests, anyway."

Garrett frowned. "I wanted to keep it."

"You can have it back after the tech guys figure it out." Max slipped the weapon into his jacket pocket.

Talen reopened the door. "Call me with info."

"You got it." Max clapped Garrett on the back on his way out. "Watch out for your folks."

"Always," Garrett said.

The door closed behind Max, and the tension in the room naturally dissipated. Garrett shuffled his feet. "Since we have guards stationed all around the building, Logan and I thought we might hit a few bars in town."

Talen nodded, his heart rate kicking up. He did require some alone time with his mate, after all. "Be home in time to leave for the airport tomorrow morning," Talen said and then paused. "I take that back. Be home tonight." He waited a beat. "Alone. Just the two of you."

Garrett blew out air. "Seriously?"

"Yes." Talen clapped him on the back. "Seriously."

Logan sighed. "Let's hit the bars anyway. I could use a drink after the fight earlier. And about five pizzas."

Garrett's eyebrows rose. "Pizza is a good idea. I'm starving."

Talen slipped him cash. They'd need a lot of pizza, knowing the two of them. He waited until they'd hustled outside before shutting the door and leaning back against it.

Cara watched him with fire in her eyes.

He crossed his arms. "So, mate. Ready to chat?"

Cara eyed her mate. For months they'd danced around this, trying to settle into a routine after the war. But that was the rub, wasn't it? Talen Kayrs wasn't a male to *settle* into anything. Even though he'd raised two kids and now adored little Hope, he was not a retired immortal but a fully trained vampire warrior in his prime.

In his fucking *prime*.

His golden eyes flared and darkened, sizzling to a vampire secondary green color. The hue of a fire too hot to touch. A vein pulsed in his corded neck, and primal dominance suddenly hardened his entire face.

Oh, it had been too long since she'd seen that look, but it was way too late to turn back now. "What did you wish to discuss?" She kept her voice level to hide the fact that her heart was absolutely pounding against her rib cage.

"What part of '*stay in the secured area*' did you not understand?" he asked mildly, the muscles flexing in his arms.

He dwarfed her and always had. While some women might've been intimidated by his size, weakened by it . . . she enjoyed every inch made just for her. He'd put that big body between danger and her more than once, and his sheer deadliness gave her a sense of security not many people in life enjoyed. Plus, he more than knew how to use that body to pleasure her.

Even so. Sometimes he made her feel too feminine . . . too protected. "I understood every word," she admitted, meeting his gaze evenly, while a shiver of nervousness caught her unaware. It had been too long since she'd poked the beast.

"Then why did you leave safety?" His voice lowered at the last. If a tone could be a warning, he'd found it.

"I heard gunfire." She winced as she hurried to add, "My son and his friend were in danger." Sometimes it was that simple.

His jaw tightened. Displeasure mingled with an unreal heat in those eyes that had turned green with temper—and passion. Even so, a golden rim encircled his green iris, making him look like something . . . other. A vampire showing his true colors.

She shivered. The storm gathered strength outside, pelting rain against the wide wall of windows across the living room.

His lids half-lowered. "Did you really think I wouldn't protect Garrett and Logan?"

She inched a step back from the barely vibrating anger in his voice. "I knew you'd protect them, but you'd moved on to challenge a helicopter." For goodness' sake. If anybody was justified being angry about their spouse doing stupid, dangerous things, it should be her. The man had challenged a fucking weaponized helicopter.

His nostrils flared.

Damn vampires. They could smell everything.

"You're both angry and aroused," he murmured, making her point for her.

She slammed her hand on her hips. "Angry, for sure. How dare you take such a risk?"

He cocked his head to the side, tension swelling from him and filling the room. "My job was to take out that helicopter."

Her eyebrows raised so quickly her skin hurt. "Your *job*? Seriously. Your job as the strategic leader of the Realm is to climb cranes and shoot at helicopters." The derision in her voice had an obvious effect on him . . . and it wasn't pretty.

"No," he rumbled, pushing off from the door. "My job, the one I take to my heart, is to secure your safety at all costs."

She swallowed and took a full step back. "Not at the expense of our children."

He shook his head, his gaze not moving from her face. "Garrett and Logan weren't in danger, not really, until you left the safety of that stairwell. At that point, their concentration could've become fractured as they worried more about you than protecting their own hides."

Well, she hadn't exactly thought of that. "I took out one guy and then I also took out the demon."

"Yes, yes, you did." He stalked her, patiently, taking two steps for every one of hers. "But I didn't want them taken out. I wanted them in custody so we could figure out what is going on here."

"So, why didn't you just capture the last guy?" She eyed the layout of the living room and then fought a yelp when her back touched the wall.

"He had a gun to your throat, Cara," Talen snapped, the band around his control obviously stretching dangerously. "That meant he had to die, and rather painfully. Or perhaps the bastard lived, but recuperating from multiple holes in his head and body from the rebar will take time."

"You wouldn't want a weak little mate who cowered while others

fought, would you?" she asked, trying to sidle down the wall and
away from him.

He stopped moving. "There's nothing weak about using strategy,
which we needed to do at the moment." His growl filtered through
the room and rolled through her body as if it licked every part of her
with just a little too much heat. "The demons wanted you, so you
needed to stay hidden until I captured them."

She frowned.

He took another step toward her, bringing warmth and tension.
"When Dage was targeted by that feline group out of Australia, we
locked him down until we took care of the problem. That's what
happens."

That was what had happened, and the king had been pissed but
overruled by his brothers. She cleared a potted plant and calculated
the distance between her position and the other side of the sofa. Her
lungs trapped her breath, and anticipation flittered through her abdomen. Her panties dampened. "So I didn't understand the plan. It
happens."

Slowly, so deliberately, he shook his head. "It will never happen
again."

She stopped moving, defiance rising fast and heated. "Oh,
really?"

His expression turned dark and foreboding. "Yes. In battle situations, I expect to be obeyed without question. Not just by soldiers,
not just by the boys . . . but by you."

Lust and denial flamed through her at his natural show of dominance. Her spirit rejected the order, while every feminine nerve in
her body thrummed to life. The man had been made for her, yet
sometimes, he seemed to forget her strength. Knowing she was
going too far, knowing she'd probably pay, she forced a mocking
smile. "Not in a million years."

She moved quick, jumping around the sofa, and he let her.

Oh, the vampire could be quicker than a jaguar striking prey, and
he could've stopped her. Instead, he rolled into motion, his steps
slow and sure, raw hunger glittering in his eyes. "You should never
run from a vampire, baby," he whispered.

Her sex clenched. "Why not?" she breathed.

"We can't help but chase, and when we catch, we're not gentle. You want gentle, right?" he crooned.

Hell to the no. She wanted Talen—all of him. "You're assuming you can catch me," she taunted, her back to the storm outside.

He was getting closer, too close to the sofa. She couldn't tell which way he'd round it, so she remained still, her legs bunched to run. The second he moved, she'd go the other direction. If she made it to the door, it'd be a miracle, but that didn't mean she wouldn't give it her best shot.

His concentration narrowed in focus just like a wild animal's as he stalked her. Sexual awareness cascaded along her arms, wrapping her in a hunger with sharpened teeth.

"I'm going to catch you, mate, and I'm taking you down hard," he whispered, coming closer. "You're going to beg for more by the time I'm finished with you tonight. Then you're going to promise to obey me next time . . . and you'll mean every word."

Her clit ached with enough need she wanted to jump him and tear off his clothes. But no. That wasn't how the night was going to happen. "Meh," she said. "We've already done the taking down hard. That all you have . . . *mate*?"

He growled, and her lungs seized. She fucking loved that sexy sound.

She smiled.

He moved then, sailing over the sofa in a graceful leap. She gasped and hesitated one millisecond too late. His arm wrapped around her waist, and he took her down.

Chapter 10

Talen's fangs dropped low as his woman bucked against him, fighting with every dirty move he'd taught her through the years as he dropped to his knees. Her elbow jammed him in the gut, stealing his breath, and he fought the urge to laugh out loud.

This was what he'd been missing all these years as she'd fought the illness.

She'd been correct that he was still treating her like fragile glass, but even now, the thought of any harm coming to her ripped his heart into shreds. Vampires loved once and once only, and she owned him, body and soul. Nothing could harm her. Period.

Even so, she didn't need kid gloves from him. Especially if that gave her license to put her life in danger.

What she did need, she might not like so much. His body thrummed in time with hers. He could smell her desire, her lust, and the familiar scent threatened to snap the small amount of control he had left. She was wild and sweet, a promise of everything good and pure in his life.

She broke his hold, partially turning.

A fierce wave of excitement surged through his veins. Her hiss of triumph rocked through him, igniting lust. He grasped her arms and flipped her onto her knees, facing away from him.

She swept her leg out, faster than he would've imagined, and knocked his knees to the side. Scrambling quickly, she made it up and around the couch.

He laughed out loud, absurdly pleased with her. With a roar only a vampire could make, he turned and cleared the sofa in one smooth motion, launching himself at his mate.

She let out a startled *eek* and flew back into the door, her hands instinctively rising.

His hands slapped the wall on either side of her head, and he inhaled her spicy scent, his nostrils flaring.

Her eyes widened. "Um—"

"Oh, baby." He leaned in, satisfied by her sharp intake of breath. "It's too late for *um*." He grasped her shirt at the neck and ripped it in two. The useless material fell away from her body.

Her eyes darkened to the color of a fathomless ocean.

"Bra," he said, lowering his face to hers, giving her a chance to save the lacy lingerie.

The quirk of her lip, the hint of defiance, was all it took.

He shredded the bra, revealing her pretty pink nipples.

Her chest heaved. "Talen—"

A quick dip, and his mouth enclosed a nipple. She gasped and grabbed his shoulders. He slid one arm around her waist to keep her upright and flicked her, allowing the scrape of his fangs along the side of her breast.

She trembled against him, need pouring off her.

He licked up her chest and over his bite mark on her neck, the one that had never completely healed. She shuddered and let out a soft moan.

"Before tonight is over, I'm biting you again, Cara. All the way to bone." He nipped at her earlobe and drew back.

Her eyes widened even more.

Oh, it was time to claim his woman once more. Sure, he'd mated her again when she'd healed, but apparently it hadn't been enough. He'd make damn sure tonight was enough to fully convince her of his loyalty and of anything else she needed convincing about.

His knee slid between her legs, and the feeling of her hot sex nearly pushed him over the edge.

Pink wound beneath her skin from her neck to her full cheekbones, adding to the glitter in her eyes. His mouth crashed down on hers, and her unique taste of honey and sunshine filled his mouth. God, she was fucking perfect.

She gasped him in, kissing him back, and then let loose with a low chuckle right before biting his lip.

Surprise whipped into lightning-hot desire. He flipped her around, his body keeping her still, and grabbed her wrists to put above her head. She struggled against him, her soft laugh stroking his lust hotter than either one of them should want.

Indulging himself, holding her in place, he traced her spine down her back with one finger. She shivered and shook her head, tumbling her silky hair over her shoulders.

He drew in her scent and tucked his finger in the waist of her jeans, giving an experimental tug.

She stopped moving.

He grinned and shifted to press his cock to her ass, feeling her moan to his balls. His free hand flattened across her abdomen. She pressed back against him, her back arching.

Sensation burned through him.

He unsnapped her jeans and shoved them down, leaving her delicate pink thong in place. It had probably matched the ruined bra. When the jeans reached her knees, he stopped and stood back up, his hold on her wrists tightening and raising her almost to her toes.

She shifted and then caught her breath, her legs shaking but unable to move.

"Yeah. You're trapped," he whispered, his breath at her ear. He curved his hand over her rounded buttock and squeezed.

Her head went back.

The skin across her hip was smoother than silk as he caressed her and moved his hand over her sex.

She moaned.

"Are you wet for me?" he whispered, sliding his fingers beneath the material. His low chuckle echoed against her neck, and his cock ached enough to really hurt. "Oh, baby. You're wet." And she was.

Her thigh muscles clenched, trying to still the ache. He laughed and set a knee between her legs, keeping her nice and open for him.

She was beyond soft and sweet, and when he stroked across her swollen clit, she gave a mewling sound that was for him. He hoped to God it was the last thing he heard when his time finally came.

Her body gyrated against him, and when he slipped a finger inside her incredibly wet heat, they both groaned.

He licked along her ear. "Now, sweetheart. Let's talk about obedience."

Her shoulder rocked back into his chest. "God, Talen," she breathed.

Not exactly what he wanted to hear. Punishing them both, he freed his hand.

She shook her head.

He palmed her ass again. "You were saying?"

Cara's entire body hungered on the fine edge of pain. Only Talen could do this to her, and by the dangerously hard cock pressed to her hip, he was in the same state. "Sex now, talk later," she gasped out.

He squeezed her butt. "Talk now," he growled.

Her eyelids flipped open, and she tried to focus on the door in front of her face. "What?"

"Obey? Yes or no in battle situations?" He stroked her ass, his fingers firm.

She stopped breathing. There was a right answer, there had to be. But what the hell. "No."

The ensuing slap from his large hand was angled up, and she instinctively went up on her tiptoes. "What the—"

Another slap. Then three more. Heat spread from his hand, right to her aching clit. Oh God. So much. She wanted more.

He caressed her smarting flesh. "Say you get me," he rumbled.

"Oh, I *own* you," she gasped.

The next slap had her crying out and struggling against his hold. Then pleasure bloomed across her butt. Another slap, and she arched her back. Four more hard slaps, each one getting her closer to orgasm. She shut her eyes to just feel.

His strong body warmed her from behind, and his hold kept her in place. Then he leaned in and scraped his tongue across the bite mark in her neck. Pleasure sparked from his mouth to her diamond-sharp nipples. His fingers brushed across the Kayrs marking on her hip, and her sex convulsed.

He nipped the bite mark. "Now's a good time to submit, baby.

Don't push me any further." His hand slid between her legs from behind and cupped her sex.

Her eyelids flashed open. The exquisite touch propelled her to a desire edged with pain. "No."

His hold tightened. "Your ass isn't the only thing I can spank. Give me the words, Cara. I'm on the edge."

She wanted him over the edge, damn it. But instinct, an awareness of his primal nature, whispered caution. Talen Kayrs had never been a male to be pushed, and after seeing her in danger earlier, the animal must be rioting for freedom inside him. He stroked his fingers over her entire sex. Pleasure streaked from her womb to her breasts and back again.

"Now, Cara." He rubbed her again.

"No," she whimpered.

Smack.

He hit her clit with unerring accuracy. She jerked from the ex-quisite pain, and tension uncoiled inside her. Her knees weakened. Pressure built inside her, and she fought against it, against giving in.

The second slap to her engorged clit had her whimpering and holding her breath. The entire world seemed to stop. He waited, his mouth at her ear, his breathing heavy.

Smack.

She shrieked. Her orgasm imploded within her, shredding the entire world. Lights ripped behind her eyelids. He rubbed her clit, intensifying every excruciating sensation, forcing her to shake through the entire climax, the pleasure almost too much to bear. Finally, she went limp with a low murmur.

The world tilted, and she found herself on her knees, Talen fol-lowing her down. Need clawed through her again, somehow sharper than before. Her hands flattened on the marble floor.

A rough hand between her shoulder blades forced her down, chest to marble. She turned her head to the side, trying to find enough air to fill her lungs. Rough hands grabbed her hips, one brushing the marking.

She arched.

The thickness of his erection pressed against her still-quivering sex. He shoved in with one hard thrust, pushing past swollen membranes and pulsing nerves, stretching her until he embedded himself deep inside her. She gasped, her body going rigid.

He flexed his fingers and then stilled. "You okay?"

Her voice was long gone, so she could only nod, and her body slowly relaxed.

Then and only then did he start to move, pounding into her with fast, deliberate thrusts. Agonizing, desperate pleasure electrified her internal tissues, and she pushed back against him, the outside world ceasing to exist.

There was only Talen and his long, demanding drives into her. Lightning arced from her clit to her womb, burning beneath her skin. A razor-sharp sizzle streaked through her, forcing her higher, increasing the pressure building too quickly inside her.

He stopped, his hold almost bruising.

"No," she breathed, her lungs compressing, her body shaking with the need for release.

He leaned over her and scraped his fangs along his bite marks. "Now. Tell me."

On all that was holy. She blinked several times and tried to clear her vision. Oh, she knew he was a centuries-old soldier, and he knew what to do in battle. "Fine," she gasped. "Next time demons are after me, and the kids are with us, I'll stay in the room."

"Not good enough. Try again." His fangs pierced her neck and dug in.

A shaking started deep inside her, and she clenched around his cock.

He groaned against her skin, and his fangs went deeper.

Pain flared and snapped to where they were joined, increasing the unreal need. Her vision went completely, so she shut her eyes. She tried to push back against him, but his hold remained absolute.

The fangs cut deeper.

She sucked in air. Her entire shoulder was on fire, but the pain didn't come close to the need still building in her core. "Fine. In battle, I'll obey." It was the only damn word that would satisfy him.

His fangs touched, and he started to pound. Hard, fast, out of control, he thrust into her, forcing her thighs farther apart, holding her exactly where he wanted her.

The chill of the tile beneath her was yet another sensation added to the heated vampire behind her. She pushed back into his demanding thrusts, her body clenching around his. So much. It was too much. There were depths to Talen she hadn't had a chance to reach yet, but now that she was whole, she'd explore every one of them.

His bite tightened just as he reached around and plucked her clit.

She exploded, shouting his name, her entire body convulsing. As she came, she could swear her entire soul joined in, lighting the room as her mate claimed her once again. He shoved inside her, held tight, and jerked with his own release.

His fangs retracted, and he licked the wound closed.

She went soft with a murmur. "Love you."

He withdrew and turned her, rolling to stand with her in his arms. "My soul is yours, baby."

Hmmm. Sounded like the same wavelength. She cuddled into his neck.

He chuckled. "Oh no. No sleeping. The claiming has just begun."

Chapter 11

The call came in right about dawn. Talen jogged down to a room in the basement of the hotel, his mind clear, his senses on alert. He passed kitchen supplies, a series of storage rooms, and finally reached a small concrete room in the back.

Max stood outside, arms crossed. "They're inside."

Talen frowned, and the smell of pickles wafted around. "Pickles?"

Max shrugged. "Storage for food upstairs. Somebody must've spilled. The Sandovskys . . ."

"What?" Talen asked.

"Not what I expected." Max pushed open the door.

Talen strode inside to see a man and a woman standing across a cement room. The guy was well over six feet tall with long blond hair and enough lines at his face to show at least a thousand years of life. The woman, petite and round, had stark white curly hair and soft black eyes. Both obviously full-bred demons. The guy shoved the woman behind him and settled his stance.

Talen kept all expression off his face. "You're Sandovsky?"

"Yes." The guy had a slightly Russian accent.

The woman poked her head around the man. "Me too. Sandovsky." Her voice was low and her tone . . . ironic?

Talen shifted his feet. He'd planned to kill them quickly but hadn't expected the woman. "You declared war on us."

The woman slapped the man's arm and tried——unsuccessfully—— to move around him. "I told him it was a bad idea and that we should just have called you. But no. The world is tumultuous and dangerous and we have to be so careful."

Talen actually agreed with that sentiment.

A rustle sounded behind him, and awareness crashed through him. "Cara." The guards had obviously not even tried to stop her from following him.

She moved to his side, her eyes tired, her body on alert. "Hello."

Sandovsky gave a half bow. "Lars Sandovsky and my mate, Fern."

"Cara and Talen. That's Max." Cara settled next to Talen, her gaze thoughtful.

Lars sobered, taking her in. "I apologize for any inconvenience we caused."

She lifted a shoulder. "We had an adventure." Then she frowned, and her eyes softened. "Talen. He's sick."

Talen glanced from his mate to Lars. "Huh?"

She patted his arm. "Lars is sick." She angled her head to see Fern. "Did you have the virus and he tried to yank it out of you?"

Fern elbowed her husband and moved slightly forward. "Yes. Exactly. Now he's ill, and we don't know what to do."

Ah, hell. Of course Cara would catch on to what was happening. Her intellect was only trumped by her empathic abilities. Virus-27 had infected many mates, and when it had gone airborne, it was freed to be yanked out. Unfortunately, the vampire or demon mate who yanked it out then got sick. "Why the hell didn't you just call us?" Talen snapped.

Lars shook his head. "We've lived on our own for so long, and we don't know the new demon rules or you. It seemed like a better idea to just get the cure and move on from there. We did give orders that nobody was to be hurt."

Cara turned and looked up at Talen. "Nobody got hurt. Well, none of our people, anyway. We have to help them."

Talen settled at the plea in her eyes. No way could he turn away from that. Besides, it wasn't like he could hurt Fern, anyway. "All right." He turned a smile on the demons. "Why don't we go up to our suite and have breakfast. There's an easy cure for you, Lars. I'll have the medicine we've created flown here within an hour."

Fern clapped her hands. "I knew things had changed for the better. Cara? I love your blouse. Where did you get it?" She shoved by her husband and moved for the door.

Cara turned and escorted her into the hallway. "There's this great store online. I'll get the link for you." The women moved for the stairwell.

Lars frowned as his mate disappeared around the bend. "Huh."

Talen fought a grin. "Guess we're allies now."

"Vampires and demons as allies." Lars strode toward the door, a hitch in his stride. "Great."

Several hours after Talen had said goodbye to their new, and recently cured friends, he finally kicked back in a leather chair, bound for Hawaii.

The private plane had three passenger sections: a bedroom, a rec room, and a quiet room with a couple of loungers and soft music. Talen sent the boys to the rec room to watch a movie and dropped into a lounger with his mate on his lap.

Her blue eyes were hazy, and dim circles marred the smooth skin beneath her eyes. He'd used her hard . . . the entire night, and then she'd entertained all morning.

Yet happiness all but bubbled from her tired form. Yeah, he should've made sure she had gotten some sleep, but they had an entire week on an island to rest.

He tucked her close and extended the footrest. "You need sleep." Truth be told, he could use a couple hours of shut-eye, as well.

The plane rose into the air, and he grabbed a blanket from a basket next to him to tuck around her.

She nuzzled his neck.

Desire flared through him, and he shoved it down. The woman needed rest, damn it.

She chuckled, no doubt noticing the erection under her ass. "I can barely walk already," she murmured, sounding at peace for the first time in too long. Leaning back, her gaze met his. "I've been struggling to find my place."

He frowned. "Your place is with me."

Her cheek creased. "Yes, I know. But I need to find my own place, too."

He leaned back, keeping her gaze. "I don't understand."

She flattened her hand over his heart. "I have immortality now, right?" At his nod, she continued. "I feel like I should do something good with it."

He ran his hand down her back, noting the delicate bones. "Okay, but you're not fighting." Yeah, he wanted to be a lot smoother than that, but in the end, Cara Kayrs wasn't a soldier. No matter how fierce the fire in her breast. "Although, you are a hell of a fighter, and I'd have you at my back anytime."

Pleasure rolled from her. "That's sweet."

"So how about we make a deal?"

One of her eyebrows arched. "A deal?"

"Yes. In battle situations, you act like any other soldier and obey commands. In every other situation ever, you can just be in charge."

She chuckled. "So I'm telling you what to do."

"Any time, sweetheart." He grinned. "Just no heading off into battles, if you don't mind."

"You are one confident male, Talen Kayrs." She rolled her eyes. "I don't want to go fight people, for goodness' sake. I'm a botanist."

He rubbed a smudge from her cheek. "Okay?"

She swallowed and glanced down at his neck. "There's some new research into crossbred plants that may have healing properties for humans. I need to teach the next generation of humans how to expand on that."

Ah, hell. The woman had handled herself well in battle, and he could continue training her. The soft heart of hers was what he loved most about her. Plus, she'd shown her skill and great abilities by just meeting the Sandovskys. She was talented and strong. How could he not let her follow it in helping people? It's who she was.

"I understand, and if that's really what you want, then we can create a safe way for you to do that. But you have to figure out the timing that works for you." His heart warmed. The woman was so sweet she wanted to help a species she was no longer even a part of.

"Timing?"

"Yeah. You're immortal. So you teach a few years like a normal career, and then you have to disappear from human life for years until trying again." He had to allow her to have a life, the one she wanted, for her to be happy. He got that, finally.

She didn't look back up. "I'll have to look at the timing, then. Do it just right."

"Okay." Heck. Maybe he could teach something at the same time.

Military strategy or something. The idea of them posing as a normal couple, both college professors, tickled his mouth into a grin.

She straightened. "I know you have money, but I've been investing, and I can float us for years. Honest."

He smiled. "My only advice would be to talk to Logan's mum before you choose a bank to invest in, if you plan to continue investing. Make sure it's not one she's planning to rob."

Cara's entire face lit up.

Talen shook his head and pressed a kiss to her nose. "You are not robbing banks with that crazy demoness." A guy had to draw the line somewhere.

"We'll see." She kissed his neck and snuggled down with a soft sigh.

Talen closed his eyes and held tight, like he always would. For some reason, sleep eluded him.

He held Cara for the entire trip, and she slept quietly. With every passing mile, his arousal grew until it was all he could do not to strip her bare and feast for the rest of the time. But she needed sleep, and he'd cut off his own arm before harming her.

The plane finally touched down, and private transport met them at the airport. Soldiers had already lined the way, so he was nearly relaxed when they reached the private villa set on a cliff overlooking the Pacific.

"Oh, Talen." Cara danced around the master bedroom, which was open to the outside. Glass doors could be closed at night, but for now, only wispy curtains billowed in the soft breeze. "It so beautiful. I love Hawaii." She eyed the large bed and bamboo furniture before giving a happy hop at seeing the pool right outside.

She was beautiful, and he couldn't take his eyes off of her.

As if sensing something, she stilled and looked around. Her gaze landed on him. Mirth filled her eyes. "You have got to be kidding me."

He shook his head and slowly advanced.

"I can barely walk." She chuckled.

"I'll be gentle." If he didn't have her, he'd explode.

She ripped off her dress. "I could be persuaded."

Thank God. He shucked his clothing and reached her just as she tossed her panties to the ground. A flick of her front-clasp bra, and

the most beautiful woman in the world stood before him, offering him everything.

He kissed her, going deep, enjoying the throaty murmur she gave. Trying to be gentle, he lifted her, his chest settling upon discovering she was already wet.

Pressing her back to a column, he worked inside her with short, smooth thrusts, taking his time and letting her body adjust to him.

She threw her head back, and her thighs tightened on his hips. "God, I love you."

"I love you more." He kissed her, keeping his hold gentle.

"Hey, Dad, you should see the—"

Talen turned to see Garrett and Logan loping up from the pool.

Garrett coughed and then backpedaled, his face a beet red. "Oh God. Oh God. Oh God."

Logan turned around and then tried to grab Garrett before he stumbled into a short white picket fence that was probably just there for show. White stakes flew in every direction.

Garrett bellowed, his arms windmilling, and fell over the cliff.

Logan ran forward and leaned over. "Um, he's okay. Hit a bunch of rocks about forty feet down." The demon didn't turn back around. "I'll, ah, go help him up." Even the tips of Logan's ears were red. He quickly disappeared down the cliff.

Cara chuckled and dropped her face to Talen's neck. "We just scarred them for life."

"Idiots should know better." Talen resumed his pounding, kissing her, truly enjoying the moment.

Yeah. Life was pretty damn good.

Cara watched the sunset spread across the sky from a cushioned lounger at the pool the next night. She wore a bikini with a sheer wrap around her hips. She had so many things she wanted to do, including having more kids, but she wanted to work for a while and play with immortality.

Talen was inside on the phone, and he had three more minutes before she interceded and got him back to relaxing. It had taken nearly the entire day for either of the boys to be around her without blushing beet red. But after eating entirely too much crab and then getting a good night's sleep, they now lounged in the pool drinking beer and acting back to normal.

She frowned and glanced at her phone.

"Dad will be out in a minute." Garrett didn't even look up. "He's just finalizing the treaty with the Sandovskys."

Logan nodded, his dark glasses hiding his eyes. "We're going to visit their headquarters after we finish the job with the Enforcers in Seattle. Alaska is nice this time of year."

"Sounds like fun. Maybe I'll come with you. I'd like another glass of wine. Be right back." Padding barefoot, she walked into the kitchen and uncorked another wine bottle.

"Mom!" Garrett called. "Dad's off the phone."

She ran out of the room and barreled straight into his arms. "We have a new treaty."

He held her easily. "Thanks to you, we have new best friends."

She kissed his mouth, pleasure overtaking her. "It's nice to contribute."

Talen lifted her up and fell right into her lounger, extending his legs. With his jeans and T-shirt, he'd probably get too warm. She moved to get up, and he tugged her closer. "You're safe now."

She blinked. "What did you do?"

Talen grinned at the boys. "We made the cure completely public in case there are any other hidden species out there trying to find it or you."

Garrett and Logan knuckle-bumped.

Cara smiled. "That's a great plan. The cure should be public."

Talen sighed. "So long as you're protected, I don't care what we make public."

There was the man she loved. "You make me feel safe."

He smiled and cupped her head. "I vow you'll always be safe."

Now, wasn't that sweet. Cara smiled at the one man she'd love forever. Peace had arrived, and she'd figured out what to do as her life's work. Life couldn't be any better. Her mate was finally seeing the real her. "I love you, Talen Kayrs."

His eyes swirled golden and intense. "I love you more, mate. Forever."

So far, the magical world of Ireland pretty much sucked eggs. Her dreams of rolling hills, rugged men, and wild adventures had given away to facts that tilted her universe, spun it around, and spiked it head first into the ground.

The world held too many secrets.

Tori Monzelle leaned her shoulders against the cold metal wall of the van and tried to blink through the blindfold turning the interior dark. Nothing. The carpet in the rear of the van smelled fresh and new, but she sat on the floor, her knees drawn up and her hands tied behind her back.

The sounds of drizzling rain and honking horns filtered inside, while two men breathed from the front seats. She hadn't recognized either one of them when they'd arrived at the penthouse just an hour before. For an entire week, she'd been held hostage in various luxurious locales after having been kidnapped from Seattle.

Had it only been a week since she'd learned the world wasn't as she'd thought?

Witches, vampires, and demons existed. As in *really existed.*

They were just different species from humans, apparently. So far she'd seen witches create fireballs and throw them, and she'd met a demon who'd shown her his fangs. She had to go on faith that vampires really existed, but at this point, why not believe?

She cleared her throat. "Listen, jackasses. I'm about done with this entire kidnapping scenario." It had to be the oddest kidnapping of all time, with her being flown across the globe and then put up in zillion dollar penthouses for a week. "I promise not to tell anybody that supernatural beings exist. Just let me go."

A snort came from the front seat. "Supernatural," one of the men muttered.

Her chest heated. "All right, so you think you're natural. Then how about I refrain from announcing that your species even exists?"

Another snort.

What a dick. Fine. "Are you witches, demons, or vampires?" If she had to guess, they were witches.

No answer.

The van swerved, and she knocked her head against the side. "Damn it." It was time to get free. "Let me go, you morons. This is international kidnapping." Did witches care about international laws? Her shoulders shook, and a welcome anger soared through her.

The van jerked.

"What the hell?" one of the guys snapped.

They tilted.

Something sputtered. The engine?

An explosion rocked the day, and the van spun. Her temple smacked the metal, and she rolled to the other side across the carpet. Breath swooshed from her lungs. Pain pounded in her head, and she blinked behind the blindfold.

The van stopped cold, and she rolled toward the front, her legs scrambling. Her forehead brushed the carpet, and she shook her head, dislodging the blindfold.

Doors opened, and grunts sounded. Men fighting. Punches being thrown.

The back doors opened, and light flooded inside.

She turned just as hands manacled her ankles and dragged her toward the street. Kicking out, she struggled furiously, her eyes adjusting and focusing on this new threat. A ski mask completely covered the guy's head, leaving only his eyes and mouth revealed. With the light behind him, she couldn't even make out the color of his irises.

His strong grip didn't relent, and he easily pulled her toward the edge, dropping her legs toward the ground.

She threw a shoulder into his rock-hard abs and stood. He was at least a foot taller than she and definitely cut hard.

Everything in her screamed to get the hell out of the area and make a run for it. She was smart, she was tough, and she could handle the situation. No time to think. Tori leaped up and shot a quick kick to his face. While he was tall and fit, he probably wasn't expecting a fight.

He snagged her ankle an inch from his jaw, thus preventing the impact. Using her momentum to pull her forward, he manacled his other hand behind her thigh and lifted, tossing her over his shoulder in one incredibly smooth motion.

Her rib cage slammed into solid muscle, knocking the wind from her lungs.

One firm hand clamped across her thighs, and he turned, moving into a jog. The sound of men fighting behind them had her lifting her head to see more men in ski masks battling the two guys from the van.

Then her captor turned a corner and ran through an ally, easily holding her in place.

"Let me go," she gasped, pulling on the restraints holding her hands. Cobbled stones flew by below, while cool air brushed across her skin. Rain continued to patter down, matting her hair to her face.

He didn't answer and took two more turns, finally ending up in yet another alley next to a shiny black motorcycle. Her hair swooshed as he ducked his shoulder and planted her on her feet. Firm hands flipped her around, and something sliced through her bindings.

Blood rushed into her hands, and she winced, pivoting back around. "Who are you?" She slid one foot slightly back in an attack position.

He reached out and tugged the blindfold completely off her head before ripping off his ski mask.

Adam Dunne stood before her, legs braced, no expression on his hard face. Rain dripped from his thick black hair, and irritation glittered in his spectacular green eyes. That expression seemed to live on him. He was some sort of brilliant scientist, definitely a brainiac, and he always appeared annoyed.

She blinked twice. "Adam?"

He crossed his arms. "It has been nearly impossible to find you."

His deep voice shot right through her to land in very private places. Then the angry tone caught her. She slammed her hands against her hips. "And that's my fault? Your stupid people, the fucking witches, *kidnapped* me."

Witches. Holy crap. Adam Dunne was a witch. Sure, she'd figured that out a week ago, but with him standing right in front of her, she had to face reality.

The man looked like a badass vigilante and not some brilliant otherworldly being. For the rescue, he'd worn a black T-shirt, ripped jeans, and motorcycle boots. Definitely not his usual pressed slacks and button-down silk shirt.

His sizzling green eyes darkened. "I have about an hour to get you to a plane and out of this country, so you'll be quiet, *for once,* and you'll follow orders."

She pressed her lips together. No matter how badly she wanted to punch him in the face, she wanted to get out of the country even more. "Fine."

He lifted an eyebrow. "We're getting on the bike, heading to the airport, and then you're flying to Seattle. You don't know who rescued you, and you haven't seen me in weeks."

She swallowed. "How much trouble are you in if we get caught?"

He turned and grabbed a helmet off the bike. "Treason and death sentence."

Everything in her softened. He'd risked his life for her. Sure, his brother was dating her sister, but even so. "Thank you."

He turned and shoved the helmet at her. "Don't thank me. Just do what I tell you."

Man, what a jerk. Nearly biting through her tongue to keep from lashing out, she shoved the helmet on her head.

He did the same and swung a leg over the bike, holding out a hand to help her.

She ignored him and levered herself over the bike and into place, anger flowing through her. Why did he have to be such a dick? She'd wanted to thank him, that's all.

He ignited the engine. It sputtered. He stiffened and tried again.

Hell. She closed her eyes and tried to calm her temper. They had to get out of there. *Work, bike. Damn it, work.* The more she tried to concentrate, the more irritated she became.

He twisted the throttle again, and this time, nothing happened.

Damn it. Why the hell did this always happen to her? What was wrong with her? "It won't work. If it's broken, it won't work." She tugged off the helmet and slid off the bike.

He turned toward her. "The bike ran just fine an hour ago."

She shrugged, her face heating. No way was she telling him about her oddity. "I know the sound of an engine that's not coming back to life, and so do you."

He frowned and tried the bike again. Nothing. "All right." He swung his leg over and stood, reaching for a buzzing cell phone and pushing a button. "I have a problem," he said.

"The woman has been tagged," came an urgent male voice. "There's a tracker, and you have about five minutes until the Guard gets there." Keys clacking echoed across the line. "Get rid of the tag and find safety. I'll be in touch with new coordinates as soon as I can." The line went dead.

Adam surveyed her from head to toe, reaching for her shirt.

She slapped at his hands. "What are you doing?"

He sighed. "You've been tagged, and I don't know where. Strip, baby."

Baby? Did he just call her baby? Wait a minute. "Strip?"

"Now." A muscle ticked in his powerful jaw. "Our tags are minute and could be anywhere on you." He dug both hands through her hair, tugging just enough to flood her with unwelcome tingles. "Not in your hair."

"I am not stripping," she said through clenched teeth, her body doing a full tremble.

He lowered his head until his nose almost touched hers. "Take everything off, or I'll do it for you."

She blinked.

He gave a barely perceptible eye roll and turned around, pulling off his T-shirt. "Drop the clothes and put this on. It'll cover you for the time being."

Muscles rippled in his back.

Her mouth went dry.

"Now, Victoria. We have to hurry."

The urgency in his voice got through to her. She shucked her clothes, kicking off her socks and shoes, shivering in the light rain. The second her jeans hit the ground, she reached for his shirt and tugged it over her head. The soft material fell beneath her thighs and surrounded her with the scent of male.

He turned around, and yep. His bare chest was even more spectacular than his back. "Everything off? Bra and panties?"

Did Adam Dunne just use the word *panties*? A slightly hysterical giggle bubbled up from her abdomen, and she shoved it ruthlessly down. "Yes."

"Good." He took her hand. "Sorry about the bare feet, but we'll get you replacement clothes soon. For now, we have to run."

A car screeched to a stop outside the alley.

"Bullocks. They're here," he muttered, launching into a run down the alley. "Hurry, and don't look back."

Panic seized her, and she held firm to his hand, her bare feet slapping hard cobblestones.

A fireball careened past her, smashing into the brick building above her and raining down debris. She screamed.

Adam stopped and shoved her behind him, dark blue plasma forming down his arms as he pivoted to fight.

She gulped in air and peered around him as three men, each forming a different color plasma balls, all stalked toward them from the street.

"Run, Victoria," Adam ordered.

**Don't miss the next Scorpius Syndrome novel
from Rebecca Zanetti,
available this September!**

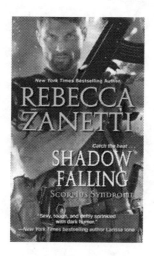

Before the Scorpius Syndrome tore through North America
and nearly wiped out the population, Vivienne Wellington was
the FBI's best profiler. The bacteria got her anyway. But she
survived. She recovered. And when she woke up from a
drug nightmare of captivity, her skills as a hunter of men
had gone from merely brilliant to full-on uncanny.
Her mysterious rescuer wants her to put them to the test.
But no matter how tempting he is, with his angel's eyes and
devil's tongue, Vinnie knows she shouldn't trust him.

If the FBI were still around they would rate Raze Shadow
as one of the bad guys. His military training can't wipe out
his association with the Mercenaries, the most feared gang in
a thousand miles. His loyalties are compromised. He won't even
tell Vinnie his real name. But there's no FBI in the new America
of fear and firepower, only instinct and risk. And the way his
arms wrap around her tells its own story. Whatever else
Raze is concealing, he can't hide his desire . . .

**"Thrilling post-apocalyptic romance at its dark, sizzling best!"
—Lara Adrian**

Dylan Patrick

New York Times and *USA Today* bestselling author REBECCA ZANETTI has worked as an art curator, Senate aide, lawyer, college professor, and a hearing examiner—only to culminate it all in stories about alpha males and the women who claim them. She writes contemporary romances, dark paranormal romances, and romantic suspense novels.

Growing up amid the glorious backdrops and winter wonderlands of the Pacific Northwest has given Rebecca fantastic scenery and adventures to weave into her stories. She resides in the wild north with her husband, children, and extended family who inspire her every day—or at the very least give her plenty of characters to write about.

Please visit Rebecca at: www.rebeccazanetti.com/
www.facebook.com/RebeccaZanetti.Author.FanPage
twitter.com/RebeccaZanetti

TWISTED

DARK PROTECTORS

New York Times Bestselling Author

REBECCA ZANETTI

SHADOWED

DARK PROTECTORS

New York Times Bestselling Author

REBECCA ZANETTI

TAMED

DARK
PROTECTORS

New York Times Bestselling Author
REBECCA ZANETTI

New York Times Bestselling Author

REBECCA ZANETTI

WICKED RIDE

DARK PROTECTORS

THE WITCH ENFORCERS

Printed in the United States
by Baker & Taylor Publisher Services